HER DESCENT

J.E. & M. KEEP

PREAMBLE

DEDICATION

BY JOSHUA KEEP

I have my mother to thank for introducing me to not only reading at such an early age, but also empathy. The first story I ever remember her teaching me to read was about a suffering animal in need of help. And while I am sure there was much more that came immediately after, the next big books she got for me were about science, nature, and greatest of all: insects. Beautiful, alien, insects. So much of Her Descent comes from those beginnings, the empathy and the alien were integral to this telling of horror. The alien is obvious, but if I couldn't empathize with Thia (and those she encounters), I couldn't have made a compelling story of her harrowing journey and suffering.

Empathy in all things. Or at least sympathy.

While it was my mother who introduced me to reading and started a life-long love affair with books, it was a certain passionate and enthusiastic English teacher that turned it into something more. Something insidious.

Here I sit writing today, a full time author, having sold more books this year than I ever dreamt possible. Yet to say I am living the dream would be a lie, because even in those days debating literature with a certain Mr. Broderick - the two of us getting so passionate about our conflicting views - I never dreamt that writing would be a career for me. It's not the kind of dream a troubled boy from a poor fishing community has.

But all the same, he put a passion for fiction and its dark corners, so I started writing with no thoughts of anything but scratching an itch.

Plenty of hopeful young writers had whittled away their lives pursuing a hopeless dream in publishing. I just happened to luck out, get into it at the right time; and bust my ass of course.

The busting my ass was all me (and Michelle, of course) but to Mr. Broderick, I owe a thanks for those dangerously fascinating discussions. They paid off afterall.

INTRODUCTION

Her Descent, despite all our anticipations, was a success.

You have to understand, the two of us went into writing as a career with our eyes open. We pursued it with the same vigor and work ethic we did our previous careers, and tackled it like a job.

So when we wrote this horror novel, we did so as a passion project on the side of our more 'commercial' writing. When the shit hit the fan, and stress got high, we retreated back into our old hobby: writing stories intended purely for the both of us.

No longer confined by thoughts of how readers would respond, we wrote the most screwed up thing we could come up with. Because that's what we enjoy. But in all seriousness, we wrote a story that pulled no punches, was something that made us cringe and whimper.

Being a story we enjoyed, it ended up becoming our longest published work. But once we did finish and sent it out into the wild, we did so with no fanfare, and no expectations. It received none of the promotional efforts we gave our more 'commercial' writing. Yet somehow it found not only sales, but fans. A lot of fans.

Reading people comparing your novel to great works of literature like the Odyssey, Alice in Wonderland, or stunning artwork, is surreally pleasant. We're no strangers to positive reviews, we've always gotten far more of it than negative, we've been fortunate to find so many readers who click with our work. But for this? Something so personal? Such a passion project?

Blew us away.

So here it is, a new special print edition to celebrate Her Descent and its bestseller status. But also to mark the occasion as we prepare to publish another work of horror. Another project of passion.

We hope you enjoy. It means so very much to us.

❧ I ❧

19TH CENTURY BRITAIN...

She could hear them. Not with her ears. Not with any mortal senses. It was something deeper and more primal than that, and it had become more acute when she moved into her late great-aunt's manor. As if reaching out of her past, from the nightmares of her childhood during those winter stays in the towering stone complex.

There was something singing to her, and she shifted in her bed once more to listen more closely. Even the sound of the thick sheets rubbing against one another made it hard to hear, drowning the voices out.

Her nights were spent so sleeplessly that she could never enjoy the days. The sun and birdsongs of the day were unenjoyable to her as she overslept to make up for a night of strained listening.

Life became a strange daze to her. Ever sleep-deprived, her mind always lingered on matters nobody else could relate to; none of her high society friends, certainly not the servants who came and brought her supplies and transferred her belongings.

Arising from a brief spate of sleep, she moaned, surprised to have woken with her hand cupping her sex, and she slipped it out of the white, lacy undershorts and rested it onto her stomach. She could smell herself in the air, and it was tinged with something beyond her reasoning.

Thia knew not what *they* were, or where they lurked, but after her fourth sleepless night, she knew she had to find them.

Slipping from her bed, the wood floor felt cold beneath her bare feet. She was a slender woman, and she stole gracefully down the hallway. It didn't matter that she was wearing nothing more than the see-through white slip, for the help was yet to be hired. She had hurried to this place as soon as her great-aunt died.

Something from her youth made her *need* to return.

$$\text{❦} \quad 2 \quad \text{❦}$$

The aroma of the tea filled the air even before the serving lady finished pouring it up. "Thank you, Mary," said Theodora, giving a light smile as she let it be known the woman could go back to the more important matters of unpacking her things, before she returned to her parent's estate where her proper employment remained.

"Of course, m'lady," said the elder maid, smiling fondly at her. The grey haired woman having served as a constant teacher and companion for so long that Theodora considered her as much family as servant.

"Is that bergamot I smell in the tea?" asked her friend Celeste from Oxford University, another woman who forced her way in where she wasn't invited.

"Yes it is," replied Thia, the two women wearing dresses that were perfectly fine and fancy, yet would've turned a few eyes had they the nerve to parade around public in them. Yet that was why Thia enjoyed her company, the both of them liked to buck expectations in their own way.

As such they both served up their own milk and sugar in the

absence of Mary, rather than keep her around for such menial things.

"Are you quite certain you're going to be alright out here by your lonesome, Thia dear?" asked Celeste, her head moving about, taking in the sight of the countryside around them as they sat upon a patio outdoors during a particularly lovely day. "I know you have always been one to skirt the norm, but... I dare say you shall be all by your lonesome out here. Nary a clever wit to match your own for miles around.

Thia's lips crooked into wry amusement. "Who's to say how long I will stay here, Celeste? But truth be told, I intend to get some of my own very special work done. Maybe write up a new treatise on animal biology, geology... once I take an appropriate trip for inspiration," she remarked with a prideful grin.

"Theodora on the Origin of Everything, hmm? Is that to be your new life's work, darling?" quipped the towering woman.

"Something like that," she responded. "We mustn't tarry putting a woman's touch to the issue, no? But first thing's first, dear Celeste," she remarked, placing down her tea cup and letting out a soft sigh as she relaxed back. "Some time to compose myself at long last."

"You've earned it," remarked her friend, smiling to her. "Don't shy from sending me a letter now and then. Especially if you find yourself off in some dark corner of the world, discovering untold wonders." She leaned over the table, smirking a bit, "I promise I won't steal the details and rush to publish them."

Thia's eyes flashed wide, "Suspicious you would even say that, my dear. I'm afraid now I shall have to hold my cards a bit closer to my chest!" They both laughed.

Thia's blonde hair was pulled back from either side of her face, curled against her head and pulled back into twin ponytails, as though she wore a wreath at all times. It was practical for the young woman, and didn't get in her way as she moved into the basement.

It was late, so late, and she knew better than to wander, but that primal pull was growing stronger every day.

Even the slightness of her physique couldn't prevent those rotting, wooden stairs from creaking, and she ran her fingers along the stone walls as she walked. They felt almost slimy, and her hand retreated in protest. Her heart pounded as she took another step, feeling the stair give a groan under her weight.

She could hear *them* calling her though, and she forced herself down onto the cold ground. It was dry and smooth, but she swore she felt things crawling towards her. Something glanced across her bare ankle and she gasped, stepping away.

"I can hear you," she pleaded into the darkness, and tried to light her oil lamp. "Please." Her hands shook before she finally ignited it, looking upon... nothing.

The basement was bare, holding little more than some preserves and rusting grounds-work materials. Thia's large, blue eyes filled with tears, and her body trembled. She was walking in a dream, it felt like, unaware of reality and the absurdity of her position.

It was only then she realized how cold she was, her pale flesh prickling as a brush of air touched along her bare arm.

She gasped and turned! For a moment she thought she saw something lurking between the shadows just before her light snuffed out.

There was nothing.

Just the void of darkness all around her.

She had dropped her lantern but couldn't feel it. Perhaps it was her panic at having just seen something—someone?—but she couldn't find the cold metal to latch onto as she groped along the ground.

As she searched, however, the sound of that crawling returned. It grew, and sounded as if it came from ahead of her. All she could do was follow it. Heed her impulse to search it out.

It was growing closer, but never quite within reach. Always out of reach no matter how loud the scratching sound of some unknown claws moving upon stone and wood grew.

It reached the point where she could no longer take it, not in the oppressive dark that left her so powerless, and she touched the cold stone of the wall and pushed herself up. What was she doing? Had the sleepless nights truly driven her to such an obscenely ridiculous state as to scramble after bugs on her hands and knees in the dirt? She had to get away.

She had to run!

As she thrust herself from the wall and bolted into the dark, her getaway was short lived. She crashed into something wooden, and it was as if all the world clattered down around her noisily.

$$\text{\Large ❧ \quad 4 \quad ❧}$$

Thia had no idea how long she'd passed out, but awaking she felt cool air brush over her. It beckoned her, but she felt wood blocking it from much of her body. She very nearly tried clawing her way through when she noticed the glimmer of light in the distance, and saw her lamp on the floor.

Somehow it had become lit again, and she crawled out from beneath the broken, rotted wood and towards it. Righting the lamp and letting the flame grow, she could see again. Her eyes fell on the gaping hole she'd accidentally created from some rotted corner of the basement.

It led into a rickety chamber, sealed only by decaying wood, it seemed. And though curiosity beckoned her, she felt a thudding pain in her skull and the stab of hunger. How long had she been there?

Her hands were so dirty, and her muscles felt exhausted. There was a tightness between her two shoulders, and she took a step backwards. This was it. This was her time, her choice, and her body trembled.

Something beckoned her from within that foreboding hole, but instead she turned to the stairs. They were partially splintered and rotted, and her entire body felt like she'd been stretched on a rack for days. It could wait.

5

She'd taken several days to recuperate from her incident, but each moment of her wait was spent agonizing over her anxiousness to explore. It had gotten beneath her skin, the surreal and strange feeling so familiar and foreign all at once. Even the light of day couldn't ease her mind of what lurk beneath her.

What was it that was happening in the manor? What was the noise of that crawling?

Even as she sat at the ancient, wooden table her aunt used to serve breakfast at, Thia's food sat idle as she stared towards the door, pondering the mysteries of the basement.

That was it, she concluded.

That weakened portion of wall she'd accidentally exposed was the key to her answers. She felt it more than knew it. It had to be. It was as though some dark, instinctual part of her had become attuned with things she didn't yet know of, and she pushed herself up from the table.

Her small stomach gurgled in protest, but it didn't matter to the young woman. All that mattered in this instant was what she didn't know and yet knew so intimately. Lost were thoughts of balls and courtly affairs, of obligation to family and the estate.

It was as though whatever secrets were there had crawled under her flesh and infested her slim body. She wore a long, antique-gold dress that brushed against her ankles as she walked and bared her shoulders, and though she knew it was impractical, she breezed past the hall leading to her bedroom on the way to those rickety stairs.

Still, she hesitated at the top, and her hand trembled as she went to the oil lamp. The help would be arriving within a fortnight, but the wait... It was torture. She couldn't hold off for the presence of more.

It was another instinct, a deep burning down in her very core. She had to be alone.

Thia had been a young scholar, an exceptional student growing up, and a pride to her family in academic matters. She had been encouraged to be more than a mere lady-in-waiting, and she excelled at it. She told herself it was the same yearning curiosity that drove her at that moment to plunge back down into that deep basement.

She reached around the corner of the doorway and found the lantern. One thing she would not skimp on was oil for it, and she filled it to fullness before lighting it and heading down that dark tunnel.

Between the groans of the stairs she heard it: that faint sound of crawling from the tunnel below. Her destination.

She plunged down, nearly toppling when one of the old wooden stairs gave way with a crunch, dropping a quarter of an inch. Thia managed to catch herself with her nails dug into a crack in the cold stone and swallowed down her anxiety.

The flickering image of some figure in the corner of the basement drew her attention until she realized it was just the misshapen shadow of an old shovel propped against a crate.

The noise of something scuttling through that hole at the

other end of the basement faded, and she felt the light, cool flow of air tickling her skin beneath her dress.

"Hello?"

Her voice echoed in the small room, and her nose crinkled with confusion. Her voice shouldn't echo, not here, not with the low ceiling and the dirt floor.

Her mouth went dry, and she swallowed as she took a step towards the shovel, her fingers touching against it. Should she take a weapon? Something within her said no, and her hand retreated.

Thia approached the hole, the lantern shedding light upon those ancient cut timbers. They looked nothing like the wood throughout the rest of the manor, not even the rotted old boards in the basement. Even those must have been replaced a dozen times since these before her were put in place, and it didn't take much for her to push the ones in the hole out of the way. They crumbled with ease, falling apart against her push, twisting and breaking, but not with the crunch of wood in the other room. These were molded and slightly damp; they peeled away like soggy bread.

Her curiosity nearly got the better of her, but she cleared enough of a space to safely get through before attempting to squeeze in. When she pushed her lantern through all she saw were the smoothly worn away walls of what was once a tunnel leading down. She could see that damp water trickled across their surface, and had turned what must have once upon a time been carved stone blocks into smooth, nearly melded surfaces.

It was an older stonework than the rest of the manor, she noticed right away. Nothing like the elegant style of the rest of her aunt's place.

Thia's heart thudded in her chest, and she felt heat rise within her, even though the cool air was stronger with the boards gone.

She had to push forwards, though. Some innate yearning to

explore, to discover, to... she didn't know what, she just had to go in. Regardless of the justifications, or lack thereof.

With careful motions she climbed through that gateway into the unknown, and as she reached the other side safely, only the sound of fabric tearing broke her triumph. Her dress had caught on some rusted, medieval looking nail and suffered the loss of a long strip of its golden fabric.

She tugged it away, but didn't frown. The loss of the rich material was nothing in the face of her discovery, and she took a tentative step forward. Then another.

Each breath felt like it was echoing around her, and there was something in the air that made her skin prickle. A thought came to her, unbidden: *I should turn back.* She shouldn't enter such a place by herself, yet not even her self-chiding could stop her foot from taking her further into the depths.

Deeper she went, the stairs twisting and turning, but in no seemingly logical fashion. There was no symmetry or order to it, it just went on and on at random. *Where did it go?* She pondered endlessly, the trip down taking her far longer than she could have imagined. It had been at least an hour, and still the stone staircase went ever down.

Every time she nearly slipped on one of those smooth, rounded stairs she felt the pangs of doubt strike back at her conscious mind. But she pushed them away, she had to find out. Had to delve deeper.

After seemingly endless descent, and still no sign of an end, doubts began to become real. She should have prepared. Should have brought supplies. Food. How long had she been gone already? Her lamp must have gone through hours' worth of oil already!

Though as she considered turning back, a tickle of a cold breeze—not just air, but a breeze—touched her ankles, and she looked down.

An open crevice broke through the stone wall and showed

through to the other side thanks to the ancient erosion of that trickling water.

The only way for her to see through it though was to crouch down, get onto one knee and lower the lantern.

The light did not carry beyond the stone of the wall itself though. She could make out nothing beyond but inky blackness.

She nearly lost hope when the idea of shuttering the lamp came to her. She choked off its meager light and stared through the crevice.

Nothing came to her at first, but as her big, blue eyes adjusted to the dark she could see it: vast cavern lie far below, carrying on for what seemed like miles.

She could see so little of it through that tiny hole, but could make out the soft glow of some fungal plumes that showed off still lakes of water. More interesting than any of that was the wall she sighted. A wall of intelligent construct. Great and mighty it guarded something, it had to. But she couldn't see. For whatever it was, it lay beneath her staircase. Right beneath her.

Her heart pounded as she pushed herself back, leaning against the wall ignorant to the water that ran down her back and soiled her dress. What was down there? How could anyone have constructed something so deep, underneath her aunt's manor all this time and beyond?

She needed to see what it was, to explore, and with renewed interest, her pace quickened.

With her unshuttered lamp back in hand, she descended further. She could feel moisture on her forehead, and brushed her blonde bangs to the side as she wiped it away. The trip seemed unending.

Distracted by that she lost her footing on the increasingly smooth surface of the stairs, and she slid down a length. The rough ride jostled her slender form until the walls ended and she very nearly toppled out into the blackness.

In a scramble she grabbed for what she could, broke some of

her nails as she tried to cling to the now near smooth stone surface. Her lantern went flying from her grasp and she watched in her panic as she clung on for dear life as that light snuffed out, followed by a clatter of metal on stone as it impacted what she swore looked like a stone house.

Her heart stopped.

Panic gripped her. But she held on. She had to.

There was nothing else but to cling, suspended in desperation.

She began to pull herself up once she felt secure in her grip, but just as Thia rose up over the edge she heard it: the sound of stone crumbling.

One hand gave way as a chunk of stone came with it, then the whole of the stone-stairs beneath crumbled and fell and she went toppling backwards to meet whatever fate greeted her lost lantern.

$\maltese \quad 6 \quad \maltese$

The sound of something crawling awoke her. The feel of some long, inhuman limb brushing her leg made her dart her eyes open.

When she opened her eyes the glow of those fungal blooms surrounded her. It was such a low glow, and could never have normally been noticed if not for the supreme darkness of the caverns.

It gave her enough light to look and see that she had broken her fall on a large outcropping of the fungus however. Some of the spongy stems broken beneath her, as the things climbed up to several feet off the cavern floor below her.

As she struggled to get up, she noticed the collapsed stairway above. A big gap remained between it and the stalactite from which it had descended above, the seemingly human-wrought stairs having been hewn from natural cave structures.

It was as if she had descended from the heavens unto earth from within a mighty icicle in the sky. She couldn't help but appreciate it, even in her dire predicament. That is, up until she descended from her mushroom bed and felt something beneath her foot rise up and stab at her calf.

A shriek passed her lips and she recoiled from the glowing bed of fungus, though her heart caught she saw it was nothing alive. Nothing alive anymore, at least.

What looked like the bone of a ribcage had pricked her leg when she stepped upon it, but more than that a whole heap of bones—human bones of all sizes, skulls of young and old alike —laid out beneath the great macabre bed that had saved her.

She was stuck down there, and that realization gripped her heart and made her breath shallow. Thia bent down and touched her leg, frowning at the dribble of blood and wiping it away from her fair skin. Her dress was torn in places, the ankle length skirt now having tears up above her knees, and she felt positively famished.

Panic began to rise in her and her eyes darted about the gloomy dark for some sign of another way. Instead she was greeted with the new reality of her situation: stone buildings, hewed from the earth itself, all about. She had landed in a veritable city beneath the earth.

The spiraling staircase had descended from within a stalactite in the cavern ceiling down into the midst of some ancient stone community.

Thia plucked herself up off the ground and shakily made her way around the nearest building. It was deathly quiet. Worn, old tattered cloths hung from the windows and doors of the settlement all around, but none stirred even in the slightest.

Those old human bones she found the only sign of life she could make, other than the patches of luminescent fungus that grew about, many of them much smaller than the great patch that had saved her life from her fall. How old was that pile of bodies that fueled its growth? She wondered, with all her scholarly learning, and could not help but think of the countless lives lost to fuel her rescue years later.

What terrible tragedy had befallen them that led to their piling up and being digested by hungry fungus? Were they, like her, victims of that worn, ancient staircase? Explorers of some forgotten time who had descended those stairs from the manor above only to slip and fall to their doom again and again until their carcasses were enough to finally provide sufficient nutrition to save her life?

The cattle-like expenditure of human life, the arbitrary, predatory nature of her salvation, it all made her tremble in the cool dark as she walked those ghostly empty roads.

An ancient blood sacrifice for the cause of cushioning my fanny.

There was no settled dust down there. Though it looked like dust, it was actually a thin layer of spores that coated just about everything, and she realized as her eyes adjusted to the dark, that the spores were responsible for much of her ability to see anything. The macabre fungus once again her saviour.

It was as she pondered this that the faint sound of crawling arose and grabbed her attention. She turned, and saw it led into some dark alleyway. She followed it, and saw there at the end a silhouette of a man in a long, black coat. He stood facing away from her, and seemed to wear some sort of hat. As she moved towards him, though, he vanished. The next moment, she spotted him moving upon the wall like some crawling spider, and he vanished once more. He was gone for good, with only the faint echo of claws upon stone left in her mind.

She rubbed her big, blue eyes as if to free them from grit. To see what was happening, to understand, but there was no understanding. Though she couldn't quite place what, something didn't seem right at all, as if it were all a dream. This place, what she was seeing, none of it made sense, not logical sense anyway, and she pinched her bared arm to wake herself.

Yet she couldn't wake. She remembered back to the sharp pain when she'd landed upon that rib cage and knew there was no waking. The thought terrified her, and she heard her own voice echo around her.

"Am I dead?"

Had she fallen to her doom and this was all an elaborate fantasy? Was this the place between life and death? Her eyes welled up with tears and she ran towards the man that wasn't there, wanting to cling to him, to find something to save her from this doom.

In her near-mad panic she saw a knotted cord, old and frayed, but thick and sturdy looking. It dangled from above, as though made of some alien material, and it looked like it would hold her if she climbed it towards the window overhead.

Was it some sign? Should she follow?

She would have to leap to grasp it, but before she could she heard something: were those voices? Yes, it must be. It came from the roadway, and though it was in a casual voice from some distance, the quiet of the mighty cavern caused it to carry to her from far away.

People. People were living here, underneath the world? The fear of purgatory gripped her. Was this a punishment? She had been a good woman, led a good life, and there was no reason she should be sent to the great beyond.

They seemed so calm, their voices so reassuring, but she couldn't stay here. She would climb to the place of clouds and happiness, and she leapt towards the rope, feeling it burn and splinter into her hands. The sharp pieces of frayed fabric bit into her soft, unworked hands as she slid down and fell off.

Her landing was off balance, and she stumbled back a few paces. Her heart pounded beneath the stiffness of her dress, and her nerves were rattled. She needed to escape!

In the quiet of the underground world every scuff of her shoes was so loud, and the voices stopped, though she could hear footsteps coming towards her. Racing in her direction.

She couldn't get to the rope in time though, and as she got

up to try and leap for it again she heard them behind her. Their voices were raspy, but speaking in some old yet familiar manner. "A lass," spoke one, and she could not help but turn to see them.

They were two men, tall, powerful looking, so pale of skin as to look sickly. But the muscles that bulged from their bare chests and legs promised strength, not weakness. One wore long, white hair around his shoulders, the other cropped and dark, but neither wore much. Just the tattered remains of pants on the white haired one, that and a ratty looking vest upon the other.

She couldn't help but stare as she backed away. The fair young woman was terrified of these outsiders, of the people that lived without sunlight or sky, and her mouth dropped open. How could they live underground? How long had they been here?

Yet her curiosity was dampened by the feeling of wrongness, by a deep understanding that this wasn't...well, it simply wasn't right! *They* weren't right!

Nothing that lived in this place beneath the earth's crust could be. She was frozen in place by her fear, by her anxiety, and she couldn't speak. Instead, it was as if all ability left her as she stared into the eyes of the two men, and her pale flesh felt drained of all colour.

As they stepped closer towards her, their features grew clearer. From a distance they looked masculine, she would almost say handsome. No facial hair she could see, though each had strong jaws. Something seemed so familiar to her, like they were walking out of a dream towards her. Out of *her* dreams.

The same dreams she awoke to with her fingers buried in her panties, and as they neared, she could see their eyes: red, malicious looking. Their lips: curved and sinister, with two downward teeth like fangs prodding their lower lips.

They were monsters. Yet they were men. They were the stuff of nightmares and dreams, and she felt drawn to them as they approached. "A ripe young beauty," rasped one.

The other responded in his old fashioned manner, "I've not laid eyes upon such a tender morsel in nigh on a lifetime."

She couldn't move. She wanted to, but her feet stayed so firmly planted on the strange ground beneath her. It almost felt like it was shifting, and she leaned forward, towards them, to balance herself. It was so precarious, and her weight shifted to the ball of her foot, pushing her closer.

It could be considered a graceful dance, the way she trembled in fear while they beckoned her body to contort and seek them out, but for her it was only horror. Their alien nature chilled her.

"I'm lost," she protested, and her voice sounded nearly as dry and raspy as theirs. "I fell."

To gaze into those red eyes of theirs was like looking into the heart of her dreams.

The white haired one seemed to beckon to her without so much as a curl of his fingers, and she stumbled into his hard body. Found it to be cold. As cool as the air that surrounded them, sapping the heat from her own fair flesh.

"Pretty doll," rasped the dark haired one, as he went about behind her, and she could feel their ravenous hunger practically radiating off them. They yearned for her, and the press of dual manhoods against either side of her as they opened their mouths and hissed through fangs was bliss.

Some part of her knew enough to be scared, and her fingers trembled at her side, but it fought with her arousal, her desire for this. For them.

She'd known of them since she was a child, spending the summers with her aunt. She'd dreamed of them in her youth, and it was a crushing realization that they were the reason her life had been put on hold. It hadn't been school, or the desire to travel.

It was them.

She'd been waiting for this all her life, and her pulse quickened as she heard the word 'yes' curl around them. It was sweet comfort to feel those strange, hard, cold bodies press in on her.

The dark haired one behind her grabbed hold of her two arms and yanked her back. "I want 'er," he said with no small amount of insistence, the strength of his pull painful, nearly wrenching her arms out of their sockets.

The other hissed, though he was poised to plunge his fangs into her. "Git yer grubby hands off her," he retorted and yanked her back with her hips. The tug of war between the two powerful fiends was painful, but somehow her mind was in a haze, and she could only be grateful for their attentions.

It felt as though she were floating, powerless over her own body. It was as though she were looking at herself from afar, and her mouth dropped open. She wanted to solve their quarrel, but words somehow felt too sophisticated for this strangely beautiful barbarity.

She swooned between them as her body ached and groaned in protest of their rough handling.

The dark haired one let go of an arm and struck the other fiend, "'ands off!" he bellowed.

To which the long haired man twisted her body to the side and discarded her like a toy, causing her body to spin and fly away against one of the stone buildings. He let loose his fangs and gave a great, animalistic cry at the other. They were fighting over her. The two beautiful men, clad in almost nothing, ready to tear each other apart over their need for her.

She could feel that pulse between her thighs that had woken her deep in the night, and her fingers trembled with need. She had to feel that pleasure, that pressure on her sex, and her hand pressed the thick material of her skirt betwixt her legs. It was just the tiny tease of sensation and she knew it wasn't enough.

It couldn't be.

Her fingertips pressed down harder on that throbbing nub and stilled it for a moment, but her entire body felt hot. She was so deep beneath the world, hidden to all but the two men, and her breath hitched.

How could terror be so intertwined with lustful need?

The two powerful bodies impacted one another again, and again. They struck out, nails and fists hitting each other with loud, dull thuds as they postured, swayed and struck out. They were so mighty, and their pale, muscular forms held such power in them as they attempted to win their contest.

Thia could only watch as they struck, and the dark haired one buried his fist into the others stomach. The hit caused the fiendish man to buckle over and hiss in pain.

Their bodies grappled together, thick, bulging limbs pressing and squeezing as they pushed and pulled one another back and forth. They were like glorious gladiators of the dark reaches of the earth, and she watched as the long white haired man struck his two fists upon the spine of the other, while the dark hammered his fist into the man's side again and again.

She wanted to tell them to stop, though she didn't understand why and her attempt turned into nothing more than a moan. It was futile. Her thoughts had so quickly disappeared as her fingers rubbed over the thick cloth of her skirt and she leaned against the strange wall to steady herself.

She wanted to flee, begged herself to get away from the brawling madmen that wanted her so badly. Her eyes drifted to the rope once more, hanging so tantalizingly out of reach, but she couldn't force her legs to move. They felt weighted down, her entire body so heavy with exhaustion and fear.

Thia waffled as her inner battle raged while the two men brutalized one another, and peering back, she saw as the dark haired one hammered the other, and she heard the sound of a rib breaking beneath his pounding fist.

It looked to be nearing its end, the white fiend breaking, exhausted and pummeled, until he lunged for the others throat and sunk his fangs into it. With a hissing cry from the short-dark haired brute he ripped out a chunk of his throat in a gory mess, shoved him to the ground and stomped him into a bloody pulp.

Her mouth dropped open but her scream was silent, and her body responded only with more heated blood rushing to her sex. Her blue eyes watered as they widened in horror and disgust, but she couldn't stop her furious rubbing, couldn't quell her dangerous need.

However, before he could look back at her—his prize, hard fought and won—her legs finally moved. She just needed to get to the rope. To climb to wherever it led.

Her feet crunched on the ground, stones skittering beneath her feet as she leapt for the hard, brittle rope once more.

Thia missed. Her legs were too much like jelly to propel her to the rope, and as she fell to the stone wall, she slid down it and turned to see the battered man coming towards her. One side of his body was clutched in hand as he limped in her direction, his handsome face now a gory mess of blood and bestial desire.

He lunged for her with his one free arm, grabbed her ankle and pulled her across the stone alleyway towards himself. "Mine," was all he managed to say in his rasping, horrid voice, so much more strained following the brutal fight.

She cried out and heard the sound all around her. Her body felt like it was boiling, her dress too hot for her even as she grabbed onto the wall to try to pull herself up and away from him.

Even in his injured state, however, he was stronger than the petite, blonde noble, and her struggles were fruitless.

Worst still, she didn't understand why her body fought. He looked every bit the monster, but her dreams kept flooding her consciousness. *Wasn't this what I had wanted?*

The futile struggle ended as he dragged her across the ground towards him, his heaving, hard chest looming over her as he bore down upon her. That look in his eyes something of pure animal need. Deeper than lust, deeper than hunger. He bore his two pointed fangs as he pushed his hand into her gut and kept her pinned.

Time seemed to freeze, and the fear of her imminent doom gripped her. He was going to gore her like he had his companion, and part of her wanted that. Welcomed it. Had waited for it for endless years, and did not shy away from such a bloody end in the bowels of the earth.

Thia did her best to war against that part of herself, but surrender or no, he had her. No amount of strength or will she could muster would change that.

She was so consumed with her dread and welcoming of her demise that she didn't notice the enhanced darkness that came up behind the fiend. Part of her even twinged in regret as a hand shot out, took hold of its long, white hair and wrenched it back from her.

Another hand lashed out at that bloody face, and a strike hit the former victor, leaving his cheek wrenched open, and a bloody mess of flesh and teeth showing through the side.

Her former violator raised a fist to fight back, but another slashing strike hit him and the horror watching the fiend's eye dangle out of its socket was nearly too much for poor Thia.

"No!" she cried, and was shocked by the word as it lingered in the air. It was too much! She'd spent all her life waiting for this moment, for this man. To have it all wrenched from her?

Yet that part of her, that deep, human pit in her stomach was filled with gratitude and thankfulness that this wasn't the end. That someone... something... had saved her. Her entire body felt like it had been torn open and exposed, yet she still lived, and could feel that thud thud of her heart reminding her of the truth.

The perseverance of that fiend astonished her though, he fought back even with half his face missing. The slender, dark figure dodged the blow though, and a swift motion—a kick?— hit him up in under his chin and she could hear bone break. His neck snapped, and he fell back to the rocky floor.

Thia was alone with her saviour in that ominous alley. In that dark pit of the earth.

She couldn't make him out though, he was shrouded in darkness. Tall and slender, he was nothing like the men—the fiends—that had tried to ravish and feed upon her. He—it?—stood over her in silence, masked by dimness and his own dark flesh, like a pillar of obsidian.

She stared at him, and her entire body fluttered like a leaf in the autumn winds. "Why?" she asked, and even she wasn't sure if it was a protest or something else. Surely she didn't wish to be eaten, to be devoured by the strange men.

Even the thought, the reminder that she had for a split second so desired it, rankled her mind and body. She felt her stomach tighten and she leaned to the side, coughing at the dirt. She couldn't even vomit with disgust, even as she inhaled the blood and gore tinged air.

It didn't speak to her, but she heard something. Some faint sound. Not like the crawling noise that first led her here, but something faintly familiar nonetheless.

It watched her in silence, then as she struggled to get up it leaned forward. She felt its hand upon her arm as he pulled her up to her feet, and then she could see something more at least. The long dark overcoat it wore was a century or more out of fashion, with a high collar, and what looked like a hat from before instead appeared to be a strange hairdo that curved up at the back of its head like a large frond.

Thia's legs were still weak, and she leaned towards him. She didn't understand what was happening, and her wide eyes pleaded with him. "I need to go home." Exhaustion washed through her and she felt her slim stomach tighten and gnarl with lack of food. How long had she been down here?

Silence still. It watched her, and as her large blue eyes trailed down its arm to where it grasped her, she felt it. A voice. In her mind. "*Going above is not easy.*" She winced. It was strange, like the words were formed in her brain by the cacophony of crawling noises so long remembered, a million little harsh sounds combining into something like a man's voice.

She gasped and her hand went to her temple, feeling along the golden strands of hair as if touching her head could help her understand. She swallowed and her head tilted.

What was he?

"You..." she murmured, and she thought back to her dreams, to the odd nights that she felt something calling for her, and the chittering that followed.

"Please... I don't understand this place."

His hand did not leave her arm, and she heard his odd voice in her head again. *"I saved you from those two, but there are more. Many more dangers,"* she heard something then with her ears, a soft noise, barely audible, like the faint chittering of an insect. That and the empty stare without a face that gazed back at her in the dark of the caverns.

Was he a danger, though?

He certainly seemed to be everything that she'd been warned against, yet he'd saved her. Protected her from being devoured, and the reminder that she'd wanted that for even a second made her stomach churn again.

"I'm scared," she confessed on a breath. She never should have left her bed, never should have come into this infinite basement with its unnatural secrets.

She felt something then, as if instead of words he spoke to her in her mind with emotion. It was strange, inhuman emotion though. Something almost like sympathy, but not. Something like an urge to protect, but not. Something like desire, but again, not.

He released her thin arm and spoke into her mind again, *"No running. You cannot run from these dangers. Only hide."* He looked up at the rope then back to her, *"Come. I will show you. Hide you. Trust."* And there it was again, that faint little chitter of noise as the backs of his dark, void-like fingers brushed her arm with their rough touch.

She had no other options, no other hope but to trust this... creature. This man that was nothing like a man, and she moved closer to him as if in response. She didn't understand how he'd invaded her mind, how those weird sounds formed something intelligible. Her fear was palpable, and her hand reached out for him. "I tried to get up there," she murmured.

With that he put his arm about her waist and held her to him. He was slender compared to those great fiends that had battled it out over the right to devour her, but he was far taller than her, his body hard. He reached up for the rope and took hold of it with ease.

There was no warning, he pulled them both up by that alien rope with some deftness that should have been impossible with only one free hand to use. He scaled that cliff-like wall at a surprisingly rapid pace, though when she peered down at the bloody alley below, she felt the world spin as she realized in a mixture of sudden fear and terrible excitement that all that held her from falling to her doom was that one strange creature's singular hold.

It was as if she were looking at life through a haze of confusion, as if it were a dream. Nothing seemed quite right, not even herself. She wasn't acting right. She didn't feel right. Her body wasn't her own, and for a moment she thought she was going to faint before she forced herself right once more.

There had been none of the fungal blooms in the alley below, only the light sprinkling of spores that allowed her to see the pale forms of those deceased attackers, but as she entered at last into the hole in the rock face above, she had to squint momentarily at the light of all the fungus. It looked to her like a cave at first, ripe with the blue-white glow of the mushrooms, though as he put her down she saw it was more than that.

Old stone desks and shelves hinted that this was a home or

building, hewed from the stone like the others below. Unlike the stonework of the stairs though, she could see that this was well taken care of. Aside from the fungus it was tidy, and the intricate craftsmanship of the bizarrely angled furniture was breathtaking, if jarringly alien.

Even as he put her down she still clung to him, as if she were afraid to leave him. The only safe thing in this twisted underworld, and she was afraid he'd disappear just like he had before. That she'd be left to the flesh and blood of the strange men with their red eyes and their powerful need.

Thia trembled on her weak knees, and her voice was so raspy. "I shouldn't be here."

His response didn't come in words, it was a feeling that swept her. It was different, but she knew the undertones of it intimately: rejection. He denied her statement through emotion, not words.

It was strange, and she turned her head towards him and up to look into his blank visage. Then surprise greeted her. In the glow of the mushroom-lanterns she could see him, albeit faintly. His obsidian flesh blended into the darkness of the caverns so well, it was hard to make him out even then. But the smooth almost boyish jawline led up across his face until it blended into something monstrous. Eyes like pools of oil, exotically shaped, not ovals, not circular, three cornered and alien. Hair like small tendrils that swept back over his head.

Her saviour was more monstrous in appearance than the fiends that had sought to devour her.

Her lip trembled, and she wasn't certain if she screamed, but felt her tongue move in her mouth. Repulsion swept through her and fear twisted in her heart. She didn't know what to make of it, of him, but she wanted to go home. To wake up in her soft bed, and know safety.

That wasn't an option though. She had to contend with this reality. Contend with him.

That flood of foreign emotion swept over her again, she could feel his response to her horror: anger? No, not anger. Something like it. Disappointment? Frustration? Very nearly.

She watched as the smooth line of his—its—mouth opened, and like those fiends below two fangs protruded. Though these were longer, more slender. Curved. His mouth trembled and a strange chittering sound emerged, like that which had called her to the underworld at first.

He pulled the rope up into the hole-of-a-home then swept past her deeper into the place. He was so odd, so alien.

"You're not going to kill me?" she asked, no longer clinging to his side like a lost child. Instead she was standing back, forcing her eyes away from the gore that lay beneath.

Why had he called her here? Made her leave the safety of her home? She'd known of him for so long, yet his terrifying visage was enough to make her squirm.

It didn't quite make sense though. The things below... those fiends that sought to devour her had been in her visions. She had felt the pull towards them. She did not feel it towards this... aberration of a man.

In his anachronistic coat, the man-thing moved about, giving no answer right away. But when he returned he had with him a bowl, filled with strange mushrooms, and at the heart a large upturned beetle, with its carapace cracked open and its meaty innards puffed out. "*No kill,*" came its chittering voice inside her brain. "*Eat.*"

She was certain she made a face, for that was the most disgusting serving of food she could have been offered. Yet still, her stomach growled with need beyond her, and she shifted with uncertainty. She hadn't eaten in so long, and her body felt so weary, her mind fogged with dizziness.

"This is a bug." She was unable to hide her disgust even as she took the bowl.

A bug and the macabre fungus that bloomed from the corpses of the dead, her mind added.

He simply echoed a "*Yes*" in her mind and reached down, pinching off some of that white, puffy bug meat with his clawed fingers and mimed eating it. He didn't, however, and instead offered it to her upon his fingers, and she felt some strange, inhuman emotion that resembled caring – was this thing capable of tenderness? – emanate from him.

Her nose crinkled, but even her disgust couldn't outweigh her very primal need for food. She took it with a ravenous craving, even as the texture felt rubbery and hideously oily against her tongue. She swallowed it with a quick gulp and nearly choked, but her need for food grew, and she took the second clump of meat on her own.

She was quiet as she devoured the disgusting meal, her body trembling as she realized just how famished she'd become.

All the while he watched her. His quiet approval was a foreign emotion that invaded her consciousness. He was a monster, and she knew not what he wanted, but she knew he didn't want her dead.

Trapped in that hellish land beneath the earth, he seemed to be utterly fascinated by her curious differences. He reached out, and with his dark, clawed fingers he stroked her straight blonde hair with a tentative sort of exploration.

She didn't move away, but she cringed as she finished off the puffed meat of the bug. She couldn't bring herself to dine on the fungus of the dead, though, and she offered it back to him with an urgency. She didn't want it tempting her, that disgusting, strange glow taunting her.

"I can't stay," she pleaded. "I don't want to be here."

She could feel his own twinge of disappointment at her words, and he reluctantly took the bowl from her. "*No easy way above,*" came his scratchy voice in her brain again, and he laid the bowl aside to stand up before her.

He was so tall, and she could see through his open coat that his chest was bare beneath. His dark black-brown flesh hard and lean, slender, but corded with muscle fibre. He lifted both of his hands to her head, and stroked over her blonde hair with each, she could feel the fondness, the... it wasn't quite right, not a human's emotions. It was different.

"You will be safer here," he assured as he tenderly stroked her head and hair. *"I will tend you. Care for you. Protect you,"* and she could see the memory of the two blood-fiends fighting over her and this... thing coming to rescue her from the victor. It was as if he replayed that memory into her mind.

She shouldn't need protecting! Tears welled in her eyes, and fear had replaced all the curiosity and desire that had forced her into that hole in the first place. She simply wanted to go home. To not know of this horrible place beneath the earth's crust, beneath her very home, if she could bring herself to stay after this.

"But they wanted to eat me," she pleaded. "How can I be safe where people want to eat me?"

His black pools that sufficed as eyes stared at her, seemed fascinated by her every little movement. He moved his own lips as if in mimicry of hers, and in a very amateurish attempt to sync his lip's movement with the words he put into her mind he said, *"Me. I make you safe."* It was followed by a quiver of his lips and those fearsome fangs of his, a chittering emerging from his mouth in time as he neared her beautiful face.

"What is this place?"

She felt so dizzy and swooned, on the brink of passing out. How much time had passed since she arrived? She reached out, grabbing hold of his forearm and righting herself. She should be terrified of him, of his alienness. He didn't look right, as if he were from not of this world, but he'd saved her. In her sleepy delirium, it was enough.

He held her, arms holding her up and steadying her. Though

her weary mind took time to realize it wasn't with the two arms she could see. He still stroked and held her head, admiring her human features with such fascination.

From within his large coat a second pair of arms had emerged and wrapped about her. This new set was like the two he held her with, save for having three hooked talon-like digits a piece.

It was as if the terror had reached its peak and no longer could she make sense of it. Her face went pale, and it was in that instant that she lost all consciousness.

It was too much.

✵ 7 ✵

hia was slow to regain consciousness, though the first thing she experienced was an alien emotion in her mind: wanting.

She felt strange physically, and it took her a while to realize she was laying down upon some flat, hard surface. She felt something itchy against her backside like fabric, but certainly not the rich cloth of her dress. Her big, blue eyes fluttered open and she looked up, seeing the visage of that dark monster over top of her.

He no longer wore the old-fashioned coat, and his body was bare from the waist up. She could see his form in all its misshapen 'glory'. The corded muscle that looked like it was woven from fibres beneath his skin, the twin sets of arms, the long, proboscis like tongue of his that was licking out from his fanged-maw over the wound upon her bare leg.

She was naked.

Thia cried out as she shifted away from him, her hands desperately moving to cover her body. She still felt so sluggish, sedated, her mind not comprehending what was happening.

An acute awareness of her former dreamy state came rushing into her consciousness unbidden. This wasn't real. It couldn't be. She'd been having a nightmare about ghouls in the dark, and strange, almost insectoid men, but that was a dream. Nothing that could hurt her... yet the feel of his tongue was so real!

The sight of him, his twisted body, was even more so.

He looked at her with those dark pools, staring in quizzical silence. She could feel the saliva of his long, white tongue like a slimy film over her leg wound. As she covered herself in that scratchy grey sheet, the only covering she could find, he crawled up over her like nothing human could.

He gave her a dark stare as he twisted his head to the side, his words invading her mind. "*Hurt,*" he said simply, and before her hackles could raise in fright he added. "*Heal your hurts.*"

"Where are my clothes?" she trembled, her voice warbling as he prowled over her. Even though her dress was tattered and dirty, it was softer and more comfortable than the itchy blanket she tried to cover herself in. It felt more like cheap carpet than a sheet, and it did nothing to calm her fear.

"Where am I?"

"*Home,*" came his response immediately, and she could only watch as that dark creature loomed over her, reached out to stroke her hair once more with one of its four limbs. "*You are safe,*" came its reassurance, and she realized she was in a different part of that hole-in-the-wall-home. Its lean, hard muscled chest rising and falling before her as it clicked softly.

Her throat felt so dry and she shook her head. "This isn't *my* home," she protested. "This is... scary." The sleep had done nothing to reignite her curiosity, as if being here were the sole driving force of it. As if she'd been born to be here, to seek it out, and to explore no more after that.

As the creature continued to stroke her hair so tenderly—so lovingly, she realized!—her horror at the place was diverted for only a moment as she realized the odd little corner she was nestled in.

No sign of her dress, though the greyish fabric that covered her was everywhere. It looked nothing like the fabric she'd found covering the home's doors and windows outside. It seemed somehow freshly spun despite its scratchy nature against her pale form. She was rested upon a bed covered in it, a bed of stone, but a bed no less. And all about her were arrayed oddities. Little trinkets, strange gems and pottery, and more of that greyish fabric fashioned into designs around her bed.

"*Not scary,*" he reassured her, his bizarre, dark face looming so close to her that made his statement almost laughable. "*Home. Safe. Yours.*" He chittered lightly, and she could feel that he—unlike the fiends—was not cold. Even his breath had some slight edge of warmth to it. "*Made you home. Special for you,*" and his two lower arms formed a giving gesture, as if he were offering her something.

She felt like she was going to cry out of frustration, of fear, of appreciation, all at once. She wanted to accept his gifts and be gracious like she'd always been taught. To be kind to those who helped you.

But that advice was given to her about people. He was decidedly not a person.

"Who are you?" she trembled. "What are you?"

He was still mouthing his answers to her, trying to imitate speech as he simply popped his words into her mind. "*Yours. Your protector,*" there was a pause, and during that she realized something... the odd grey fabric patterns on the walls? They were fashioned into bizarre imitations of her life above. One threaded image looked so much like the manor her aunt had bequeathed her it was uncanny.

"*Your husband,*" came his final words that struck a chilling stillness in her, as if it took him time to root through her mind to find the appropriate approximation he wanted to express his alien meaning. For as much as he was easily mistaken for a man in his coat, to see him bare and exposed before her, the oddities of his alien heritage were simply unignorable.

Her arm stretched out towards that strange, familiar replica, and she felt that longing to return to the manor. The familiar, safe wood that kept out any threats. She smiled until her hand faltered.

He knew where she lived. Where she'd grown up.

Her gaze shifted, and she saw anew all the little replicas of her life, of the doll she slept with as a child. The familiar, warm mementos of her childhood, twisted and morphed by this alien being.

Her mind couldn't handle the shock, the true realization of what he'd been doing for all these years, and there was only blackness to comfort her.

8

The warm summer breeze blew across her face. Thia could feel the heat of the sun build on her body as she lay in the grass down by the river near her academy. How she loved that spot.

Opening her eyes she saw beside her the visage of Edain, the handsome, dark haired student she shared so many classes with. He reached over to her, put his arm about her form and smiled. His face always lit up when he smiled, and those cheeks of his dimpled a bit.

He didn't say anything, but he leaned over and kissed Thia's thick lips, his thumb stroking along her side.

He tasted like fine, rich sweets, like the truffle chocolates she always had as a child. It was exquisite, and his body was so warm and comforting. Everything else drifted away from her consciousness as she felt his protective arms tug her into his hard body.

Her lips were so full and they tingled with sensation, as if every nerve were reaching out to feel him, to respond to his tender affections.

Edain had always been so nervous and cautious, but instead he pushed himself over on top of her, his much larger body pressing down upon her slender frame. She could even feel the prod of that masculine bulge as he tongued her mouth and stroked a hand down her side to her skirt, methodically fingering the fabric and curling it up over her thigh.

So forward, so wanting. He was just filled with adoration, she could feel it. He wanted to be with her in every way, and he ground that needful swell against her groin as he tugged her dress upwards.

Some part of her knew it was *wrong,* but she forced it away as her mouth parted for his. Her tongue lashed against him, tasting him so eagerly as her legs spread to make room for him. So often she'd dreamed that this would happen, that he'd finally get over his apprehensions and just touch her, feel her.

Thia's heart pounded heavily and she could feel how wet she already was, her sex pulsing with its overpowering need. "Take me," she murmured against his throat.

The low growl of desire he gave was so husky and masculine, so full of need. He lifted her skirt and, brazenly, she was wearing nothing beneath. Edain touched her tender quim beneath, finding it so slick and willing. He tasted her on his fingertips, gave such a groan of satisfaction!

"I need you, Thia," he groaned out the words, and she heard his belt coming undone, the slap of flesh as his manhood struck against her bare slit. She could feel him squeeze her breast as he rocked his hips and nudged himself against her cunny, dousing his shaft and bulging crown with that vaginal honey.

It felt so *good!* Sparks of electricity ran through her, excited her body to levels she'd never known before, and she moaned so wantonly. She'd never been with a man before, but she couldn't imagine a more perfect start, a more perfect man for her.

There was no concern of getting caught, no fear that her parents might stumble upon them. She knew, instinctively, that they were all alone on that open field. She desired him so greatly that she knew nothing could stop them. He wanted her so badly that the world would have to end before he'd take his attention from her. Just the thought made her pussy throb harder.

As he finally lodged that thick crown inside her, he gave a deep "Ahh" of satisfaction though she had a twinge of pain as in the act he snapped her hymen open. The thin sheath of her virginity broken forever as he slid inside her deeply. "Yesss," he hissed out, and his voice sounded a little odd. Rough. Scratchy.

Though the feel of him pushed into her depths completely was so perfect, despite the remnants of pain that reminded her of her former virginity. That was nothing, after all, compared to the squeeze of his hands upon her pert little breasts, the slow pump of his manhood into her, and the feel of his tongue against her lips and mouth as he stroked her hair...

Stroked her hair... squeezed her breasts...

❧ 9 ❦

I t took her too long to realize, but her body tensed. It was a dream. It wasn't real. She willed Edain's vision to remain, for it to be his body pressed against her, but it wasn't right. Everything about it was off. How quickly he'd seduced her, how willingly she said yes. Edain's eyes opened and they were pools of black. It wasn't right, and her mouth opened into a scream.

Reality flooded back in and she was pinned beneath that tall, lanky monster. His four arms all holding her down, grasping her chest, one in her hair, another on her shoulder.

He was crooning his enjoyment in some strange rhythmic manner as his body rocked back and forth. The sight was so obscene, so vulgar. He had shed his clothes to reveal his uncanny nudity, and his alien cock was pistoning in and out of her slick cunt rapidly, the slaps of their bodies filling the chamber.

His body was so tough, so hard, and he was doing such a poor imitation of a kiss as he lashed his pale tongue against her pouty lips, coating them in his saliva.

She screamed again, squirming beneath his multiple hands,

feeling his entire body pin her down. This wasn't happening. It wasn't real. She willed herself to be home, to be safe and secure once more, but he held her so fast into the present that she couldn't escape.

He felt so *off*, so inhuman, even as his body rutted into hers in only the faintest recollection of the man from her dream. Such an act was made to seem so human and so alien all at once.

The thing's rock hard body moved at an increasing pace, his dark flesh such a stark contrast to her fair skin. She could hear its rasping breathing, feel its organ swell within her. Its one hand pawed at her hair with feverish haste, and she heard its inhuman voice reverberate in her brain, *"Love."* Again, *"Love."* It echoed repetitively as she watched his lips move, those great snake-like fangs bared as he licked at her mouth.

She squirmed beneath him, but there was no getting away, and she felt like she might pass out once more. Somehow she stayed conscious, but she wanted to go back into her dream. To feel the masculine hands of her school day crush. Instead she felt the not-right body of her protector, and terror washed over her in waves.

That obsidian monster thrust into her with erratic, almost savage momentum. He hilted his inhuman loins up into her and she felt him swell even wider. That movement inside her tight, deflowered canal was next to impossible.

His clawed fingertips dug into her pale flesh, and he lashed his head around, his tongue hanging out as she felt him reach his climax. Still that singular word *"Love" echoed* in her brain, but with it she was flooded, invaded, by the emotion of his joy and satisfaction. That more than anything was close to her own understanding, the pleasure of his release as he flooded her depths with his seed in long torrents. It was almost enough to make the act of being bred by a horrifying monster bearable, but his long, sustained ejaculation carried on and he hissed his pleasure as every muscle throughout his hard, lean body went taut.

Her scream lasted as long as his orgasm, and the pale blonde beneath him was on the brink of passing out. That strong emotion, that repetitive word, however, kept her awake and aware of every second that he was inside her. There was no escaping him, or his member, and she shuddered violently beneath him as her arms thrashed.

Dying at the ravenous, savage hands—and fangs—of those fiends outside would have been more pleasant, for they emitted something that she now realized had tricked her brain into wanting it. Here, she had none of that. Just the sharing of his pleasure as he quaked and spurt his alien seed into her.

When at last he finished, he lay atop her, and his hard, tall physique did not seem to weigh upon her much as he chittered his fondness and licked his long, pale tongue all over her face. He lavished his affections upon her so, and his inhuman voice crooned in her brain, *"Love you. Safe here. Where you belong. Have waited so long. So long... never leave."*

The feel of his tender, monstrous heart enjoying such near-human satisfaction welled in her.

Even as he forced her to feel such things, to know such intimate details about his emotions, she couldn't replicate them. There was no way for her to feel anything more than fear and revulsion at him, and when her scream finally died in her throat, her entire body felt so heavy.

It was as though she were being weighted down, and as the tears welled in her eyes, she knew none of his pleasure.

She must have fallen asleep, though the only way she knew that was because she awoke.

Returning to consciousness, the first sensation she became aware of was the remaining stickiness between her thighs. Next was the scratchy feel of that alien, subterranean fabric, as a thick blanket was rested atop her, heavy with whatever stuffing filled it.

To look around she saw the reminders of her protectors watching. His mental intrusions.

The knitted fabrics that replicated her life above. So much of it from her younger years, when she was not a woman but a girl, and still fancied dolls. For the first time she looked up and noticed he had created a mimicry of a canopy bed, like the one she had at her aunt's. To the side, one of the stone cabinets was even fancied up like her dresser from back home.

All around her he surrounded her with gifts. Tokens of his alien affection. Including two new bowls, one filled with water, the other with another of those giant, disgusting beetles, cracked open and displaying its white innards, surrounded by more macabre corpse mushrooms.

Finally her heart leapt to her throat in realization: he wasn't there. And she didn't sense him nearby.

She shuffled up out of bed and felt how heavy her limbs were. She was still exhausted, but she reached down and grabbed the bowl of water. She'd never been so thirsty, and she guzzled it, spilling some of it over her slim chest.

She could escape. She *would* escape. She grabbed the bug and as disgusting as it was she began to feast, her eyes working over the room in search of her dress.

Thia's search turned up nothing until something obvious occurred to her. She went to the 'dresser' and pulled it open. Inside she found it. All her things, arrayed with such reverence and care. He had even attempted to fold her things in a fashion resembling that of what her favourite maid did, though it was not quite the same.

Getting dressed, she found that the tear was crudely repaired. More of that itchy grey fabric in place of the rip she had sustained, though it did nothing to improve the look or feel of the golden garment.

Exiting out of the room through the grey curtained doorway, she came into a hallway. The stone home he'd brought her up to was bigger than she had realized, and there were three other door arches leading from it. Though at the end of the hall she could glimpse what looked to be the room she had first climbed up into with him. Her protector.

If he'd been human, if he'd been someone close to her, she might have been touched. She could have felt appreciation and maybe even adoration for the way he doted on her. The way he said he loved her.

Instead, all she felt was fear. Terror.

She was being held captive. He'd taken her in her sleep, convinced her it was someone else, and there was no coming back from that. She knew what lay beyond the rope, but she was still convinced there was a way out. He'd said it was too hard, but she'd find her way, and she moved down the hall stealthily.

As she went to the side, she found the rope was already let down. Did he leave while she slept? It only made sense. The thick cord was knotted, and she found it easy travelling, despite the danger. Though swaying along that high up rock face without anyone to support her was terrifying in itself.

She swallowed down her fears and when at last she dangled from the end, she dropped to the ground and toppled to her rear.

In that familiar, dark alleyway, she saw no signs of the two attackers. They were gone.

Renewed strength coursed through the young woman's body, and she knew she'd escape. She'd find a way. She had to.

The terror was pushed aside and replaced, instead, with a burning need to get back home. To leave this horrid place and never look back. She knew that the staircase was a dead end, but she also knew that the bones of the fallen would make a weapon if she needed it, and instantly she began moving back.

As she made her way there she paused when she caught sight of something that halted her breath.

Dangling from one of the larger buildings was a big, grey cocoon. Or so it looked. It hadn't been there on her way through the first time, she was certain, though when she looked again she that: a thick head of white hair hung from the bottom, though only the maimed side of the face could be seen.

It was the body of that fiend that had seduced and attacked her, hung lifeless in a ball of grey, web-like material.

The revolting sight was not enough to distract her from another realization: that material looked so much like what was used to stitch her clothing up.

Her face contorted in disgust as she stared, and her head spun, but she knew that she had to keep going. No matter how much he thought he was protecting her, he was keeping her prisoner. She would leave and never look back, and so she turned from the strange sight of her would-be killer.

Conflict raged within her about her captor, and she was disturbed to realize that his assault was even being justified in her mind. His cruel, horrible use of her was something sick and twisted, no doubt, yet it bothered her less than being trapped in this underground town.

She couldn't be sure why she didn't feel his presence in her mind. He had shown plainly that he could drop his words into her head from immense distances, yet here she was, making her way towards hoped freedom with no sign of him.

Thia found the great bloom of mushrooms, and the pointed rib that had pricked her leg. As she bent down and plucked it up, she was reminded of the cut it had left on her leg. Though touching herself there on her shin, she found no sign of it but a patch of itchy scar tissue.

She shivered as she remembered that he'd said he was healing her with his tongue. The thought made her gag when she remembered that same tongue lashing her lips, but as she clutched the makeshift weapon, she felt more certain of herself. She'd get out of this. She looked up over the stem of the mushroom and knew that way was hopeless, but it didn't matter. She'd seen the wall, she knew how large the place was. Surely there were more entrances. More exits.

She began moving from her hideaway, towards the unknown sections of the eerie, unknown town.

The heights of the ancient buildings grew higher, more imposing as they led towards the center of the town away from the wall. She delved that way further, though as she went a change in the area became more prominent: the roadways looked darker. It took her a while to figure it out, but as she entered into the larger part of the city it made sense: the spores were not coating everything here, though they were just as thick —if not thicker—the further in she went.

As her feet carried her onwards into the dark unknown it became apparent as she noticed the faint patterns on the stone: the roads were more travelled the further she went. Inhuman feet trod upon this ground far more regularly, and scuffed the spores away.

The timing was unsettling, for she felt that now familiar sensation of foreign-feeling wash into her like a sudden tide. Though this time it was unmistakable, nothing unknown about it. It was fear. And fear gave way to panic, *"Don't go!"* Came his strange imitation of a voice into her skull.

"I have to," she thought back, though she had no idea if he could hear her. If he knew her thoughts like she knew his. Her heart pounded, but she figured that the more people there were, the more likely there was a path out. As the buildings grew taller, she hoped to be able to climb one, to reach further up and find an elusive exit.

His voice came on again, though that panic did not wane. *"No! Don't! Not there! Cannot protect you there!"* and his terrible voice was wrought with distress, she could almost sense him tearing at his own flesh in frustration.

Her footsteps paused.

Why did it frighten her that he couldn't protect her? How could she want him to, after what he'd done to her?

Yet she couldn't keep going. She took a step backwards, and the rib bone felt cold against her clammy hand. She hadn't even realized that she was sweating, but her heart thudded louder. *"Get me out of here,"* she demanded, and she hoped that her anger came through louder than her fear.

She had barely time to think those few simple words before she felt it: that subtle tug. That soft little pull to go forward. That something so much more satisfying, someone so much more charming and desirable awaited ahead, if she'd just keep going forward.

Perhaps the mournful wail of that monster helped hold the appeal of the notion off. Such sorrow filled her mind from him, *"Turn back! Turn back! Anywhere but there!"* He pleaded with her so desperately. *"Will work things out! Promise! Swear!"*

She knew that feeling, that compulsion, and she turned and ran while she had the chance, before it could sink its fangs into her and make her fate irrevocable. She kept hold of that weapon as her other hand lifted her long skirt to her knees. She needed to be away from them, from those beasts of men that wanted to devour her.

The appeal, the desire to turn and head back didn't diminish though. In fact it seemed to grow stronger, and she felt her legs grow wobbly with weakness. *"No no no!"* came the voice of that thing in her mind. Though it had no more but the discordant wave of emotions; panic, distress, fear, anguish, concern.

Thia couldn't help but look back, and the whole of reality seemed to warp around something off in the distance. With the lack of illumination it was too far to see, but it was almost as if existence shifted and magnified and she could see: a man, walking towards her. Casually. Slowly.

He was stunning.

He strode not in tattered rags like the other two, but in boots, pants and jacket, that only showed a strip of bare chest, muscular and pale. The smile on his face was framed by shoulder length dark hair.

She faltered. She wanted him, with a strange and primal urging that she'd not felt before. Her heart pulsed as she stared, and she knew she had to keep moving but her legs wouldn't obey. How could anyone in this wretched place look as good as him?

The frantic protests of that monster that had violated her waned to dust then, no more than a slight, chittering annoyance at the back of her mind. This Adonis that strode towards her demanded her attention in full, and she stumbled to a halt, ready to give it.

Time itself seemed to move to his rhythm, and he came towards her at his agonizingly slow pace, and she wanted him to speed up. To come take her and ravish her immediately!

There was barely anything left of the clever woman inside her that knew it was wrong, but that tiny voice protested. Tried to get her attention back to her need to leave. Memories flooded back to her of what the other two had tried to do to her, the savage cannibalistic fiends ravenously intent on killing her, but it wasn't enough to dissuade her.

Her feet carried her towards him. Shakily at first, but they grew more steady as she neared that dark beauty. He was so strong, so masculine in his ruggedly dark, old fashioned clothes. He'd take care of her far better than that *thing*.

She could see him so clearly, that strong jaw of his, the smooth, pale face with those almond-shaped eyes, so bright red. She wanted to bury her face into that hard chest of his and be comforted.

Thia reached out as he was still meters away.

She was too lost in her desire to see the lanky dark figure bound along not like a man, but as a beast on four—no six— limbs. It gave no cry as it leapt at the charming fiend, it simply flung itself at the alluring man with all it had, every ounce of strength and momentum, its two fangs bared.

Thia caught glimpse of the things attack and started to cry out. It was going to ruin her chances at happiness! At fulfill- ment! At –

The charm faded as the tall, gorgeous man savagely struck the creature. He was not caught unawares by that attack, but her captor's distraction had weakened his charm upon her. Thia couldn't help but notice though that the six-limbed saviour went sprawling against a nearby wall, nearly limp and lifeless from that crushing blow.

He was trying to help her, again. And she knew, for a wonderful moment, that she needed it. It was then that she forced her body to move, to hold that old bone like a dagger.

She hated part of herself as she ran towards that gorgeous man and prayed that, perhaps, he wouldn't kill her. That he'd instead protect her like that alien beast had.

That blood-fiend was massive, taller than her would-be saviour, but bigger, thicker, so obviously strong and a better fighter after laying the creature out with one blow despite his disadvantage of surprise. As Thia came up to him he turned towards her, fangs out and a look of hunger on his face so very like that of the first two she had encountered in this hellish place.

She could hear the weak protests of the near-unconscious creature in her brain. *"No good... can't fight him. Tricks do not work on them when alone... when..."* He had turned their psychic seduction against each other before.

The human-like creature grabbed hold of her neck and bent her head back in one smooth move. He hissed at her, "Mine," the only word as he sunk his fangs deep into her neck.

She screamed, but it was garbled, and she forced that old bone into his side, to the soft flesh near his stomach. She wasn't his. Her body swooned and she thought she was going to pass out, but instead she managed to pull out her weapon and plunge it once more into the pale beauty of his body.

The fiend pulled back, and blood spurted from her neck as he glared at her in surprise. He did not shake from the stab wound, but he shoved her away with such force that she went flying to the ground in a heap.

Gazing down at the bloody mess in his torso, he moved to seize the bone from her, but before he could yank it out that black phantom image of her protector raced back into the fray.

He climbed atop that mountain of muscle and sunk his own two fangs into his neck, as if in revenge for what he'd just done. Though it didn't seem to affect him much, those long, snake-like prongs sliding back out as the dark haired man head-butted back against him.

This time, however, her monstrous protector did not dislodge. He had his four sets of claws sunk into the man and was hung on, even as the great fiend reached back and struck the much smaller form.

It was no match, Thia realized as she stood. Even with the wound in his side, that monster could not hope to take down this sorcerous devil.

As though proving her thought, he grabbed the thin neck of that creature and yanked him off his back, heedless of the furrows of flesh gouged out of his body. He lifted him up and with both hands she could hear him choking the life from her kicking and flailing protector.

She grasped her bleeding neck as she stood, and ignored the head-rush as she pushed herself forward. She lowered her body so that she was charging like a bull, and she aimed for his legs as she dove.

Such a move would not have normally fazed the titan, but with the wounds all across his torso, and the struggling creature held out from his body at a distance, her strike set him off balance. His knees buckled and he toppled backwards. Her dark protector went rolling across the stone street away, choking and sputtering for air through a partially caved-in throat.

Thia had somehow braved the crash to be the only one with any sense left, and she saw that rib poking out of the man's guts. With panic filling her, she grabbed it, yanked it out and plunged it in again. Then again. She lost count of how many times she sunk it into him, she just knew she couldn't stop.

When the torso before her looked like a mauled lump of flesh, however, he struck out and knocked her away.

She couldn't believe her eyes as she watched him rise up from the stony ground and touch the empty gap where his guts were tore up.

He glared at her while coughing up some blood. *What could kill this man?!* she thought in a panic, and immediately the chittering inhuman voice of that dark monster entered into her thoughts: *"Nothing. Run!"*

She saw he was forcing himself weakly, battered and bruised as the misshapen creature struggled to get away from the seemingly immortal demon.

But she'd seen them killed. One lay in a cocoon not far from her. Nonetheless she finally heeded the monster-man's cry.

Her legs pumped fast under that long gown, her steps uneven and warbling as she tried to put distance between her and it. Them. She lost track of time, of how long she'd been running until that searing pain in her neck reminded her of the gaping wound.

Throughout the chase she felt the tug of that insistent charm, but it receded again and again, as if it were fought off. Finally, though, after her endless flight, the exhaustion and wounds she'd suffered took their toll. She had to stop. She crouched down beside a building to catch her breath and try to staunch the flow of blood.

It was then he came beside her, walking funny and with two of his arms clutched to his wounded chest, he looked to her with his big, black eyes. *"Go home. We go home and hide!"* he insisted – no, pleaded. He was hunched and in pain; she could hear his breathing, and he no longer sounded so silent and quiet as he did before. His throat was injured from that choking and his every breath was a noisome chatter.

"I don't belong here!" Thia begged, and even in her desperation, she knew enough not to shout. "These things are everywhere. I can't stay cooped up in your den all the time!"

Bent and hunched as he was, he reached out to her in a

humble manner. Two of his clawed hands reached out to gently tug and pet at her hand, trying to coax her into going back to his hole in the wall. *"Safe. Safest!"* he insisted. *"Can take care of you there. Keep them from ever finding you. Promise!"* He was trying to convince her, she realized. He couldn't keep her locked up, not when she could escape so easily. Or perhaps he just didn't want to force her. She had no way of knowing what went on inside such a monster's mind.

She felt so exhausted, and even though she knew she'd try again, the loss of blood had made her body weary. She needed to rest, to heal herself, and so she gave the slightest of nods. "For now," she hissed as she looked at her blood soaked hand. "And you're not to... to... do that again," she added, thinking intensely of her rape.

Surprise and sadness flooded from him and he twisted his neck and hung his head. She could feel the confusion and objection rise in him and cross into her, though he didn't say anything. Instead he led her back.

❊ I I ❊

Climbing the rope was so much harder with the both of them wounded and hurt. He carried her up, but she had to cling to him, for he was in no shape to spryly clamber up it as he before. Though in retrospect, she understood why he had such an easy time. Though he held her in one arm, he had three arms to spare that she simply hadn't noticed at the time.

Returned to his home, he hobbled off down the hall. *"Food. Heal,"* and she could remember him licking her wound when she woke up, *"Rest."*

She nodded her consent and felt no greater need than sleep. Her attempted escape had left both of them in worse shape than before, and she felt crushed with the knowledge that from here on out, she couldn't do it alone. They could find her, and they'd eat her.

And she'd want them to.

He returned without his thick overcoat on and a bowl clasped in each pair of hands. Ushering her into the room he had prepared for her, he offered them up, the usual fair eagerly on display. *"Eat. Rest. Heal,"* he urged, ushering her towards the bed and looking to the uneaten mushrooms in her disregarded bowl. *"Good food,"* he said, then balancing the food bowl with one hand he mimed eating a mushroom. *"Very good. Eat,"* and she could sense something like pride amidst his feelings of concern. He thought he was providing a rich banquet for her.

"They grow out of dead bodies," she protested as she grabbed the bug out of the mushrooms and reluctantly began to eat that. She'd been able to push aside her disgust at eating a bug, but to eat something that grew out of decomposing bodies was something she couldn't fathom. She paused before she put the first piece of meat into her mouth, as if about to say something, but instead she ate in silence.

He mimed eating the mushroom again, *"Very good food,"* as if the fact that the mushrooms growing out of corpses was evidence of how good it was.

The dark creature watched her with its inky eyes, and she could see its gaze trail to her bleeding neck. *"Heal,"* he said, and conjured the memory of his licking at her calf. He was a vile thing, and terrified her despite its attempts to rescue her, but she could not say it didn't seem concerned for her physical well-being.

It had worked before, and she was feeling dizzy from the wound. She swallowed and the pain stung and burned, and so she nodded. Even that was hard to do, the barest motion causing her body to tense and protest.

He climbed up onto the heap of itchy grey cloth beside her, though his movements were noticeably slower and pained. He got to her side and leaned in, his mouth parting and showing those strange, inhuman fangs. They looked more terrifying than the ones those fiends bore, but she knew to fear them more than his.

The feel of that slimy tongue licking along her bite marks, though, was both soothing and repulsive. She could feel the thick, viscous mucous coat her wounds as his words intruded upon her thoughts again. *"Made special home. Just for you here. Knew you would come. Knew you would heed their calls, but need safety from them."* He was almost like a dog with the way he licked at her, if she could ignore his humanoid body and monsterish features.

Turning towards him to speak she noticed his dark body was marred with several great lumps upon his shoulder, arm, chest and jaw. He'd taken more of a beating than she'd realized from that fiend.

Yet he'd done it for her.

The conflict raged within her once more, for she knew what he'd done to her was wrong. He'd done something unforgivable to her body, and she knew she should flee from him.

At the same time, though, he'd saved her. He'd protected her against things that would do much worse, and she trembled against his licking tongue. A chilling thought presented itself. "Did you make me come here?"

He ceased his licking and backed off. A tremble went through him but she got the distinct feeling of rejection. He did a mimicry of someone shaking their head, perhaps plucked from her memories and mouthed a *"No"*.

Scurrying to the corner he picked something up and brought it over to her. *"For you,"* came his voice into her mind, and he held out the bent shape of her lantern. The glass around it was shattered on one side, and the brass was bent in two places, but it looked mostly intact. *"Went out to get while you slept,"* he told her, a twinge of regret through him as he remembered that was when she had taken off and nearly been devoured again.

The fact that he could make her feel his emotions so powerfully wasn't helping her confusion. It almost seemed like she was the one feeling the remorse, the sorrow, the rejection. It itched at her mind as she took the lantern in her hands, caressing the brass.

She felt her tears begin to well up and she wondered if this was the last relic she'd ever have of her life before the underworld.

He reached out and stroked her blonde hair as she wept so tenderly. She realized then why that feeling was so familiar. It reminded her of years gone by when her father would coddle and hold her, stroking her hair and telling her how special she was. It was amongst her most fond of memories of the man before her studies took her from her family at a young age.

"Will protect you. No matter what," he said, as if that chittering mind-voice of his were an echo of the past.

A tear splattered against the lantern and she set it aside. "I can't stay underground," she pleaded once more. "I need the sun. My family. Why am I here?"

He stared at her blankly, that face, part human, part something else, just unfathomable to her. *"Do not want you to leave,"* came his voice, and it wasn't a demand. It was simple, sombre, and though his feelings were so alien to her, that feeling of loneliness was unmistakable and overwhelming. More than anything else, he felt alone.

It was strange, but that thought kindled in her something other than sympathy. An epiphany. Was this strange creatures psychic abilities what reached out to her? Perhaps inadvertently? Did it latch onto the sorcerous charms of the blood-fiends and create some pull she couldn't resist, much as he used their own abilities against them when the two attacked her?

Her breath paused and she licked over her lips thoughtfully. Why wasn't she more frightened of him? Was it just that the alternative was so much more dangerous? That the cruel liberties he'd taken with her—from her—were far better than the death that awaited her elsewhere?

It didn't make sense to her how neutral she'd felt about the assault, about his touch. It seemed almost familiar and safe in some ways, but still, fear swam in the pit of her stomach.

But then... of course she'd be afraid. She was trapped, away from home.

"How did they find me?" she murmured.

He had mostly confusion to offer her, though his head twitched as he seemed to think of something as he knelt beside her, still stroking her hair in that familiar yet strange manner. *"Strong ones,"* and she saw a memory of that powerful fiend in the streets that had nearly been the end of them both. *"The strong ones have great powers. They lure victims from above. Feed. Make... slaves,"* it took him a moment to pull the word from her brain.

It made her heartsick to know what a foul creature the gorgeous vampire was, how cruelly he wanted to treat her. Even the thought of his beautiful body made her lashes flutter for a moment and her pulse quicken. "Why couldn't they find me here, then? If they're so strong."

"Protect!" came his answer, and he forced himself to sit up straighter as two of his hands touched at his chest, indicating himself. His lips, so human—even attractive if you could ignore what lay further above—contorted into an imitation of a smile. *"Protect you here. Protect you when am nearby as well!"* Though he grew a little grim then, *"Though take concentration. Hard when by self."*

There had to be more to it than that, and she figured there was something about how he had set up her home. Before she could voice that he scurried to the bowl and held it up to her and mimed eating the mushroom again. *"Good food,"* he insisted. *"Help protect you!"*

"But it's rotten people," she protested, though his words made her falter.

She needed protection. She needed to be able to get out of this place, and she needed her strength for that. Her hand trembled, and she reached for it, trying to remind herself that most food came from decomposing matter anyway...

Still, she fought a gag as she swallowed the first strange, spongy mushroom down.

Focussing her mind as she forced down the vile tasting fungus she thought on the home he had prepared. The whole place was packed with those mushrooms; they grew on the walls, the floors, in every crevice between those things he had prepared for her. It was as if they had all grown to a design. No, she realized, it had to have grown to **his** design.

The thoughts of him using blood or gore to paint the walls of her "marital home" in anticipation of her arrival was sickening.

Her nose crinkled as she pushed it away, her head falling to the side, and she wondered if it had been those beasts or if other innocents had died for his cause. "Where did you put the other one of those... those... things? I saw one hung up outside a house."

A flicker of something crossed over his eyes. Was it shame? She couldn't see it, for the nictitating membrane moved too fast. He simply stared a while though, before he answered her. *"Food for me,"* he said meekly, aware of how it would disturb her. He looked to her bowl and pointed at it, *"Not good food for me. But very good for you! Promise."*

She made a face, but she slowly put another mushroom in her mouth and forced herself not to gag. "That's gross," she admitted, and her shoulders slumped. How had she gotten so tired? The loss of blood and the exhaustion of the fight, of stabbing a man...

Had she actually stabbed someone? She'd never had a violent thought in her mind before that night, and the shock was palpable between them.

As her eyes descended sleepily, he stroked her golden hair once more and she heard his voice in her head, quieter, almost soothing—if such a chittering voice could ever be said to be soothing—as he said, *"Take care of you. Think of everything for you. So you live and be with Tar'kul forever... if you not run from it."*

Tar'kul. It seemed to fit him, though she couldn't place why.

"I can't stay here," she said, but already she was curling up on that strange approximation of a bed.

He retreated from the bed itself, wary it seemed after her earlier chastisement, but continued to reach out and stroke her hair gently. "*You can. Tar'kul could make it work,*" he reassured, insistent as always to keep her company. "*Tar'kul could make you safe. Comfortable. Happy. If you let. Not mean to make you upset ever.*"

"I need the sun," she insisted, but her voice was weak and soft. She yawned, and her finger went up to the wound in her neck, touching it curiously and feeling the strange mucusy film.

She dreamt again that night of the sun on that grassy field, and as she bathed in its radiance she suddenly felt Edain's presence. She looked to the side and saw him smiling at her apologetically, looking as handsome as ever, though guilt tinged his features.

"I'm sorry for being so forward, Thia," he said in his smooth, soothing voice. "I got carried away, and... cost you something special." The look of sadness on his face was palpable, his almond-shaped eyes downcast. "I never thought we'd regret it," he confessed.

Thia glimpsed through his lips two elongated, inhuman fangs and awoke a moment later when she heard the soft chitter of Tar'kul approach. He held out two familiar bowls again, and his voice rustled in her mind, *"Morning,"* as he mouthed the word.

Her hand went back to her neck, feeling where she'd been bitten and nearly drained by the fiendish and terrifying vampire, but found no more holes there. She swallowed and found that the pain was simply residual – a memory of anguish, not anguish itself.

"Morning," she muttered back, surprised at how well she remembered the dream. But then, it wasn't so much a dream. It was him, invading her mind in order to apologize. To pretend he was a man rather than... whatever he was.

His full, manly lips contorted into a smile, and she could see his two lower limbs were still clutching his sides, but no longer looked so helplessly limp as the day before. He was healing fast after his brutal ordeal the other day. It had been a miracle he survived at all.

"*You relax. Rest easy. Grow stronger each day,*" he spoke into her mind, miming the sounds with his mouth. He rested the bowls beside her then shuffled over to the wall. There beneath some mushrooms he pulled open a stone cupboard and took out a curious thing, wrapped in the same grey material most everything in his home was. "*Will show you fun way to pass time afterwards,*" he declared with an eager smile.

She thought back to all the things that she had done in her large home and frowned. Frolicking through meadows, swimming in lakes, devouring books and studying different cultures and places. How could anything ever compare to that in this dim, foreboding place?

Yet her head hurt from sleeping too much and she needed something to take her mind off of how heavy her entire body felt, and she nodded to him, helplessly.

He unwrapped the object, and how bizarre the device beneath was! Made from some kind of ancient metal, it looked like nothing made from the hands of humans, but seemed to fit in well with the hollow, stone city of the world beneath that she'd stumbled into.

There appeared to be two handles on it, and he extended one to her, his hand wrapped about the other. "*Pull. Twist!*" he beckoned excitedly in his chittering voice.

Thia hesitated, her pale features so much more drawn and aged from when the vibrant young woman first entered his lair. The lack of sunlight and the loss of blood had weakened her mind and body, but still she obeyed his suggestion, her fingers wrapped about the cold handle and pulled.

From the strange mechanical center of the device she heard gears grind and then… it blossomed open. Weird lights emerged from the center and a bizarre series of sounds played. It was the toy of another world beyond her own. Queer and wondrous, yet frightening all the same. For the shades of light were not comforting, but ominous. The sounds not pleasant, but grating and harsh.

She stared with a strange curiosity, but it wasn't the same sensation she was familiar with. Prior, when seeing something foreign, from another culture or time, it was akin to childish wonder. Pure amazement.

Now it was mixed with fear and apprehension, as if nothing were quite right about any of it.

Her blue gaze rose to his inky, black pits. "I can't stay here, Tar'kul."

His smile fell a little then perked right back up. *"Look!"* he gestured, and began to twist the handle, and from out of the center of the device the sounds and lights began to change. She realized then the whole of the room had taken on a different atmosphere, the lighting colourful yet dark, filling the chambers as the sounds started to form a certain sort of twisted rhythm.

"Do like me," he beckoned, going through the twisting motions slowly, demonstrating for her so she could try and replicate it.

Her eyes began to water with frustration, but she followed his motions, even if she didn't look away from his face entirely. "Please, Tar'kul! I'm going to die down here!"

He frowned over at her, even as her mimicry with him helped produce such haunting music. The devices metallic noises sounded very nearly like a violin as it filled the chamber with its macabre melody. Like a dirge for her former life.

❧   13   ❧

Thia knew it was a dream, though how she couldn't say, because it was like no other dream she had ever had. She was on the surface once more, surrounded by men. Military men, in long dark overcoats.

The skies were not sunny, overcast in fact, but they seemed so bright to her. The men all seemed familiar with one another, and they toted their muskets over their shoulders as they trudged on.

"Up ahead," one called, pointing to some rocky cliffs across the meadow.

A tall, handsome man beside her said, "Those bastards'll pay fer what they did." She had trouble making out the words at first, the accent and style of speaking so very old it would have made her own grandfather sound modern. Yet the speaker himself…

She awoke to the familiar, haunting tune of that device Tar'kul had shown her four days earlier. She had come to understand the thing was left by whatever people built the near-empty city below, and that her strange companion treasured it.

Somehow he had mastered its workings, and could produce such beautiful—if morbid—melodies and light shows with it.

Yet the entire time she'd spent in those days, 'resting' and 'healing' as he'd insisted, she'd also been plotting. She knew that she couldn't escape on her own. She needed Tar'kul to help her, to protect her from the call of those vampires. Just thinking about them made her heart beat faster, made her want to go find the nearest one and offer herself up to them.

But she struggled with how she could get him to help her. She kept hoping he'd let something slip, through her dreams or the strange, shared feelings, but she knew so little of the expansive world she found herself captive in.

The vile food he was giving her somehow helped her heal more quickly, and over time was slowly growing less repugnant. The slick chewiness of his beetle-meat didn't seem like it would ever grow palatable, not compared to what she was used to anyway, but all the same, it made her stronger.

The music stopped and she heard him shuffling down the hallway. As he passed before her room, he simply walked on by. It struck her as odd, but took her a moment to realize why.

He'd always seemed to be aware of her presence, her awakening, before it even happened. Before he should be able to be. Yet for the first time, she awoke without him arriving immediately to greet her.

She calmed herself and waited. Perhaps he was just fetching her 'breakfast'...

But when he shuffled back on by, not stopping at her room, it only seemed to confirm it.

Was the food doing its trick then? Was it not only protecting her from the pale men's mind control, but Tar'kul's invasive mind-reading?

Hope filled her, for the first time since she fell into this horrifying world. Her heart beat faster and it was so hard for her to sit still. Suddenly, instead of dreading the food, she wanted it, craved it.

It would protect her.

It was her key to escape.

She would be patient. Wait for him to slip into his own strange slumber.

A smile formed on her lips as she lay back down, a small sound escaping her lips as she pretended to just be awakening and drawing him to her.

❦ 14 ❦

Tar'kul, she came to learn, did not sleep so much. Yet when she came to understand his patterns, it was simple enough to put her plan into motion.

Slipping into the pantry he used for storing their food, she grasped a grey-cloth satchel and began to stuff it full of the mushrooms and bug flesh. Vile as it was, the protective edge it offered would be her only means of survival.

Once she had that, it was an issue of escaping down the rope outside again. This time, however, she had much less issue with it. Shimmying along its length until she dropped back to the stone alleyway of the ancient city.

As she made her way towards the thoroughfare, it dawned on her that either the glow of the luminescent spores was brighter... or her own sight had improved dramatically since arriving in the subterranean hell.

She could see much further into the distance, even able to sight the apparent exit from the city at the end of the street.

Following the road down, she tread carefully, though it

wasn't so much the noise she made that made her afraid. It was the gentle tug of those familiar feelings.

Whatever it was that kept Tar'kul out of her mind, was not enough to entirely block the power of those savage men. As she approached the archway at the city walls, she could feel the urge… the pang of lust for them. Their siren's call.

It felt so tempting, yet… unlike before, it was nothing more than an unwanted thought. Like a sickly urge to do something vulgar that she tucked away within her breast as she sat primly at the dinner table.

It never quite faded away, but as she stepped from the confines of the city and out into the open caverns beyond, she felt a certain triumph. She had broken free.

Though the long dark expanse before her gave her no promise of anything but a near blind search.

15

She had felt Tar'kul reaching out to her after what had seemed like ages, though she knew couldn't have been long at all. He never seemed to sleep for more than two hours, but Thia felt like she had wandered the inky blackness of the caverns for a day, at least.

Where she could resist the desires of the vampires, though, she found herself pausing at his call.

She understood him on a level she'd never understood anything before, and it was inexplicable since she barely knew him. There were no lies or falsehoods. He couldn't hide his emotions from her like the others she knew, who prized themselves on their ability to deceive.

He loved her, and longed for her, and some part of her felt bad that she was escaping his strange, alien sanctuary.

Still, she knew that what she had said was true. She would die down there, wither away to a grey, pallid old woman without a mind of her own.

I'm sorry, Tar'kul. I have to do this.

His words reached her, but it was so much weaker than

before. It was as if he merely spoke to her, instead of implanting the meanings so deeply inside her mind.

It isn't safe! No! You are in danger! Danger!

She could feel the panic from him, the deep concern as he awoke. Could easily imagine the frantic way he doubtlessly tried to find some sign of her passage.

Still, Thia pushed on, urgency hurrying her along through the darkness of the cavern. His warning gave her a chill and she wondered if she should eat again, but didn't want to stop. Not yet. Not when she was so close to her freedom.

The cavern floor wasn't particularly rocky, though at times great boulders stood in her way, small stones threatened to trip her.

Tar'kul's voice returned to her.

There are dangers! Dangers other than the pale men! he implored. *The caves beyond the city are treacherous. Evil! Unknowable!*

The words had barely reached her before she heard the sound of running water ahead. It was so gentle, delicate even, yet in the still silence of the great underworld cavern it was so powerful as to be unignorable. It was the first real sound she'd heard other than her own footsteps in so long!

She didn't falter as she pushed herself towards it. Her limbs were sore after being unused for so long, her legs tired and aching, but she didn't care. She made them work, to keep her going forward, towards that distant noise.

As she neared the source of it, she noticed the cliffs, a dark row of precipices that would have summoned her to her death had she not developed the gift of such adept dark-sight. From the edge there she saw an incline that led down, and she followed it.

Before she even reached the halfway point she made out the surface of water below – the refreshing sight of crystal clear water!

She'd glimpsed nothing like it in so long, and the sound of it pouring was like music to her ears.

It was so exciting, she almost didn't realize how strange it was for the sound of pouring water to not be accompanied by the sight of it. There were no waterfalls, no spillage of it nearby. Just a shimmering pool of water at the bottom of the precipice, the only access point a smooth ramp that seemed to be hewn by time and great use.

Her feet slowed, her brow furrowed as she began to look around more carefully. Where was it coming from?

Thia's heart thudded so loudly it almost drowned out the sound of that beautiful water pouring constantly from... where?

Was it like one of those strange hot springs? She didn't understand it at all.

As she hesitated, the water rippled strangely.

Then, seeming to act of its own accord, it rose up as if something had splashed amongst its refreshing waters.

Panic set in as the pool moved like thick tar, taking on the form of something wholly alien and terrifying.

Like a great ape that had begun to melt, it loomed tall over her, and the sounds of pouring liquid distorted, becoming like a growl. Yet its mass looked like nothing but inky black water.

It lurched out towards her, and she could see the smooth indent it had occupied was void of anything. The pool she had witnessed was nothing more than the prone, waiting form of a hideous monstrosity that now advanced upon her.

"No," she barely had time to gasp before she began to run. She wasn't even sure of the direction, whether it was back towards the den or somewhere else entirely. She moved only on pure instinct, fleeing from a creature that she never could have fathomed in their wildest nightmares.

It did not move like the ape-thing she had initially thought it to resemble, and once it lunged for her, its shape had changed wholly again. It was a thick odious sludge creature, and as she ran back up the ramp she found its smooth surface hindering her climb, like some aberrant pitcher plant trap.

It had been so easy to descend upon, but the smooth, steep curve gave her no traction, and she stumbled as her feet slipped again and again. The only saving grace was that the thing took a while to push up from its first failed lunge, taking on some new, hideously random appearance as it loomed high once more, overshadowing her petite frame.

"No, no, no," she pleaded with no one, with nothing rational. It couldn't end like this. With her, making her escape and being devoured by something from the deepest pits of hell. She would have rathered the vampires suck her dry. Then, at least, she'd have had some sick, hypnotic pleasure to calm her end.

It was the only way out, though, and she struggled to regain her footing, moving onto all fours to lower her centre of balance and help herself climb up.

The creature crashed to the stone of the ramp with what sounded like a tidal wave wiping out a village. As she scrambled up its smooth surface, she glanced back and saw that though it had missed her once more, it was still for a moment.

Any hope or reassurance she may have taken from that was short-lived, as the thing rose up the path behind her like the rising tide. It climbed the path with ominous purpose, closing in on her like a malevolent river defying gravity.

She turned straight ahead and refused to look back. *Just climb, Thia,* she told herself, her fingers already feeling a bit raw as she tried to force herself up the smooth surface. It was almost impossible, but there was no turning back.

It was a desperate struggle, and her poor slender fingers clawed at the stone, nails breaking and hurting as she sought to pull herself up out of the trap. She didn't know how close that murky creature was to touching her, though when she felt a tug at one of the frayed strips of her dress she had an idea.

Desperately she grew closer – too slow, she thought – to the rim of the pit, fighting against the smooth, treacherous surface and the gravity that fought against her momentum.

Freedom seemed to be so close, too close to give in now! With what energy she had left she propelled herself up and over the rim.

She stumbled onto the flat stonework, and heard the sound of her dress ripping.

A glance back showed her some of that yellow fabric being sucked into the liquid mass of the creature's body, devoured into its form as it sizzled and the cloth seemed to melt.

She was panting hard as she backed away from whatever strange, terrifying thing that former-puddle was. She nearly collapsed to the ground, but she wouldn't allow herself the luxury. Even though her body ached and her legs pained, she needed to escape.

Now.

It was wise of her, as it did not satisfy itself on her scrap for long before reprising its trickling approach. She tore another scrap free, tossing it near to the creature to lure it from her just a little bit more. To buy precious more seconds.

Though now upon flat stone and dirt, she had merely to overcome her weariness to push to her feet and outpace the thing. Her only battle was with herself as she fled into the darkness to escape its clutches.

Panic was pushed aside by adrenaline. She didn't have time for thought, for fear or worry, and she forced herself to move through the anguish, the burning in her lungs.

She wouldn't die down here in these pits.

She couldn't.

16

It was only after the unearthly sound of its watery form had finished that she dared let her pace falter, and came to a halt beside a great stone. Her heart pounded, her legs ached, and it was all she could do to keep herself from collapsing.

She'd not eaten since she left, and the exhausting escape from that creature left her drained, her stomach groaning in empty agony.

She quickly moved the grey bag into her lap as she sat down, her bloody fingers trembling as they grasped for the disgusting meal.

Thia felt fear like she had never known. Not the high impact rush of danger, but the gnawing sense that she would never escape, never free herself from this place.

Perhaps it was hell.

Perhaps she was already dead.

The thought haunted her as she ate the spongy, flesh-like mushrooms, and the slick, chewy flesh of the bugs that Tar'kul had caught. It took her a while to realize that the incessant thrumming at the back of her head was not merely a headache, but also the stuff of her former caretaker's pleas.

Let Tar'kul in! Let me find you! he pleaded vigorously, and she suddenly became aware that he had been trying to reach out to her all along.

You won't take me back, she argued, but she was weaker now. Exhausted and frightened and tired of running. Her limbs burned, but she knew she had to push through it. The alternative was not an option. It never had been, not after she'd gotten so far. Survived so long.

His voice chittered into her mind, *I will protect you! Not force you! Do not go alone!* he pleaded so desperately. She had witnessed him leap to her defense before, had seemed to self-lessly put his own life in danger to protect her. Though she couldn't say for sure what went on in the mind of such a monstrous figure as him, could she? Her feelings of under-standing could just be an illusion.

She ate quickly and then pushed herself up, her legs crying out in protest.

There was still as of yet no sign of escape. The gaping cavern continued onwards into the pitch black of the unknown. As she pushed on ahead she saw before her scattered mushrooms among the rubble and rocks. The further she went, she found more and more, and noticed the temperature growing warmer, almost balmy as the humidity rose.

Soon she came upon a vegetation that covered the floor of the jungle, not merely the grotesque mushrooms and spores that coated the place, but actual, greenish-yellow vegetation. Vines mostly, that coiled and curled into shapes like trees, that seemed to spiral up to the cavern ceiling like pillars. Or perhaps they hung from there, she couldn't be sure, but that seemed to make the most sense.

Thia had seen nothing like it before in all her time below. It was a marked shift from the fungal nature of all plant life she'd seen thus far.

They resembled jungle plants from far off colonies that Thia had seen pictures of and read described in books. Vegetation grew from everything, dangling from the surface of rocks and in absurd places it made no sense for such lush life to grow.

More than that, life seemed to bristle from within the greenish-yellow jungle. The sounds of rustling and curious cricket-like noises. They were more subtle than the sounds of life in a meadow of the world above, but they didn't need to be anything more. The still quiet of the underworld made it seem like a symphony.

Some small buzzing insects of strange, alien design even flew by her on their way to perch upon bizarre flowers dangling along green vines and strange, pseudo-trees. The curious trunks of which were more like leafy branches, thick and winding with greenish-yellow life as they fanned out across the ground. While up above they became roots that reached for not sunlight but the cavern ceiling. To what end she wasn't sure. To collect minerals and water from the rock ceiling?

It was reality inverted. It was madness to behold and took her some time to realize what purpose it could have.

When she moved further through and the day passed, and in the distance, there it was... pools of bubbling yellow liquid that created smoky plumes.

It had to be the source of the heat, and as she approached she could smell the ripe fumes and how strange they tasted upon her tongue. It was repellant, but there seemed more to it than that... her mind began to work.

She saw the smoke move in a fixed sort of pattern. It didn't simply waft up and fill the cavern, it all headed off to the side and...

As she moved towards it as quickly as she could, she saw the truth of it. The smoke was following some sort of path through the stone. It meant air current. And the caverns were so still that meant it had to be a passage to the surface, didn't it?

Still, she quickly remembered what pools of water may become, and she tried to temper her excitement with caution. Her blue-eyed gaze followed the steam, slowly sidestepping and looking up, trying to find her escape. Her freedom.

The way around the pools was precarious with the numerous stones, mushrooms and vines, but she did not let the macabre beauty of the purple-red flowers upon the vines distract her. As she rounded the oddly shaped pools of yellow, she saw it… a slowly sloping tunnel that snaked upwards into the cavern wall. Along it travelled the smoke, confirming her suspicions.

She was focused and intent, studying everything as carefully as she could in the strange, dim lights. Her eyes had adjusted to the dark, but it was still difficult to pick out the little nooks and crannies she wanted to be familiar with.

The yellow pools below offered some extra light, but the smoky fumes only grew thicker. The further she climbed, the more of an irritant it became and she found herself coughing, having to swat at the air to wave it off.

Further she pressed, able to feel escape so close… yet the higher she went, the thicker the smoke became. When she peered back, it stunned her to realize just how little of a distance she had travelled.

How had she only gone so far in all that time? She coughed and felt herself sway a bit. The noxious fumes were getting to her.

As she pushed on she saw that the caverns narrowed up ahead, but continued on. The smoke got worse and worse, and the harder it was to see… to breath.

From inside her mind, she heard the insistent pleas of Tar'kul. *Do not leave Tar'kul alone!* and his chittering words were beyond sorrowful. *Anything you say! Anything! Just do not leave Tar'kul alone! Help you leave!*

Tar'kul, she murmured, and she wasn't sure if it was a thought or the word spoke aloud. She was getting so dizzy, and her body was so tired. Was she being poisoned by this noxious gas?

But freedom was so close...

She muttered something softly, dizziness beginning to overwhelm her, and she knew she only had one option. She couldn't keep climbing. Not into that thick, pungent gas.

Thia turned, or at least tried to, but her head was spinning with the intoxication of the fumes and a turn became a full whirl.

It all seemed to happen in slow motion, like the world around her moved as slow as her great aunt's molasses. She didn't feel any pain as her head struck the ground, but she felt consciousness bleeding away... fast.

It wasn't a conscious effort on her part. Not something she planned on doing, or wanted to.

But in those brief seconds before she passed out, she reached out for her monstrous saviour.

She felt something slip into her. An unwanted presence. Yet so very, very desired.

❧ 17 ☙

Thia awoke in the plush bed of her great aunt's former manor. Now hers. Immediately her eyes went to the window, and she saw it was opened, unshuttered, and though it wasn't day, the brightness of the moon seemed to sting her eyes for a moment.

The relief at seeing that was but momentary as she heard the sounds of laughter and revelry from outside her door. Men's voices, jovial and spirited.

She rubbed at her eyes, trying to free them of the painful grit, blinking to restore her vision but it didn't clear her mind. Who was outside her door at this hour?

Thia slipped to her feet, surprised to find that none of the aches and pains remained in her legs as she made her way to that door. Though as she pulled it open, she saw not the hallway she expected, but a dining hall. Full and lavishly attired as if for festivities, beautiful, pale skinned men wearing not a stitch of clothing sat about, upon benches, on tables, joking, smiling laughing.

Each one a gorgeous specimen of masculinity, with bodies seemingly carved from stone by the most masterful of sculptors.

As if she was an expected guest, all their eyes turned towards her. Their gazes were brighter still as they beheld her, as if she was some beacon of hope, come to bring them greater joy still.

Her eyes went wide and she shut the door, sure that she was seeing things. Dreaming some wicked dream, like she had before, and her blood rushed to her head. Slower, this time, she cracked open the door, as if expecting to see them all disappeared from her home.

They still lingered there, watching her through the crack. Only now she noticed one, the biggest and clearly strongest, was rising up from his seat. He looked so familiar to her, with his long hair, beautiful looks, though it was hard to figure out why... especially as the sight of his stirring loins caught her gaze.

He curled his fingers in beckoning for her to come to him while his thick, vein-ribbed cock moving at his groin. "We've been waiting for you," he said in a deep, deliciously masculine voice.

The other men bobbed their heads, some of them brushing hands back through their hair of various lengths, and all responded with that same, heated response in their groins.

Her body tingled with pleasure, but there was something foreboding about it all. As if it were too good to be real. Her mind was always clouded by them, though a nagging but uncertain feeling warned her of them.

Thia blinked her eyes, harder this time, but still they remained, their bodies on display so openly. "Who are you?" she asked, glad that her voice didn't feel as meek and frightened as she felt.

The tallest one approached her until he was so close she could smell him, his delicious musk, that male scent that originated at the dark tuft of pubic hair nestled over his stiff, throbbing cock. "I'm yours," he said invitingly, his voice so deep and appealing as he extended his large, strong hand to her. "We're all yours."

With a sweep of his other hand behind him he gestured to the room of gorgeous bodies, all the men nodding their affirmation enthusiastically, as one even wrapped his hand about his girth and beat his fist in excitement over the sight of her.

"But, why?" She didn't want to argue. Not really. Though she found it all very embarrassing and strange, something weirder nestled beneath her rib cage; a sense of foreboding about it all. It seemed too familiar, though she couldn't put her finger on what, and yet she felt drawn to them. As if she deserved some peace, some affection.

Yet she wasn't the type of woman to simply follow the easy path. .

She took a step backwards and tilted her head, her golden hair piled around her head like a wreath once again. "I need to be alone."

She stepped back into the door, finding it closed behind her as two of the men moved in towards her, behind the towering alpha of the pack. "We'll comfort you," he said, a twitch of his cock before her, the thick, purple crown poking out of its sheath, glistening at the tip with precum, so eager for her. "Massage your aching legs," he purred, and she felt the ache again, "satisfy your needs." She could feel the pang between her thighs then, that urgent desire to feel them.

As she did, she also noticed the air between her legs, and looking down saw that her slender form was as utterly nude as they were.

"Ah!" Her arm went instinctively across her slender bust, her other palm cupping her sex as she tried to back away, feeling the door press against her pert behind. This couldn't be happening. This wasn't real.

It was all so wrong, even as so much sensation bombarded her. Pain, need, desire, it all coalesced through every fiber of her body. "You all have to leave me alone!" she shouted, anger penetrating her voice.

She was a swirl of emotions as those men approached, for as the fear mounted, so too did the desire. It was unnatural, and did not originate from herself, but it was unignorable. It was a struggle to refuse, but she had to… didn't she?

The two men by the alpha's side reached out, touched their smooth, strong hands over her body, feeling her slender physique. They rubbed her calves, they fondled her shoulders. "Let us comfort you," they beckoned, and she could see every little ripple of muscle, the twitch of their hard pecs.

She gazed at the pinpricks of red in their eyes as their leader insistently held out his hand, beckoning her to take it. "I'll bring you so much pleasure," he promised, and she knew it to be true, even if all the other feelings of foreboding were right… that statement was so unmistakably honest.

Her hand lifted towards him, the slender stalk of her arm barely holding it aloft, as if she was a mere puppet to him, her master. Her lips twitched and her waifish body swooned as she felt her head become heavy and dizzy once more.

Something told her she had to resist, to run from them, but they were so inviting.

And she was so tired of running.

Her body was on fire where they massaged her, the nerves wallowing euphorically in their touch on her aching muscles.

As she slipped downwards towards the floor, two of the men came in around her, catching and lifting her. Holding her dainty body against their hard, muscular physiques. Those powerful hands rubbed and fondled, and she felt their twin throbbing shafts brush against each hip, pulsating with blood as they squeezed her small, perky tits. One even leaned in and suckled her neck, the other nipping her earlobe and tugging it.

Yet the largest one still stood before her, beckoning her, not closing the gap but holding out his hand. "I want you so badly," he said, his full lips contorted into a smile that made his perfectly chiseled jaw tense. "You're absolutely perfect," he remarked, and she could see two little pointed teeth protrude into his lower lip as he smiled at her.

No. No, no, no. She remembered, vaguely, in some tucked away part of her mind that this was going to end poorly if she didn't resist. If she didn't find some reserve of willpower.

But she was so tired, and their bodies all felt so inviting. Thia didn't want to worry, or fret, or run from them. Not with how her body pained all over and hungered for their touch. The desire was nearly driving her mad, but it still didn't seem to originate from within her. There was no passion, yet there was something deeper and darker that called to her.

"No," she finally managed, but her struggles were in vain. Her slender body was weak and exhausted, and they were so strong. So very strong.

"Take my hand," he insisted, jutting out that strong palm even as the two men rolled her breast flesh under their fingers, and slid the other hands down, parting her thighs and massaging her mons, across her slick, puffy, needful labia…

It was such a contrast of pleasant desire, and ominous threat, but the man before her was quickly growing impatient. "Take my fucking hand!" he demanded, and it seemed he was nearly ready to strike her cheek with his palm as those eyes burned bright crimson.

"No!" she finally managed to cry out, her struggles becoming more earnest. That flash of anger had been enough to rejuvenate her, or perhaps it was that strange, horrific feeling of fingers against her sex.

A faint memory surged back to her.

Tar'kul! He'd saved her and abused her, yet these fiends would sooner devour her whole than protect her.

Her fists and feet began to flail, her form rocking and arching as if she were a crashing wave of the ocean, seeking a means of escape.

The men holding her vanished into smoke, and before her that angered alpha seemed to turn into a malevolent apparition as he hissed his anger at her.

Then they were all gone.

$$\maltese \quad 18 \quad \maltese$$

She awoke to the sounds of her own mumbling, her eyes feeling so heavy she had to force them open.

Thia could see little but the ashen-coated floor of the tunnel, though she could hear a smooth sliding sound. It took her a moment to realize it was her that was sliding, being dragged back down the tunnel by her feet.

The stench of those yellow fumes still filled her nostrils but she was being pulled from it to safety… slowly downwards… though she drifted out of consciousness quickly once more.

❧ 19 ❧

She found herself with that wandering troupe of soldiers once more as they approached a cave opening.

"This is the place," said one of the men, and the tall, handsome man beside her nodded.

"Muskets at the ready, lads," came his strong, youthful voice as he led the way inside.

She heard them raise their weapons, affixing their bayonets dutifully.

They advanced through the opening of the cave and found but a small little area around a fire, a living space that seemed to have been occupied by a half dozen or more people. Fur sleeping mats, coarse wood trunks, and a hare roasting over the fire.

As the soldiers explored the area, one of them spotted a tunnel leading deeper into a dark recess, and he called out. "'Oy, there's somethin' more back here, Lieutenant."

It was scarcely said a moment in time as Thia witnessed what came out of the hidden passageway.

"Muskets up! Fire!" came the handsome Lieutenant's orders as the occupants of the cave came at them.

The charge of scraggly bearded, half-clothed barbarians that emerged out from within the inky blackness came as a terrible surprise, they cut down the man who called the initial warning. Yet with his loss, there was time to open fire and the sound of metal and gunpowder filled her world until it faded.

❧ 2 0 ❧

Thia's eyes slowly opened as she left the world of dreams and illusions. Her ability to tell what was real and not seemed to be eking out of her. Reality was a horrible nightmare, her dreams often much better. Which was real and which was the stuff of delusion? She wasn't sure she could tell anymore.

It did not help that the first thing her still dry and irritated eyes beheld was a room that appeared fashioned from jungle vines and trees. Was she back on the surface? Had she been rescued?

"I do believe she is awakening," came a very regal sounding voice that seemed wholly unfitted to the subterranean nightmare world she was lost in.

"Oh," stated another voice, this one feminine, sounding somewhat disappointed. "I suppose she will not be ready to join our court quite yet, more's the pity."

Thia had trouble making out the figures precisely, her vision still not back to full, and the fact an actual light was lit in the room only hindered her efforts more. They seemed to be but candle flames, yet they were such a terrible fire upon her eyes which had not beheld a glimmer of true light in many days.

"We can go ahead and cancel the garden party for now then," said a portly sounding man with a heaving sigh.

One thing Thia could tell for certain was that these were the voices of refinement, of culture. Voices of the surface world, her home. Civilization.

When she tried to move she felt constrained, and looking down revealed that rather than being restrained, she seemed merely to be tightly wrapped in some sort of blanket. The soft material was a jarring change from the scratchy grey cloth Tar'kul had.

Who were these people? She struggled, but that quickly tired her while she tried to blink the grit from her hazy, blue eyes. This didn't make any sense. Her mouth fell open, and though she thought to speak, nothing came out but a gasp of air.

"She looks terribly exhausted," said the woman's voice.

"Should we not bring her some water then?" said the first man.

The portly male's voice rose once more, "I don't know, Vanessa does not seem too keen on the idea of calling off the Garden Party."

"Oh pish posh," said the first voice, and she felt someone hold a cup to her lips. "Drink up, my dear. You look simply parched," he said, and she felt his hand guiding her head gently.

It was so hard to drink in such a strange position, and her head swooned, but she quickly swallowed back the liquid. She almost choked herself on it, in her hurry to quench that dryness in the back of her throat as she willed herself to look at her captors.

Where was she?

"Does she even speak?" said the woman with some exasperation.

"Perhaps she inhaled too much of those fumes. It's quite toxic, don't you know?" said the portly man.

"She shall be fine," said the first man once more, and she could feel him lean in close, even if his face was all a blur. "Won't you, my dear? Tell us, what's your name? I am Sir Reginald Farthington."

Thia blinked her eyes, very slowly, trying to clear them before she breathed out her name on raspy breath. "Thia... Thia Suthers."

The portly man chortled a bit, "Suthers? I do believe I recognize that name."

Vanessa added in a terse voice, "Of course you do. Upstart lot, them. They marry all about and spread their coin with them." The hint of derision was unmistakable, and of course Thia knew from her great aunt that such feelings had been quite common place against their family at one time.

"Well miss Thia Suthers," came the first man's voice, and she thought she could make out a smile on his face, but her vision was so very, agonizingly slow to adapt to the bright lights of the chamber. "You are quite lucky I stumbled upon you out there. Those fumes out of the tunnel are quite poisonous. Had you not survived...well, you certainly would not be the first unlucky soul to fall to them. You should count your blessings."

"Are you going to hurt me?" Her voice sounded a bit distant, but slowly she was adapting and waking from her state. She shifted again, swallowed a bit harder as she tried to push herself up.

"Take it easy," cautioned Reginald, a supportive hand at the back of her shoulder as he helped her sit up. "You're one of us, dear. Do you really think we would bring harm unto you in your current state?"

Why were her eyes not adjusted to the light yet? It was as if they were no longer meant for such a bright source of direct light.

"It would have made matters a great deal easier if you hadn't woken up just yet," chided Vanessa, sounding annoyed.

The portly man said, "Hm, indeed. We could have carried her up top for the Garden Party, instead she stirs and we have to drop everything and tend to her mid preparations. Quite a spot of bother."

"I don't mean to bother," she murmured. "Why can't I see? Where am I?"

"You can't see, dear?" asked Sir Reginald with concern.

"Ugh," said Vanessa, "she's damaged goods. So we carry her up top and she proves an invalid for the rest of her days? Truly that would be a wretched waste. Of our time," she said bitterly.

"She does have a bit of a point, Reggie," chided the portly fellow.

"Hush up Harold," Reginald retorted back before quickly amending, "Duke Sarlow," to a grunt from the portly Harold. "She's just got some of that stinging smoke still in her gaze, that's all, I'm sure. Besides, she is one of us, hm? How often do we run across one of our own down here in need of our aid? It's always those monsters or at best some base-born scoundrel."

The other two went silent at that reprimand and she felt Reginald move away for just a moment before returning with what seemed to be a basin in his hands. "Here, splash some of this in your eyes, lady Suthers."

Her mind still rolled over a phrase they'd used: Damaged goods?

Her body flushed and her pulse raced with fear that they were right, and she tried to do as instructed. Still, she knew it was no use. It wasn't the smoke.

Her eyes had adjusted because of those disgusting corpse-shrooms.

"I don't mean to be a bother," Thia repeated. "Please do not hold up the party on my account. I have to be finding my way." Her old way of speaking came back to her so quickly in the company of other nobles. Even if they were monstrous to behold.

"Finding your way?" said the portly Harold before chortling with amusement. "Did you hear that?" he said. "Finding her way."

"She is quite the spitfire, this one," said Vanessa, as if she was in equal parts impressed and astonished at Thia's stupidity.

Sir Reginald gently guided her hands to the basin. "Here, just try to splash a bit of water into your eyes. And what do you mean find your way? You mean to go on alone? We were planning to take you up. You could still make it in time for the Garden Party, it shan't begin without us I assure you. And besides, this is no place for anyone to go wandering about alone. It would be… madness."

She scooped up a handful of water from the basin, then stilled, as if just realizing what they were saying.

"Wait... you know a way up? To the surface?"

"One step at a time, child," said Harold as he chuckled some more from his belly.

Vanessa butt in quickly, "She's a bit slow. Are you sure those fumes didn't damage her brain along with her eyes?"

It took her a while to blink the water away from her eyes, but it did ultimately help. The lights in the room were still so painfully bright, even though she recognized them for what they were: oil lanterns.

She turned her gaze back upon Reginald as he spoke to her. "If you're eager to go up, I'll take you. Once you've been to the Garden Party you'll be feeling in tip-top shape, I guarantee it," he said cheerfully, a broad smile across his deformed face.

Deformed was the only word she could think for it at the time, for though he looked vaguely like a man in all the superficial manners, his skin was not made of flesh, but seemed to be constructed out of plant matter. It was as if he were a man pieced together from leaves and bark in a very crude fashion.

A glance at the grinning, leering face of the portly man showed him to have the visage of something between a decaying corpse and fetid jungle foliage. While the sneering Vanessa had pointed thorns running along her cheekbones, and hair like a massive series of rose petals.

They were a menagerie of grotesqueness, a mockery of the human form.

Suddenly, the garden party sounded like the most horrifying thing she'd ever heard of, and she cringed away. "I'm sorry, I can't stay. I feel fine. Thank you." She shifted, feeling her head swoon and ignoring it. "I just have to go up now."

What were they? She wanted to scream, to cry, to break down, but she refused herself the pleasure.

Their voices were so perfectly human and rife with nobility, their clothes she noted were even exquisite noble style yet thick with moss. Either they were old clothing from above that was covered with the foliage, or made from it entirely, she could not tell. Certainly not then as panic filled her.

"It's okay," assuaged Sir Reginald, his cheeks two thick flaps of bark, his lips like two leaves stuck between them. "I'll guide you up," he offered, reaching out and taking her hand with his smoothly flexible, wood-like hand. He helped her to her feet, and made no effort to hinder or deter her.

Thia did not miss the disapproving looks of the other two.

Vanessa chided once more, "I told you she would be trouble. It would have been better had she not awoken at all."

Then Harold harrumphed and nodded, "She's a pretty lass, but full of sass." He chortled at his own rhyme and Thia swore she saw some flecks of decaying plant matter fall from his jowls.

"I'll be no trouble at all," Thia argued, taking in a deep breath. "I simply can't enjoy a party right now."

She managed to suppress her fear, only because she had been surrounded by terror for so many days. How long had it been since she'd seen the sun?

Thia had to squint her eyes as she walked. The chamber she was in looked like a dining hall of the surface world, yet covered in jungle vines and flowers. It was a perverse emulation of the noble courts above,

"You needn't fear," said Sir Reginald, looking upon her with a warm smile on that odd face while guiding her along towards a door. For though it looked comfortingly assuring compared to the harsh faces of the other two, it was alien and horrific to her none the less. "I shan't let a thing happen to you on the way up. And once there… well, you'll be all set. Safe as houses." He beamed at her as they climbed some spiral staircase.

"Don't go getting all smitten, Sir Reginald," came Vanessa's voice. "You look more a squire with a crush than a Knight of Court," she said derisively.

"Keep out of it, Grayfol," he retorted back to her, pausing their ascent up those stairs that so resembled the secret set she had taken down in the first place. "You owe me that much at least, despite all ranks and privileges, do you not, Baroness?"

The silence from the thorned woman and the way she turned away from him with her arms folded over her chest said it all.

Thia felt like she swallowed a cup of sand, her throat still so raw and scratchy as she tried to whisper. "Please, please don't hurt me. Just take me home. Up above."

He gave her a warm smile, and she saw the way the leaves upon the top of his head lay in such a way it so closely resembled hair. "Fret not," he said, giving her hand a reassuring squeeze so that she heard the groan and creak of wood shifting, "I'll see you up safely."

She was so frightened, so confused and uncertain about what she should do. Was this just a hallucination?

"Why are you down here? How did you come here?" Why would anyone willingly descend into these depths of horror?

Of course, she thought with a pang of retrospective regret, she had.

He gave her a curious look, "Why? It wasn't exactly a choice. Who would choose to come down here?" he asked with a whimsical laugh.

She had. Albeit at the call of forces she did not understand. Some seductive pull of monstrous yet enticing men that lured her into the pits of an underworld that would terrify anyone.

"But if you can go back up..."

The stairs were ever winding, spiralling up and up, yet such were the stairs she had taken down. This stairwell was coated in greenish moss and vines, so fully intertwined with the stone itself that she couldn't see anything but trace remnants of rocks among them. Nevertheless, the hard, tree-root like material it was constructed from made for sturdy stepping upwards.

"Do you truly believe we could go back to the world above as we are?" he asked her with a raised brow, as if dumbfounded by her question. "They would call us monsters. Slay us. Or worse still, cage us as specimens to be studied or gawked at in a circus by rabble."

"I thought I was seeing things," she muttered, and felt a wave of pity and sympathy go through her. What had happened to them to make them into such caricatures of humanity? "But surely you have large manors you could hide within instead of this hellish place?"

He stared at her a while, curiosity burning through him. "You do not understand," he remarked as they move upwards, and the smell of vegetation grew stronger. "We ended up here because we had died. Our bodies buried and brought back by a force both holy and magnificent," he said with a gentle smile forming. "You're the first of our ilk we have ever seen down here alive. And it's quite exciting."

Her steps faltered as she looked at him, fear in her gaze, but something more as well. Reverence, perhaps. "I am? You are?" It all ran through her head so fast, and she scrambled to keep up, some unknown emotions taking hold of her body. "How?"

They came to the end of the stairway, and she found herself atop some sort of tower surrounded by a parapet. Beneath her she could see what looked like a castle from the world above, yet like the twisted individuals she found herself among, it was purely constructed of the jungle-like fibres of plant material. A twisted mockery of the civilized world. As if nature itself had copied all that humanity had made in its own image to show that its power knew no bounds.

The castle towers were connected by walkways and shielded by parapets, yet she saw no further stairs going upwards.

She beheld such monstrosity with blue eyes that had been so innocent not a month before. Her pale lips parted and she blinked once more, trying to ensure that what she saw was real, and a terrible tremor ran down her spine.

"This is as high as it goes?"

Her barrage of questions struck him silent a moment as he guided her along the walkway. "Not quite," he explained to her in even tones. "And yes. I died, in case you were wondering. In battle I presume, against a noble house. I don't remember the specifics, but I know I was leading a charge against the right flanks of the Lancaster lines. I can only presume I fell in the process," he said quite casually as he guided her along. "Pray tell, how did you get here if you were not buried dead? We very rarely see other humans down here."

"There was a tunnel," she said, thinking back and closing her eyes for a moment. It felt so very long ago, and despite his current... condition...she realized it was nice to see another human. Almost a relief.

Almost.

"Through the basement of my home. I followed it down, and... It ended with a cliff. I couldn't get back up."

His brow raised at her story, "Interesting. To think such a place existed in the basement of a noble's manor." He shook his head as if what she said was pure madness, yet there he walked, a living undead creature made from the stuff of plants and trees. "This next part is the tricky bit," he explained and extended a hand to her.

Absent the bright, glaring light of the oil lamps she could see much clearer. The way his fingers were made from wood fibres, the knuckles like knots in a tree trunk, the nails like stubby little hard leaves.

He saw her staring and said, "It's not so bad, you know. Truly, the only downside is the small social circle I walk in," he said with a humorous grin. "Aside from that, I suffer from no ailments. I live on immortally for all I can see." That explained the part about dying in battle with the Lancaster house, for Thia knew there had been no open warfare between noble houses in her lifetime, "And my senses are enhanced in many, many ways."

"It's not that I think it's wrong, what you are, it's fascinating...but the last time I became curious, I fell into this place." She would have to curb that in the future, she knew. But still, as her fear gave way to intrigue, and the beat of her heart returned to normal, she couldn't help but want to know more.

With his hand still extended he smiled and nodded. "It is quite fascinating. I've had a long time to ponder it, and I would relish the opportunity to share with you my observations. I was something of an aspiring scholar before duty to my family called me forth to go to battle. Pray tell, are you a thinker too? You're certainly a lovely girl, the makings of a beautiful lady of court. Yet looks can be deceiving."

"I was drawn down here because of those thoughts, that burning desire to know more. And yet I feel ill-prepared for the horrors I've faced, and dare say I would have died numerous times if not for chance." And Tar'kul, but then, how could she explain him... that... to them?

Perhaps they'd seen others like him, other beasts that lurk.

"Do the fiends not draw you to them?"

He furrowed his brow as he studied her. "Fiends?" he looked quite confused. "The only other beings we come across are the monstrous beasts of the dark, and those pale creatures that wander by from time to time. They have no interest in us, nor we them. I theorize we are much alike in some ways. For they do not seem to live. Not as you do."

"The pale ones," she hissed with a shudder. "They are the ones that lured me down here, into this trap. Have you seen their city?"

"It is not their city," he said with some certainty. "They merely inhabit the space. That place is something ancient, created by hands inhuman. Even more so than they."

He smiled a bit unevenly at her look of surprise, "You wonder how I know this. For one, we have noticed they do not understand fully all the implements of that place, the clearest mark of foreigners. They are usurpers. Killers. Enslavers. They feed off of life. Human life. Which is why they summoned you then, I would wager."

Reginald mulled it over a moment, "I suppose that would explain a lot, if I'm correct. They must have some psychic pull on the living. An ability to lure them to their doom. I always did wonder how they managed to find living beings when they so hated light."

She felt lost in the conversation, ignorant to the other two nobles as she spoke with Reginald. "Is it just the three of you down here? If you died as part of an army, why so few?"

"Oh, they did not die in battle with me," he explained with a soft laugh. "No. Duke Harold Sarlow died in bed from a wasting disease. Hence his current state. Even the miracle that sustains us could not revive him hale and hearty once more. Vanessa claims she was poisoned. None of us passed at the same time and I am oldest here, though I died the youngest," he explained so casually, as if speaking of his own death were as normal as what he had for breakfast. "What we had in common was that we were buried. And I presume in a particular plot."

Tilting his head he pointed up, and for the first time she gazed upon the ceiling of the cavern fully. She could see the thick vines and tangles of brambles and flowers that covered the area, dangling downwards. Amid the mess she could make out some coffins and skeletons, dangling down, caught up in the tangle. The macabre underbelly of a graveyard suspended over her.

Another chill went down her back and she looked at him, her blue eyes narrowing in concentration. "Help me get out of here. I'll find out where and see to it that the cemetery is used once again, to bring liveliness to your parties."

His brows raised in surprise at her proposal. Or at least those woody, moss-coated ridges that resembled a man's brows. "Would you now? Even for your own burial? To live again, forever?" He smiled broadly, "I would quite like to get to know you better. You're a beautiful and interesting lady. Quite adventurous. That's the sort of thing this place could use. The other two never venture beyond the borders of our castle. And as lovely and vast as it is, it's quite limiting after an eternity."

Immortality didn't sound so bad. An endless time to explore and search out this place that had haunted her since she was a girl, to come back stronger and better equipped to handle the den beneath her ancestral home.

"I think I would enjoy that," she agreed after some thought. As long as she could get away now, she'd be willing to consider it more seriously later. Who cared to die truly?

It was a bizarre thing to believe after the nightmares it had inflicted upon her, yet knowing the pale ones had no interest in their kind and they seemed so safe and secure despite their predicament… it was almost invigorating. Empowering.

He reached out to take her hand then, "Alright. Come with me. There is but one way up that we know of, and it is neither pleasant nor guaranteed. Yet I say it is your best shot." He grasped her soft hand and rubbed his smooth, woody fingers over it, "I look forward to an eternity to get to know you, my lady."

Her lip quirked and she glanced at him again out of the corner of her eyes. He was a monstrosity, a sham of a human male just like the rest of this place. It filled her with a sense of unease, and yet she found it thrilling all at once.

Perhaps it was just that compared to the rest of this horrid underworld, he was the first glimpse of her old life that she had found. Not just the remnants of his half-decayed body, but his mannerisms and speech.

"I've made it this far. I won't fail or falter now."

With a firm nod he began to guide her along the narrow suspended walkways from one tower to the next. It wasn't until she neared the center that she determined what it was exactly he led her towards.

There, suspended from the ceiling itself, were a thick mass of dangling vines, like tentacles from the great forest creature above. They were massive, coated in great thorns ranging in size from fingers to arrows, with bright blood-red flowers upon them. It was terrifying to gaze upon but he pointed to it across the two foot gap.

"This is the way up," he indicated. "It's perilous, and the same thorns that could kill you will also be your only method of climbing. It will all rest with you whether you make it or perish," he said firmly, turning to the side and making room for her. "I can't help you past this point. The added weight on the vines would not be a service to your benefit, my lady."

Her knees were trembling and her lips thinned into a straight line as she looked up at the obstacle with growing resolve. She wouldn't fail.

"Thank you," she tried to say confidently, but it came out as weak and small. "I will make it. Please enjoy your party."

Touching his hand to his chest he bowed down low before her, a very elegant, courtly gesture that she could recognize the grace of. He rose back up with a broad, pleasant smile. "Good luck. I do hope to see you again, my lady. Life is long down here, and I do pray for some worthy company." He touched his fingers to his lips and blew her a chaste kiss, like the young men and ladies might toy with behind curtains.

She smiled but couldn't spare him a curtsey or other niceties that a lady of her class should have. Her knees were buckling and she could barely hide her fright as she looked back at the vine and took a running leap towards what could be her demise or her salvation. The way she quickly jumped from terror to bold exploration never ceased to amaze her own self, though part of her wondered how much longer she could endure the wear of it all.

Thia had wasted no time, did not let the moment drag on in doubts. She simply leapt.

Whether it was pure chance, or her own desperation, she made the leap and miraculously avoided being impaled by the thorns. She grasped at the thick, hard protrusions, her heart racing in her chest as she clung onto the slightly teetering vine.

The green tentacle like appendage was thicker than her, yet that didn't assuage her much. It still felt perilous to entrust one's life to such a thing.

Knowing delay would mean her strength reserves would only be depleting rapidly, she climbed upwards, grasping from one pointed thorn to the next. Her slender, petite frame only helped in this effort, she realized, allowing her to move at a greater rate than a heavier individual could, due to the precariousness of the position.

As she climbed higher she could hear voices below, muttering. It sounded like the other two nobles had joined Reginald, though to look down now would be to risk it all.

Thia pushed on, the vines getting thicker as she went, and

she could see they extended across the ceiling for quite a ways, dangling over the castle at many points. The one she took just happened to be the lowest hanging, and easiest to reach from the towers themselves.

As she slowly climbed higher towards that macabre scene above of broken coffins and skeletons, a cry pierced the air. A wailing moan of pure agony from human lips.

Her head darted upwards and about to find the source of it immediately. There, immediately above her she saw the body of a man. Or at least, half a man. He was alive still – or was it again? Twitching in agony as plant-matter consumed his flesh. Replaced it.

He gazed about, unable to see her it seemed as he lay rooted upon the vine, thorns piercing his body and keeping him in place. "Help! Oh God above put me out of my misery! Kill me!" he shrieked in hellish agony, twisting and flailing as much as he seemed able, which was barely at all.

Just accept it, she silently bade him, not allowing his cries to distract her as she climbed. She steeled herself against the pain in his voice, the fear of that happening to her one day. *It won't hurt forever*.

Thia caught herself, realizing how she had changed so much in so short a time.

She kept pushed herself up, her muscles beginning to quiver with the exertion, but stopping wasn't an option.

As she pushed onwards, the man's wailing turned to sobs. "Damn you merciless monsters!" he said, though he still seemed able to see nothing. "Damn you, damn your Garden Party!"

Her mind lit up at that. Garden party. They'd not shut up about it the entire time. Of taking her up to the garden party.

Was this man then not one of the corpses from the graves above but a living victim of this... alien intelligence? The court of undead fiends? Had she offered herself up willingly to its grasp?

It stilled her body but not her mind. Yet what was she to do? Turn back? Return to those strange creatures? Either way she would be taking her chances, and though her body burned with agony, she refused to be afraid of what might happen once she reached the top of the strange, thick vine.

It took reserves of courage that the girl she was back home would have had trouble fathoming to push ahead. Moving from spike to life threatening spike, feeling the shake and sway of the vine, hearing the wails and moans of the man above.

As she grew nearer, the man above began to shriek and cry. "No! No! Not again! Dear Lord not again!"

What was it now? She thought, though as she gazed above she need question no longer.

There, amid the great tangle of death and greenery, was an immense blood-red flower. As its petals parted and opened up, she saw not some stamen, no earthly organs of plant anatomy. Instead, within was a great beast's maw, coated with sticky mucous.

Her alarm at seeing it began to rise as the vine she was on began to sway of its own accord. She had been still as she gazed up, not jarring it at all, yet it was swinging more, moving as if it were the tentacle appendage of some great beast.

Thia's slender arms instinctively clung tighter to that organic mass, her hands gripping tightly. She knew what was happening.

The vine lived.

And not in the way that most plants on the surface did.

"Sir?" Thia tried to keep her voice level and calm, but instead it was shrill and frightened.

Reginald's voice called out, "It's the only way I know of."

Cutting in sharply Vanessa stated loudly, "Oh just get it over with already. There's naught to do but go up. You'll become one of us or die… and then become one of us. Either way."

The idea of escaping up that way somehow seemed less and

less likely as she dangled there, and as she clung on for dear life she saw another swinging vine nearby.

As the whole mass was becoming livelier, like the great body of a single being, more of those thick vines began to swing. Ultimately, they seemed to be trying to pull her up towards that waiting maw.

Might it possibly be a way out? Looking upon it, she saw nothing like an escape, only a way to join that half-devoured man in misery and perhaps eternal life as some undead being.

Her blue eyes gazed about as she did her best to shut out the panic, and she saw that one of the vines that brushed against hers swung close to another tower of the castle. If she could get onto it, it'd just be a four foot drop or so onto it…

She was nearly in tears. Her muscles screamed and blood rushed through her. Adrenaline helped her along, stomping down her panic just enough for her to plan her trajectory, though jumping from a living, moving thing was much less reliable than jumping from a true vine, she'd imagine.

Still, it was her chance to flee her two nightmarish options, and timing it just so, she leapt.

Her luck was not so great.

She grasped the thorny vine but it pricked and stabbed into her torso, making her cry out as the voices of those twisted nobles below yelled at her to stop.

She knew she was doing the right thing then more than ever, and she pulled her body from the pointed thorn with a cry. Blood ran out of the wound, but she had no time to worry about it, she had to press onwards.

The vines were swinging more and more, bringing their tips closer to that flower-like maw to feed her to it. She had made her move none too soon, as she saw the previous vine nearing it at a quicker rate.

From below she heard Sir Reginald call out, "Don't do it!

You're still beautiful and young, you can be that way forever! Why fight it?"

She came closer to that other tower, the backswing actually helping in that regard. She would just need to time her fall and tumble into it to make the drop in good shape. Time was running out though, as the other two nobles were moving along the parapets from opposing directions. Their long route of interception would buy her some time, but she had to move fast.

Twisting about to the other side of the vine, she took a deep breath and made her leap.

The hard wood of the faux-castle was rough to impact upon, but she rolled and took the bruising.

"Stop her!" cried Baroness Vanessa Grayfol shrilly, though the shambling Duke was unable to make great strides despite the urgency.

Thia saw her avenue for escape, or what she dearly hoped would be. At the nearest tower was a set of stairs that spiralled down.

Everything in her body screamed for her to find some relief from the stress, but she wouldn't. Couldn't! Her lithe legs pushed her on faster, her upper body so thankful for the break, and she made dexterous, quick motions towards the stairs.

Beautiful and young, she lamented coldly. As if she were just a body to be disposed of, preserved at just the right time and twisted into something horrifying. She could prepare for that, have herself become one in her old age once she passed on, peacefully. But not now.

Now, she had to get to the surface and... She didn't know what, but she had to be free of this place.

The two cruel nobles were closing in on her, but she was faster. She ran down the stairs, clutching her bleeding side. A sort of dizziness began to take hold as she went down It spread a sort of cramping feeling through her torso and when she lifted her hand to look at the blood, she could venture a guess. Her wound was taking its toll.

The thorns must have been poisoned with something, as her blood was stained with some strange greenish-yellow fluid.

There was nothing to be done but push onwards though, and she did, racing down and down the spiralling staircase.

With one hand against the wall to support herself she finally reached a room. It wasn't the one she recognized from when she awoke, but it had a distinctly familiar feel to it. As she moved through it occurred to her: it looked like a strange imitation of the pantries in manors above, and she moved through it into what was the recreation of a kitchen. Though what she found there made her come to a shocking halt out of fear.

The three nobles were apparently not alone, not completely. The kitchen housed two mangled forms of what were once human beings.

One had no lower body whatsoever. Her torso came to an end with a tangle of roots and moss as she was propped up atop a stool. In constant agony it seemed as she swayed and moaned, oblivious to Thia's entry.

The other lacked both arms, and swayed in place miserably as a basket hung from his neck.

From behind her the voice of the bellowing Duke called out, "Stop her!" And with that, both of the tortured servants came to life out of their stupor and locked their alien gazes upon her.

There was nothing to do but run through them, and Thia did, shoving the one over off the stool as she grabbed for her, and then kicked the leg of the other to keep him off balance as she dashed through a door.

The castle was labyrinthine, like the manors of the world above, yet she'd walked many and used what instinctual experience she'd developed from it to guide her way.

Coming to a great hall her wounds nearly had her swooning, but she clutched her side and carried on. Past the bizarrely carpeted central hall, lined ruby red with curious petals, out through the immense doors to the foyer beyond.

It was there before the exit that she found her grey satchel, suddenly that coarse grey fabric Tar'kul had created seemed so much more welcoming. She grasped it up and pushed her shoulder into the doorway, slowly edging it open until she was free.

The excitement was short lived as she entered into the court-yard and found herself staring across the field of mossy-grass towards the gateway.

"Lower the gate!" called out Sir Reginald, and as she dashed for the exit it crashed down. Great hardwood bars shutting off her escape. Her hands went to the bars, her feet trying to push her up, but it was no use. "I didn't want it to be like this, lady Thia," he called out from above. "But you have no idea how much the loneliness tears at a mind. The longing for one's equal."

"I said I would be back," she screeched, her mind slower than it needed to be for such stress, such an escape. Her eyes darted around quickly, adrenaline making her wound a little more tolerable, though not much.

"And I believed you," he called from above, leaning over the parapets. "But the truth of the matter is, my lady… that there is no way back above. No way that one might survive. Only the pale ones seem to know of a way, and they guard it jealously, for it is the source of their sustenance and succor." He sighed sadly, "Won't you please give in? You could stay here awhile as you are if you wish, and when you are ready become as I am. I mean it faithfully."

As he spoke her eyes darted about and she saw a door in the side of the archway into the gatehouse. She went to it and pulled it open, but upon doing so she was greeted by a terrifying sight.

The man—the thing—that stood on the other side was immense. It was well over six feet tall, with a body that looked to be like the suits of armour that adorned her manor's hall-ways, spiky and terrifying. As he trod towards her it was like the ground shook.

"Don't hurt her," called Sir Reginald, "she is my honoured guest."

Yet Thia's mind did not entertain surrender. She would not become a captor once more, and so she thought if she could just get around the armoured brute she could find some way from inside the tower to get out.

"I am not your honoured guest! Guests may leave whenever they wish!" She darted back two steps and felt her body reel with the motion, her balance thrown off by the wound in her side. She was so lean and usually dexterous, though her limbs were responding seconds too late to her mind's commands.

Her eyes sized up the beast of a man, and knew he would be slow. He was too bulky, and she was too quick.

She could get past him.

The world spun as she back-stepped away, the giant knight advancing upon her with such earth-shaking footfalls. She had almost every disadvantage then, as not even her agility could aid her much when her mind reeled from the effects of the poison inside her.

Thia swayed, swooning forwards and to the left, while the knight lunged forward to catch her. Except she turned away and stumbled to the right. She crashed to the gates and bounced off as she used every bit of strength and willpower she had to dash for that door.

The lumbering knight was off balance himself though and couldn't turn to grasp her in time, and she slipped inside.

His footsteps were not far behind though, and she only had one way to go: up.

Up she went, unwilling to give in until all other options were exhausted. The stairs spiralled up and she couldn't recall how high the tower went, not with her head pounding, though thankfully it proved much shorter than the towers when she came to a window.

It was unshuttered, and as she went to the edge she saw a vine dangling down towards the ground. It stopped six or so feet from the underground jungle's floor, but it was all she had.

As the sounds of frantic cries from the monsterish Sir Reginald rang out and the heavy footsteps of that lumbering knight grew closer, she slung her grey satchel over her shoulder and lifted her leg out the window.

It was a long drop she realized, and if she couldn't keep a firm grip she would undoubtedly fall to her doom.

There was no room for hesitation. She pushed out and put all her faith in her resilience and determination. She felt the burn of the vine on her hands as she slid down faster than she had intended, her feet kicking in the air to get at the castle wall and stop herself.

"No! You'll crush yourself!" he cried in terror. He did not fear her dying, it seemed, merely her damaging her body so much that... what? She could not be revived as a whole being. Perhaps like one of those torturous servants?

She slowed her descent and tightened her grip, though quickly ran out of vine to hold onto.

Thia dangled there for a moment precariously but eventually she knew she would have nothing to do but drop and try to brace herself for the landing. She had no way of knowing that in her fuzzy-headed state she had grossly underestimated the length to the ground.

It seemed to take an eternity, falling through the air as the frantic man's voice cried out desperately above until...

Thia crashed through bushes and branches, feeling them break off and scratch and scrape at her skin as she tumbled along. Painful as it was, the brush broke her fall somewhat and rolled her trajectory away from the ground. She nearly lost consciousness until she found herself dumped into the moat, the cold water jarring her senses as if a shock of electricity had started her all over, renewed.

The fuzzy headedness faded and though her body ached and pained, she felt excitement fill her once more. She was alive, and she was free.

Off to the side she saw some vines and roots that looked to make a good escape out of the moat, something she might climb up over and began to swim towards it.

She'd never known weariness before that moment as she pulled herself up out of the water, her yellow, tattered dress now such an immense deadweight as it was infused with chilled wetness.

There was no time to delay though, as she heard Sir Reginald call for the gates to be opened and more urgently still something else was splashing in the water.

Looking back was not wise. She curled her fingers around one root and grasped a vine, pulling herself up with a loud series of grunts and groans.

She had to make it, she'd not be stopped now.

As she pulled herself slowly up, pouring water behind her, she managed to catch sight of such a monstrous vision. A creature that was perhaps once man, but now looked more like a jungle-shark, a creature of imagination, flailed through the water almost limbless as it gnashed its gnarled teeth toward her.

Tugging her legs out of harm's way she watched it flounder and flop in the water, wailing its frustration at having missed such a delectable meal.

The grinding sound of the gates raising filled the air, and Thia knew she had no time to count her blessings or catch her breath. She clutched her gray bag and began to run in the opposite direction. No clue as to where it would take her. No idea of where it was in relation to her previous journey. She could have been heading right back where she came from, but all that mattered then was finding escape.

How long had she been fleeing for? She cursed herself for her curiosity, for trusting such horrific creatures, even if they did look to be human, once upon a time. Then again, so did the pale ones, in their own terrifying way.

Would she ever find her way out?

She was becoming more and more convinced that she never could, never would, but she knew that she wouldn't stop trying until she was dead.

The jungle slowly gave way to mushrooms, greenery replaced with pale, fleshy sponge. Some of it translucent and glowing, exuding a faint powdery residue that filled the air beneath their sometimes towering plumes. Other times they were purple and dark, nearly invisible to her sight until she was tripping over them.

She had to rest, her body was in agony. She was exhausted and weary, having never had a moment to recover from any of her experiences after fleeing Tar'kul's lair.

Ahead she found a copse of fungal trees, the tallest of which must have been seven feet tall or more, while other shorter ones bloomed near its base. Together they formed a nice little hollow beneath which she thought she would find some rest and comfort. A moment to eat some of her disgusting food and replenish herself.

It looked like heaven, and she had to police herself so that she wouldn't become too hopeful. Everything she'd seen so far had taught her that no matter how innocuous something seemed, it could be cruel and deadly. So despite her enthusiasm and joy at having found such a place, she proceeded with caution.

The bed of smaller fungi made for a soft mat beneath her, and as she got in under the haven of the larger blooms it seemed perfectly secure and safe. She nestled in and found the area to not only be soft and spongy thanks to the mushrooms, but warmer than the rest of the caverns. As if the fleshy fungus sucked all coolness from the air, or gave off a heat of their own.

Thia nestled in and dug into the still moist grey sack she carried. The mushrooms and bug flesh were unharmed by being dunked in water, thankfully. The water didn't even affect them much at all, and she was able to eat them same as ever. It made her wonder at the nature of the cloth Tar'kul kept.

Though she noticed now the food no longer made her recoil as it had in the past. Perhaps it was merely just her exhaustion and hunger that was driving her, but she devoured the fleshy bits of both and even found herself genuinely enjoying it, despite herself. She had no idea how long it had been since she'd last eaten, but her body was desperate for the sustenance.

She had brought enough of it to last herself a while longer, but still she realized just how much she had devoured in that one stop. She'd have to find a way out before long, or else things would get even worse for her. She had little to no idea what might be edible in the wilds of the cavernous dark realm. Tar'kul had showed her what she could eat, but in just a few days of travel—was it truly days?—she had seen such drastic shifts in the life she'd come across. These mushrooms bore little resemblance to the ones she'd found inside his home, after all.

As she mulled these things over, she felt weariness and exhaustion take over. Keeping her eyelids open took more energy than she had left to give, so she could only give in.

Thia found herself back in her dream. It felt so distinctly like a dream, yet she retained a lucidity she did not ever have in her own dreams. Instead it was like she stood witness to another's dream, with the clarity of awareness that came with it.

The soldiers were moving through dark stone tunnels, down and down. The Lieutenant held a lantern out, though now she noticed there were a few of the men missing and some of those that remained looked distinctly more disheveled and injured. A few had blood soaked bandages about their arms or legs.

"Can't we just leave 'em to rot down here, Lieutenant?" asked one of the men.

"No," came the Lieutenant's terse reply. He kept his eye strained ahead as much as he could as they pushed downwards into the inky black. "These savages have been responsible for countless misery above. IF we leave 'em be to these tunnels then they'll climb back out an' claim more innocents before they're caught again." Clearing his throat he raised his voice enough so that all the soldiers could hear him, "No, men, we see to it this job is done now, and that nary a maiden, child, or innocent traveller is harmed by this lot again."

The stone tunnel was not like the stairway Thia had taken to the underworld, but she knew exactly where it was headed if not exactly why she was sharing these memories through a dream. These men had ventured where she is now… in the past, not now, for their weapons were far too old to be in use anymore.

From behind them a cry rang out in abject horror, and the Lieutenant turned about, shining his lantern light upon the direction.

Illuminated by its light she saw the pale flesh of a man – no, not really a man. One of those wretched beings held a soldier in arm and had ripped his throat out, blood running down over his pale chin and throat as he savoured the taste.

The soldiers recoiled in horror before the Lieutenant shouted, "Take aim!" He kept his cool and rallied the men, "Fire!"

In the tight confines it was deafening, but when the smoke from the muzzle blasts dissipated there he still stood. The metal slugs lay embedded in the pale leaches body, but he looked unfazed. Dropping that soldier he advanced towards them on the next nearest.

"Bayonets!" cried the Lieutenant and the soldier reacted on trained instinct to stab the tip into the creature. It did nothing. Even having the pointed tip of the musket embedded in his gullet did not slow or hinder the creature as it grasped the soldier with one hand and lifted him like a toy off the ground.

"Everyone, charge!" ordered the Lieutenant, and many of them did. Though it was fruitless. That lone, pale beast batted them away like flies, and the crack of bone against the stone from one of them boded he would not rise again.

It was then the soldiers morale broke, and one dropped his

weapon and ran deeper into the cave. The Lieutenant was left with no alternative as others were to follow, "About! Into the caves! Retreat!" he called out, and with great relief all that could adhered in their abject terror. Consigning at least two of their brethren to the mercies of that monster.

❦ 23 ❦

Thia felt trapped, she couldn't see much of anything. Her exploration into the old servant's quarters against her caretaker's wishes had resulted in a messy situation. The old floorboards had given way and she'd fallen to the root cellar beneath, where there was darkness and cobwebs, but little more.

"Help!" came her voice ringing out and back to her. "I think I hurt myself," she whimpered, clutching her bleeding knee to her chest.

It wasn't long before she saw some light above through the hole she'd fallen and a familiar voice call out. "Thia?" it was Edain. A moment later his head looked out over the edge of the hole she'd made. "Are you okay?" he asked with concern.

Looking up at him, he appeared angelic, his face ringed in white light, looking so beautiful. Her saviour.

"Not really," she admitted, her voice strained. "I think I'm really hurt, and I don't know of a way out." Her long dress was torn and stained from the fall, the light blue contrasting against the bloody red so terribly. Her blonde hair had been pulled up, braided around her head and out of her eyes, but stray hairs touched against her pale cheeks and forehead.

"Don't worry, Thia," he said in his reassuring voice, so steady and calm. "Just sit tight and I'll be right back to get you out of there." He radiated such control over the situation. Never fazed by any misstep, even the largest disaster he took in stride. The worst he had to offer a frown, and then only in sympathy. "Don't move, or you could risk getting yourself in more trouble, okay?"

"Fine." She hated having to rely on anyone, to admit her own defeat, but Edain never made her feel patronized about needing his help. For him, it was just a simple understanding that everyone required aid from time to time, and there wasn't any judgement on his part.

Her soft smile quickly turned to a cringe, though, as she shifted slightly felt a twinge of pain in her knee.

"I won't be long," he promised as he pushed himself back up to his feet and disappeared, leaving her to the quiet solitude of the old root cellar.

❦ 24 ❦

Thia awoke from the dream and back to her reality, and existence so bleak and horrific she could never hope to make a person above ever believe her without first showing them. It occurred to her that if she ever tried to write or talk about it, she would be committed to an asylum without a doubt.

Her first thoughts upon awaking were of her wound. She hadn't tended to cut from the thorn before she drifted off and she immediately began to worry. Though as she looked down through the whole in her dress, she could see the dried blood and… the puffy red flesh where it was closing over.

How could such an injury—one poisoned, no less—be so quickly healing?

She was still groggy, but her fingertips brushed over the wound, curious about it. How had she changed so much down here? Her body, her eyes, her mind. They all felt different, as if she no longer belonged to herself, and she was frightened about what that meant for her return.

The thought of Edain lingered, and she wondered if he had missed her. If he'd been looking for her.

She prayed not, that he wouldn't have followed her trail into this pit of hell, yet at the same time she longed to see him again and how his care and concern for her still lingered.

Looking around her the little nook the mushrooms made for her were exactly as she had recalled them before falling asleep. Things seemed much the same, except she noted a soft sort of rubbing sound from outside. Try as she might, she couldn't see the source of it from within her hideaway.

It was such a soft, delicate sound it didn't seem like it could come from anything bigger than a cat or dog.

Yet who knew what tortures this underworld could convey through a cat or dog would be capable of, considering what she'd seen already.

She hesitated before slowly reaching into her bag, taking out one of the disgusting mushrooms and chewing it thoughtfully as she considered what to do.

She knew she'd have to leave, and that if something else had detected her presence, no matter how innocuous, it was only a matter of time before more things were attracted her way.

So she had to leave, and quickly, all while ensure she was not caught by whatever that thing was outside her hideaway.

Finishing her 'morning meal', Thia found another way out. It required her to squeeze in beneath the thick mushrooms, but the spongy flesh-matter gave way to her slender frame as she forced herself through.

Coming out on the other side, she could hear the soft shuffling noise clearer. It was as if her mushroom hideaway had been dampening the sound of the external noises, letting her rest peacefully, but also disguising the extent of the sounds.

All about her she saw the source of those noises, though it wasn't instantly apparent. Through the field of mushrooms she saw some of them moving. They were oddly shaped, not completely circular as most of the actual mushrooms, but ovular and segmented. It was like watching a field of giant sow bugs shuffle about quietly.

The nearest one was within just a couple dozen feet of her, and she could make out its limbs beneath. Were they some kind of fungal animal? Evolved from mushrooms itself? Or perhaps some sort of bug that evolved to disguise itself amid the fields and forests of underworld vegetation.

Regardless, she didn't want to take her chances with any of the strange creatures that filled this world, and she instantly set her mind to the task at hand. Escape. Always escape.

There had to be some way out of this den of horrors, and the rotten, half plant people had given her a clue as to where. The pale ones guarded it greedily.

She'd agonized over calling Tar'kul for help. Struggled with doing so for so long. Could she trust him to deal with her fairly? She felt she could, but she no longer trusted her instincts on such matters here. Though one thing was certain, she didn't think her odds of surviving alone remained that good anymore. Not when her own trail to freedom was so vague and illusory.

Tar'kul, she thought, her mind reaching out for her monstrous ally. She hadn't heard from him in so long, and knew that he wasn't invincible any more than she.

It took just a moment for his words to enter her mind, *Coming! Stay put, stay safe, find you soon. Help you.*

Perhaps she was going crazy with need for human contact. It had been so long, and she had so wanted to trust those... those... corpses and trees. She wanted to come back to them, get to know them. She was desperate, and the only thing that kept her going was the fact that she was more desperate to escape and feel safe again.

Was that why her heart leapt with relief that Tar'kul was okay?

All about her were fields of mushrooms, and she had no idea

where to go. Perhaps it was because of that reason rather than an urge to trust Tar'kul's words that she turned back towards her hiding spot.

Whatever the reason, when she turned around to go back whence she came, she found herself staring at three of the little mushroom crawlers. They had shuffled in behind her, one atop her former mushroom fort, and two on each side.

They ranged in size from about three to four feet long and as she looked upon them they shifted. And rose.

Beneath their mushroom-like backs moved the gremlin-ish forms of spindly little beings. Like miniature, impish humans with pointed, deformed figures and gnashing jagged teeth and claws. They had no eyes she could see, but large noises that snuffled in her direction.

Each one was smaller than her, but as she noted, there were dozens of them surrounding her throughout the field, all told. And those jagged teeth and claws looked like they could do more harm to her than she cared to take after her perilous journey.

Would the tortures of this land never end? Her muscles were still sore, her mind still fuzzy, and yet somehow, the adrenaline still kicked in. Her body still knew it had to escape, and would work towards it or it'd be her demise.

She hoped it would not be the latter.

She was surrounded, looking out at a field of those... things. So she did the only thing she could do.

Thia ran, as fast as her legs could carry her, seeking asylum from these beasts that thrived in the dark that nearly blinded her.

The sound of her feet tearing up the bed of mushrooms and thumping upon the ground alerted more of the creatures that had yet to notice her. All about her she could see those things rising up, like a wave on the ocean it crested. First their pointed ears would dart out to the sides and then they would slide back upright, like pieces on a playing board. A sea of them all about.

Her heart leapt to her throat as she noticed the larger ones actually carried implements. They were not merely mindless little animals; they had fashioned crude spears and clutched them in their sets of four arms.

Thia didn't let that thought overwhelm her though, she kept moving, veering away from her current direction when she realized it took them into the thick of the creatures, and away to an area that was sparser. Though as she did so, they began a cry. The little fungaloid beings starting some chatter in an indecipherable language as they issued a war cry in furious little chittering voices.

Some of them threw their spears, and though their reach was longer than she would have suspected, their aim was far worse. Their shots landed wide of her, missing her calves, which seemed to – be their target. Now, though, her calves were no less valuable than her heart – if her legs became wounded, she knew she'd never make it out of the subterranean hell alive.

She leapt over two of the creatures as they lunged forward to grab her. They lacked sight, and that gave her a bit of an edge, but with how close their claws came to raking over her pale flesh, she knew not to get cocky about that. They very nearly tore her inner thigh out!

Her lungs already started to burn with her quick motions, her torso leaning forward as she ran to propel herself on faster. She'd hardly realized how much of her dress had been torn off, leaving her calves exposed, and though it was a blessing for quicker motion, it also left her feeling vulnerable.

Tar'kul, what are these things?

She felt confusion in return, his confusion. He had no idea what she referred to, and it dawned on her he could not read her mind so thoroughly. Either he never quite could, or he was now restricted to those words and messages she directly allowed him.

As she ran further, she found their numbers did not seem to thin. They were covering the entire field in every direction she looked. Like an army on the march all of them seemed to be headed in the same direction before she caught their attention.

More of their barbed spears came at her and she had to veer away to avoid them, the sudden change in direction nearly making her topple over and lose all momentum, but she narrowly avoided it and carried on.

She felt a faint hint of curiosity, about where they were originally headed. If they, too, consumed humans, then perhaps they knew of a place to hunt those that the pale ones were unable to nab. But there was no time for her to ponder it at length, and she knew she simply had to keep moving.

The fungus monsters!

There was a moment of quiet before she heard him inside her head once more. *They will not harm you if you avoid them! They are fearful and protective, but only fight to defend selves.* It was not exactly the assessment she would have thought to give them as she ran from their spears and cries.

But then, the plant people were left to their own devices around the pale ones. Perhaps these fungal people didn't care for Tar'kul, but had a prominent interest in her.

"I won't hurt you!" she cried, but she didn't know what good it would do as she veered out of the way again.

Tar'kul spoke words into her mind again, but she never heard them. The horde had come to an abrupt silence, and an overwhelming sense of dread stilled her.

Abruptly they all seemed to lose interest in her and resumed their former course, except now they no longer did so slowly and inconspicuously. They ran. Upright and without inhibition they ran around her, avoiding her entirely and giving her a wide berth.

Thia should've come to the conclusion based on that alone, but the imminent sense of impending doom that washed over her was not natural. It did not spawn from herself or the events around her. It clouded her mind and slowed her from stopping and assessing the situation.

Once she snapped out of her nightmarish trance, she looked about and saw its source. The source of the fungal people's fear. What undoubtedly must have been driving their sudden flight and made them so defensive at her intrusion.

Of all the horrors she had witnessed in the hellish depths of the cavernous underworld, there were none so alien, so damning, so gut-wrenching—so damn large!—as that creature that moved silently over the fungal fields.

It was nearly two stories tall at its highest point, and about two to three times that in length.

Words could not describe the menace of the thing she saw with any adequacy, but its motion was in part like a great crane, or perhaps more like a titanic insect. Its many long, multi-joined limbs moved in succession as it carried it quietly along.

Its head was like that of a hornet or wasp, but coloured in bloody-hues. Its fore-limbs worked ceaselessly, going about its foremost diversion. For though it had a great and fearful maw, somehow both insectoid and reminiscent of hideous monstrosities out of sailors folklore with writhing tentacles, it instead was focussed upon the most macabre act of preening all the hells could devise.

Its great, segmented body curved down from its head then back up to its peak at the rear of its abdomen, but all along its form great spikes grew from its chitinous hide. Thia's first thought was that this armour must serve as its defense, like the hard shell of a beetle, but she reeled as it began very methodically and silently grabbed the fungal people from the fields and then impaled them upon its spikes.

It did this again and again with machine-like regularity. Four of its pincers at constant work plucking up their little bodies then reaching back and thrusting them over one of its bodies spikes so that very quickly its visage became naught but a grotesque menagerie of corpses for armour.

Through all of this she only rarely saw it pluck one of the fungal creatures up and feed it into its maw. It was a messy affair, and tentacled tongue-like protrusions lashed out from the giant's mouth to lap up the fluids that spurted horrifically from its prey.

It was only then that Thia realized she was screaming, for the beast had turned its black gaze upon her and began to redirect its methodical course. All she could do was join the fleeing creatures and head in the same direction they were, too terrified to even notice they no longer gave the slightest damn about her.

She felt like she'd lost something of herself, something very important. She couldn't think, couldn't do anything more than run ahead, her cry still filling her ears. She'd seen into the deepest face of madness, and there was no convalescence from that.

It didn't even register to her that she'd seen at least one human's body impaled on that walking charnel house's spikes.

She hurried on, finding resolve and energy in her limbs that she didn't know she still had after everything else she'd been through.

The immense horror that chased them seemed to move so slowly, yet it managed to keep pace with them, lumbering along in absolute silence as it continued to harvest a crop of flesh and blood. She'd never imagined these almost serene fungal fields could be witness to such a terrifying reaping, but more alarming still was that the fungal people were coming to a halt ahead of her, panic seeming to take hold of them.

It didn't take long to realize why when she glimpsed the great gaping chasm that lay before them. Their escape was cut off by a sheer drop into oblivion.

Whereas so many of the fungal beings did crouch and hide beneath their mushroom hides, hoping for that camouflage to protect them, Thia had no such optimism. No final recourse as she stared out across gaping nothingness.

Was this it?

Was this her death, to the great, horrifying creature that lumbered after her?

Her life flashed before her eyes. Her childhood, spending time in that old manor. The first time Edain smiled at her and set her heart aflame. The photographs of her parents. The long days studying, reading all she could about a myriad of subjects.

Thia had never been satisfied with her lot in life. The notion of simply being a lady of leisure repulsed her, she wanted to learn, to accomplish, to be the equal of any other. She had read stories about adventurers in the jungles of Africa, or sailing to islands in the far off Indies. Yet she had lived something more fantastic by far, and her years of studying zoology and botany and helped prepare her for much of what she encountered.

Yet, what plant in her textbooks could have prepared her for walking undead plant-people? What Bengal tiger or horned rhinoceros could compare to the abomination before her?

Her blue eyes glazed over for a moment as she pondered her demise before she forced herself to assess her surroundings. Deep, focused breaths to calm her heart, and tiny bursts of air to energize her brain.

She couldn't discern the purpose behind this strange, disgusting, terrifying armour of carcasses, but she knew it was large and moved with steady, sure footedness. She just had to learn its rhythm.

She saw it then, her glimmer of hope. Down the edge of the chasm she could see something moving. Some*one*. A tall, dark figure that leapt and bounded with an alien grace that had grown all too familiar to her since arriving in the dark under realm.

Thia began to run past the fungal people cowering in fear and hoping for the best. She ignored the approach of the immense monstrosity and focussed only on getting nearer to her dark saviour.

Come here! came his plea, and she saw him climb a mushroom on the other side that was a good six or seven feet tall, right along the edge of the precipice.

Thia did all she could to get closer to him, though once she reached the opposing side she found herself gazing across a chasm at him helplessly all the same. She wanted to call out to him, but she knew better than to raise her voice again; that monstrosity was drawn to sound and she could feel the doom of its approach without so much as glancing in its direction.

What do I do? She asked Tar'kul in desperation.

Catch me, he responded, just a moment before he did the unthinkable.

Running across the top of that mushroom he leapt, and though she knew him to be quite nimble and flight of foot, the gaping chasm was too great a divide.

Soaring through the air, Tar'kul flailed out his arms and legs —all six limbs in total – - as he jumped towards her, and for a heart-pounding moment it was like time slowed down to a crawl. She watched him rise, arc and begin to fall just beyond the edge.

She didn't know what possessed her to do it, but she reached out to grab him, to catch his hand and help him. Perhaps it was the knowledge that even if she didn't, she'd only live long enough to become impaled upon some spike. To perhaps avoid spending her last moments writhing in agony with the knowledge she was a new gory adornment atop a hideous beast's hide.

Whatever the reason, she knew she didn't have the strength to not only grab and stop him but pull him up, and reality proved true.

She caught his dark fingers in her pale hand, and clutched on tightly, and him to her. Then when the sudden force of his weight yanked her forward, she was dragged across the gravelly surface, the coarse material digging into her knees as she went plummeting over the edge with him towards the promise of dark and final oblivion.

Everything seemed to come to a halt in that moment, just like it had when she first watched Tar'kul leap. She could feel the cool air rushing up from the furthest reaches of infinity beneath her. The wicked cackling howl of its winds far below like some presiding daemon eager to devour her.

At least, she could comfort herself, it would be a quick and painless death. She'd not come back to live in as some undead plant creature, but at least she would not suffer the agony that came with such a transformation.

As they fell together, Tar'kul wrapped two of his arms around her, clutching her to his hard, dark body. The flap of his trench coat so loud as the two of them flailed through the air.

Somehow in that hopeless moment, he gave her a smile on his dark lips and squeezed her tighter, clinging to her as he chittered into her mind, moving his mouth in mimicry of normal human speech as always. "Hold on."

She could do nothing else but dig her hands and nails and fingers and legs into the monster's body, knowing this was it.

The end.

She'd die in the arms of her monstrous saviour, captor, rapist, and protector, a mere stain on the bottom of the world.

Perhaps death wouldn't be so bad. Perhaps it would be the release that she'd been looking for, the absence of horror, of fear, of the constant threats made against her. Her body was exhausted, but more than that, she knew her mind couldn't take much more of these unearthly horrors.

Just when she thought she'd be safe, find some silver lining, she was dragged back into the pits of hell, forced to flee from another beast that had no right to exist.

Death could be the sweet absence of all that, a reward for a battle well fought, and as they fell, she tried to make peace with that. An old prayer came to mind and she started reciting it silently.

It was a long moment later that she realized they were not falling directly down but curving through the air. More than that, curving back towards the side Tar'kul had come from.

She hadn't seen it in the darkness, but he held rope made of that gray fabric corded so thickly it was dark and nearly invisible in the subterranean dimness.

A heartbeat after that realization, they crashed into the opposing cliffside and she heard the loud sound of cracking like bones breaking. However it was Tar'kul who took the brunt of that impact as he clutched his rope with two hands.

She could see the look of anguish on his face from that impact as they jarringly settled against the cliff walls, his teeth gnashing from the pain. Yet never did his grip loosen.

Every moment with him, she felt like she understood him less than she thought she had. He was so foreign, so alien to her, and yet he seemed to care. Truly, and more honestly than most humans she knew, even if the ways he showed it were something beyond her comprehension.

She didn't look back at the thing that had chased her, and hoped that she'd never have to see that vision of nightmares ever again.

"Thank you." Thia echoed off the wall, the exhaustion more than evident in her voice.

Without delay, he was pulling them both up the cord, his arms strained as he inched them closer towards the ledge after his brutal impact. She had no idea of what went on inside that alien mind of his. So compassionate and caring at times, then others...

She tried not to think on it, not while she relied on him so much and his mind was so near.

Slowly he overcame gravity and the tug of that infernal pit to reach the edge of the cliffs, and he used his lower arms to try and lift her up to grasp on. *"Take hold,"* he beckoned her, *"will support you."*

Her arms were weary and exhausted, but still she managed to find the strength to reach out and grasp for salvation. He gave her a boost up over the edge, and she scrambled atop it, panting heavily as he climbed up to join her.

He hardly looked any less worn and weary than she, Thia instantly noticed. He was breathing heavily, throwing himself to his back once he was up to rest. Did he even rest while he was searching for her?

Likely not. And even though she wanted to enjoy the momentary reprieve, her eyes searched for new threats, new horrors that sought to snuff her out.

"What was that?"

She didn't dare speak the words aloud, afraid she'd attract something else.

Tar'kul didn't look back across the chasm. He visibly shivered as he slowly caught his breath and pushed himself to his palms. *"Soul Reaper,"* he responded in kind, the words inside her mind even though he mouthed them. *"Evil. Pure evil."*

As she listened, she inspected the area, and though her first gaze showed it to be much like the other side, with the field of mushrooms growing as far as she could see, amongst the fungus she saw the occasional bits of stone. Carved stone.

They were as a whole sort of conically shaped, with a hole in the tip, though most seemed to be in various stages of degradation and destruction. They bore a resemblance to the architecture of the city where Tar'kul hid and the pale ones lurked.

Her exhaustion couldn't keep her still as she pushed herself up, moving towards and inspecting one of the pieces of architecture. She kept her back to Tar'kul as she 'thought' to him.

"You now understand that I cannot stay here, and I will get out of here if it costs me everything."

He stilled at first, but then she heard him shuffle in behind her. He had obviously both exhausted and injured himself badly in coming to her rescue. Yet all the same, he responded to her words simply, *"Understand."* His expression fell, those human-lips frowning even as his bizarre fangs marked him as so inhuman.

As she studied the stone work she began to see a pattern in how they were laid, they were like road markers that led the way. When she scuffed her shoe over the ground, brushing aside the silt and spores, she saw stonework beneath. A roadway. Confirming her deduction.

But to where? Surely it couldn't be back to the city she had fled, was it to another?

"I was told of a place the pale ones guard, a way out of here." Thia looked to him, then motioned to the ground. *"Do you think this is a path there?"*

Tar'kul's shoulders slumped and he visibly shrank before her. *"Maybe,"* he responded, *"but should not go there. Not safe. Treacherous. Vile pale ones. Never honest. Never to be trusted. Only want to feast upon you. Make you food."*

"Well, the plant people want to make me one of them, the mushroom people wanted to take out my legs, and that devourer of souls... There's no shortage of things that will kill me down here." She dusted off her hands, quietly, and felt her body swoon a little bit. She needed rest. True rest.

But that was a luxury now.

Tar'kul reached out and braced her with two of his arms. *"Need rest. Both of us,"* he urged. *"Come. Know place. We rest there and decide what to do after. Yes?"* he asked, the tall, strange man staring at her with his inky black eyes.

She nodded wearily. "*No... touching,*" she mentally spoke, staring at him coolly with her clear, blue eyes.

Slowly he retracted his arms and tucked down his chin like a scolded puppy, in stark contrast to the unsettling visage he made. "*Understand,*" he replied as a whisper of a thought before shuffling off in what seemed a random direction. "*We rest. Need it for journey. Too hard to travel like this.*"

She'd not seen him limply lope along so badly before, not even when the pale one nearly ripped him to pieces.

A part of her cringed, beginning to feel bad for her treatment of him. He was the only one who had done anything for her that wasn't entirely selfish and self-serving, and was definitely the only thing that hadn't tried to kill her.

Yet, he'd violated her, and in some ways that was almost worse.

Still, she followed after him with careful, measured steps, eager for sanctuary.

The journey to the safe area took quite some time with the both of them in the condition they were. Despite the urgency they couldn't make much of a pace, and dragged their heels the entire way there.

"That's it. Up ahead," he told her, and what he indicated seemed like nothing more than a pile of rocks. Though the closer they got, it was more accurate to say it was a pile of rubble. Old stonework of the like that made up the ancient city.

She was too exhausted to even comment. It took everything she had just to force herself forward, and she was surprised by the reserves of energy he seemed to have. Not long ago, after all, she'd rested within a safe cocoon. It was likely more than he'd done.

Her feet began to scuff but she forced her legs up higher, nearing his secret hideaway.

There seemed to be no way into whatever hideaway Tar'kul had, but that just meant it would be an even better hideaway, she reckoned. He led her around, and tucked away towards one of the mighty stone stalagmites nearby, he led her into a small hole that led to a doorway.

The place inside seemed to be the basement of the ruined building above, and as Tar'kul led her in, she could see that it contained a full harvest of those mushrooms he had fed her.

"*Safe, secure,*" he recited to her in his chittering mental voice as he slid the broken stone doorway back shut behind them. There was little inside, two rooms, many mushrooms, and series of shelves and stone slabs in the larger back chamber. Though off to one side she heard a dripping and saw there was a source of water there in some strange stone basin lined with a brass-like metal inside.

She realized just how thirsty she was, walking towards it. "*Safe?*" she asked curiously, her throat feeling so gritty and sore as she forced herself to swallow.

Even in her exhaustion, though, Thia was fascinated with the subterranean home. Who had lived here before? Humans? It was terrifying to think that there was once civilization that could live in such a horrific place.

There was nothing reminiscent about humanity in the style and design of these cities, though. Their strange design was so ancient yet advanced, and completely, utterly otherworldly.

Tar'kul nodded to her, "*Safe,*" he affirmed as he dragged himself over to the wall where the mushrooms grew thickest. He very meticulously studied them, picking them out. "*One of many homes. Never safe to stay in one too long. Would show you them all in time. Teach you how to survive,*" he explained to her. "*Only want you be strong and safe. Be with...*" he trailed off morosely and plucked one mushroom before continuing his examination.

Her heart panged again and she pushed it away. She simply had to remember what he'd done to her, yet it was hard for her to steel her heart to the only thing standing between her and death.

"How long have you been down here?"

"Many years. Lifetimes," he said to her, his chittering voice softer as he found a shelled bug rooting through the mini-orchard. Plucking it up it wriggled its many limbs and made a whining noise before Tar'kul broke its exoskeleton along its neck and removed the head with a twist. *"Too long ago to remember,"* he admitted, implying he was not always a subterranean dweller.

It confirmed something she didn't want confirmed, and she looked towards him, her words cautious and spoken aloud. "Were you once something else?"

Tar'kul froze in place as if the question upset him greatly, though it was just momentary. He turned towards her with mushrooms and the recently decapitated bug in his arms. *"Good food,"* he waffled. *"Very fresh. Very potent. Best for you. Make you strong and... and..."* he struggled, his face contorting as he sought out the more complicated word, *"resilient."*

She sighed audibly, walking towards him and making a bit of a face as she accepted his morose gift. "What about the pale ones?"

Handing her the food he cringed at that. *"They were once men. Alive. Now they are... walking dead. No soul. No..."* he struggled again for his next word, but it wouldn't come, and his face showed the pain of lost words, lost memories. However long he had been down here, he seemed to have had little opportunity to speak with others and exercise his language.

After a pause he looked to her, *"Tar'kul not thing. Am..."* he lifted a hand, pointing a dark finger at his own chest, tapping his hard body as he struggled for the word. The struggle was a different sort, this time. His lips moved and he formed the words with his voice, albeit poorly and with great struggle. There were curious hisses and popping noises, but at least he said, "Man. I was born man," each syllable a struggle for his malformed mouth, so starkly changed from what it once was, "still… a man."

Part of her expected that, especially after seeing the grotesque transformation of the plant like people, but half of her felt revolted by what he had become. By what this place had done to him.

Her face fell as she forced some of the dead bug flesh into her mouth, but it only increased her need to gag. She held it down, but new emotions swelled within her and she sensed such a sense of loss for him.

How mad must he have gone in the decades that must have passed, loneliness and fear and exhaustion driving him as it drove her. And she'd only been down here... She wasn't entirely certain. Weeks?

Tar'kul stood watching her a moment before he turned and shuffled to one of the benches, sitting himself down then curling his legs up beneath him. *"You are… resilient. You will survive. Only wish… you did not have to go,"* he said in somber, confessional tones of that chittering, mental voice.

"Did you have someone help you when you first... stumbled into this place?" Her weariness was replaced with that damnable curiosity, and though she sat down and felt her limbs thank her for the rest, her mind wouldn't quiet.

He took a while to think on it as he wrapped his lower arms about his legs and rolled into a ball. *"Yes...almost,"* he said in response. *"Did not know the way of things here. We learned together. Until..."* he shuddered from the memories. *"Until Tar'kul only one left."* His dark eyes flickered as he gazed across at her. *"You, first living person seen in..."* he mulled it over, as if mentally calculating the time, *"many, many years."*

A heavy burden was placed on her shoulders, and she felt a great pity for him rise up again. She was clearly dredging up things he hadn't thought of in a long time, and she couldn't help but want to know more. About him, about how this place existed.

About how long before she'd start to warp into a monster like him.

Instead, she mentally asked, *"Have you met the plant people?"*

The question had been asked silently between their minds, but he hissed aloud. *"Enslavers. They… they sought to …put me in chains,"* he struggled to say, exercising his linguistic faculties with her as he dredged up long forgotten words. *"Remember when they were but one. De…delusional, alone, he thought himself… King of Underworld."* She couldn't be sure, but she thought Tar'kul rolled his eyes. *"Now… even he has company."*

She wondered if he was speaking about Reginald. It would make sense. Perhaps that company is why he was still so well spoken, and Thia frowned at the thought. *"Why did your body change?"*

His grasp went rigid about himself and he clutched at his form more tightly, as if sheltering from the question. *"Don't wish to talk about that,"* he said to her quietly. Though she wished to know if a similar fate awaited her.

"Will it happen to me?" she asked.

Tar'kul paused a moment then shook his head. *"If you leave… then perhaps no. If you stay… teach you how to avoid it. Stay same. I… like you as you are,"* he confessed to her. *"Bring memories of life above, looking at you. Bring pain. But glad."*

She didn't realize there was a tear rolling down her cheek until it dripped from her chin to her chest and she had to look away. She was sure she looked horrible. Pale and exhausted, and she knew her hair was a mess, for what that mattered down here. Not to mention her ripped and torn dress, which was once so regal and beautiful, what seemed like so long ago.

She didn't feel like she could remind anyone of life, and she swiped at her eyes angrily as she forced herself to look away. "We should rest."

The huddled creature Tar'kul gave her his simple reply, "*Rest well. Tar'kul will protect.*" It was his pledge to her, and despite what he had done, she knew it to be sincere.

And even though her brain was still buzzing, she rolled onto her side and sleep quickly overcame her.

❧ 26 ❧

Thia stood watch over the troupe of soldiers as the Lieutenant huddled, arms around his knees. He was weary; he'd not been sleeping much as of late. Pushing himself as they were lost in the underground world. Without him saying it, she could sense his feelings of obligation and duty, his thick, long dark hair shimmering in the faint glow of the underworld as he bowed his head.

One of the few soldiers remaining to him came shuffling up, "Lieutenant," he said in a low voice, trying to remain quiet. "Lieutenant?"

Lifting his head, their leader said in a gruff voice, "What's the report, McMillan?"

"I ain't sure, but... up ahead a ways, there's some kind of... well, it's odd, but... a road, Lieutenant."

"A road?" he echoed, brow raised.

"Aye," responded the soldier with a nod. "Stones, obviously shaped to bricks, linin' the ground and leadin' off deeper into the chasm. Weird stone cones along its edges. They got these hoops in 'em, not sure what for. But I guess… I guess it must lead ta somethin', right?"

The Lieutenant's deep, dark eyes stared off in thought, and Thia could feel him concentrating. "If there's a road it means someone musta built it. It probably isn't the bandits, because they looked far too hard up to build anything, even shoes." With a nod he dusted himself off and rose, "Let's get ready. The longer we sit here, the more vulnerable we are, lads."

Thia was becoming gradually accustomed to this, living another's unconscious dreams. Or perhaps simply their memories. Some faint psychic shadow of events past that had transpired in this dark pit.

As the soldiers moved on and found the roadway it was like time sped up a bit, but she noticed for the first time that the Lieutenant looked to her directly. "I'm sorry I got us into this, Corporal. I never thought we could come across such madness…" his head hung low. "How could any man?"

She felt the urge to reply, but it wasn't easy forming words in that dreamscape, though just before she felt she was about to get one out she noticed the look upon the dashing Lieutenant's face. Her gaze followed his, and she saw it… their destination. She only glimpsed it momentarily, and though it was reminiscent of the city she had come upon after first arriving below, it was at the same time nothing like it.

The unholy look of that spiralling citadel-city was the stuff of nightmares. Like the throne of hell itself. Yet never would she ever find words to describe it exactly. Words were but the tools of mortals to put shape to the doings of nature, yet what she saw had as much relation to nature as the sun and stars did towards the hopes and aspirations of a squirrel.

❧ 27 ❧

Thia awoke with a start in the dimness of the chamber, a gasp escaping her lips, her body clammy and cold. She had been sweating profusely in her sleep, and it couldn't have been a very long one either. She felt no less weary and exhausted than before she slipped out of consciousness.

It took her a moment to relax, calm her breathing and notice that Tar'kul was rising up and watching her. A troubled expression marked his once-human face.

"It's nothing," she hissed into the darkness that her sight could now cut through, and she let her body go limp as she strained her ears. She swore she heard something, a scuttling, but perhaps it was simply her mind playing tricks on her. Enemies were everywhere, danger was never far.

"Sleep. Rest. Will need all your energy for what is to come," he both urged and warned her as he settled back down wearily.

Yet something was unsettling her.

Whose memories... whose thoughts were they? Or were they simply a strange manifestation of loneliness and anxiety, being stuck down in this pit for so long?

The thoughts and memories of the dreams troubled her as her clammy body struggled to rest once more.

She only knew that this place had a way of seeping into her in every way. Into her body, changing the way her eyes saw and wounds healed, and into her mind with the way she now dreamt and thought. It only punctuated the importance that she get out immediately.

28

It wasn't often that Thia had got to see the inside of Edain's room; such things were considered the height of impropriety for two young nobles. An exception was made on only two occasions. Once when he was seriously ill. The second time when he feigned illness.

As she strolled into his large room, so elegantly decorated with exotic, foreign silks and drapery, the sun poured in from outside, bathing his immense bed with golden hues as he lay there reading. He hadn't heard her approach, so she got to see him peaceful and quiet for a while before he looked over to her and smiled. His handsome face lighting up so pleasantly.

"I like it better when I come visit you," he said to her softly, looking nothing but overjoyed at her presence despite his words. He wore a black silk suit for lounging about in, and it made him look like some far off exotic prince of the East to her eyes, that had never gazed beyond her homeland. "How are you Thia?" he asked.

Her lips turned up as she walked towards him, her own dress large and cumbersome, the blue matching her eyes. "Quite fine, compared to you." Her golden hair was left down, the tresses lightly teasing her collarbone as they spilled over her shoulders in soft waves.

He shut the book in his hands and set it aside. The room was so large and opulent and the warm summer breeze through the open doors onto the balcony made it the absolute perfect setting to recuperate. Or lounge and chat, as it were.

"I'll be okay," he assured her as he pushed himself up in bed and straightened his silk jacket over his dark flesh, those almond-shaped eyes of his glittering pleasantly. "You have no idea what it does for me just to see you smile at me like that," he remarked in his charming voice. "It's like I feel my battered ribs knitting back together already," he said, which struck her as odd, as she was told he'd suffered an injury to his thigh. "Thank you for coming."

Her eyes narrowed but her smile only grew as she pulled up one of the chairs to his bed, settling down and crossing her legs at the ankles.

"Ah yes, your poor ribs. It must hurt to even sit up as you are."

A hesitant sort of smile formed on his face and he rested his hands in his lap. Very sheepishly he lowered his gaze, and his dark hair fell before his eyes before he brushed it back. "I'm so sorry about what happened before... I know what happened between us was wrong now, but... I was so caught up in the moment, and you seemed to be enjoying it. I..." he stammered, sounding so troubled, "I should've controlled myself better."

It felt as if all the blood drained from her body and she sat back in the chair, blinking away her confusion. Her dreams... they were so strange. It barely felt like a dream at all.

Almost as though her mind were simply vacationing in the skull of another.

She swallowed, her fingers beginning to nervously tap-tap-tap on the arm rest.

"I should have stopped you."

He shook his head and gave her several fleeting glances. "It was too soon. No matter the passions involved, I should have proved myself a gentleman and waited until we were both properly and formally ready." He swallowed heavily, "You're a beautiful and refined lady, Thia. You deserved better than a moment of passionate abandon. Now... now I fear I've ruined it all for good." His words so sombre and resigned.

And she knew it wasn't Edain. Edain... he was simply the dream portion of what really happened, of what she thought she was experiencing.

The truth was much darker.

Yet it was also tinged with sorrow and anger at the depths of insanity this place could push on someone once a man. Someone that, on some level, could pass for her dear Edain.

She didn't know if it was true or not, but the dream was too real and too fake to ignore. Tar'kul was somehow manipulating her mind, yet he did it with precision, with eloquence that mirrored her own.

Thia stood from her chair, looking down on the supposedly broken man, and her smile held no joy. "We can talk about this when I'm back home."

The implication was, of course, that she'd still talk to him. Even when she was safe.

He looked up at her, wounded and sad. "I can't follow you back there, of course. You know that, Thia," his voice so resigned. So sullen. He wrung his hands together in his lap, fidgeting nervously beneath her gaze.

"You can't be seen. You know what my manor looks like. And it needs to be guarded so that no others can fall into the pale one's lair. I can only do that for so long." Thia fidgeted, playing with her hair as she took in a deep breath. It wasn't an easy conversation for her to have, but she believed him.

Believed in the loneliness that drove him to such horrific lengths, even if she didn't forgive him for it.

He stilled there a moment before resuming his fidgeting. Looking like the beautiful young Edain, his troubled expression was all the more impactful. "I can't travel across the open ground," he confessed. "Not anymore. If… when we find you a way out, you'll have to travel under the open skies. I cannot go there."

"There's still the entrance I came in through. With enough rope…" she said softly.

After all she'd been through, all that had happened, she'd never want to condemn someone to this place.

The tortured visage of Edain gazed up at her with quiet disbelief before he nodded. "Very well," he said in that familiar voice of her once beloved. "Thank you," he said softly, lowering his gaze once more. "After all that has happened… thank you from the bottom of my heart. Thank you in ways I can't express. These deformities of the body prevent the expression of the soul ever but when we are entwined mentally."

She stared for what felt like a very long time, her breathing becoming deep and steady as she considered his gratitude. What could he have been like, before all this? Someone dapper and charming? Perhaps he would not be so possessive, certainly not so desperate and alone.

"Things will seem better in the morning, Tar'kul." Her smile was sad, for though she pitied the monster before her, she still longed for those brief reprieves and conversations with Edain.

At that name his brow furrowed and he looked as if the very sound of it bothered him. "I hope someday you will forgive me," he said at last, though already the dream was slipping away and she awoke to the dingy little hole in the ground they hid away in.

The sound of water lapping against something awoke her, though it felt too loud to be simply the nearby basin. When she looked around she saw that the floor of the basement was coated in a quarter of an inch of water, and the basin well overflowed.

Tar'kul still slept across the room from her, huddled into his ball.

She glanced at him, that mixture of pity and something deeper crossing her face before she went towards the basin. She didn't want to feel so much apprehension at something as innocuous as water flooding their area, but she couldn't help it. Everything down here seemed to have a purpose - to kill her.

The dripping into the basin was much steadier now, and more than that it was running down the wall from the crack it built from. Whatever the source, it was obviously increased as it began to fill their little hideaway.

Before she had time to do anything more, however, the crack in the wall widened and she watched as more of the cool water poured in with a gush. At the rate it flooded in the chamber would fill before long.

"Tar'kul!" she hissed. "We have to go." Yet even in her fear, her instincts kicked in, and she dunked her hands into the frigid water and bringing it to her lips. It was still clean and crisp to her lips compared to the wickedness that pervaded all else, and she knew she'd need it in the time to come.

With her warning, the obsidian man rose up alert, he darted his head about and noted immediately the situation. "*No!*" he chittered into her mind. "*The flood season is here early!*" Thia saw the panic in his movements as he got up, quickly grabbing mushrooms from the walls and shelves, stuffing them into his trench coat pockets as quick as he could.

Yet all the while the water rose and Thia could see that the exit, which lay at the other end, was at a slope and was faster growing buried beneath water than they were at the opposite end.

She tried to drink, even as she plotted her exit strategy. Running around in a wet dress wouldn't do, but it was already too late to worry about that. And her more immediate concern - *their* more immediate concern - was going to be food and drink.

Yet even in her panic, his words slowly seeped into her mind.

Flood season?

Spring?

As Tar'kul broke the head off another beetle she called out to him, *"The door!"* And he immediately snapped his head towards it.

"No!" he cried as he stuffed what he had into his pockets before splashing through the rapidly rising water towards the door. It was of stone make and quite heavy, and Thia could see he was struggling with it as the water pressure added to the burden. *"Not good, terrible,"* he muttered mentally to her.

She ran towards him, trying to help. She remembered what he'd said in her dreams, about his ribs, and she knew what terrible pain he must be in. Her desperation forced out the anxiety of drowning, even as the water threatened her collarbone, the dress weighing her down.

Together the two of them strained to move the door, but every time they budged it a little, the rush of water trying to get out helped push it back closed again.

"Too soon," he lamented. *"Should have had much more time for safety here!"* and gnashing his teeth he put all his strength into the action, and together with her help they shoved the door open enough for one to squeeze through. *"Go! Get out,"* he said as he used all six of his limbs to both push against the door and support himself against the wall.

She didn't hesitate to push her way out, nearly stumbling forward with the rush of water, her slender body easily slipped between the rock door. The runoff was getting trapped at the exit, splashing back around and sealing the door in its path, and she risked losing her fingers if she tried to pull.

"Tar'kul!"

All that dark sinew of his muscles bulged and shook with the strain, the door that had been such a secure seal over their hide-away now a deadly trap. Straining himself, he kept his head over the water as he inched forward, pushing it open wider gradually until… he was knocked back a few inches and cried out in pain, a hideous sound. His injuries were only compli-cating matters.

Thia knew then his life rested with her, if there were any chance at all. She had to find some way to jar open the door and so she looked around.

Rubble lay everywhere – the home above was a pile of it, after all, so she grasped a thick chunk of melded stone and metal. It was heavy, and before she started her journey she'd never have bothered even trying to lift such a weight, but she did it this time without hesitation.

Her slender arms strained and she carried it back to the doorway. "Watch out Tar'kul!" she warned as she dropped it down into the water and used it to jar open the doorway.

It came not a moment too soon, as the obsidian man's arms gave way and the crack of the door striking the stone boomed afterwards. He hissed in gasps of air as he squirmed through the tiny opening, getting stuck in the process.

She was amazed it had worked, that it didn't just crack, but so thankful for it all the same. "Give me your hand!" she ordered, surprised by the reserve of strength in her voice. "Suck in your breath, we can get you out."

He grasped her hand with two of his foreword arms, clutching tightly as he wriggled and squirmed. Though tall, he had a slender and lean build. That saved him as she pulled him out through and the two of them waded up onto dry ground.

Tar'kul slumped onto his hands and knees, chest heaving as he sucked in air. Those dark, alien eyes of his turned towards her and he chittered to her, *"Thank you."*

She stood guard as he caught his breath, nodding. *"I couldn't leave you there."*

She took a deep breath. *"My bag is lost. Did you make out with much?"*

He was slow to recuperate fully, but nodded to her. *"Enough for few days,"* he responded as he finally pulled himself up, his trench coat sodden but stuffed full of the harvest he'd grabbed on their way out. *"This not good,"* he remarked as he stood up, looking off. Though the ground was mostly flat in the subterranean world, there were gradual slopes and inclines in the plane, and Thia could see that there were some streams of cool water over the mushroom fields ahead, and the temperature had indeed dropped because of it.

She shivered in her wet dress, her arms wrapping around herself. *"What does this mean?"* She was so afraid that it was spring up above, the snow melting and flooding them out. Worse, it meant that far too much time had passed with her down here. More than she expected.

Tar'kul looked to her with some hesitancy, and though his visage was so otherworldly she could read the subtle signs of reluctance upon his face. There was something he wanted to say, and something more he didn't. *"Journey much more dangerous now. Great peril ahead. Worse than expected,"* he said before reaching down to wring the cold water from his trench coat as best he could.

She mimicked his actions, trying to get out as much water as she could from her dress as her lips turned down in a frown. *"If the water is getting in from the surface, then maybe it could make a passage way."*

"Maybe," Tar'kul replied as he went about draining as much of the chilled water from his clothing as he could. *"In a lifetime or two. It is…"* he struggled for the word in a way he didn't seem to have to in her dreams, *"seepage from surface. Many little trickles join,"* he explained.

She frowned deeper as she nodded. She knew him to be telling the truth but desperately wanted it to be false.

"So we need to move fast, then." Thia stood tall despite her dress pulling her down, and squared her shoulders.

"Too late for that," he said with resignation. *"True danger is not water, but what it brings."* He limped wearily away, rounding the corner and pointing off in the distance. *"With water comes the Death-Lamps,"* he told her, sounding defeated, as if there were nary a worse fate to march into but he knew he would agree to accompany her regardless.

It sounded almost comical after facing the Soul Reaper.

"Death-Lamps?" They sounded almost quaint.

Perhaps he felt her mirth in the tone of her psychic words, for he looked at her sullen and sad. *"Death-Lamps are..."* he struggled for the word, *"unknowable. They blind with their eyes. Never seen one. Not directly. They travel in packs... monsters. Devour everyone who come near to water."*

She deflated at that, and took a step from the pouring font of water behind her. *"I can't live like this."* It was too much. A constant stream of terror. Her noble body wasn't made for such stress.

He immediately looked to her, as if perhaps there were some hope. *"Let... let me take you somewhere safe. Wait out floods. Stay in shelter, safe, warm. Never have to go into danger. Tar'kul care for you, bring you foods and water until time to go. Then make journey in safety,"* he was hopeful, practically pleading with her to take his offer and wait out the new danger.

It was such an enticing idea after all she had been through, yet to look at him and what had become of him, to think of how fast she was changing already. She was speaking to him with her mind alone! Would there be much of the original Thia left by the time the floods had cleared? However long that took?

"Tar'kul, we don't have time. I... won't be able to return to the surface if I stay down here much longer. I'll change." And how terri-

fied she was of changing, of losing her own humanity, of being condemned to this hell for eternity.

Those thick, human lips of his turned downwards and he felt that hope of avoiding almost certain death fade. *"You are beautiful,"* he said, reaching up a hand, nowhere near close to touching her, but miming the gesture of stroking her cheek nonetheless. *"You are resilient. You can make it. But... can't survive being ripped. Gutted. Eaten."* He tapped his chest with a free hand, *"Survived so long by being wary. Avoiding danger."*

And surely any path up would be dangerous. Filled with water and fraught with horrors.

She logically, rationally wanted to agree. To let him guide her to safety, the slow and cautious route.

But she was too desperate for that.

"I can't risk becoming a slave to this world down here."

His expression fell and he nodded. *"Okay,"* he surrendered, knowing there was no further arguing with her. As tall as he was, he appeared stooped and resigned. *"We can move along this way,"* he indicated over the damp fields before them, though she couldn't really tell one area from the next. *"If we run into Dead-Lamps... at least we can run and hide into tunnels nearby."*

She was amazed by how much his speech was improving. He was becoming more fluent and articulate with practice, and that broke her heart. How much had he forgotten just to survive in these pits?

"Do the pale ones... Do they go above?"

He looked to the side at her, *"Sometimes. When darkest. Do not like..."* he struggled for the word a moment, *"day. Hate day. But venture above to lure victims when darkest."*

"Can we follow them?"

"Not time for that yet," he said to her with a slow shake of his head. *"Must reach... reach,"* he struggled, perhaps the word was forgotten, or he simply feared to speak of it from some dark

memory, she couldn't tell from the way he flinched. *"Must pass floods first. Then worry about such things if still alive."*

That didn't sound like a great bid of confidence, but she nodded, resigned. Her wet dress still clung to her form, but she didn't have the backpack to weigh her down, and she had gotten at least a little rest in that fitful night of sleep.

"Lead the way, Tar'kul."

29

Thia had not imagined the dark depths could get any more ominous, that their looming presence could chip away at her psyche any more than they already had. Yet as she walked through the mushy, cold bogs of the now flooded regions of the underworld, she realized just how wrong she was.

The mushroom fields had become a teeming marshland, the smaller mushrooms now part of the spongy wet floor that she walked over, squishing unpleasantly beneath her with each step. All around, the larger ones stood up among the mists dewy with condensation, ominously dripping wetness into the soggy bog beneath their plumes.

That and the ever present chill of the runoff from the world above would have been enough to dampen her spirits. The uncomfortable wetness against her feet made each step so unpleasant, and knowing each noisy squelch she made drew attention to the two travellers had a fraying effect upon her mind, every moment wrought with paranoia. Was this the moment that they would be found? Was there some new horror about to pounce around the mushroom-tree ahead?

No, if that had been all of it, she might've stood the new horrors well enough.

Added to the dreary paranoia and uncomfortable cold, there were the absent yet omnipresent Dead-Lamps.

Looking back at her initial dismissal of them seemed so jarring now that she'd walked in fear of them for so long. Never had she seen one directly, yet she felt like she knew the fear of them more intimately than anything else.

Only rarely did she catch sight of them out over the bogs. Some brief glimmer of pale-white light far off in the distance, long and almost rectangular. They only ever seemed to show up for seconds at a time, enough to notice them and stare, to make their strange shape known before blinking out of existence again.

It was their cries that affected her most. Shortly after their lights would blink out of existence, an unsettling clicking noise would carry through the underworld, seeming to echo off the waters. It was like two rocks clacking together, but Tar'kul reassured her that was not what they were doing.

Yet she could scarcely imagine, and loathed to try. She was constantly shivering, her body so damp and cold to the very core. She resisted the urge to sniffle and could only imagine what a sight she was, walking through the cold, clammy air beneath the surface of the earth.

Her stomach was clenched so hard that it was becoming difficult to eat, her appetite lessening even as she tried to force herself to keep up what meagre strength she had.

It had been so long since they last rested, with no convenient and safe locale in sight. Tar'kul gazed back at her, and she could read the concern on his alien face for her. "*We rest as soon as a place can be found,*" he chittered.

Though something else greater than rest began to dominate her mind. Even in her weary state, she was in deep concentration, thinking of their environments. It slowly dawned on her that the appearance of those lights and the clacking noises the Dead-Lamps made had a certain pattern to it. They weren't random as they first seemed, no.

Some were closer than others, while some were further, and she assumed therefore it meant nothing, yet as she thought on it she realized that they were hunting as a party. They were coordinating their efforts and closing in around them and making sure they were ready to intercept them on their current course.

Thia felt her stomach roll and she thought she'd be sick, if not for the fact that she had nothing in her.

She said to him, silently, *"We have to be erratic. Throw them off our trajectory."* She'd been forcing herself, as much as she could, to talk. To use the words she knew, to keep her vocabulary strong.

Already, she knew her attempts were failing, but she wouldn't give up. Perhaps it would even help Tar'kul...

Tar'kul looked at her with confusion, but slowly she could sense the gears turning in his head as he figured out her meaning. *"They are hunting us,"* he said to her, his dark eyes darting about the underworld. He was troubled by the realization and more so by the fact it had not occurred to him sooner.

Swallowing heavily he began to lead them off their course through the muck and mire, their footsteps slowed and heavily laden down by the cool water and soggy bottoms beneath it.

It wasn't long before her theory was proven correct, and those eerie white lamps appeared closer to them, making her eyes sting with their light before they flickered out and more clacking noises followed.

She was going to die down here.

Never had it seemed more apparent to her, and she just

wanted to delay it. To keep fighting for another footstep, to get just a little bit further.

To get closer to freedom and know that, even if she died, she did everything in her power to escape. She would die fighting, figuratively speaking.

As that impending doom neared upon them, Tar'kul reached back with one of his hands towards her. One of those with the still human fingers up on it, *"We need to run now,"* he said to her with urgent insistence, and though things were so very, very quiet and still, she knew that he was right. They were out of time. *"Do not look at lights. Shut your eyes when they appear."*

She glanced around as quickly as she could, trying to take in her surroundings and where they could run as she grasped his hand, before beginning to pump her legs. She was so thin and frail, just lean, sinuous muscles, and it gave her speed, despite her lack of food. She couldn't keep it up for long, but she tried to manage her pace between a sprint and a jog, each footstep a threat of slipping on mushy bog.

Dangers lurked everywhere, and even the cave floor looked like her death with its slickness, a trap set just for her.

Tar'kul kept a tight hold upon her hand however, and helped keep her going. They made more noise trying to run like that, but it was already too late to worry about it. They were long past the point of hiding their presence from the Dead-Lamps, and their bright lights began to flicker about around them.

As luck would have it, they had picked a good direction to run in, and the blinding glare of those white, unnatural lights came mostly from their backs and sides, yet still they did the trick of making Thia's world an impossible daze. She could see why Tar'kul had advised her to simply shut her eyes, because it made no real difference. She couldn't see anything with them open, so why not close them? It at least lessened the stinging brightness that was like staring into a thousand suns.

Their path could not be precise running like that however, and it occurred to her then that her life was but a matter of moments away from ending. For how long could they truly hope to run from a pack of hunters that they couldn't see? How long before they slipped upon some spongy mushroom or stumbled into a rock and then became helpless prey to their hunters?

"Keep running!" Tar'kul urged to her mentally, though her cold, frail body was so weary and exhausted, and the futility of it was crushing.

"We're going to die," she responded, more of an outcry in her thought-speech than a statement, even as she kept pushing herself forward. *"I'm sorry I took you with me."*

"No!" he wailed, both at her and to himself, she realized. She could feel the flood of emotions from the monstrous man, the deep despair, the crushing sense of failure. The guilt, not for her death exactly, no, but for failing to make it up to her while she still lived. *"I'll not let you,"* he insisted, and she felt rocks beneath her feet amongst the soggy mushrooms.

She stumbled upon them, and he struggled to right her, to help get her back up and moving at the same rate, yet her weary body wanted to give up.

She couldn't cry. It wasn't that she didn't want to, for her eyes stung and her mind was filled with anguish. She just simply didn't have enough water in her body to spare on tears.

"I can't," she whimpered, even as she pushed herself ahead, reaching deep down into her reserves for that little bit of strength and quickly exhausting it.

Tar'kul paused for just a moment and pulled her to him, scooping her up into his four arms and then beginning to run once more. The world was a bright unknowingness to her still, the light from the Dead-Lamps piercing her eyelids enough to make her see its white, unnatural glow even then. The only way to lessen it to bury her face in Tar'kul's shoulder as he ran with her.

She could hear him breathing, his strange, rasping breath strained as he struggled to keep up their pace. *"Just need to keep going,"* he chittered to her insistently, holding her against his hard, obsidian chest.

Thia sobbed, a rush of emotions filling her frail body. She tried not to tremble, but it was so hard. The fear, and the anxiety, and the impending doom all felt so close, so crushing, and she clung to him as if that contact could somehow protect her from her own demise.

The whole struggle was so fruitless, she could feel Tar'kul slowing down as he wore himself out. He was just as weary as she when they started running, and she knew he couldn't possibly carry them both for too long like that.

The end came not with a whimper, but with a bang. He stumbled into a stalagmite and fell forward. As he did, he twisted himself about, trying to shield her from the fall, but it succeeded only in smacking himself against another stalagmite, and together the two of them tumbled into a copse of those stone pillars.

All was at an end for her then, Thia felt, but without her realizing it, they had reached the cavern wall. As the Dead-Lamps closed in, their blinding light making the stone wall gleam in its dark hues, a rush of limbs came out from the tunnels built into the walls.

Thia couldn't see them, but her burgeoning psychic senses gave her some impression of where they were and what was going on.

The creatures reaching out for them were not humanoid at all, and possessed ten limbs each, like great human-sized insects. They scuttled after the source of the lights and the Dead-Lamps clacked out their alarm, as if ordering some kind of retreat to one another.

The new creatures on the scene pursued them, drawn to their

light as they surged out of their tunnels and a great battle was fought.

Though for all the Dead-Lamps' fearsome prowess as hunters, she knew how it would end. With her eyes shut to the world she could sense the relative numbers through mental powers she scarcely understood, and knew these new creatures far outnumbered them, and more were coming all from their tunnels quick as a disturbed beehive.

The gore and gnashing that occurred left them untouched, as they were hidden from the light by the same stones that had stumbled and tripped them.

Tar'kul held her close, his heat easing the chill of the flooded underworld as he stroked her hair. *"Hush,"* he urged her. *"Be quiet. Not a move, not a sound,"* he pleaded with her mentally as they cowered and waited out the carnage.

He was once a man. She didn't know where the unbidden thought came from, but perhaps it was a condolence for the comfort she took in his protective body. An acceptance for how she accepted his soft, consoling strokes of her hair and flesh.

An awareness of how much she craved human contact, kindness, and how he was the closest thing she'd come to down in the pits of hell.

The great ruckus of combating creatures continued on, the horror invisible to Thia as she clenched her eyes shut still.

Only after the glowing whiteness slowly tapered off did she dare to open her gaze once more.

The Dead-Lamps had retreated, and she could see once more into the murky gloom of the underworld. She was shivering cold but the sight of those creatures made her quiver deeper.

They had so many limbs, like long, spindly tentacles with how fast they moved, and though they had features of both a squid and insectoids like an ant, they resembled neither at all. They rushed about as if possessing a singular purpose, a hive mind.

Tar'kul roused her and spoke into her mind, *"We are stuck between them. They are both fearsome... but the Whip-Legs are safer."* He gestured towards their tunnels in the rock wall, *"We can sneak into their hive. Use it to get around the bog. They can't see without light, so if we stick to darkness..."* he didn't sound entirely sure of the plan, but after so long of crawling through muck and mire with impending doom closing in on them, it sounded like their best shot.

She nodded, but only because she was too exhausted to argue. Or, for that matter, to do anything more than just... tremble, and what felt like a long minute passed before she pushed herself away from his comforting body.

"Thank you."

He looked to her, his glassy black eyes studying her a moment before he nodded in return and climbed up onto his feet with the aid of his four arms. *"We need to go now, before they are done clearing area. Safest to get inside when they are busy,"* he urged, still holding her head as he tugged her towards the nearest tunnel.

Her legs felt like cooked noodles but she still forced herself to stand with his help. She'd never known exhaustion like this. Thinking to her past... She realized she could barely remember it any more. What her life was like, back when everything was simpler and her worries were so trivial.

She pushed out her fear at the forgotten memories and moved on ahead, back into the dark.

Tar'kul was cautious, and peered around the corner before he edged inside and took her with him.

Once inside the tunnels, she could see that they were smooth, as if worn away by countless aeons of use. The circumference was too perfectly ovular to ascribe its origins to natural erosion from water. Except along the tunnels there were gouges in the wall. Little pits to her left and right at the same distance. It looked far too planned indeed.

Despite the tunnels branching off into countless directions, Tar'kul guided her along knowingly, as if he had some compass by which he navigated them. Up one sloping tunnel, down another. It was endless.

"Must be quiet," he urged her. *"Whip-Legs do not see in dark, but have good hearing,"* he cautioned her as the sound of the returning horde echoed through the tunnels. She noticed the strange sound of their scuttling legs stopped once they entered into the tunnels properly and was replaced with a less natural sound, like fast-moving whips.

Perhaps it was her familiarity with this underworld in coming to this den, but she understood it. The little gouges in the walls, the cute nickname for the creatures – she shuddered. Nothing in this world was as it should be.

The sounds seem to be coming on faster, and Tar'kul grabbed her hand tight, tugging her against the wall and down into a crouch. *"Duck!"* he warned, shielding her body with his own. It prevented her from seeing what happened entirely, but she saw enough.

Their name was so very appropriate, the creatures hooked their long spindly limbs into those pits and used it to propel themselves forward along the tunnels with whip-like motions of their arms. Like that they moved so much faster than they had out in the bogs themselves, and appeared so single-minded.

Despite the fear of the moment, they didn't pause or take any notice of the two of them. They merely whipped on by, the strange scent of those creatures violating her nostrils and lingering in the air.

It was like an endless train of them, and train was the right word, for Thia felt like she stood beside the train tracks. Her curiosity was only put off as she witnessed that some of them dragged the corpses of what must be those Dead-Lamps, and her stomach turned.

They were hideous abominations, as far as she could tell

from the glimpse she got of them as they skittered by so quickly. Their shoulders so broad and thick, their heads atop bulbous necks and sitting horizontally. Their mouths to the right side, their eye… their single eye on the left.

A sickly pale colour, they had errant, prickly hairs sticking off of them and were utterly repugnant. Their slithering back ends looked like twin tadpoles that oozed blood-like fluid onto the tunnel floors.

She closed her eyes. She couldn't take any more of the horrors that this place contained, and she held her breath so that she couldn't smell them any longer either.

But it didn't help.

She had the knowledge of what they were, what they looked and smelled like, and it burned into her brain, just like everything else.

Even if she did get back to the surface, how could she live surrounded by people that would think her insane?

It took some time, but finally the long train of Whip-Legs came to an end, and the sound of their movements disappeared up the tunnels, leaving only the cool, stirred air in their wake.

Tar'kul had sheltered her from them in case they took notice, but after it was safe he loosened his grasp upon her and checked around. Those long, thick tendrils of dark hair he had tickled against her pale skin before he rose up and helped her to her feet.

Knowing he was once a man, it was easier to see those aspects of him. The handsome jawline, full lips, broad shoulders. Even his monstrous appearance had almost seemed to fade a little to her eyes, now so used to much more horrific aberrations.

"Do not know how long before we find a place to rest," he cautioned her, *"but must not stop until we find safety."* His open trench coat showed his lean, muscular chest still heaving with his heavy breath. He'd taken a heavier burden on the journey

thus far than her, and she'd not seen him eat in the entire time. Saving the food for her it seemed.

She didn't know how he had developed such stamina and endurance, but she was thankful for it.

"Are they gone far?" she silently asked, not waiting for an answer before continuing, *"Have you been in here before?"*

He shook his head to the first part, *"They are all about. As long as we are quiet, we should be fine. And I have been here before just once. Studied… learned their ways then. But never came back,"* he said, taking her hand and leading her down the tunnels. *"Not sure of way, but we will head in general direction,"* he explained to her, shattering the impression he knew precisely where he was going.

Yet still she trusted his sense of this world. It was his world more than hers, and without her faith in his abilities, she'd have crumbled and perished. She was certain of it.

In his absence, she almost had.

One thing fleeing the underworld brought her was walking. Endless walking.

The tunnels were much safer than the wetlands that they had faced before, or so it seemed, but they entailed no less walking. In fact, navigating the honeycomb-like network of passages demanded much greater effort. All the ups, downs and arounds as they went through the great hive built into the cavern walls only took an even greater toll upon the weary young woman.

As exhaustion threatened her with unconsciousness she nearly stumbled over something, only catching herself at the last instant.

From the ceiling dangled two thin strips, but at a closer look she traced them up to the ceiling and found them to be the spindly limbs of those bizarre Whip-Legs. There, one rested upon the ceiling, motionless and still, two of its slender limbs acting like some kind of detection system for the creature while the rest worked against the sides of the tunnel to keep it suspended there.

"*Watch out!*" she warned Tar'kul, and the tall man pulled away from the limbs at the last moment.

The agonizing quiet seemed like a constant threat to their security, the danger of accidentally making a sound that would give them away hounding them at every turn.

Walking beneath one of the creatures to progress further only made matters worse. She could hear its quiet, wheezing breath. See how its gelatinous underbelly was protected by a stiff outer shell, which it used to protect itself by curving its elongated torso in under it.

"*There will be more of them,*" Tar'kul cautioned as they passed the creature undetected.

She tried to stay more alert, force her eyes to be keener, but she couldn't help but find her mind wandering. How far had they moved? When she went up to the surface, would she even be anywhere near her own home?

Perhaps more disturbing still was the realization that her guide, whom she relied upon so much, hadn't seen it, despite being in the lead.

The thought filled her with dread that she could only force away.

They came to a point in the tunnels where some moisture dripped, which was peculiar as the rest of the tunnels had been quite dry. Tar'kul turned them down there and spoke to her, "*Whip-Legs don't like water. We can rest in here perhaps.*" He was weary, so weary. She could detect that even from his mental voice.

And she knew that, no matter where they went, they'd never be safe. Never be completely shielded from their enemies.

"*What about the Dead-Lamps?*"

"*It's deep inside the tunnels, they should not be a fear here,*" he said, though she suspected it was just a guess and he had no genuine idea. The fact of the matter was they needed to rest, and without that, the two of them would keep making stupid decisions and fumbles. If this was one of them, it was just inevitable.

The tunnel was becoming less smooth, Thia noted, growing rockier and more natural. It was still obviously hewn by some creature, but seemed to see less use.

The further they went the craggier it became, until it was clear they were entering into a natural crevice. There a big crack in the earth itself appeared that split the tunnels, creating a gap in the ground that was about two feet in width. From out of it came the sound of echoing droplets, and the thick feel of humidity in the air.

It was cold and unpleasant, but therein lay a nook big enough for them to nestle into and hide, and seemed about as good a place as they could hope for to rest.

She motioned to it with her head and her mind, giving him a soft smile. Or what she could muster to pass for one, in such a terrible scenario as they were.

"As good of place as any."

Tar'kul looked to the spot and gave a weary nod, helping her down into it. She could sense him about to say something, likely offer to hold up guard, but even he realized he was too weary to possibly do it. They would sleep, and if they were caught and killed, that was all there was to it. Neither of them was in any shape to keep watch. Saying otherwise would only be kidding themselves.

"We will rest. Looks safe. Doesn't seem Whip-Legs come here… and we are too deep into their tunnels for Dead-Lamps." He nestled down into the nook, and there was fortunately room enough for them both there with some to spare, even if the chill of the flood season was in the air.

She was soaked through to her bones, surrounded by horror, and yet she felt strangely at ease.

A chill ran through her when she realized she was growing

more accustomed to this place and the pain and horrors it afforded her. A brief reprieve in a dangerous cave seemed like a relaxing stay in her warm, comfortable bed.

Still, it only took her a moment before she was completely enveloped by a deep sleep.

$$\text{❧ 30 ❧}$$

To gaze upon the unholy city was one thing, to walk among its angular roads and be steeped in its claustrophobic streets was another thing altogether. It was as if those smooth, dark walls were watching her and the rest of the soldiers as they marched through.

The stonework—if indeed it was stonework, because it looked more like black metal—resembled that of the city she met Tar'kul in, yet it was only superficial. As if this smaller place was but an imitation, a forgery by amateurs who despite their craftsmanship could not—or did not care to—emulate the ominous nature of the original.

Great obsidian towers extended from the ground like stalagmites only to meet with the immense cavernous ceiling above. The more she stared at it, the more it seemed less like the twisted construction of some alien race and some measure of another dimensions reality bleeding over into her own. A perverted nature of another universe.

The soldiers marched on, but they were terrified. She could sense it, as could the Lieutenant.

"We should turn back," uttered one of the soldiers around the perimeter, his voice shaken with fear.

"This is an unholy place," agreed another in the same fearful tone.

The courageous Lieutenant rebuked them. "There's no way but forward, men. You all saw what we faced back in the tunnels down. Those things would pick us off one by one. We at least have some hope if we push forward. Don't be shaken, you're good men, all of you. We'll make it back above somehow, by the Grace of all that is good and holy. We have the training, we have the fortitude, and I'll lead you through hell itself to survival, even should this be its foulest of pits."

He said it all with such certainty, but Thia was close enough to see just how much his hand trembled holding the flintlock pistol. The aura of madness had seeped into him no less than anyone else; whatever bravery he had was purely for the sake of those men he was responsible for.

The Lieutenant saw her look, and knew his secret was discovered. He raised a finger to his lips to quietly caution her not to say a thing to the soldiers that might betray his own weakness.

She didn't quite nod in return, but it was an acceptance of his terms. They needed strength, and the Lieutenant was stepping up to the job despite his own terror. She'd feel worse about him if he weren't afraid, down in these pits.

She didn't understand the... dream realm. The way she walked another plane of existence, conversed with Tar'kul fluently, joined these men in their horrific adventure. Yet she was growing accustomed to it. Their terror, it was an escape from her own.

No amount of knowing that the city wasn't real could eliminate the feeling that it didn't belong, though. That it was twisted and unnatural and had no place in her mind, let alone her reality. There was no describing it fully, nor even that aura of wrongness it emitted; she couldn't even attribute it to the stuff of her surely diseased mind.

It was simply otherworldly.

Pushing ahead, the soldiers came to a grand boulevard, wrapped around an immense obelisk. The centerpiece not set in the ground itself, but hovering. Motionless. Its stillness was jarring, as if it were out of phase with reality. It drew attention to how the rest of existence seemed to hum with some sort of life.

Was it the splinter which stuck into existence? Which made her universe red and infected with its foul nature?

Thia had to tear her gaze away from it, because she felt her mind slipping fast, as if staring into its nothingness were causing her to precarious sanity to siphon away with each passing moment.

Looking to the Lieutenant, she saw him with his eyes bulged, gaping at it with rapt attention. Though his body convulsed and he seemed to be struggling to look away. "M-men," he muttered, his handsome face contorting, "Look away. Look away!"

The terror she heard in his voice was something that would stay with her into the waking world, she knew. Hopelessness flushed through her body, and she knew the depths of terror... Of darkness.

Of eternal damnation.

Forcing his gaze away from it he went up to the soldiers, grabbing their shoulders and forcing them to look away. "Let's go! Stop!" he cried, and some of the soldiers were convulsing violently. One dropped to the ground, suffering a violent seizure, another expelled the contents of his stomach.

The Lieutenant turned to her, panic in his eyes, "Sergeant! Help get these men away!" He pointed to a large building along the boulevard, "Over there! Pull them away from it!"

She ran, just as she would have in the real world, and touched the very real shoulder of the man next to her. He was half buckled over as if he'd seen something that shattered his soul, and she hauled him away. She was surprised by the amount of strength it took just to move him as he resisted her saving tugs.

Still, she managed to turn him about and push him forward, but he was in a daze.

He'd seen something there was no recovering from. At least not quickly.

Some of the men were able to be rallied, and together they slowly dragged those others with them. The Lieutenant holstered his pistol and took hold of a man himself, hooking his arms in under one man's shoulders and pulling him. Yet all the while it was like that obelisk was pulling their gazes back towards it, its existence seeming to hum to them incessantly the longer they refused.

Even *she* felt it, and she knew better than to stare into the pits of eternity, or hell, or horrors beyond her ability to comprehend.

The building they went into provided some shelter, as thankfully, once it was out of sight, that pull to stare at it was far weaker. Though the open door and windows did not make it easy to escape it. It was like the place was designed to facilitate gazing upon that dimensional splinter.

None of them were fast to recover, though some were worse than others. Those vomiting, convulsing fools scratching their fingers upon the floor as they tried to claw their way to a window or the door to gaze back upon it. It was a struggle just to keep them from destroying themselves like that.

It was then they realized they were not alone.

The Lieutenant saw it first.

His eyes widened in what she thought at first was abject terror, but quickly realized was utter sadness and despair instead. His eyes welled with tears before she dared to look back.

Far from escaping the terror of the pale men and their unstoppable villainy, they had marched into the heart of them.

At the rear of the great hall were ringed half a dozen of them, gloriously nude but staring away, their backs turned.

They were worshipping something. Some hulking mass of a creature. A female, she realized, as her gaze travelled over its bulbous hind end towards the top, which still mimicked a human woman's torso.

She convulsed and writhed as if in agony as one of the worshippers rutted her inhuman lower-end, that squishy, pale sac. Her head flailing about, her long hair whipping madly. It was the most grotesque of orgies Thia could have ever conceived. The muscular creature that fucked her letting loose his moans of ecstasy as he came up inside her grotesque hind end.

The mad goddess let loose a banshee's wail and twisted about. Though she looked like a woman from the waist up, she was large, much bigger than any of the men, and her mouth opened to inhuman proportions, lined with jagged fangs. She tore into the throat of the man she was mating with, ripped it out and let his head tear from his neck to roll upon the ground before he'd even pulled from her.

Yet despite the blood and gore that fell from her ravenous maw, the other worshippers seemed anxious for her anyhow. They stroked themselves and knelt before her, seeming to hope to be next despite the heinous arachnid betrayal in their disgusting orgy.

Thia stared. Unlike the obelisk to oblivion, the thing which she could feel chipping at her sanity, this was something... else. She couldn't quantify it, with its terrifying monstrosity, yet they were flesh and blood and even though it was horrific, it felt ...somehow more familiar, more of this world.

Still, she knew better than to get comfortable.

The dark altar might steal her mind, but those pale ones would just as easily steal her life.

"We need to get out of here," Thia muttered beneath her breath.

The Lieutenant was in tears, but he nodded to her, grabbing the men and hauling them to their feet. He didn't speak but he signalled them to leave, even as they were caught between the maddening obelisk and the sinister orgy, there was no choice but to go back out.

Yet as the men rallied, some of them began to moan and call out in unintelligible voices towards the freakish pale woman as she feasted upon the carcass of her lover. They clawed towards her even as they shook and wailed.

The Lieutenant tried to stop them, but it quickly began to feel hopeless, and the pale men were starting to notice them, even if they did not seem keen to step away from their demented goddess.

There was so much noise now that quiet no longer seemed necessary or smart, the Lieutenant ordered, "We retreat, let's go!" and he began to shove one man towards the exit, his eyes still glassy as he was forced to order the men to leave the others behind. "Avert your eyes and run!" he commanded.

The worshippers praised their lord, a chant rising up as she finished devouring the flesh and bones of the last man with loud crunching and wet gnawing. "K'ray'ah!" they shouted repeatedly, putting their hands up in the air as she selected another who eagerly strode up to mate with the monster.

The Lieutenant grabbed Thia's shoulder and dragged her to the door. "We have to go," he hissed, as some of their comrades writhed across the floor in their own excrement to join the orgy.

The fetid smell filled her nostrils, and she wondered if she'd ever wake up from this nightmare.

She looked to the Lieutenant and felt such a deep pity, a horror that crept into every fiber of her being.

He was doomed. And so was she.

It was always harder to tell it was a dream when it was hers, and not some bizarre psychic interference from the underworld. It became harder so when her thoughts of sunny vistas and grassy fields were so pleasant and calming.

Thia basked in it, relaxing and luxuriating in the warmth. She only clued into its nature as a dream after what seemed like hours. She instantly regretted the realization. She had been happier before realizing. Afterwards it was as if a cloud had cast a pall upon her relaxing day.

Lifting herself up from the grass, she looked about. For it was lonely, if still pleasant. No sign of another. Until she saw far off in the distance a man. Edain.

He sat beneath a tree almost beyond sight, and only her intuition told her it was him. Though in truth she knew it was Tar'kul, sharing her dream.

He didn't come to her this time however. He sat there among the blowing blades of grass, soaking up the memory of sun which had doubtlessly been forgotten by him. All while giving her space.

She clung to herself, her arms wrapped about her waist as she watched him, and just like pity she'd felt for the Lieutenant, she felt for Tar'kul.

Once they'd all been free, living blissfully unaware of what lurked beneath their very feet. They'd sang songs, and felt the blades of grass between their toes. They had known emotions other than despair and terror. She moved towards Tar'kul, drawn to him. To their shared sorrow of what they'd lost.

And she knew his loss. He'd experienced more in his eternal life than she could imagine, and already she felt her mind begin to bend and warp in the underground lair of demons and monsters.

A place where he had survived.

Edain—Tar'kul—saw her coming from a distance away, and rose at her approach. He was dressed in one of those lovely suits he would always wear. The height of cosmopolitan fashion, but with a little flair of his own. The collars of his shirts exotic, a style from his far away land, the buttons of some curious make that drew the eye. His silk kerchief a bright red against his black velvet vest.

Did Tar'kul take on the visage of her handsome beau of old simply because he was so present in her dreams? Or was it something else? Did he feel some kinship with that figure of her memories? Were the two, so separated by time, place, and circumstance as to be wholly alien, have some common thread beyond their longing for her?

She couldn't say for sure, but he gazed upon her with wide, expressive eyes, hope and sadness written upon them.

"Do you remember the sun?" she asked, gathering her skirt as she sat next to where he stood, gazing up at him against the harsh glare of the warm sun. It was hidden by clouds now, but there was still a bright filter all around her, straining her eyes in the most pleasant of ways.

Lowering himself down into the grass beside her, he curled his legs beneath him, heedless of his fine pants in a way Edain never was. "No," he confessed with a shake of his head, a single tear upon his cheek. "I had forgotten what it was before you came along. What it felt like. That it had even ever existed." His gaze dipped sadly to his lap before he forced it back up, staring at the sky, its shades of blues, whites, greys and the yellow of the sun.

She smiled softly, gazing upwards as well. "I know this must be hard for you." To feel all these new things, to know of her hope and her need to escape.

To know how hard he must have tried before he turned. Before he lost the person he'd fallen into this trap with.

Gently he shook his head, "I don't remember ever being happier than I was when you appeared below." He brushed the back of his hand over his cheek, wiping away the tear that trailed down. "I felt you above for so long. That presence... of a real person. I thought I was crazy for a long time. That my mind had finally slipped entirely... imagining a real person directly above me." He shook his head then buried his face into his knees as he lifted his legs.

She thought back to all her dreams, the thoughts that called for her. Maybe it wasn't entirely the pale ones. Maybe their power had only amplified Tar'kul's longing, his desperate need for someone to save him. Yet instead of feeling angry over his bringing her down here, she now only felt sorrow. Sorrow that his life had gotten to such a spot that he needed someone in his life so bad.

"We can get out, Tar'kul."

He was huddled in an almost fetal position, though she saw that his gaze marvelled over his own physique. The body of Edain as he remembered it so perfectly male, such an incredible form. "I was like this once," he remarked dumbly. "Maybe you don't believe me entirely, but I was... I looked like this. I talked like this. I was even respected," he said sorrowfully. "But if we get out, I'll forever be just a monster."

She didn't know what to say. He was right, of course. There was no going back to the man he was, or could have been.

Her gaze dropped to her lap and she played with a frill of lace along her dress, thoughtfully.

"What is it you want then, Tar'kul?" she asked, after the silence had stretched so wide between them.

He had no words for her. What was the point?

She knew what he wanted.

For as horrible as the place was, it owned him now. He simply lifted his gaze to her a moment, peered at her miserably before returning to look at sky. He wanted to enjoy it for as long as it lasted, at least. Before they would have to return unwillingly to the reality of the underworld.

❧ 32 ❧

This awoke to the sound of dripping water. The first droplets were sparse and light, but in the echo chamber of the crevice, they were exponentially doubled up again and again.

Tar'kul still slept, his tall lanky form balled up beside her. She knew he must've been even more tired than her, and to see him still slumbering wearily affirmed it for her again.

Her stomach gnawed at her though and she saw some of the food bulging his pockets.

Reaching over, she very gently slipped some of the food from his coat. The rubbery mushrooms and beetle flesh were still her only nourishment.

It didn't make her gag, or feel much of anything anymore. It had become routine, something she had to do to get through the day. Food wasn't a pleasure any longer. It was simply something that provided her the energy to keep moving.

As she ate, her thirst grew, and she knew she had to drink. Perched right beside the crevice she peeked around the corner and saw into the inky black there. Next to the edge she noticed a bit of dripping, and she could lean around just enough to catch it in her mouth.

It took a while to drink enough to sate her thirst, and as she pulled back from the edge she saw the most surprising of sights.

Across the gap in the tunnel on the other side was a young girl. A simple young girl, no more than seven or eight at most. Dressed in some dingy clothes, both pale and thin, but a young girl nonetheless.

As Thia spotted her, she scurried back down the rough tunnel and out of sight.

Thia stared at that spot she had stood and blinked, wondering if her eyes were playing tricks on her. She drew her lower lip into her mouth and knew better than to feel anything but dread and foreboding.

Nothing was as it seemed down here.

She looked across at Tar'kul, but dared not wake him. Instead, she tried to enter his dreams, even as she remained awake. The notion of doing so troubled her for a split second, but she reminded herself that he had entered her dreams – and nightmares – many a time. Though her reasons for doing so were pragmatic. She wanted to master her abilities, to grow more powerful and capable, to not be victim to the horrors of the under realm any longer.

Controlling her new psychic abilities proved harder than she anticipated. Though transmitting thoughts had come easily enough, the rest had all been stumbled upon. With some effort she managed to get a vague sense of Tar'kul's feelings as he dreamt, but if she had any ability to consciously enter his dreams, she could find no hint of it.

Instead, all she got was the sense of fear and loneliness he felt as he slumbered. He seemed to dream of walking the under-world alone once again.

She found her hand moving to his jawline. It was still so human, and she wondered if that would someday change as well. Become harder, more monstrous. She wished to soothe him, to bring him some type of peace that she didn't know if he was capable of feeling any longer.

He'd said in her dream that he'd once been a man like Edain, and if those small hints of the man he once was were any indication, he wasn't lying. His jawline and those lips still held some masculine appeal. He was both tall and strong. Even his curiously thick, dark hair wasn't too heinously altered. It was those monstrous aspects to him that marred it, the fangs, those alien tri-corner eyes of his, the second set of arms.

Tar'kul gently stirred from his position and nuzzled into her hand, his smooth dark flesh grazing over her palm while fully asleep. She could sense his emotions easing, her gentle touch bringing some measure of peace and warmth to his dark dream world.

Though something out of the corner of her eye drew her gaze back to the tunnel across the gap, and she saw the brown hair of a human girl there peek out and stare at Thia. The child looked more surprised than Thia before ducking back around the corner.

She couldn't let him sleep any longer.

"Tar'kul," she mentally nudged him, her touch remaining on his jaw, trying to ease him from slumber as gentle as possible. Yet still, she knew her mental state wasn't calm. Not with a girl lingering so near in these dark pits.

How could a child survive down here?

Her dark guide roused from his sleep, his eyelids flicking open to stare those inky-black pools at her. She could still sense his emotions, the surprise, the warm fondness, the hope as he gazed longingly to her.

She'd not awoken him jarringly, so it took a moment for him to clue in that she was distressed and she simply wasn't awakening him tenderly as if out of a dream. *"What is wrong?"* he asked, unfurling his limbs and slowly pushing himself up.

"There's a girl. A young girl. Around the corner over there," she replied silently, motioning with her icy blue eyes towards the location she'd seen her last.

Tar'kul didn't know how to interpret her words at first, and he blinked in confusion before he was up on his feet and gazing across the gap towards the other end of the tunnel. *"Not possible,"* he said simply, such an idea simply beyond his reckoning. *"No others down here. Definitely no little girls,"* he said with a shake of his head. *"Must be trick."*

"But not one you're familiar with?" A small part of her wanted that little girl to be real, and innocent, to be unscathed. If a child was here, there was also a hope that there might be an entrance nearby that she had scuttled down, but Thia knew better than to hope.

Tar'kul hesitated, looking fidgety and uncertain. He didn't like new mysteries, she realized. After so long down here relying upon caution and carefulness, a novelty was a big risk.

Those inky-black eyes of his turned towards her she felt, and he looked about to argue against checking it out. Though by now he was able to anticipate what she might argue. The little girl might be her best chance of getting out, after all.

"Must be careful," he cautioned her, leaping across the two-foot gap then reaching back to take her hands and pull her across with him securely.

She clutched his hand tightly, the damp dress changing the balance of her body and throwing her off slightly. Still, it was nothing she couldn't handle, and she smiled at him gratefully. Perhaps the sleep, even filled with terrors as it was, had done something to rejuvenate her.

Her monstrous guide looked surprised by the small gesture and gave a pleased grin in response. Those long fangs marring his otherwise handsome lower face. "I will lead," he said, pushing in front of her and rounding the corner.

Together they moved forward, though they saw just a

glimpse of the child dashing out of sight up ahead. Tar'kul looked nervous about that, but together they went on. The child was fast and they were hesitant, so they never did quite catch up to her. Always a little out of reach.

The tunnels grew increasingly strange as they went. Rockier, craggier... though upon reflection Thia realized it should've seemed more natural than it did.

The tunnel began to open up, getting wider, more erratic and uneven. It seemed that they had entered into some more naturally shaped cavern, though all along the walls and floods there were still grooves from some instruments, something akin to picks.

"She won't stop running," Thia silently said. *"Is she leading us into a trap?"*

"Probably. Yes," Tar'kul agreed quickly, his suddenly justified paranoia taking over as he grabbed Thia's hand and turned to leave. *"We must go,"* he insisted.

Though when they turned around to flee they discovered it was too late.

In the midst of the larger cavern's upper reaches were tunnels that came out of the rock, and perched up there were men. Human men. Dressed in scraggly clothes or none at all, but men nonetheless. They gripped crude weapons and pointed them down at the two of them. Spear-like weapons crafted from stone, and simple rocks.

They were pale and sickly looking for the most part, but she saw in that flicker of a moment that they were shocked by the sight of her. As surprised to see her in the underworld as she was to see them.

A loud voice called out in fast, bizarrely accented English, "Halt! Hol' yer places!" And as Thia traced the voice back to one man, the biggest of the bunch, broad and bare chested, thick and muscular—at least compared to the others—with only a pair of trousers on. He leapt down from a tunnel above, some metal-crafted weapon in hand as he stared at her, looking as if he didn't believe his own eyes.

Her heart pounded in her chest and she felt almost dizzy. Less concerned for herself, she clung to Tar'kul, suddenly protective of him at the sight of her own.

She was right to fear for Tar'kul, as the dark, half-man, half-monster was crouched and fidgety. He was terrified of the new humans that had approached, and that feeling only grew as they broke out some strange sort of lamps. They did not give off much light, and the source of it seemed not to be fire but a phosphorescent stone that they kept shrouded until need be. Yet still it was enough to irritate Thia and Tar'kul's eyes when so many of them lit up at once.

Were they really her own?

"I am Thia Suthers!" she spoke loudly, trying to hide the quiver in her voice. "We... we're not here to hurt you."

The men all broke out into surprised chatter and hushed gasps at her speaking to them. Perhaps her ability to speak, more than her presence, was quite surprising to them.

Their 'leader', if that's what he was, approached, grey eyes wide as he stared at her in astonishment. "Ya speak th'tongue?" he asked in that same quickly spoken garble of English. His head was shaved bald, with a few nicks and scratches upon it that she could see in the glow of the lanterns.

"Yes," she said, wincing at the soft light that burned her eyes. "Are you from above? Is there a way out? Please, we just... we're looking for an exit."

A furrowed brow and a gaze of curiosity crossed the man's face, and many confused mutterings from the other men penned the two of them in. She couldn't make out any of the words, they were too far away, the words too quickly spoken and in such a bizarre tongue.

The leader was almost as tall as Tar'kul, but much more broad. He was an intimidating presence as he strode close towards the two of them. "Thia," he said, repeating her name curiously. He thumped his chest with a large, powerful fist, "Jremy," he said gruffly in introduction.

Though his eagerness to introduce himself to her did not ease Tar'kul's anxieties. *"We need to go!"*

"If we run, they'll pursue," she replied silently, even as she gave a smile to the leader.

"Jremy," Thia repeated. "Do you have a way out?"

A smile formed upon his lips in response to hers, a big toothy grin as he curled his fingers in the air. "Come'long," he beckoned in his strange English. Though he cast a sour glance towards Tar'kul, "Mus' leave th' devil though."

She could feel that dark hand squeeze hers tighter as Tar'kul cowered and shook. *"No good, must go!"*

She squeezed him back and shook her head. "He is a friend. He has helped me live in this place for many..." she trailed off. She didn't know how long it had been. Weeks? She dreaded it having been longer.

"He is my protector and will not harm anyone," she finished.

The men around them gasped or gave unintelligibly angry shouts, though the leader raised a palm and brought silence to them again as he looked at her, brow furrowed not with anger, but concern it seemed. "We are protectors," he said, and she could tell he was struggling to speak carefully for her sake, to slow down and draw out the words as she did. "We can no le' a devil through. W'be a sacrilege."

She didn't dare close her eyes, even though they burned, and something within her started to break.

She knew she wouldn't leave Tar'kul. She wouldn't be so cruel as to abandon him to his fate, his loneliness, and she squeezed his monstrous hand. "Then we will not enter," she replied, and her heart burned. She was turning her back on people. On real, honest-to-god people.

Beside her she could feel Tar'kul's astonishment, her psychic powers giving him greater empathy with the fallen man. Surprise gave way quickly to gratefulness. Then to sorrow. For her.

Before anything more could transpire between them, the great uproar of the men around them was calmed again and their leader looked to her so confused. His grey eyes travelled down over her body, that damp, shredded dress and the waifish figure beneath. "You no kin survive dow' 'ere wit'out us, girly," and he truly did sound concerned for her as he said that. "Ya nee' yer own kin'."

"I don't want to survive down here. I want to find my way up there." Her voice quivered a bit, her breath catching and for a moment, a brief, flicker of a second, she wanted to stay. To give up, to have someplace that resembled what she'd lost.

But it was an imitation, a compromise.

More muttering went on, and the leader stepped in closer, leaning down to talk with her more privately.

Thia could feel Tar'kul tense and grow ready to lash out to protect her. He bristled at the approach of that big, burly man. Feared for her.

"Ya rally wan' turn away 'cause a one a tha devils?" he said, confusion on his face as he studied her. "Do he control ya mind? Trick ya?"

"*There are more like you?*" she asked Tar'kul, urgently.

She could feel no deception in him, just confusion. "*Like me?*" he asked, baffled. "*No others. All alone.*"

The men watching them grew impatient with her delay, and the large man reached a big hand out to touch her shoulder reassuringly. "We kin protec' ya. Save ya from 'is tricks," he urged.

"He has no control over me, and is the only one of his kind. We have seen no others like him." She was trying desperately to remain calm, though she was almost overjoyed at the ability to talk aloud.

She knew it wouldn't last, and enjoyed it while she could.

The man spared Tar'kul only a glance, as if he were a mere thing rather than the twisted man he was. "Th'devil take many forms, but he be all over th'place, girly," he said as if reciting scripture. Giving her shoulder a gentle squeeze, he nearly begged her, "Come wi' me, girly. We'll take care o' ya."

"Not without Tar'kul," she said, brushing off his touch and looking at him sternly. "He's no devil. He was..." she paused, her throat feeling parched despite the damp air. "He is a man, twisted by this place like all of you. Like all of us."

That caused a true uproar among the men, and one of them tossed a rock at Tar'kul that he was barely able to avoid in time. Thia gasped and tried to protect him before she even realized what she was doing, her fear for him greater than it ever had been. Perhaps because she was dealing with the one thing that was familiar to her here, her one constant for so very long.

The mob was moments away from unleashing an even greater fury upon them before their leader wove his arms in the air and shouted, "Nuff a dat!" His bellow filled the caverns, loud and booming.

Once they were quieted enough, he turned back to Thia, a hard look on his face. "I'll offer ya passage on me honour. Ya devil... ya fren," he amended, "kin come. But shoo he harm anyone, or do 'is tricks upon any o' our flock... not'in' more ta do." He said with some finality, before extending his big hand towards her again, "Won'chu come now, girly? I dunna wan' ya ta 'ave ta go wit'out our protection."

She softened, slightly, as she stood up from the huddled, scared monster she now called a friend.

"He shall not be harmed?" Thia paused a moment, her blue gaze turned towards the crowd, "He will not hurt anyone." And she believed it. Despite their past.

Tar'kul clung to her, fearful for them both she felt, his voice urging her not to trust them. But the large Jremy nodded his head to her. "Fer now it'll do," he said. "Sort out th'rest later."

Her hand stroked along the strange, coarse hair on Tar'kul head and nodded her agreement. "I think the three of us should go talk somewhere private."

"Talk t'much," he said as he gestured to the other men. "Take you back now," he said firmly as the men all filtered back around through the tunnels hesitantly. He walked back to the rope that dangled from the tunnel he came out of, climbing up it before reaching back down, offering his hand to Thia. "Help ya up."

The fear she felt wasn't solely Tar'kul's, but she accepted his offer working to pull her waifish form up. Her gaze travelled around as she did, trying to study the layout now that the glaring lights had disappeared.

The cavern was big, and stretched up much higher than she had first realized, with many tunnel exits opening up onto it. There was little more to note about it other than the fact that it seemed to have been carved by someone rather than formed naturally.

Though all the while Tar'kul muttered to her, fear tingeing his words, *"We should not go with them! Can't trust them. Will betray us!"*

Jremy pulled her up with ease, into his welcoming arms as he gave her a big, warm smile. He had the look of a lower class workman, but he was not unpleasant to gaze upon. His smile was even handsome as he held her against him for that brief moment before helping her back to the tunnel.

He surprised by bending down and offering Tar'kul his hand next.

Gratitude filled her as she stepped aside, her head a bit fuzzy from the hug. Human contact. It was like a drug she had been deprived of for so very long.

"What is this place?" Thia asked, some urgency in her tone as she sought to find out all she could before venturing too deep into their lair.

Tar'kul refused the offered hand, and when he saw Thia had no intention of turning back, he climbed up on his own. Those six limbs of his were quite adept at clambering up surfaces so that he had little trouble getting to her, then reaching out to take her hand again.

Jremy shrugged it off and turned down the tunnel. "Jes' the p'rimiter," he said as he guided them both down the tunnels.

He didn't seem in a very talkative mood now that they were agreed on a destination at least. Taking her through the twists and turns, avoiding others, knowing the path intimately until he guided her to it…

There, like a single, great shaft in the rock, was a village. There were holes dug into the rock wall, and out of them people came. Many more pale, scraggly human beings, looking malnourished but very much uncorrupted. They came out to stare and talk excitedly about the newcomers.

More striking still was the curious glow that came from the top of the shaft. It was bright and stung Thia and Tar'kul's eyes, very nearly like the sun, but not nearly strong enough. Was it some crack that eventually led to the surface, and through some twists and turns reflected the light of the day above in a weak form?

It had to be, she thought with awe, as she realized plants—real plants!—grew on the gravelly walls up above. Not fungus, not mushrooms, but plants. Real green plants. And there was moisture in the air, but with so many people and their fires, it was not cold in that little village as it had been out in the dark under realm itself.

"Welcome ta Haven," Jremy said with a broad, proud smile as he turned to Thia.

Thia squeezed Tar'kul's hand and quickly swiped at her eyes as she realized she was crying. How lonely, how desperate, how frightened she had been. And then to be shown this…

It took her breath away, and even though she tried to choke out words, they were but whimpers.

Tar'kul had a harder time than her with the faint reflected glow of day in the cavern, and he crouched, sheltering his head from it with his arms. *"No! Awful place! Bad! Must go! Never return!"*

Jremy extended his hand to Thia, "Come. Take ya ta my place. Stay in m'spare home there," he offered with a bright, cheerful look to her.

She tried to smile, but Tar'kul...

He was frightening her.

At first she'd written it off as paranoia, something they were both familiar with. But now, she wasn't so certain.

"I need a moment," she said to Jremy, acting like she was simply too choked up to continue on before she started communicating telepathically with Tar'kul. *"Calm down. Tell me what happened."*

Tar'kul kept a hold of her hand with one of his, but all three other arms were wrapped about his head as he crouched on the ground beside her. The light hurt him, and moreover he was terrified of the place. Unintelligibly so. She couldn't tell if it was merely because of the light and the many glaring, hateful pairs of eyes upon him, or for some deeper reason.

Jremy looked impatient, peering around at all the gaping viewers before he looked back to her. "C'mon. Sh'get yer fren' inside an' out o' sight," he said, and there was wisdom in that. "Coo' show ya 'roun', or get ya some food'n'stuff if yer starved."

She bent down, her knees aching against the hard floor as she levelled herself to Tar'kul's face. She was practically ignoring the man as she instead stroked Tar'kul's boyish jaw, trying to coax him back to reason.

Out of the fright and sadness, she managed to make out some of Tar'kul's chittering worries. *"Not a place for me,"* he said so morosely. *"Not a place for you,"* he added, giving a sort of whimpering out loud as the tall, lanky monster knelt beside her. *"Let's go…"* he pleaded.

Jremy bent down behind Thia and said to her softly, "Really need ta get ya inside," he said urgently, and the noise of those watching grew louder. More angry at the intrusion of a 'devil' into their midst. "Ya kin take all th'time ya need in there," he said, putting a hand on Thia's shoulder and tugging gently.

She did something that surprised even herself.

Standing, she turned towards Jremy, at his rugged handsomeness, at the kindness he'd shown her. She felt some call to stay with him, to be with those like her, but instead she forced a resigned smile to her face.

"It's not the time for us. I'm sorry."

Jremy looked aghast at her, his hand still on her shoulder as he peered into her blue eyes. "Ya can't be serious," he remarked as the sound of so many quickly chatting voices around them filled the air of the tunnel. "Come up ta my place an' sort ya stuff out. Think it through," he urged with a squeeze of her slender shoulder, worry upon his face.

"Tar'kul is afraid." It was simple. It was direct.

She wouldn't go with Jremy because Tar'kul was terrified. Whether that meant there was really trouble or not, she'd rather talk to him about it later. When he had calmed down.

In his dreams.

The burly man looked between her and Tar'kul, "He be less 'fraid up in th' room I gots fer ya. C'mon. I'll bring ya both lotsa greens," he promised, trying to edge her up the ramps, made of some strange material that resembled wood but could not possibly be wood.

"We'll leave," she said sternly, "and return once we've thought this through. On our own terms. Thank you." Thia was being earnest in her thanks, but harder in her refusal, and she backed up, tugging Tar'kul with her. "There was a girl. She was the one who found me. Why was a child let loose in this place?" Thia asked as she began to back up, away from Jremy's strong hands and body.

The commotion grew in the tunnel, and Jremy was starting to look anxious. "She got loose," he said, "We was all out lookin' fer her." His eyes darted around and he was quite plainly uncomfortable having this conversation with her then and there, "C'mon up," he tried again in a calming voice. "Ya can't come back if ya go now. Won't ever find ch'other, an' won't be able ta let ya back even if ya do," he explained.

Her stomach turned and her tears had dried only because she hadn't enough water in her to waste. But she felt a heartache she couldn't remember, and for a moment, she blinked her eyes, and he looked like someone she knew. An old friend of the family, someone familiar and kind, and then she blinked again and it was gone. Her mind playing tricks on her.

"I'm sorry," she said again, and his insistence only made her more certain that she couldn't stay.

Jremy's gentle expression hardened, and he reached out for her with irritation. When his strong hands grabbed a hold of her roughly, Tar'kul leapt up. Despite the pain from the glowing light and his complete inability to see, he was a maelstrom of savagery as he launched himself at the larger man.

Lunging into Jremy he knocked the man over, and the two of them were instantly entangled as they fell back into the tunnel, Tar'kul's claws and slashing, the big man's fists pounding.

"Tar'kul!" she screeched, her eyes wide as she ran forward, trying to tug him off. There were too many eyes, too many people, too many everything for him to escape.

For them to escape.

What he was doing was suicidal!

The two big men were a confusing tangle of powerful limbs, and she could only make out snippets of Tar'kul's chittering words for her through his tangle of emotions, his urge to protect her. *"Won't let him hurt you!"* he cried.

Though as he struggled to disentangle the two she was struck in the face with Jremy's elbow and knocked back, striking the back of her head against the wall.

All was dark after that.

❦   33   ❦

A ll around her the soldiers of the lost platoon were huddled and weary. They had escaped the madness of the orgy… but only in the strictest sense.

The Lieutenant sat with a troubled expression upon his face, staring at some of the men. They were growing paler, fast. Too fast for it to be lack of sunlight. Yet they didn't seem to be acting sick.

The room they occupied was round, circular. It overlooked much of the unholy city, with columns that stretched up overhead before twisting and turning and forming an odd roof.

The dashing Lieutenant caught sight of her as if surprised, then gestured for her to approach quietly.

Even though Thia knew, on some level, this wasn't real, it didn't stop the ache in her muscles or the chill in her bones as she joined the man. She squatted before him, her hands resting on her lap while peering at him curiously.

The Lieutenant brushed back his long dark hair and leaned in, murmuring inconspicuously to her. "Sergeant, you still look healthy," he remarked, giving a final once-over of her appearance, and when she looked down she noted her body was neither petite nor feminine. She had a man's physique, and wore a uniform, much as he did. "By my count we're missin' a man with this morning's tally," he pronounced ominously.

She nodded, glancing away. "It's not surprising, I hate to admit. We're being picked off by the horrors in this place."

The Lieutenant's hard gaze studied the men around the circular room. "I don't think it was one of the horrors of this place," he said. "Not entirely," he wet his lips and looked about with such a troubled expression. "A few of them have been on duty down below, keeping watch. We've not checked on them in a while." He turned his gaze on the Sergeant hard, "Back me up. We need to go check it out."

"Yes, sir," Thia replied in a voice not her own. "Do you have suspicions of what happened?"

The two of them got up, and the Lieutenant checked his flint-lock pistol. "I do, Sergeant, but," he hesitated looking around as they made their way back towards the stairs that spiralled down. "If I'm right, it's too horrible to discuss."

They climbed down the bizarre stairwell, moving down, down into the bowels of the building. As they neared the point where the guards were to be stationed on guard, they could hear some whimpering cries and some disgusting noises of moist flesh.

The Lieutenant's eyes widened and he urged her to be quiet as he crept up on the wall. Peering around the corner he then immediately lunged back and nearly threw up. Thia felt compelled to look, and what she saw did not help.

There she found three of the soldiers—all abnormally pale—pinning down one of the others, muffling his cries with their hands and keeping his limbs in check. While another crouched down, biting into his torn open stomach, gnashing on his bloody intestines and organs, feasting on his blood and flesh with a look of absolute bliss upon his face.

She knew these men. Not well, but with a hazy recollection, a passing familiarity.

And she observed with a muted sense of dread.

The pale ones are made from mortals.

Her hand grasped the Lieutenant's jacket, tugging him hard as she muttered urgently under her breath, "We need to run."

The Lieutenant swallowed hard, colour drained from his own face, but in a different manner. "They've turned to cannibalism because we ran out of rations long ago," he said, eyes wide in disbelief. "We can't just abandon the men," he muttered dumbly.

"This isn't cannibalism. They're... no longer human." She pleaded with him to understand, her hands grasping him tighter. "Listen to me, they're one of *them* now. We have to go."

It was hard keeping her voice calm and steady, but she somehow managed, even as her pulse raced furiously.

The Lieutenant grew stern and pushed her off him before drawing his pistol. "Back me up," he insisted before storming around the corner. "Enough of this madness, men!" he shouted. "We'll not behave as animals here," and perhaps some shred of their old selves remained, as they looked to him and paused what they were doing, looks of guilt on some faces. A couple even seeming horrified by what was happening as they ate a man alive.

Yet Thia knew better. Those faces, those features... They didn't have the magnetic pull of the pale ones she'd encountered, but it got stronger with time. She'd experienced that herself.

A ball of fear formed within her as she stared at the men.

Is that what could happen to her? Why did it happen to them and not Tar'kul?

She swallowed as she pulled her musket from her shoulder, her hand shaking. "Lieutenant?"

"Think of your families back home, lads!" he shouted at

them, the madness of the place fraying his mind like the others, even if it wasn't to the same extreme degree. He hauled the men off the dying one, whose tortured screams carried out into the unholy city, so shrill and agonizing.

He put his pistol to the young soldier's head and ended his misery.

Thia awoke inside what looked like a cozy little hovel. She was covered in coarse blankets, and was warmer than she'd been since she entered the hellish underworld. As she lifted her head the pain there stabbed hard and she had to rest again, unable to get up entirely. She looked to her side and saw two things of interest. The glowing stones from which the heat in the room seemed to emanate, and a scrawny young boy that watched over her with wide, curious eyes.

"Y'awake girly?" he asked, even though she must have been double his age.

He wore no shirt, just some scratchy looking trousers, and his body was very lean. It was obvious he wasn't as well cared for as a boy on the surface world should be, but he didn't look as malnourished as some of the others.

'Where's Tar'kul?" She didn't dream of him. There was no brief reprieve from the tortures of this world, and of her mind. She pushed herself up and her world spun, her eyes burning and gritty from sleep and the hazy light.

The young boy got up and ran out of the room, his yells so

fast she couldn't make out what it was he said, except that he seemed to be telling someone that she was awake.

In her time alone she had to contend with her spinning head and her body's uncooperativeness. Bizarrely, she felt a tingling numbness in her legs, and to her alarm she realized they wouldn't respond at all to her attempts to move them.

At last after a long stretch Jremy returned, a little cut up and bruised, but with a hopeful smile on his face as he looked to her. "Yer awake at las'," he said with some relief as he pulled the curtain that functioned as her door aside and stepped in, crouching down by the mat that was her bed.

"Where is he?" Thia swooned as she sat up too fast again, and she reached out for the wall to try to balance herself. Her body ached, and dread was heavy in her heart.

"Easy nah," he urged her, holding out his hands to try and steady her. "Ya took a real hard knock to the noggin', be careful," he still had that look of concern on his face, quite obviously worried for her well-being.

Pushing herself up, she realized she was nude beneath the thick blankets as they fell away, her ratty, torn dress gone from her.

Her eyes bulged, in part because of the violation, but in part by how thin she'd gotten. She was all lean muscle down her legs, and her stomach concaved in a way she'd not noticed before. She'd gotten out of the habit of looking at herself, but now the changes were there before her, and the difference was stark.

Quickly she pulled the blankets back up, shame of her body and shame of her nudity both enraging her.

"I'll calm down when I know where he is and why I'm naked!"

The large, bare-chested man did his best to try and appear calm as he attempted to get her to relax. "Ya dress was all bloody an' hard from tha blow ya took. We had ta tend to yer wound an' clean ya up," he explained in a slow voice, trying to speak more at her rate than his own. "Ya took a real nasty hit, ya loss a lotta blood, an' ya weak an' frail. I got 'em gettin' some fresh food ready fer ya right now. You'll need it."

Tears lingered in her eyes but refused to spill as she stared at him. "Where's Tar'kul?"

She didn't have the energy for this. Most of his words, even when he spoke slowly, just fluttered through her brain unabsorbed. She was panicked and alone in a strange place, in a strange bed. She was so vulnerable in the closest thing she had to a real room since she stumbled down into hell.

His expression turned a bit harder and he sighed, rubbing the back of his neck as the young boy from before brought in a large bowl made from some strange, heavy material. It was steaming and Jremy nodded to him, "Run'long, git ya later." He turned back to her and held out the bowl.

The smell of the stew inside it was the closest thing she'd encountered to the world from above in her entire time down there. It was rich and fragrant; it smelled tasty. Though she knew a large part of that was just psychological. It wasn't more mushrooms and bug guts.

"Eat d'is first, then tell ya everythin'," he said in a firm voice.

Her face tightened with frustration and even as she tried to just quickly get it over with, her body was too weak to even push itself fully into a sitting position. How much blood had she lost?

With how dehydrated she felt, she was surprised it had affected her so badly, but she couldn't argue with how numb and dizzy and pained she felt.

"I can't," she whimpered, and hated having to rely on this stranger to care for her.

"I'll git ya," he said reassuringly, and he used the crude spoon-like implement to lift some up and bring it to her lips.

Despite his size he managed to be gentle as he slowly feed her the underworld stew.

When she tasted it she was disappointed to find it was not nearly as palatable as it smelled, yet it was still far better than the mushrooms and beetles. There were chunks of something like a potato, bits of meat and a lot of greenery in it that resembled parsley.

She didn't take as much pleasure in eating it as she knew she should have, but it warmed the dampness from her bones and she was grateful. Yet with every spoonful, her pleading eyes were upon him, knowing the worst was yet to come.

Tar'kul was dead. He must have been killed, if not my Jremy, then by the mob of townsfolk.

Killed for trying to protect her from a threat that only he understood or saw.

As she finished the meal he gave her a final smile before he said, "Did wha' I could ta save 'im, but... Ya fren' died attackin' the folks tryin' ta save ya. I'm sorry." He hung his head down sadly.

And there it was.

Plain and simple.

After a life of misery and torment, she'd come into his life like a sun and burned him out so fast. Her brows furrowed, her lower lip quivered ever so slightly.

When she'd come to realize more about her dreams, about her role in them, she had begun to understand Tar'kul. About what had happened to her, what he'd done while she slumbered and they shared... some form of connection that she hadn't been aware of at the time.

And once she'd come to know that, she'd come to forgive him. Empathize with his need to find a safe place, to hide from all of the terrible things that this place held.

She didn't realize she was crying until her eyes blurred over completely and she had to blink them free of the salty water.

Laying back she turned away from Jremy, overwhelmed by such a sense of loss. Threatened by anger at those who had slayed her friend.

"I'll give ya some time ta mourn," he said quietly, rising up and retreating from the room, leaving her to its now hollow warmth and comforts.

❈ 35 ❈

Thia found herself sleeping a lot; she'd truly been in rough shape. Her body was malnourished from such a limited diet and no sun. All the blood loss. They brought her a lot of food, each and every day, and Jremy fed her personally each time. Though after giving her the bleak news, he'd been quiet as well as warm. Disturbingly she found herself often throwing it up upon awaking, but the large, muscular man was always there ready to give her more of the precious, hearty food.

Though she slept, she didn't dream, not as before. And her attempts to reach out with her mind were fruitless.

In her grief she had to come to terms with another growing fear. The tingling numbness in her legs was not going away, and she'd not moved them since she'd awoken that first day.

He crouched before her as usual, that big bowl in hand as she was propped up on a rough mound of fabric stuffed with something spongy.

She'd put it off for so long, it felt. Asking about her legs, her ability to walk. She'd tried to push it from her mind, to not dwell on what it meant, but every waking moment was filled with that stomach churning dread.

Yet she knew putting it off wasn't helping. Silence wasn't healing her, and neither was the food.

She looked up at Jremy with her sodden, red-rimmed eyes, and her lips trembled as the question pushed forth. "What's wrong with my legs?"

His brows furrowed and he looked down over her, the outline of her legs through the blankets. "I'll git tha doc," he said simply, getting up and going to fetch him.

When he returned shortly thereafter she found out the "doctor" was an older man, with white hair to match his skin tone. He wore thick robes to cover him, and he looked little like she would imagine of a man who bore that title.

"Wha's a matter?" he asked, and reached out to pull the blankets from her legs and inspect them.

She cringed as he revealed her nude, fragile body, and tried to cover her chest and genitals from him as best she could. "I can't... I can't feel them." Her voice cracked and strained, her breath so shallow.

What could a doctor do other than tell her what she dreaded?

She could barely feel his touches as he lifted one leg, bent it at the knee, moved the slender limb about in a show of testing it before moving onto the other. He inspected the both of them in detail, and just as she saw, there were no marks or signs of anything that might indicate why they didn't work.

True to her prediction he could find nothing. He gave a shrug to Jremy then said to her, "Mussa been th'hit t'yer head," he said quickly as he stood up. "Lossa rest an' hearty food," he said. "Will put special herbs in stew fro' now on."

Jremy stood up, patted the old man on the shoulder then made room for him to go to the door as he frowned sympathetically down at Thia.

"I'll see ya git tha best," he promised.

She didn't want the best. She wanted to be able to walk. To escape this place.

This new pit of despair was beyond anything she knew. It was helplessness, and hopelessness, and it felt eternal.

$$❈\quad 3\,6\quad ❈$$

The days became a blur, even more so than usual in this nightmarish underworld. Thia slept so much, puked her guts up as often as not upon awakening, and ate more and more of the hearty food they brought her. Still, her legs never improved, even as her body filled out gradually.

One day Jremy came into her room with a curious contraption; it only took her a momentary thought to realize it was a makeshift stretcher. He bore a wide smile on his face as he greeted her good morning. "Thought ya migh' like a look aroun'. Change o' scenery," he said.

Her bitterness showed with a sullen roll of her eyes, yet at the same time she wanted nothing more than to get out of this bed. Her back ached and her skin felt constantly raw and itchy, and she became more and more detached from this waking hell hole.

She had no more hope of escape, nothing to drive her forward, and she wondered why she simply couldn't have died.

But instead, she sighed and said softly, "Fine."

He pulled a wrapped bundle off the stretched and unfurled

it, offering a very simple dress to her. Despite the shabby cloth it was made from, it was superior to her own in that it was whole and untorn. He even had leathery looking shoes to go with it, not that she needed such a thing being unable to walk. "Made special fer ya," he said pridefully. "Shou' fit like a secon' skin." He laid it out for her then backed to the door. "I'll give ya a moment."

She took a moment when he left to look at it in wonder. Never had Tar'kul's warnings left her mind, but more and more she was finding it hard to believe they would care for her in her state if they were as fiendish as he warned. Evil.

Down here, it was hard to tell.

Still, as she tugged on the clothes, she felt a bit better, a bit more like herself, and she called out to let him know she was ready.

Jremy came back in with a broad smile and looked her over in her clothes. They were simple things by the judging of the world above, yet below where most of the folk she saw had little to nothing to cover then, and what they did have was usually of poor make, her outfit made her look like a queen.

"Ya look real purdy," he said, kneeling down and wrapping his arms about her, those thick biceps and forearms pressing into her chest and sides as he pulled her onto the stretcher.

She both shied away from and craved his embrace, the warm, human body against hers. She felt so lonely, so lost and uncertain without her sole friend, and now that she relied on Jremy for such embarrassing, basic human functions, she could never see their friendship as anything more than a burden on him.

For his part, Jremy certainly didn't act as if she were. He tied her onto the stretcher securely then pulled her out into the main shaft where the village lay. Once outside she could hear the sounds of chatter, of humans at work. The numerous voices of the small but busy little village.

He pulled her up along the ramp, round and round he went upwards closer to the glow that stung her eyes. But as she got up there, he pointed out, "See?" He indicated the men who climbed up the wall with ropes around them, plucking some vegetation from the walls and putting it into baskets that others then lowered down. It looked like dangerous work, but since the reward was food a little closer to that of the surface world, it seemed a small price.

"We have good food here. It's a safe spot," he stated to her, full of confidence in their little corner of the dank underworld. "Even have light. We're protected here from danger. Hunger, too."

"How long have you lived here?" What she really wanted to ask was how long ago they'd given up their own hope for return to the surface world.

It struck her as odd, then, that she thought of her home that way. As the surface world. As though it needed clarification.

He looked down to her and replied casually, "Whole life. Was born here." He brought her closer to the edge, but safely secure. The whole shaft stretched down far, beyond her sight from her angle, though she could see so many men going about their business talking, crafting things, harvest, cooking. "You weren't?" he asked, crouching down to her level, his ripped physique, so lean and without excess fat, bulging with pec muscles, biceps and abs.

"No. No, not at all."

How long had she been down there?

Her hand went to her face, feeling out her skin as if it would hold some answers. Then down along the frayed and slept in blonde hair, but it was too mussed up to see how much it had grown.

He inspected her curiously, as if there might be some evidence in her appearance to give away her place of birth. "M'dad's dad said he was born elsewhere. Place wif a lotta light," he remarked as if recounting ancient history, his thick forearms rested on his knees. "Said he dug holes into ground. Whole buncha fellas. Then got stuck here," he remarked with a shrug of his bare, broad shoulders as if the tale might be nothing but fancy.

Though Thia didn't need another look around the shaft to think it held some truth. Were these the descendants of miners who got were buried in and forgotten?

"You've... none of you have ever found a way out?"

The thought chilled her to the core. Generations of people who couldn't escape from this underground dungeon.

But then, she wasn't escaping anywhere. Not without her legs. Not on her own.

She felt like she could scream, but instead she swallowed it down.

All the while Jremy studied her curiously. "Ya really come from above," he said as if only then truly coming to believe it. "Yer not happy 'bout bein' here, I kin see that," he stated in his low, husky voice, those grey eyes of his studying her. "Will ya come eat sup' with me family tanight? Maybe ya not think so bad on it if ya get ta know us."

And what more could she do but accept? Her loneliness, her desperation... it was all taking such a horrible toll on her mind and her body, and so she reluctantly agreed.

Whether Tar'kul's warnings were real or not, she had to come to accept the fact that she was stuck here.

$$\text{❦ 37 ❦}$$

When supper time came, Jremy came and got her, pulling her to his place. It was the last of the homes in the town going up, near to hers. It was, however, far bigger, and actually consisted of several hollowed out rooms.

The biggest was beyond the main room when entering, which contained strange trophies of the underworld. Pelts and heads of fearsome creatures, some she recognized like the ghastly, lopsided head of a Dead-Lamp. There, she came to the biggest chamber, filled to the brim with life.

Ringing the round room were four young boys, including the one she saw upon first awakening after her injury, and two older men. They all stared at her with excitement, unable to contain their eagerness at a new addition to the family meal. A familiar young boy was most excited of all as he bounced upon his haunches, grinning at her.

At the center were more of those glowing hot stones, and on top of it some strips of meat sizzling, and in the center of the stones a pot brewing.

"E'ryone say a nice slow welcome ta Thia," Jremy said, and though some did just that, a lot of them let their excitement get the better of them and shot out in their fast, bastardized English welcomes and good wishes to her.

It was hard to put a pin on what exactly she felt, but she smiled nonetheless and brushed some of her hair from her face. She'd tried to run her fingers through it a bit, cleaning out the snarls, but it was difficult without a proper

There were so many people, as if it were one of the dinner parties she used to attend, and warmth combined with bitterness in her heart.

Jremy gave her a prime seat at the head of the gathering right beside him, and he made sure to prop her up in a way that gave her a good view of the room. "M'sons," he said to her, introducing the entire room in one simple phrase. A couple of the older ones didn't look all that much younger than him—Jremy couldn't be past his 30s, could he?

The young boy who had watched over her pushed forward and grabbed up a bowl, "Kin I serve her da'?" he asked excitedly, as if the mere act of serving her some food would be quite a treat.

"You kin take her up some stew," Jremy said with a warm smile to him then to her. "Bu' first, we give a lil' pray," he remarked and put his hands together, and the whole room bowed their heads solemnly.

She followed suit, her gaze still upon them through her descended lashes, a strange emotion filling her that she wasn't familiar with. It had been so long since she felt anything other than despair that she wasn't entirely sure she remembered anything else.

"Thanks be ta the watchers, fer keepin' us safe. An' bless the tunnel o' light, our home an' haven. Our flesh an' blood, our souls, ta keep an' preserve our people. Amen," it was a strange prayer, but then what could she expect from the descendants of low class miners trapped in the underworld?

Jremy leaned forward and took up a large piece of fried meat, putting it onto a stone slab that passed for a plate before handing it to her. A moment later, the boy quickly took up some of the stew and scurried over with a toothy grin to hold it out to her. As the ritual went on and he handed out more and more, it was clear she made off with the lion's share of the meal.

It took her a long time to understand the new sensation spreading through her body.

Gratitude.

It had been absent from her since she arrived at this hidden village, despite all they had done for her. All they continued to do for her.

Jremy had always been warm and kind when he visited, and she had looked forward to them every day, yet never felt grateful for them. Not like she did now.

Though as he dished out the food to his sons, it was clear some would get very little. He'd been so generous with her that she didn't assume there was any shortage of food to go around.

"We're all real happy t'see ya here wit' us," the young son eagerly stated, and others bobbed their head to the words. They were all so excited by her presence, watching her, though whenever she looked to them most would quickly avert their eyes bashfully.

"Thank you for having me." It was strange how quickly her old mannerism could come back, given the right circumstances, since so often she struggled to remember her old life. Still, the way she met their eyes, confidently and with such self-assurance was so natural despite how fearful she remained that Tar'kul was right about them.

Even though they had been served last, they finished the fastest in their hunger and then excused themselves one by one, bowing to both their father and then her. It seemed like she had taken on some sort of special role beside him as a figurehead for the family as they dined.

Meanwhile, she had been given altogether too much food. The hearty stew and fried meat—although not exactly delicious—were incredibly filling.

"Did'ja enjoy?" asked Jremy, slowly finishing his meal beside her with his legs folded beneath him, smiling broadly at her, seeming so happy for her feminine company in a family full of nothing but men.

"It was great," she agreed, because food only had to give her strength. No longer was eating something she thought to be pleasurable, but just a natural thing she had to make sure to do in order to continue living. "Quite filling. I... I would have shared if I'd realized."

His own meal finished at last, he reached over and squeezed her slender shoulder reassuringly. "Yer special guest. M'sons wouldn't take any food from yer mouth. Ya need it ta get'n'stay healthy," he said in their peculiar way of speaking, and with that the last of the sons exited the room leaving them there alone.

She leaned back, staring at him so curiously for a long moment. She didn't know him. She didn't understand what drove him, that made him carry on his existence down here, despite the hopelessness of escape.

And yet... perhaps she did.

His family, the warmth, the comfort of his home. Isn't this what the lower class people had above? The simpler things in life, free of education and higher expectations?

She mulled it over for a long while, but she knew that wouldn't be enough for her.

She needed to see the sun, even if it burned out her eyes.

"Do you mind if I ask a question?"

"Ask any'tin'," he said immediately, happy for her interest it seemed as he leaned forward onto his knees and smiled at her happily. He seemed to be most at home, most comfortable there surrounded by his sons.

And why wouldn't he be?

Still, she licked her lips and approached the topic gingerly. "Have you seen... ah, I know them as the pale ones?"

Jremy's brows furrowed and he thought, pointing out to the entry room, "Like th'trophy?" he asked, referring to the hideous Dead-Lamp head.

"No," Thia replied. "They... look like us. But incredibly pale, and very dangerous. They... charm people to them, lure victims to them."

He stiffened almost imperceptibly at that description. He reached back behind the sort of religious altar that lay to their backs, a curious construct that was part Christian cross, part bizarre underworld oddity. He pulled out a strange jug and poured some of the pungent alcohol inside into the bowls for them to drink. "D'ey try ta lure away our girls," he said very sadly, offering her the bowl. "We're protected here, but if th'girlies wander out..." he shrugged glumly, "Nothin' we can do but try'n chase 'em down."

She nodded thoughtfully, staring down at the remains of her food as she took a breath. He wouldn't know the answer to her question. But she had to try, didn't she?

Thia took the bowl in her hands, her thumbs playing along the rim, feeling out the texture of it while she articulated it.

"Have you... seen anyone become one?"

His brows furrowed again in confusion. "Become one?" he muttered before shaking his head. "No. M'dad told me long ago of somethin' like that, but..." he shrugged his broad, hard shoulders in helplessness. "Was long ago, an' he were no' sure."

She felt somewhat validated that there were at least rumours of it, yet she didn't know what that proved.

Taking a sip of the liquid, she failed to hold back a face

despite herself. Still, it filled her with a strange sense of warmth, and for that she was grateful.

"Tar'kul... my friend. He had once been a man. But he didn't have other people around him."

Jremy was quiet but nodded. "Why, ya should stay here with us. We take care a ya, keep ya safe, secure. Happy," he said with a smile, lowering his hand down to hers to gently squeeze it as he sipped the pungent fermented brew. "Ya no change inta nothin' else if ya stay here. I promise it," he declared with certainty.

"Have you ever met anyone, recently, from above?" she pressed again, still trying to drink that brew without making a disgusted face and failing. But it felt so nice, that little bit of light headedness, the excuse to keep talking and learning more, her own paranoia dimming.

He shook his head to her, "No," he said firmly, clearly nothing more to add on the subject. "I have a noshun for ya," he said as he cozied up beside her. "Dun gotta decide now, but... m'sons could use a new ma, an' me..." he lowered his head a bit, smiling sheepishly, the look so ill fitted on the large, strong, powerful man's features. "Well... yer the purdiest girly we've ever had here," he said as he lifted his head to her again. "I'd take th'best kinda care a ya. An' would'no have ta worry 'bout yer legs, even if they never did come back."

Thia thought her eyes might bulge out of her head.

All her life she'd resisted and resented the calling of becoming yet another noble matron, a 'lady of leisure' who devoted herself to frivolity and breeding. Yet here she was, in the filthy depths of the earth... being offered a proposal to become a brood-sow to some low-born, inbred brutes.

Yet what he was proposing, more than marriage, more than motherhood, more than anything, was giving up.

That she would no longer strive to reach up higher, to get

back to where she came from. To the familiar tastes and sights and places of home.

Her hands trembled and she put down the bowl for fear of spilling it, and her hands laid numbly in her lap. Her mind reeled. She was of marrying age, of course. Well above it, many would say. But she wasn't ready for that. She was still so young, and there was so much to explore and see, so much of the world to experience.

She couldn't. She was caged in the underbelly of her potential experiences, trapped and forgotten by the very earth whose unexplored corners she wanted to revel in.

"I have to think about this," was all she could squeak out. Not because she was tempted, but because she didn't have many options.

He nodded to her understandingly, not a hint of disappointment in her reluctance. "'Course," he said pleasantly, giving her hand a squeeze before he let it go. "Ya thinkunnit. But if'n ya choose ta do it, know m'sons an' I will love ya an' protect ya. We's the most respected clan, an' ya would get th'best o' every-t'in'." He gave a big toothy smile, "Th'boys are dyin' ta spoil ya."

"And... if not?" she asked, her head tipping to the side and her blonde hair gathering at the nape of her neck.

Jremy shook his head, "We won' kick ya out or none," he said with a bit of a crooked smile. "Ya won' have it so good as ya might, but y'll still be taken care o'. Ain't many o' our kind down 'ere. Too few ta waste."

"Jremy, what did you mean when you said that if I left, I'd never find you again? It's been bothering me, as you don't seem to be a nomadic people. Ah, I mean, you don't travel to different places without settling."

He took a while to understand her question but then chuck-led. "Ah. Tunnels change. Big maze that the, uh…" he struggled to find a way to describe what he meant. "Long-legged ones?"

he checked to see if she knew what he meant then went on. "'Cause 'a them, things change. Tunnels get hidden. Can't find us easy if ya leave."

She furrowed her brow thoughtfully, but she couldn't imagine how that could happen. "How do they change things?"

He gave a shrug of his shoulders, "No' for me t'say." A simple way of saying he did not understand the machinations of such alien creatures.

Still, she boggled at the craftiness of it and slowly went to pick her bowl back up. When she sipped it, she didn't make a face, and inwardly smiled at her minor success. "Has anyone escaped, that you know of? Do people try?"

That question brought a sour look to his face immediately, and he took a deep drink of the fermented brew, whose flavour she couldn't place. "Only the girls," he said morosely. "Miracle ya survived out there long enough ta find us."

Because of the pale ones. Her nose crinkled and she glanced away for a moment. She didn't understand why they only lured the girls, but she knew their call quite well and she hadn't felt it since she arrived.

"Has anyone ever gone up that shaft? Towards the light?"

That question too seemed to strike an awkward nerve, but he showed no hesitation to answer her as such. "Only fool boys who no longer care if they live'er'die," he said, his expression a little hard as he downed more of the powerful alcohol. "Th'fall down shaft an' die."

They were all trapped, then, and they were all going to die down here.

Jremy was born in these pits, though, so he must have made peace with it. But Thia... Could she ever?

She took another sip of her alcohol before putting it back on the floor and smiling at him with closed lips. "It was a very nice dinner. Thank you for having me." Yet even through her facade of kindness, the knife she'd used for her meal found its way up along her forearm, hidden away as he drained the rest of his drink.

He smiled at her in return as he placed the empty bowl down. "Hope ya join us each night fro' now on," he said as he rose up. "I'll take ya back, 'less ya care ta stay here th'night. Got room, an' if ya need anythin' we be close by."

"I need time to think," she said earnestly, and felt so incredibly vulnerable. She relied on this man to be kind to her, to do as she bid him. Yet without the use of her legs, it would be so easy for him to take advantage of her, to make her stay.

The thought left a sour taste in her mouth, more so than did the alcohol.

"O' course," he complied congenially, bending down and hoisting her stretcher up with little effort. Unlike the rest of the dark realm beneath, night and day had some sort of meaning. The faint glow from above—which still stung her eyes—faded into completely darkness at night when the village quieted down.

It wasn't long before he was lifting her out of her stretcher and placing her back in the spare spot he had lent her, his thick arms carrying her petite but increasingly thickening body back into her bed. "We be jus' aroun' the corner if'n ya need us," he said with a smile as he laid her out gently.

"I know. Thanks again," she replied, but never had she felt so helpless and uncertain of herself as she did then. She was being offered something she craved - normalcy, hope, a purpose - but it was wrong. She was reliant on him in a way she never wanted to be, and as he left, she looked down at her legs and willed them to move, as she had so many times before.

There was naught but the numb tingling in response.

⁂ 38 ⁂

hia's dreams were so mundane and ordinary since Tar'kul had passed. She'd not experienced any of the psychically augmented dream-walks. She had nightmares quite often still, but what was she to expect in a hellish underworld?

Yet she found herself wondering, more and more, about the connection between the Sergeant and the Lieutenant. The dreams had faded along with the ones of Edain, and she wondered if they had been Tar'kul's dreams. If he had been the Sergeant and he was replaying what had happened to him so long ago.

She'd experienced so much terror through those dreams, but now she almost longed for them. She reached out for that mental contact, that connection with someone else, and never did she find it.

What she assumed to be days passed, the rhythm of the underground world filling her with its oddly mundane routine, and more and more she wondered if this was it.

She couldn't escape. Physically, she'd simply be food for one of the horrors beyond. To accept that, though she had to shut down something very important to her.

She had to deal with the fact that she could no longer hope for escape.

It had driven her for so long, powered her through such terrors, and now she was an invalid, relying entirely on a man she barely knew.

One that she constantly caught herself wondering why Tar'kul had reacted with such violent fear. She'd been dying to ask that monstrous being so many questions since he passed, and she felt another wave of regret.

It was her fault he'd died. She'd forced him to come explore these humans, these new places, and she'd gotten him killed because he wanted to protect her from harm.

And she was going to accept the harm she perceived as her new family.

What other options did she have? But she held off telling him for as long as she could, trying with every last ounce of her hope to move her legs. That little bright spot in the future she was always moving towards got more and more distant, but it never entirely fizzled out. Sometimes she thought it would be easier if it did.

Another meal with Jremy's family passed, though she swore there was one of the boys missing. He'd always been last and least to be fed, so perhaps he'd simply gone to try his luck elsewhere.

Before the last of the boys headed off, the young one—Rufus—came up to her at the end. "Ah know da' said not ta say anythin' 'bout it to ya, but..." he sheepishly glanced over at his father, who was glaring at the young man over his bowl of alcoholic brew, "but I r'ally hope ya stay wit' us an' be our new ma." He gave a big grin, his cheeks dimpling as he avoided a swat from his father.

"Git gone," Jremy said in a terse tone, though he broke a bit at the end and looked a little amused.

Despite her own mixed feelings on it, her heart swelled at the sweet words and she had to hold back the moisture from her eyes. She never asked what happened to their real mother - or mothers - as she thought it would be too difficult of a topic, but she couldn't help but be curious.

"Well thanks, Rufus," she said softly, her voice cracking with emotion as she leaned back in her makeshift chair, a half smile on her face that didn't entirely reach her eyes. Her mind felt like it was slipping away from her.

His father shooed him out after that, and he scampered off, grinning back at her intermittently before ducking beneath one of the rugs that served as a door.

Jremy offered her a bowl of the warming alcohol, "Sorry 'bout that," he said affectionately. "Don't let 'im pressure ya none."

She accepted the bowl and took a sip, her body slowly getting used to the swill. "I won't. I've been thinking about it a lot. I just... I'm not certain what I could really do. I'm not in much of a position to be a wife, or a mother, and I've never been either. And... this isn't entirely how I expected it to happen, either."

But then, her wedding dreams on the surface had long ago been quashed.

"I s'pose up above ya got ta do all sorts a thin's. Whatever ya wanted to," he mused, sipping his drink. "But, now... I was thinkin' we might try somethin' out. I know yer strugglin', an' hopin' ya legs start ta work again. So in case thin's do work out, well... why don't ya come stay 'ere wit' us? I mean, live in d'is place. Don't gotta sleep wit' me or nothin'. Don't gotta be a ma exactly neither. But... jus' be 'round for th'company, an' see how it fits ya. An' d'at way if ya legs get better..."

Jremy gave a shrug of his broad shoulders and a warm smile, as if he was just trying to be helpful.

Truthfully, she craved the company as much as the solitude. Loneliness was something she wanted to feel, and she knew she was punishing herself for Tar'kul's death. For her curiosity.

It was as though the second she was safe, she wanted to make herself pay for all the things she'd messed up along the way.

But she was tired of feeling that way. Of being left alone with her bland, macabre dreams without the feeling and emotion she was used to. She was tired of thinking and analyzing and dreading and hoping.

She needed to move on, to accept what was happening to her life, to her body, and so she looked at Jremy and nodded.

The large man's face slowly lit up and he gave a nod in return, forcing his lips shut. "I'll tell th'boys. You'll 'ave the nicest spot in th'place to yerself. Like a queen o' the manor," he proclaimed as he stood, referencing things to which he couldn't have the vaguest grasp of beneath the earth.

When she thought back to her home, the big house that she'd had all to herself, she nearly laughed at the absurdity of his words. But instead she took a sip of alcohol and closed her eyes, taking a deep breath. "Do you have a brush and a mirror down here?"

He didn't even know what she was talking about.

It didn't take long for him to inform the house, and she could hear their excited chatter, the sound of them talking even quicker than usual and then the rushing about. They truly were ecstatic about her, it seemed, it was almost overwhelming.

Jremy kept them at bay though, and pulled her into what must've been his bedroom.

It truly was much bigger than the other areas, excluding the place they all ate—she refused to call it a dining room—with many thick blankets, and a rather large, heaping bed big enough for several. He laid down her stretcher and then, in that now very familiar manner, wrapped his arms around her from behind and lifted her up, hoisting her onto the bed.

He'd laid out a big heap of coarse cushions for her, some with a furry sort of mat that was a little nicer than most of the fabrics they used.

The scratchiness of the material always reminded her of Tar'kul, of how he'd first wrapped her in his blanket and tried to comfort her. Looking back on the memory, it felt so strange. As if that had all happened when she was a child, naive and innocent.

She didn't know how long had passed since then, but she felt like she'd aged a life time, and the thought swept a melancholy over her. This was her life, now. The rest of eternity sprawled before her, and darkness was all she could see.

And still she forced a small, grateful smile at Jremy, because there was little else she could do. Whether she liked it or not, she was a prisoner of this world, and reliant on him for the most basic and humiliating of needs.

With a broad smile, the large man reached out and patted her shoulder. "Sleep tight," he bid her with a gentle squeeze of her slender arm. "Yer safe an' welcome here." He rose back up to leave, and she licked her lips, as if to protest.

The loneliness, the fear or being abandoned had grown since her injury, but she bit her tongue, holding it at bay for the evening as she laid back and once more willed her legs to move.

There was naught but the tingling.

                                   ❧ 40 ☙

The days went by at an agonizing pace by Thia's
reckoning. So little to do but sit and watch the family
of men work around her. They were all eager to tend
to her, trying to entertain her in their own way. The young Rufus
brought her a ball and some strange dried bug carapaces,
emulating a game of jacks with a bizarre underworld twist.

He noticed the dispassionate look on her face, and his ever-
present smile faltered a little. "What's it like where ya come
from?' he asked, the more he spoke with her the more he
learned to slow his tongue and refine his words.

She didn't want to think of home, but her mind kept going
there anyways. To the warm beds and fresh food, haughty party
goers and drunken rivalries.

Of books, so many more books than she could ever hope
to read.

Of libraries and roaring fires, of overstuffed chairs and hot
tea to soothe her frazzled nerves.

Thia licked her lips thoughtfully and looked at the young
boy, her arms instinctively moving to cradle herself, to console

her weary body against the onslaught of memories. "Warm," she said softly. "Dry. The sun..." Her voice choked a little and she knew why. The last time she'd seen the sun was in her dream, right before seeing that little girl. Right before Tar'kul died. She'd touched his face and she knew that the small act of affection had caressed his soul.

He'd forgotten what the sun had looked like, and she forced herself to remember through the hurt and the pain it caused, even though her voice was weak. "The sun is like a giant light in the sky, making things warm and comfortable. It helps plants and animals grow." And the blue of the sky... How could she ever explain its simple beauty to someone who never knew what it was? Would he even understand the colour of a pale blue, stretched out for eons and marked with puffy, white clouds?

She swallowed, trying to gather herself before a thought occurred to her. She opened her eyes wide and looked to him. "See the colour of my eyes? That's like the colour of the sky. A light blue."

"The sky..." he murmured to her, the thought a foreign concept to him entirely though he pieced together her meaning from her insinuations. "Looks a bi' like yellow," he remarked, and she froze.

"No. The center," she stated, pushing aside her worry at discolouration in her own eyes.

"Are there lotsa folks up there?" he asked curiously as he shifted close to sit right beside her, eyes wide, some concern there. "Do ya miss 'em?"

She couldn't look at him after that. She didn't have many people to miss, really. Her parents had long since passed, her aunt more recently. And Edain...

Her eyes watered and she tried to swallow the lump in her throat. She didn't miss many people, but she missed society. Safety. Civilization.

There was still so much she wanted to do and explore, and now she couldn't even walk on her own.

"I miss it," she admitted with a heavy heart.

The shaggy young Rufus studied her as he nodded his head, looking both thoughtful and innocent in his youth. "I'd like ta see it. I bet life up there's easier, huh?" he said, a bit of her sadness eking into him. "Prob'ly got no shortage of things."

"I didn't. Some do, though," she responded just as introspectively, knowing her large manor and yard could have housed dozens of families, and instead it was reserved for her alone. The thanklessness and lack of understanding of what she had embarrassed her now, and she looked at it with a new light.

Rufus nodded along in understanding. "S'like here then," he said. "Some 'a the families don't get s'much food as us," he said, and she knew even they let some of their family go hungry on a fairly regular basis. Though they never shorted her in their bid to make her both welcome and healthy. "I'm glad yer here," he said, "though I'm sad ya can't go back if that's what ya want."

"There's no way back," she said, and she tried to make herself believe it. Resigning herself to her fate is surely easier than continuing to fight it, to struggle against her bindings.

"Well I'm glad yer here with us. An' if I was old enough, I'd wanna be yer fella," he said a bit cheekily, and she couldn't be sure if he was fully serious or trying to lift her spirits.

"But since I'm not I'd be happy if ya were m'ma," he remarked with a bashful grin.

She felt that strange, confused sensation flutter about in her chest again and she took in a deep breath. "I've never been a mother. Never even thought of it. I certainly have no idea how to be a good one."

"Oh," he said simply, a little surprised by her response. "Well I think ya'll do grand," he said with determination as the evening drew to a halt. Jremy had come back inside, his pants hung low off his hips, body a bit sweaty as he smiled about the large room and then to her. He'd been gone that day, but warned her he would be.

With all the time she had to think she even finally realized 'Jremy' was a bastardization of 'Jeremy'. The miner's dialect was a fast-spoken mauling of the English she knew.

"Good evenin' ma'am," he said to her as he strode around the meal hall towards her and the boy, placing a large palm upon Rufus' shaggy head of hair.

"Evening," she responded in kind, and she wasn't sure if she was glad he was back or not. So many strange feelings for him tumbled around in her mind, and though she felt gratitude and affection, resentment swam within her as well. She couldn't entirely make sense of it, but she would be foolish to deny it.

The large man very roughly tousled Rufus' hair and ushered him out, "Run 'long." The boy jumped up and scurried away, his simple toy beetle in hand as he left them alone in the room.

Jremy smiled back to her warmly, "Had a good patrol 'round the tunnels," he asserted, crouching down beside her and reaching his hand to touch her paralyzed calf. "Did th'boys take care a ya alright while I was away?" he inquired, that strong hand holding her familiarly as she saw the concern in his eyes.

"I'm fine." Thia kept having to remind herself of the gratitude she felt towards him and for everything he had done, but the bitterness of being unable to escape seemed to mar everything.

No one above would have ever believed her, but now, the issue would never even come up. She couldn't warn the others to stay away from this pit of damnation, and she cursed inwardly that there could be others like her. That there *would* be others like her. Others that listened to the demons' beckoning under the ground.

He gave a hesitant nod. "Ya ready fer bed then? Prob'ly a bit sick a sittin' here huh? I hope th'boys made 'emselves 'vailable ta cart ya 'round when ya wanted to." He never failed to project a congenial disposition, warm and friendly. Avoiding impositions and awkwardness better than she'd have expected such a base-born, underworld raised man to do.

He was trying to make her prison more hospitable. It was all she could do to keep from crying.

"They were princes, I promise," she said instead.

He gave a satisfied smile and lifted her cot, carrying her back into what was once his bedroom. The large area filled with a growing number of underworld gifts, intended for a lady. The old her would have recoiled in horror at the bizarre display of colourful stones and crude carvings the young men and, primarily, Jremy had given her. Though below she had learned to recognize how special these things were. These oddities, they had value here that would be beyond understanding above.

Jremy helped her take care of those embarrassing necessities and then lifted her onto the bed with gentle care. "While I was out, I got ya somethin'," he remarked, reaching into his low-hanging trousers. "A lil' gift," he said, and she expected some other new knick-knack, so she forced a smile to her lips.

It was the same one she wore when her relatives had invited someone she didn't like over, or when she had to do something she hated. But she was a lady, so she was always smiling in public at the inconveniences of life, and now she smiled at him, because she hated her life here but he was only trying to make it better.

To her surprise, he pulled out a rather amazing artifact. Though a bit tarnished, it must have once been a dazzling necklace. Gem encrusted, it was the stuff of pure nobility, rich and lavish; no one but a wasteful noble could ever deign to have such a thing crafted. "Got it a while back," he said lowly, "was savin' it fer when ya accepted m'proposal, but I figured… why wait?" His broad jaw a bit tensed as he tried to suppress a bigger grin.

A sob caught in her throat and her world spun for a moment.

For one blissful second, he looked like Edain, that boyishly handsome face replacing the more rugged and masculine one. The hands softer and more pampered, the necklace gleaming brightly before it all dropped away and she was left with reality once more.

"It's beautiful," she murmured, her fingers reaching out to touch it gingerly.

Jremy unclasped it and reached for her, "Lemme put it on."

She lifted her blonde hair out of the way as he used those strong hands of his to wrap it about her neck and secure it firmly. That central azure gem was so heavy against her chest she could feel it. And though looking down she was able to discern some minor nicks and damage done to the thing, it was but minor, the necklace still was original, unique. And priceless in that underworld hell.

"Looks gorgeous on ya," he remarked, brushing his broad fingertips over the chain, lightly grazing her milky skin beneath.

Her eyes watered and her chest swelled with emotions she couldn't rightly articulate. It was just too much, and she threw herself into his arms and let all that pain pour out of her. Her head was hazy and full and she couldn't hold it back any longer.

Those thick, powerful arms of his wrapped about her, the bare muscles squeezing her warmly. Jremy embraced her readily, nestling her head into the crook of his shoulder as he murmured to her softly. "I wan' make ya real happy with us," he said, kissing the side of her blonde hair as he stroked a hand down her spine. "Know it ain't what ya used ta, but I'll do m'best to make ya my pleased lady."

She didn't know if that was possible. If that was something he could do or control.

She would always be looking for a way out.

No matter what she resigned herself to.

"I don't know how to be a mother," she whimpered into his

ear, and that was so true, but moreover, she didn't know how to be a wife.

Especially without the use of her legs.

Very slowly he withdrew from the embrace enough to look her in the eyes, that gray gaze of his so intense as he stroked one hand along her side to her hip. Her figure fleshier, softer now than it had been since she first descended into the underworld. "Ye'll figure it out," he assured her softly, and leaning in, he tilted his head forward to plant a kiss of his lips on her full, pouty pair.

She trembled against him, but didn't pull away. Her heart was in her throat, her body shivering with anxiety, but the closeness, the humanness of his mouth was welcome against hers.

Without Tar'kul, she was alone if she didn't open herself to someone, right? And now she was crippled. Unable to move of her own accord.

Those thick, strong arms of Jremy's though bore no limitations, it seemed, he squeezed her and probed his tongue into her mouth. That big, brute of a man pressing her body to his chest as he sat on the edge of the bed, his thumb brushing in over her hip towards parts long untouched.

His desire was undeniable. His intentions so clear.

And even though she was conflicted, she knew she wouldn't stop him. Not then. Not when she was feeling so vulnerable and needed so desperately to be touched by another person. She needed to feel some connection, some happiness...

She needed something to live for, and it wasn't going to be what her life had become.

Jremy's rough hands rubbed over her body, feeling her figure out as he lifted her dress up further, inching over her motionless legs. He was gentle for a man of his size and raised in savagery, but still the feel of that powerful physique was intimidating.

Very slowly he rested her back atop the bed as he leaned over her, his broad, bare chest heaving as he slowly tugged her coarse dress up over her hips and kissed his way down her neck.

He'd seen her nude before, of course. And left her feeling vulnerable.

This, though, was something different. Different from her fantasies of Edain, of her strange... She wasn't sure what to call what happened with Tar'kul's dream shape, not as she came to understand more of the dream world and how things worked.

She was breathing so hard it was almost hyperventilating, and her skin responded so eagerly to the tender touches even as her mind wrestled with her.

This was giving up.

She knew it.

Jremy moved up the bed over her further, that thick, muscular form looming as he tugged her dress up nearly to her shoulders, unveiling her breasts to his mouth as he descended upon them. His moist lips hungrily devouring one nipple and areola as his strong hands rubbed over her mons and then down along the cleft between her thighs.

He was ravenous and so strong, tugging his trousers downwards and showing the tuft of dark pubic hair above his manhood, growling for her with excitement.

Her baby blue eyes fluttered closed and her head tilted back. Though her nipples hardened, a knot in her stomach developed and she whimpered in return to his more masculine noises. It was like a frightened deer was being cornered by a wolf, and still she clung to him as though he were both her predator and her saviour.

In a sense, he was. He was another Tar'kul.

Jremy represented an awful fate for her, yet a better fate than she would face on her own, crippled and alone in the dark bowels of the earth. Those strong, powerful hands of his caressing her flesh, so soft and vulnerable beneath him. Her helpless legs still limp and unmoving.

Those trousers of his slipped down a little further and out burst his thick shaft. It was a large, veiny totem, pulsing with blood from his arousal as he poised himself over her atop that crude yet spacious bed. Lifting her pale legs and positioning them to the side with care as he parted her thighs, his eyes drank in her cunny.

The low thud of his hefty manhood against her mons drew her attention, that bulbous purple crown leaking its sticky precum against her flesh as he felt up her sides and towards her pert little breasts. A simple look at his face betrayed the excitement and lust etched deeply into his expression, so long constrained.

And even though she was drawn to look at his masculine form, she was equally compelled to avert her eyes, and in the end she turned her gaze to the side. A sob stuck in her throat, and her pretty mouth trembled with trepidation and uncertainty.

Jremy's large, muscular form bent down towards her and he put his arms reassuringly around her slender frame, cradling her as his lips kissed upon her cheek, then the corner of her lips. He coddled her gently against his chest as he murmured unintelligible words of comfort, that throbbing member grinding against her slit all the while. Moving down and down until that tip was pointed directly at her narrow cunt.

He felt so heavy atop her, but there was comfort there. Warmth.

A sense of peace and human contact she'd so long denied herself. And part of her wanted it, this natural, obscene, horrible, and wonderful act.

Yet the other part could only remember the strangeness, the volatility, of her first time.

She'd assumed that Tar'kul had known what he was doing when he took her in her sleep. Yet the longer she spent in that subterranean hell, the more she doubted such things. Her own ability to discern what was happening around her while away was deteriorating, how would his be after so many years all alone?

Such thoughts were pushed away as Jremy thrust himself up inside her, that thick organ splaying her delicate folds around his girth as he gave a lewd, low groan. The large, brutish man took such visceral pleasure in penetrating her as his length nestled to her depths, her narrow canal stretched taut about his circumference.

Her breath held as she fought back the rush of emotions. She could feel him. Everything. She had known that she would, for she would sometimes pinch her lower body to see where the sensation dulled, and where it simply disappeared, but it was still surprising to her in some manners. It was still so new and different, and it was like her body wanted to take some meagre pleasure from the act, but she refused it such luxuries.

His lips kissed upon her continually in their warm fashion, trying dearly to soothe her, but his powerful hips began to rock irreverently as he promptly pumped that thick girth into her. The low sounds of his moans and grunts coming out between smacks of his lips as he reached down, lifting one of her two powerless legs up over his hip to let him plunge into her more easily.

"It's okay," he said in a gravelly, lust-laden voice. "Yer m'girl now," he said to her in that deep, possessive tone as his hard body rocked atop her softer, slender form.

Thia barely cared.

Out of everything else in this moment, that realization bothered her. She would have been insulted, aghast that she was considered anyone's possession. The thought of relying on another was repugnant, yet what choice did she have down here in this pit of hell?

So she'd be his girl, until her damned legs would wake up from their slumber.

His spine arched, that thick chest made up of bulging pecs and abs, pushed out towards her as his pace worked up. The slap of his heavy balls against her ass filling the room with his monotonous grunts of pleasure until…

Jremy shuddered atop her, his head and neck twitching a bit as his dick spasmed and jerked within her. His climax came and went inside of her, pumping all he had into her depths as he lifted both of her limp legs up in the air with ease.

She felt like a doll, and anger made her pale skin flush. A doll to be rearranged as anyone saw fit.

Her blue eyes fluttered shut and she took in a deep breath, trying to find calm and balance within this nightmare. To focus on her gratitude and appreciation rather than her bitter anger, but it wasn't easy.

She barely knew if it was possible.

What lack of pleasure she took from the act was more than made up for it seemed in how much he did. His hard body coated in a thin sheen of perspiration as he breathed heavily and twitched out the last of his orgasm into her.

He pulled that thick organ of his from her puffy red folds, letting the creamy white fluid drool out of her as he kissed her forehead then slumped down onto the bed beside her heavily. His thick arm moving to wrap around her as he leaned over to kiss the side of her head. "You'll be a great mom," he said in a gravelly, weary voice.

She tried not to cringe. To let her face be neutral, even as the waves of fear crashed through her. Yet looking at him, she knew she had to ask. "What happened to their birth mothers?"

He hesitated a moment as he looked to her, then said matter-of-factly, "The fiends." He squeezed her to his side, moving her about with such ease as if she were indeed only a doll. "Don't worry. We'll keep ya safe from 'em. We know better now," he added, tugging the coarse blankets up over them both.

A cold chill went through her, and she wasn't certain it was just the sweatiness or if it was something else.

A confirmation of her fears.

She forced her eyes to him and smiled placidly. "How do you mean?"

He shut his eyes at the question and relaxed back, giving a deep sigh, keeping her in his grasp. "We take care," he said lowly. "Watch the tunnels 'round the area closer. Make sure no girlies go off alone no more." It was said with a certain finality, as if that were the whole story, no more questions necessary. All said in a much more abrupt manner than she was used to from him. Almost terse or curt.

She nodded, but the feeling in her gut and the memory of the girl she had followed here told her there was something far worse. Far more dire.

It wasn't the conk on the head that had rendered her legs useless.

She'd only thought that in the darkest of her moments in this hovel, and she'd every time pushed it away as being paranoid. She'd never asked, because she was afraid of the answer.

And now... What more was there to do with the information?

❧ 41 ❧

The suspicions of what was being done to her only made Thia's life worse, yet it gave her some purpose at least. Didn't it?

Jremy finished with her in the morning, a broad smile on his face as he pulled out and stood up. "Ya ready fer breakfast?" he asked as he pulled his coarse pants up over his still wet and turgid member.

It was something so horrific and they she was dulled to it all. She willed her legs to move at the same time she wished she couldn't feel his intrusion.

Yet Thia was a survivor, for better or for worse, and she gave him a bright and cheery smile that she hoped looked genuine. "Oh, maybe in a bit. I think I might try to get a bit more sleep today."

He gave her a broad, toothy smile in return and bent over, kissing her on the forehead. "I'll have ya food brought in fer ya then. I got some work ta take care of today, so I'll leave Rufus 'round ta see ta yer needs," he remarked, stroking her hair before he rose back up. "Ya rest good, ya need all yer health," he said affectionately as he tied his pants up tight.

"Thanks, Jremy," she replied softly, repositioning herself in the scratchy bed. "Have a good day at work."

She'd noticed, of course, how vague he'd been. How vague he always was. She'd never questioned it, and she knew it had almost as much to do with the belief that he'd abandoned her as it did with the fact that she'd given up.

Why had she let herself give up?

Why hadn't she spent this time gaining her strength, working her arms, getting used to these dead limbs and finding a way out?

She'd been so tired, and she dearly wanted a break from the horrors of her life, but now she seethed at her apathy and swore she was going to do something about it.

He wasn't gone long before the big heaping bowl of break-fast stew was brought to her by the grinning Rufus. He came in quiet, but grinned at her. "Here ya go," he offered softly. "Da' said ya wan' sleep some more so I'll leave ya be," he said with a bright, cheerful expression. He at least didn't seem to hide things from her. Perhaps because he was too young to know better. Or was it all a ruse?

She hated being suspicious of him, but it was hard to deny that he was the tipping point that brought her over. She was tired of fighting, and he was so adorable. She wanted to give him the world, if only because it had been denied for her for so long.

"Thanks, Rufus," she replied softly, her breathing a bit shallow.

He shuffled off quickly, undoubtedly under orders from his father not to bother her while she planned to sleep again.

She cleared her throat, though, and her blue gaze fell upon him. What could she say that could be sufficiently probing but not suspicious?

"Rufus, have you ever had a sister?"

He froze near the exit and turned to look at her with wide eyes. He paused a moment but nodded, "Ya, 'course I do."

Was the present tense of his response intentional?

She smiled, but her fingers trembled beneath the blanket, "Will you tell me about her? You know I love you and your father, but I've not seen another woman in so long."

His big round eyes fell, and she could instantly read the reluctance upon his face. "I shouldn't say," he responded a bit glumly. "I ain't seen 'er in… ages," he confessed, and she could tell how disappointed he was with that. He missed his sister.

"I'll keep it my little secret, Rufus. I promise." She hoped her desperation wasn't visible, her absolute need to know more.

He shuffled in near to her, albeit with a reluctant glance back towards the thick hide covered doorway. Sitting upon the edge of her bed, near her feet he said, "We used ta run an' play all the time," he said in fond remembrance. "She was real funny, and we were the best a friends," he reminisced, his feelings obviously conflicted.

Thia smiled, reaching out and taking his hands. She remembered the shy girl that had led them here, even though she'd not thought of her in some time. "It'd be hard to not be best friends with you, Rufus."

The lively boy gave her a bright smile and squeezed her hands back. "Ya wanna play some games?" he asked enthusiastically, and it made her think that perhaps the reason he was so drawn to her was that he her femininity reminded him of his now absent best friend.

"Well, sure. Just don't let your pa know or he might think you were a bother."

He ran off excitedly, returning before long with some of his underworld knick knacks that he fashioned into games. One of which was like a crude form of cribbage, with a stone slab etched with markers that you could slip the pins into.

Rufus was positively overjoyed to play with her, shuffling the extremely worn deck of cards that seemed to be missing a few in addition to the dog eared and clipped status of many in the deck. "I'm s'glad yer with us," he chimed, dealing them up. "I wish't yer legs didn' have ta be like that though," he said sympathetically.

"Me too. Is that what happened to your sister?" The question slipped from her mouth before she could stop it or phrase it more innocuously, and she gulped in air as if to swallow the words back.

Rufus nodded to her but then froze, probably realizing just how foolish it was for him to admit that. He glanced up at her then looked back down, finishing dealing up the cards. "I dun wan' get in trouble," he muttered quietly.

"You're not going to," she said and softly brushed his hair with her fingertips. "I'm just curious. Like you. Remember, I told you about what it's like up above, right?"

He nodded his head sheepishly to her, emboldened just a bit by her reassurances. "Wish I cou' see yer place up 'bove," he changed the subject softly, giving a light smile. "I bet ya were free ta run about much as ya like," he said, his imagination starting to get working. "Nobody ta tell ya what ta do or no'."

She laughed, leaning back on her forearm. "Well, not exactly, but there were definitely a lot more safe places to go. Am I the first one you've met from up there?"

Her mind was churning, and she knew she had to keep him talking. Obviously they were supposed to keep these things secret, and the thought of all these women, all over the town, suffering from the same fate as her made her stomach churn.

It took him a moment to respond, "I ain' s'posed ta see the women from up 'bove." He was trying so hard not to let loose a personal secret of his, she could tell, but his very refusal confirmed it for her. There were others from above.

"You're allowed to see me though, right? So why not the others?"

Rufus screwed up his lips and hung his head low as he looked aside at the back wall. "Yer special," he said simply, shrugging his slender shoulders, playing a card that won him a very generous amount of points in the lead of her.

She was too distracted to concentrate on the game, though she still groaned in good humour. "Well... thank you, Rufus. You're pretty special too. Though I don't know what I did that was so special."

"Da' likes ya," he said without hesitation. "But I like ya too," he added on with a warm smile as the game continued on hopelessly in his favour. "Yer real nice an' pretty. The others ain't real happy t'be here," he remarked glumly, lowering his face again to stare at his cards.

If she qualified as happy to be here…

She didn't want to push, and yet at the same time, she was desperate to know more. How did they get in? Where did they stumble in from and could she leave through the same way?

Her pulse raced and she played in silence for a few more turns before speaking quietly, "Are you happy to be here?"

He didn't give a quick response to that one, his brow furrowed and he had to mull it over, she could tell. "I'm happier now that yer here," he said to her affectionately. Which of course translated as 'no'.

He'd had his sister and best friend taken from him it seemed, and he quite often got little food at the family gatherings. Why would he be happy?

"Did you want my breakfast, Rufus? I'm not very hungry today," she said, still holding that maternal tone for him. He seemed so honest, and just as much a prisoner in this place as she was, even if he could walk.

He perked up a little for just a moment, but then deflated. "Da' said he'd beat me real hard if I ate a bite a yer food," he responded glumly. "Says I can't even lick the bowl when yer done," he tacked on with a sigh as he played another impressive hand.

Anger flooded through her but she thought she understood. She hoped she didn't.

"Is... is the food why I can't walk, Rufus?"

He lifted his head and looked to her, but she didn't get her answer from him in words or in his expression. He looked a bit confused by the question... but also ponderous. Was he thinking the same thing as she was? He was but a boy, but he wasn't dumb. For the lack of education and the circumstances, he was perhaps even clever.

His gaze trailed to the still steaming bowl and he quietly stared at it, wordlessly.

"I have to admit, Rufus. You're too good at this game for me," she said somberly, for she knew she had to find some way to stop eating. She didn't want to get Rufus in trouble by getting him to help her, but there were so few options. Rufus, for his part, seemed to be picking up on the same line of thought.

His eyes darted back to her and he blinked, his mind shifting back to the game. Then failing. She could see his Adam's apple swell. "D'ya think da's poisonin' ya?" he asked in a hushed, morose tone, the game all but forgotten.

"I think he wants to keep me here, and doesn't trust I'd stay if I could walk."

Thia watched as his eyes dipped in a troubled expression at that thought. Though then they flickered towards the back wall once more. What she thought was just an idle stare into the distance started to seem like something of greater significance.

She turned her gaze. "What's back there, Rufus?" She didn't have the faintest idea, but something... hope... swelled in her. Did he know more than he was letting on?

He looked embarrassed at being caught so easily. "I ain't s'posed ta say," he repeated nervously. It was obvious the young boy wanted to help her, yet he was reaching his limits. As much as he liked her and wanted to help, he was anxious. Afraid. Very afraid.

He got up, leaving his cards and playing board. "I shou' go," he said quickly.

If he shouldn't say, then it was a way out. An escape.

It had to be.

She nodded at him as he gathered his things. "Thanks for the game, Rufus."

The poor boy scurried off hurriedly, leaving behind those precious game pieces and abandoning her in the room.

She knew none of the other men of the household would bother her; they never did. For all his feigned niceness towards her, they were all terrified of Jremy. Of that she was certain.

It should have clicked in her mind sooner what that meant, but she had so much to grapple with that she'd pushed it from her thoughts.

Without the use of her legs it was a bit of a struggle, but it hadn't been so long since she was scrambling through the underworld, and her arms were still strong enough to do the trick. She pulled herself along, off of the bed and across the floor.

At the back wall hung a great pelt of some horrible creature she cared not to know better.

Thia's legs snaked lifelessly behind her across the floor as she clawed her way nearer, trying to muffle the sound of her grunting as she neared the wall. She grasped the furry hide of the creature and pulled it back.

Behind it she saw nothing out of the ordinary, just more of the stone wall, that was, until she drew it back far enough. There at the center was an opening in the stone, covered up by some strange material like corkboard though most likely fungal. She'd seen the material used in some manners before, and when she pushed it, it gave way and showed a smooth tunnel beyond that gently sloped down.

Crawling her way to it, she could see that rather than going up as she might have hoped, it went down and down into darkness so she couldn't see where it ultimately led.

So what will it be, Thia, she silently asked herself. *A life with a man who cripples you without remorse and tells you it's for your own good? Or the great unknown.*

She couldn't believe it.

She almost smiled as she felt the rush for freedom flood her system once more, pushing her onwards. She only had to find a safe place, outside of Jremy's clutches. Just enough to restore her legs, and then she would be fine. She remembered what he'd said, about the moving tunnels. Once she passed though, she'd never find them again, and she felt a pang of sorrow for all the people she was abandoning and couldn't help.

Thia replaced the spongy board behind her and began her wriggling descent down the tunnel. It was slow going, but the downward incline helped her. She realized quickly that the reason she couldn't see far was that it wound around. Though as she went further, she could hear faint sounds in the distance.

The tunnel served as an echo chamber, then, but whatever the source, it was either very muffled or exceedingly far away.

Instead of frightening her off her daring course, Thia pushed ahead faster, scraping her elbows and forearms upon the stones surface as she pushed down.

She was used to blind descents into the dark unknown, though this time it couldn't possibly end up as bad as the trip that brought her to the underworld itself.

The sounds grew a little louder as she got near, like the sounds of people muffled through a wall. She saw the reason why that was when she reached the end of the tunnel, and found another spongy wall in her way.

Pressing her ear to it she could hear on the other side the

source of the muffled noises. It was so hard to make out anything clearly, but she could tell they were people. Women in fact. The voices feminine, so stark and clear after seemingly endless days with only male company.

Was... was this just a service tunnel of some sorts? Her brow furrowed, but it was the only path. Her only options were to turn back into the arms of her captor, wait here for him to find her missing, or push on ahead.

There was only one thing Thia could rationally do at the point, and she began pushing away the strange wall.

She exercised a surgeon's precision as she slipped it out of place, though on the other side another thick hide kept it from falling out of her grasp entirely. She was able to tug it back in and rest it against the tunnel wall.

Except... the sounds that greeted her were among the most unwelcome she had heard in the whole of the dismal dark below.

The sobs and moans of women, young and old greeted her. Such pitiable noises that drifted upwards. A few women whispering to each other, the faint hisses of the indecipherable words carrying up to her. For as she looked out she could see that she was on some raised area that overlooked the horrible series of cells below.

Cells, because she could think of nothing else to call them

There were half a dozen women and girls, each in their own little three-walled section. There was no door barring them in, but she knew just by looking that none of them would be leaving their prison.

Two of them had legs so atrophied and frail they were little more than thin bones. Worse still were the three oldest women. Two had no legs at all and moaned in pain, while the last was bereft of all limbs, staring lifelessly up at the ceiling.

Thia didn't realize she was shaking in anger until she felt her hands almost give way. Tears burned her eyes and never had she been filled with so much hate.

This wasn't done by monsters, hellish fiends warped by this dark pit.

This was done by men just as sane as she.

And the leader had claimed her as his own.

As she trembled with rage, the sound of footsteps filtered up from below. It was lucky that her position shielded her from easy view below, because her ears had been so ringing with anger that she'd not heard those men until they were already within sight of her.

Thia recognized them as the older sons of Jremy, sporting scowls as they approached one of the legless women. She was moaning the loudest, writhing in agony. Judging by the red stains soaking the bandages, she'd only lost her legs to them recently.

Following their fast style of speaking through the echoing chamber was hard, but she made it out. "Tell us where she is," said one of them as he knelt down beside her, stroking her dark hair. "C'mon ma," he pleaded, though the other son stepped up and kicked her.

"Ya know we can't afford ta lose a girly," the other brother said harshly. "Ain't tha many ta go around."

They weren't talking about her. It was far too soon. So who? The girl that had first led her to this place?

Her ears strained as she held her breath, trying to calm her rage and focus her attention on their dialect.

The woman said nothing, but broke into sobs at the boy's abuse.

"C'mon ma," persisted the one stroking her hair, not that he was really any better. They were all psychotic. Sick. He kissed at her face, though it did not comfort her, nor Thia. "Jus' tell us. She shoul' be safe here wit' the fam'ly. So she don' get e't up by them freaks."

"Ain't no use," insisted the other before prodding her bloody stump where her leg used to be, making her wail in pain.

"I ain't givin' her up ta you animals!" she shrieked between her sobs of pain and anguish.

Rufus' sister? Is that who they were looking for?

If that really was the boy's mother...

Was she the same girl she'd followed?

Thia's head swirled with trying to put together the pieces while listening to the man interrogate the poor woman.

It was as if a light went on in her head, though it did nothing to calm her nerves. If this was what happened to women... why wouldn't this happen to her? If she went back to Jremy's home, how long would it take before he relegated her to this prison, this torture?

As Thia thought the predicament over, a horrifying sight occurred beneath her. The two sons began to strip away their trousers as they loomed over the sobbing woman, her cries ringing out.

She couldn't watch. Couldn't be witness to what was happening below her. For of all the horrors of the underworld, to witness the acts of villainy people visited upon each other turned her stomach most of all.

She had to back away, to escape such darkness. She wished, for a moment, to have never come at all. To remain ignorant to the horror and despair of the other women, to never have known how much worse things could get.

But Thia couldn't abandon them.

Still, she had to return to her room before Jremy realized she was missing.

Climbing back to her own prison chambers was much harder than it had been going down. Though she returned to the sight of the empty room, the bowl of now cooled stew awaiting her and the bed covered in old, beaten playing cards.

It occurred to her that if Jremy was poisoning her with the

breakfast meal that he would not allow it to go uneaten and left there, and her new hideaway offered her a convenient place to dump it. Surely the cracks and oddly perforated holes in the rock would absorb it before it ran all the way down, but it was incredibly hard to dump it in.

She did it slowly, one spoonful at a time so as not to allow it to cascade down to the other woman's prison.

It would be a mess next time she had to go down, but there weren't many other options in her small room. She fixed the wall and pulled herself back into her bed. She didn't know how long she could get away with not eating, but it gave those women down there the best chance they had if she was fit.

❦ 42 ❧

T hia worked her arms in preparation for her escape. She needed to be strong enough to get out once the time came, and she did everything she could to practice lifting her body with her slender arms.

Though of course without food, it would all be for naught.

When time came for supper—they only ate two meals a day typically, though food was brought to her more often, as she liked—Rufus entered her chambers, edgy and nervous. He clutched her meal in trembling hands as he murmured, "I thought ya might like ta eat in here."

The young boy brought her the meal to the side of her bed, looking at her anxiously.

She reached out and stroked his hair, giving him a soft smile. "That's very thoughtful, Rufus. How was the rest of your day? Why don't you come up here and tell me about it?"

The thought of what his brothers were doing, what his father must have been doing, turned her stomach and she wanted to shield him from that. To protect his innocence and let him grow into a full human being and not some horrendous, monstrous person that would abuse women who couldn't even run away.

He cozied up to her a little and gave her a smile, despite looking troubled. He cast a glance towards the door then leaned in to her, murmuring quietly. "I watched 'em make th'food. I didn't see 'em put nothin' in there. Least ways, nothin' they didn't put in the rest o' the food," he explained to her, his round eyes hopeful if still bothered.

She slumped back and looked at the stew thoughtfully, stirring it with the spoon as she considered it.

Could she trust him?

Her heart broke that she even had to consider it, and held him a bit more protectively as if to ward him from her own dark thoughts. "Thank you for looking out for me, Rufus."

The waifish boy wrapped his thin arm around her and hugged her back tightly. He had a certain fondness for her, it was certain, and he didn't seem to know the depths of what was happening at all.

His eyes fell upon her empty bowl from the morning and he pulled back. "Ya e't the breakfast?!" he said more than asked, sounding startled.

She kissed his forehead lightly and nodded. "It's hard not to eat, even when you don't want to." She hated lying to him, but it was to protect him.

Thia cringed at the thought. Isn't that what the men were doing for the women, in their mind? Lying and 'protecting' them? A shiver ran down her spine and she felt her stomach clench with a profound indignation.

His expression sank low, and he looked quite sad to her. "Hopefully we was wrong," he said as he bent over and picked up the empty bowl, cradling it in his lap. "But from now on I'll give a watch an' see if I can tell when they does somethin' dif'rent with yers," he said with an edge of determination to his voice.

She stroked his hair down to the back of his neck, enjoying the feel of the human contact. He was so sweet.

"Thanks, Rufus. Did your dad say anything?"

He shook his head, "He ain't been 'round t'day." At the mention of his father he twisted the empty bowl in his hands anxiously. "Though he's usually back b'fore bed time. So he should be 'round any time now," he explained.

"Well I'm feeling much better after your visit. What did you do the rest of the day?"

Rufus gave a weak shrug of his slender shoulders. "I took a look about. See if I could find out if they was poisonin' ya, and…" he hesitated, not wanting to say it. Though without further prodding he murmured to her softly, "I tried ta see if I could find where was they keep Sharn." He hung his head sadly, batting his long lashes and looking to her with glossy eyes, "M'sis."

Sharn? Was an odd name for a girl, but Thia figured it was probably a bastardization of Sharon.

"How old is she?" Thia asked, not even certain if they could keep track of things like that down here.

He furrowed his brow a little and scratched at his shaggy head of hair. "'Bout th'same as me," he said. Tracking the years didn't seem to be a big deal with them all in general, let alone the young boy. "We was always together. Best a friends," he said, growing sadder as he spoke.

"Was she the girl I saw when I first showed up here? With the brown hair?"

Rufus' eyes lit up and he stared at her agape. "Y'saw her?!" he asked, grasping onto her arms tightly. "Where to?!" he insisted, shaking her a little in his overpowering concern for his sister.

"I only saw her when I first arrived. She was wandering around the tunnels with the…" she couldn't remember what they called them. "The whip-legs," she finally recalled. "I didn't get to talk with her, but she was nearby."

Rufus deflated before her very eyes, sinking back into melancholy. "They said she was kep' safe here..." he said, and she realized it wasn't sadness but worry that made him sink in upon himself. "So ya sayin' she's out there by her lonesome?" he asked, tears suddenly welling up in his eyes.

What Thia wanted to say was that she was safer out there, but how could a child understand the depths of human pain and suffering? Especially at the hands of his own family?

How could he understand why Sharn would rather run than stay here?

She looked down at her bowl of cooling stew and inhaled deeply. "I think she's safe, Rufus. She's cautious. I'm sure she's fine."

That didn't calm him down.

Rufus stood up, balled his fists in frustration. "I gotta go out there an' find her!" he declared with that same determination he'd had for protecting her food, but amplified a thousand fold. "She can't be lef' to her own! She'll get e't or... or... worse!" he said, pacing the floor beside the bed in a near panic.

She reached out and grabbed for his hand, her eyes wide with fear and beginning to water. "Please, Rufus," she hissed. "You can't do that. You can't bring her back here."

He froze in his tracks and stared at her in disbelief. "Wha' ya mean?" he said, the wind out of his sails and the words nearly dumbfounded.

Would telling him the truth be too much for him to handle? Would knowing what was going on make him freak out? Would it make him think that his brothers and father must be doing what they do for a very good reason? How could a young boy like him deal with the reality of the situation and keep his psyche intact? He needed to know, this collective passivity couldn't be allowed to breed, but still...

"Do you trust me?" Thia asked, her pale face so dire. She had let the anger and hate for the men well up within her, give her strength, but now she had to hold it back. To protect him.

He looked her over, and she could see his fondness for her warring with his concern for his sister. "I ain't gonna give up on 'er," he said in a tone of finality, and she knew that his concern for Sharn was greater than all else.

"Don't give up on her. Trust in her," she pleaded softly. She was going to ask how long she had been gone, but she didn't even know how long she had been here. "Rufus, how long before I got here did she disappear?"

"Like a coupla days!" he said; he was impatient. He looked almost ready to rush off and find her then and there. "They said she had ta go inta special hidin' with th'other women! To keep 'er from gettin' taken away an' e't," he said, the sting of betrayal mixed with his urgent need to go after his sister.

"Honey..." She was getting choked up, her heart in her throat as she beckoned him closer. "Rufus, please listen to me. Listen very closely. We're a very, very far way aways from those beasts. She'll be safe, I promise."

It wasn't entirely true, but if she told him about the other women, he might let it slip that she knew more than she should.

He shook off her grasp and stepped away. "I ain't givin' up on her!" he repeated his chant, this time too loudly, risking being overheard. The doors were but flaps of hide, after all. "I'm gonna go out an' find her, an' if it means I gotta leave on m'own an' never come back I don't even care!"

Tears were streaming from her eyes. What had she done? She cursed herself, over and over again as she leaned towards him, almost spilling her stew onto the floor. "Rufus! If they find her, they're going to make her like me!"

He backed away out of her grasp and looked her over with a hard gaze. "I'll tell her what's what, then, an' if she don't wanna come back fer that, then I'll stay out there an' live with 'er!" He was adamant, there would be no convincing him of otherwise, she realized.

The sound of footsteps approached, and Thia knew her time was nearly at an end before they were caught talking about something they shouldn't.

She quickly swiped a hand under her eyes to wipe away the tears and her breath hitched. All she could manage out was a weak, "Please. Don't."

Of course it was Jremy who pushed back the hide covering the doorway, a look of concern on his face before he saw the look of upset on Thia's face. The towering man turned a hard look to Rufus, and grabbed for him, his big, meaty hand clutching onto the frail boys shoulder as he tugged him close and shook him.

"What'd ya do ta upset her?!" He demanded angrily as the young boy winced from the pain.

"I'm sorry da'!" he cried out in response habitually, sobbing from pain after his father smacked him across the face.

"Stop! He didn't do anything!" she cried out, thinking quickly. "I had a nightmare of the Whip-legs from the cave, and Rufus was just trying to cheer me up. I was only frightened."

Jremy heard her and froze, ceasing his shaking of the boy as he looked to Thia. "That true?" he asked her softly as his son sobbed from the pain and worry.

"Yes, I haven't had a dream like that since... well, for a while I guess. It just... I had nearly forgotten about all the terrible things out there, and I was crying when I woke up." She peppered in a few sniffles and hoped she was convincing, for she knew the stakes to be high - for the both of them - if she was caught lying.

The large brute stared at her a while, blinking, until at last he looked embarrassed. Turning his attention to Rufus he guided the boy to the door, releasing him just in time for her to catch sight of the red mark upon the boy's face.

"Git 'im to bed," Jremy said to one of the older sons outside, undoubtedly, before letting the hide door drop and turning back to her. The angry man was a little red faced still from his outburst, but calming down as he approached the bed. "I'm real sorry about that," he said apologetically, his voice resuming its usual tone. "I jes' don't want 'im upsettin' ya. Yer a real important part a this fam'ly now," he explained as he sat down on the edge of the bed beside her.

"Rufus is sweet," Thia said in a shaky but sincere voice. It was all she could do to hide her anger at conversing with this monster." I don't think he'd ever do anything to hurt anyone."

It was with great effort that she tried to retain her slow tone, even around these quick speaking people. She'd seen what had happened to Tar'kul's vocabulary as he was unable to practice language, and she didn't want the same thing to happen to her.

"Ya care for 'im, don't ya?" he said, a faint little smile showing on his broad face as he reached out to take her hands in his. "M'boys are real fond a you too, all a 'em," he said, rubbing his rough fingers over her hand. "We ain't had such a special presence wit' us in so long. Maybe never," he said, that charm coming back to him so easily, the man oblivious to how she knew the reality of the situation.

"I do. He takes good care of me when you're not around. Always makes sure I get my food on time, plays games with me. He's a good child," she stressed, and she believed it wholly. Adjusting herself back in the bed, she took a few longer breaths, brushing the last of her tears away even as she worried about what Rufus was going to do.

What would happen to him if he took that same dive into the unknown that brought her here.

Jremy reached up, that big, powerful hand of his stroking through her blonde hair in a tender sort of gesture, though it was hard to see it as anything of the sort since her discovery. His eyes trailed down to her bowls of food, seeing the one empty one and the one full. "Still hot an' everythin' when he gets it to you?" he asked, turning his steely eyes back upon her with that faux-consideration. "Don't sneak none a yer food? It's always big an' heapin' when it gets here?"

She forced a laugh that sounded tight and constrained, as her hand rubbed over her stomach, "I'm bigger than I've ever been!"

Her captor gave a big smile and stroked his hand over her hair to the back of her head before leaning in and kissing her forehead. His voice was lower, a little gravelly, "It's good. Ya look healthy. An' ya need ta be so ya can be strong an' walk again someday." He smiled at her warmly, but she knew the truth. It took on such a dark meaning, that smile of his. "An' before long ya will be havin' a child a yer own inside ya," he said, his other hand reaching out to touch her stomach as he leaned in, head tilted as he went to kiss her lips.

The thought made her gag and she had to fight back the flood of tears. She didn't want to give birth to this wretch's spawn. She didn't want to contribute to this world, to this sick and backwards community, filled with so much horror.

And yet she forced herself to smile a soft smile, her mind racing.

Amidst her broiling thoughts, an unexpected notion surfaced while she stared into his eyes.

If he'd lied about what had happened to her legs, had he lied about Tar'kul's death?

The thought redoubled her pain, because she knew that if they treated humans so horrifically, they'd never let him live.

At least...

She forced the thought from her mind.

Thia suffered through his kiss, but as he pulled back the blanket and climbed atop the bed closer towards her, it got harder and harder to stomach. The way his powerful hands that had inflicted so much suffering on others rubbed over her body, feeling out her flesh through her dress, his intent so clear and obvious as his trousers tended with a bulge.

Yet she knew she wouldn't resist, wouldn't rouse his suspicions that she knew what he really did to his last 'wife'. What he did to his children, both male and female.

What monsters he's made of the boys, what tragedy he'd forced upon the girls.

So she pushed aside the bowl of food along with her repulsion and closed her eyes. She forced herself to remember, to think back on the world above. About Edain, and his sweet, kind eyes. About her dream, how he touched her, and instead of the rough and possessive hands, she fantasized about the soft, pampered and curious touches of her girlhood crush.

After all that had happened with Tar'kul, those memories were now changed. The monstrous man infiltrating her fond memories as that brute Jremy pushed down his soiled trousers and mounted her.

He hoisted her legs, the very same ones he had made so lifeless, and moved them out of the way as he positioned his now repellant girth at her cunny. His lips smacking noisily as he rubbed himself against her, feeling her breasts as he grunted softly. "Missed ya real bad t'day," he muttered to her as he tried to work her loins into a heat by merely grinding the tip of his organ atop her slit.

It wouldn't work. It hadn't before, and it certainly wouldn't now that she knew what was happening every day. She knew it would hurt and she tried to plead that it be over quickly, that he find his sick pleasure and leave her be for the evening.

Her breath quickened, her anxiety and emotions broiling within her.

The low, gravelly grunts as he forced that thick organ into her punctuated the stillness of the cave-home's air. His member painfully splitting her open as he rocked his hips, bent upon his own satisfaction between her two paralyzed legs.

That broad, muscled chest of his just another reminder of how much strength her captor had in him to use against her.

"You're so pretty," he growled as he forced her womanhood to respond to his intrusions.

She wished he wouldn't speak. That he wouldn't keep taking her back to this place, stealing her away from her tainted fantasies.

Down in this little hole it was harder to remember that terror surrounded her from all sides. This felt somehow more real. She was dealing with humans, with real men, not the strange and foreign beasts of the underworld.

She'd almost forgotten the rotting plant people, the half dead human...

Her dreams of the Lieutenant and his Sergeant.

She'd wondered, many weeks ago, if they had been Tar'kul's dreams, like the ones beneath the sun were hers, and it filled her with such sorrow. And now, she longed for them again, to see what he'd gone through and understand him better. Her demonic looking friend.

Those thoughts got her through the torture of the moment, though his shuddering, noisy climax reminded her once more of the unpleasantness of the situation. Reminded her of the unavoidable risk she was forced to take with him.

His lips kissed upon hers once more and he pulled from her, sounding so smugly satisfied. "Glad we got this moment," he remarked, tugging his trousers up over his filthy groin. All the underworld grime suddenly seeming so much more noticeable to Thia. "Seein' as I gotta go back out there. See to the security in the tunnels 'round here."

That was odd. In all her time there he'd not had to be away from her so much tending to such matters.

"Oh?" she asked groggily, as if just waking up, her breath ragged and throat raw. "Are you on a rotation or something?"

It was the kindest way she could think of to probe him further.

He bent down and kissed her forehead again, smiling at her warmly while he tied up his pants. "Not really a rotation for th' chief," he said with a touch of pride before grabbing her now cooled bowl of food and offering it to her. "I'll have the boys heat it up for ya, love. Gotta stay strong an' healthy fer the babies ta come."

"Thank you," she said kindly, but her mind was reeling.

Did Rufus' mother tell the boys where the sister was?

"Will you be back at all tonight?"

He gave her a touched smile, as if her question were meant in as some sign of her missing him. "Dunno. Prob'ly not, but we'll see." He kissed her once more on the forehead. "I'll do m'best to git back fer ya. But don't be upset wit' me if I can't, please hun?"

"Promise. I know you wouldn't leave unless it was important," she said, still trying to ferret out a hint of the truth.

"'Course," he nodded to her as he walked towards the door, bowl in hand. "I'm out there makin' sure yer safe, an' ain't gotta be concerned for the boogadies that wander the world," he said with a confident smile. "So rest up tight. Ya got yer part ta play too."

With that he left her, though it wasn't long before one of the elder sons came with her food. A grin on his face as he offered her the steaming bowl. That expression having such a darker meaning as he recognized him as the one who'd violated his own mother.

"Ya need someone ta keep ya warm tanight?" he asked her brazenly. "I know da' can't be doin' it… but it's my turn ta stay behind fer now. Look after the homestead."

The bile in her throat nearly choked her as she took the stew. "Ah, he said he'd be trying to hurry home."

Please no. Please just go, she pleaded with him silently. Why was this happening to her? How did this group of people come to behave like this?

He hesitated, his beady eyes roaming over her for a moment before he nodded. "If'n ya change yer mind, I'll be outside. Call if ya need anythin'," he said to her, staring at her awkwardly up until the last moment the hide flap shut.

She had power. Some measure of power that those women down the tunnel didn't, and the thought nearly made her laugh. She was a captive and thought herself to wield more power than others simply because Jremy had claimed her as his own prize, something that he had earned and deserved and would defend.

It was sick.

Thia waited in her bed for what felt like a long time, listening to the 'manor' settle and when she thought it was at last safe, she shifted herself towards the floor and reached beneath her mattress, removing that long hidden knife she'd taken when she first met Jremy's family, and placing it against her thigh.

Something then gave her a moment's hope. Though her legs still refused motion… they began to tingle. Sensation returning to them in the form of annoying little pinprick sensations that travelled from her thighs, weakening towards her knees, like the blood rush one got after sleeping on a limb the wrong way.

Was the poison they had been feeding her wearing off already? Before the passing of even a whole day?

Why hadn't she realized sooner? Why had she hoped so hard that humans living in this horrid place could still be kind and decent to one another? Why did she believe that there could be some type of solidarity between them?

Tears stung her eyes as she crawled towards the hidden escape, pushing herself in and down over the disgusting bits of discarded lunch. The descent was easier, but the strange pinprick sensations were distracting her. Exciting her.

When Thia arrived down at the horrible dungeon, she heard no sounds but for the moans and laments of the women.

Looking down from that high entrance above, she saw them. Pathetic sights all, with missing or shrivelled limbs. None of them looked able to escape, even if they were given help.

Right there beneath her was the poor mother, her limbs amputated, staring vacantly at the wall to her right.

She hated the idea of giving them hope, of promising things that she couldn't deliver. But still her heart bled for them, and she cautiously pushed away the spongy fungus and part of the tarp.

The cavern area was large, and the clearing of her throat went unnoticed by them. Her only chance was to climb down, and her stomach growled as she pushed herself forward, her arms aching and her legs prickling with new sensations.

Down the ramp she went until she came to their level. The mother's was the second 'cell' from her, and she went unnoticed by the other slumbering woman as she crawled by before coming to the poor mother, staring off in her silent agony. It was an exhausting journey with only her arms to propel her forward, but she made it there beside the woman, the smells of blood, sex and excrement ripe in the air.

This time Thia got her attention, and those nearly vacant eyes turned towards her. Confusion filled the woman's gaze as she muttered weakly, "Who're ya?" Her words were slow from weakness.

"No one can know I was here," Thia said, her voice murmured and quick. "I want to help you, but they've put something in my food. I can't walk. I don't know how long I've been here even." Now that Thia was finally here, she barely knew what to say. "Please, I saw what they've been doing to you, tell me how I can help."

The woman stared at her blankly, a tumult of confusion and hopelessness upon her face. "They put th'pollen in the stew. Makes yer legs give out…" she said in her weak voice. "I figured that out too… didn't help me in th'end though." There was no humour at that remark. She simply lay there, the truth of the matter her existence.

Thia's eyes fell, defeat drooping her shoulders as she looked at the other woman. She wanted to hug her, to tell her it would all be okay, but instead the tears she'd been holding in for so long started to fall. "There has to be a way."

The mother's eyes returned to her. "Out? There's a way out," she said with finality. "S'only a question if'n ya can stay out. Ain't nowhere out there fit ta survive... an' if ya stay close... they'll only bring ya back. An' they'll make ya pay."

Thia's hand went to the woman's shoulder, squeezing it, as if trying to comfort her through pain that even Thia could scarcely imagine. It was one thing for her to be betrayed by these people, but this was her family!

"I've lived out there. I can do it again," she insisted eagerly.

That sparked a remarkable change. The woman's eyes betrayed some hint of hope as she stared hard at Thia. "Ya lived out there?" she asked in some disbelief. "Ya mean ya weren't taken from up above?"

It gave her pause, then she shook her head. "I've been down here for... months. Out there. I've been chased by everything, almost killed by everything, but I lived. I had a friend, he... They called him a demon when we arrived, but he used to be a man. We saw a girl. I think you know who I'm talking about. We came here to find her, and they took us in. But my friend tried to warn me, to protect me against the men here, and I was knocked unconscious. They told me he had died in the struggle, and I have been here ever since, unable to walk."

Thia's story seemed too much for the woman to take all in, but one thing she did hang upon was, "Girl? Ya saw my..." Her eyes welled up with tears forming, but through some miraculously undepleted well of willpower she forced back her sobs. "If'n I tell ya how I got out... will ya take care o' m'Sharn? Git 'er away from 'ere an' never come back? Teach 'er 'ow ta live out there?"

"Yes," she hissed eagerly. "Her *and* Rufus, he's talking about going after her. Please, I don't know what to tell him. He wants to find and protect his sister so bad, and I'm afraid he's going to do something stupid before I regain my legs."

The torn woman hesitated, thinking. "You'll need yer legs ta git out. Ain't no crawlin' yer way outta here," she said firmly. "Drink lotsa water. Git 'em ta bring ya as much as ya kin, an' you should be able ta in less'n a day maybe. An' once ya did that ya go – "

The sound of a footsteps approaching could be heard from some tunnel around the corner. Heavy footsteps. And the mother's eyes trembled and went wide with alarm as they bored into Thia, nothing able to be said. Not even a gesture to warn her to be quiet.

Pity, regret, and fear all battled within Thia. If she got caught down here, she'd be punished. She'd be forced to live like this poor, destroyed woman.

Thia's blue eyes glanced around, searching for escape, but found nothing. All she could do was scurry into the corner, trying to make herself as small as possible and hope beyond reason she wouldn't be seen.

She didn't know who it was, but she could only imagine that it was Jremy. Was this what he was doing on his night patrolling? Torturing other women?

She tried to drag herself as quickly as possible, become more compact, and squeeze into the dark recesses of the cell.

In that moment of panic she felt her legs respond to her, just a faint twitch but it was more than she'd felt in days. She pulled her legs in against the wall with her, but those footsteps grew closer. Closer.

Scuffing upon the stone floor they neared the cell she was in until… they blessedly stopped. Though she had no idea for how long.

"'ey there girly," came the voice, and she recognized it as the older son that had brought her food not long before. He stepped into the neighbouring cell, and Thia could hear the woman there stir awake.

"Oh fuck, John, no," came the pathetic whimper of the poor woman therein, much younger than the mother that stared at Thia in quiet concern. "No' ag'in."

"Aw c'mon, dun' be like that," he said, more sounds of feet scuffing. "I was missin' ya. All alone. Don't like it none that da' ordered ya put down here wit' the rest."

She couldn't listen to this, but there were no other options. No other way but than to stay still and endure.

Could she have spared this woman by accepting that man into her own bed, asked him to keep her company for the night? The thought nearly broke her, the responsibility for these battered women nearly driving her mad. She had more strength than them, more opportunities, even if she was still caged.

As the conversation in the cell next to her grew increasingly disconcerting, she noticed the mother gesturing her towards her with her chin.

Thia was reluctant to move, but she did so, slowly getting closer.

The older woman murmured secretively, "Th'way out is back where he come from. Go. Go now. Ya ain't got yer legs back yet, but… find th'strength in ya ta git out if ya got it. Jes' go an' rescue me girl," she pleaded, eyes watery. "There's a room halfway down th'tunnel. The escape I used is up 'bove. Ya need ta reach up… dunno if ya kin do it without yer legs, but… try. Sneak past 'im now. It's m'girls only chance."

The sounds of the grunts and groans from so close by was disgusting. The pathetic whimpering, those mewlings of dissatisfaction and pain the same sort that Thia had repressed not long ago.

That reminder was more than either her or Sharn's mother could take it seemed.

"Thank you," Thia whispered, her hand hesitating above the older woman's shoulder, knowing how much being touched was a curse down here more than a comfort. "Stay strong. I'll protect her for you, always."

With another fleeting look, Thia struggled to make it towards that exit as quickly as possible, favouring speed over silence with the grunts filling the chambers.

Thia couldn't look, not even to see if he saw her escape. What difference would it make? She couldn't run away if he caught her. All she could do was drag her body forward hurriedly as she saw that tunnel to here scape.

The noises of the other woman's violation provided a sick symphony to mark what might be the moment of her freedom.

The dull slaps of flesh on flesh, pounding one into the other, filled the air as Thia pulled herself along and into that hall.

She got through without being caught.

Though how long could she possibly have?

His torture of the other woman carried on as she pulled herself along that upward incline, becoming a fainter noise in the background until she reached that small chamber.

There was no sign of what the mother had referred to, and Thia's heart started to fall. It was just a strangely shaped natural cavern in the rock, it seemed, unlike the carved tunnel she had just crawled through.

Finally her vision led her to see it. It was hard to see in the uneven and erratic natural grooves of the cavern wall, but there it was. A little nook. It looked like no more than a foot deep, but it had to be a trick of the dim lighting, right? There was nothing else the older woman could've referred to.

The sight was a short lived victory, though. Very quickly

Thia realized that she could not hope to reach it without the use of her legs. It was beyond the meagre reach she had from the ground. Still, the dull smacks of flesh behind her pushed her onwards.

Crawling to the wall, she tried to pull herself up its surface. First sitting up, she then did her best to find some grooves in the wall to grab a hold of, to dig her fingers into and use as supports.

The closest thing she came to that were a few small indentations, though they failed to hold, and she slipped back down onto her ass with a grunt.

Onward again and another fall. It seemed hopeless. Utterly so.

Though the prickling tingles in her legs seemed to have grown lower still, she could feel sensations just below her knee. Through sheer force of willpower she tried to make her legs move. Her fists smacked her traitorous thighs, and she managed to make them twitch.

A single twitch.

That wasn't enough.

She could cry with frustration!

The sounds of violation from the chamber were growing lower. Was he finishing with the poor woman?

Thia's time was short. She turned back to the wall and tried to force herself up.

Using those shallow grooves she pulled herself up higher, supporting herself on one arm as she reached down with the other. She grasped a hold of her leg and tried to position it beneath her. Her thighs were of some help, she could tense them a little, hold them in place, even her knee maybe, but her feet were dead weight. They lay askew against the floor in a position that looked quite painful.

There was no time to worry about possible damage though; she had to get up to that crevice or else all was lost! She'd become like one of those horribly mutilated women back there. Used and abused as less than human.

Thia was able to grab a hold of that ledge, though almost instantly she slipped…

It seemed nearly like she'd lost her grip entirely, and she braced herself for the hard strike against the floor, but she clung on. Her desperation gave her strength she didn't think she had as the sounds of abuse in the other room came to an end.

She had moments more, that was it.

Using all the strength she could muster in her arms, she pulled herself upwards. Her muscles strained, they ached. They burned. She could barely do it, but she got herself up there. Pulling her upper body onto that ledge, with only her dead-weight legs dangling out behind her.

It was then she could hear the sound of footsteps over the pumping of her own blood in her veins. Impending doom approaching as she desperately tried to crawl forward, though the slipper, naturally worn grooves of the tunnel made it much harder than the other, man-made ones.

She had no idea just how close she was to being caught, only that she had to pull her legs up and retreat in deeper, as deep as she could get! Though when his footsteps began to recede again, his pace never changing… she knew she'd done it.

Escape.

Yet it didn't taste sweet, or like freedom at all. It felt like the start of a new struggle. Nonetheless, this was one Thia welcomed. She had to push herself forward, and find a place to hide for when Jremy realized she was missing. She had a clear objective now, a sense of purpose with those women locked up behind her. With the children she wanted to save from their hideous father's influence.

She'd not eaten all day, and after so long on such a rich— albeit poisoned—diet, her stomach rumbled in protest. The recessed tunnel she crawled along gave her no mercy. It was narrow, uneven, and tilted upwards with smooth, worn rock that she slipped upon every few minutes without constant diligence and exertion.

In all her time beneath the surface of the world in what could only be described accurately as hell, she had not felt claustrophobia so intensely as she did during that crawl. Stalactites dug into her back at times, and the air was so still and heavy.

How had that woman crawled through here with a child in tow? The poor girl must have been hysterical.

Her sobs must have echoed dreadfully in there, because Thia's eardrums seemed ready to burst from the simple sounds of her own grunts and breaths. It was all the tension of the moment, of course. The echoing noises of her own lips and throat mixed with an eerie underworld presence that chilled her to the bone.

It got so dark in there. So very dark. Thia's eyes could barely adjust to the darkness, seeing only faint traces of outlines, missing many a little stalactite or stalagmite that jabbed into her.

Yet she had to push on. Claw her way upwards towards freedom, as ill-prepared as she was.

Her dark vision was weakened from her time in the hut, but she knew she'd adjust. Eventually she'd be able to see through this pitch black world again, but it would take time. Time, of course, was a luxury she didn't have now, and she found herself thinking back to her first few days, in the intermingled safety and terror of Tar'kul's lair.

Never did she think she'd ever reminisce warmly upon that security, but she was beginning to understand why he'd kept to himself and secluded himself from the rest. Why he steeled his heart towards escape.

From out of the darkness she finally saw something ahead, some faint light that only got brighter as she went. Brighter and brighter until at last… through a crack she saw a trace of reflected sunlight. It was so bright it hurt her eyes!

Though quickly her enthusiasm was dampened when she realized that out through that crack, in between the calcified columns, she was looking at the shaft through which Jremy and his fellow miner-folk lived.

Pushing her face to the bar-like stalactites she could see the people down below, and her heart nearly stopped.

They couldn't see her, though. It was too bright down there, and she was surrounded in darkness. Still, she glanced around, keeping an eye out for Jremy or Rufus or any other familiar faces.

She waited a while to catch her breath and watch the goings on. It was uneventful at first, until she saw some of the pale miner-folk rush out of one home and race along. She didn't recognize them, but then some voices sounded and right beneath where she was more footsteps could be heard. They had to be coming from the upper reaches of the tunnel, perhaps at the top level where Jremy's brood resided.

Something seemed to have gotten them into a tizzy, she realized; was it her escape? Were they all looking for her?

Thia waited a while longer, hoping to see more, but whatever it was that got them moving seemed to end. Though just as she was about to crawl on ahead she heard muffled voices beneath her hideaway.

Pushing her ear to the door she could hear what sounded like Jremy's older son. His creepy drawl now so familiar to her, though it was hard to follow all that was said with how fast they all talked.

"So wha's goin' on now?" asked the elder son.

It was hard to make out the response, but she picked up part of it. "... S'all gone ta hell. Da's in a rage. Lost a couple now."

There was a derisive laugh and the older brother spat, "Jus' after 'e got in a good mood from fuckin' that new girly a his. 'e ain't never gonna be 'appy no more," he whined.

"Well ya better get da fuck out there," came the younger's

voice again, though she couldn't make out a word more as both of them left the area beneath her hideaway.

Whatever it was that was happening, it sounded like she got out not a moment too soon, and feeling a bit reinvigorated, she pushed on ahead. Quickly, though, her body reminded her how tired it was and how little she'd eaten, and she was back to struggling through the claustrophobic tunnel.

Hope filled her as she moved upwards; she had to be nearing the surface, right? Though in her distracted state of mind she didn't see the dark pit before her, and went sliding down the smooth stone face first into unknown danger.

❧ 43 ❧

Thia looked about her, though it wasn't necessary. She knew exactly where she was by the feel of the place alone. She was in the dread city. That unholy place that was like a splinter of another dimension, lodged stubbornly into hers.

There were so few of them now. The handsome Lieutenant looked dishevelled, but determined. While the other men were exhausted, injured, or worse. Only the Lieutenant showed any semblance of being in control; the rest were all hanging by a thread. Down below she could hear the sounds of struggle. Like people tied up and unable to move.

They were still in the tower. That damnable tower where she'd witnessed the men tearing into their comrade, devouring his flesh. Not out of dire need, but like it was some macabre ritual. Eating a man while he still lived.

The faint glow of the cities strange lights illuminated the Lieutenant's silhouette, drew Thia's eyes to just how attractive a man he was, even if so long below left him a little thinner, his jaw marked by a little more stubble.

She didn't want to say it. She knew the Lieutenant would refuse her, but still, in a soft voice she murmured, "We can't save them all. We have to flee."

His eyes dipped a little, one hand upon his hip, the other hanging down. "So we should just pack up an' head off from here, is that it? Save ourselves while we still can?" he said to her, his eyes travelling back to hers, that gaze so intense. So genuine. So pure.

He wanted to save the men, more than anything else. More than he cared for his own life. It wasn't feigned. Thia could read it. She'd had enough practice reading the face of a liar recently.

She inhaled deeply and nodded, her own gaze sullen. There were so many terrors here in the realm beneath the world, and she was so tired of fighting them all. Yet at the same time, she wanted to live, to save those she could and protect them from this hell.

He rubbed a hand back over his shiny black hair and exhaled sadly. They were close together, their talk quiet, the other men with them were unconscious or asleep so they didn't hear. "You're right," he conceded with a sullen nod. "You should go. Get word back to the surface of all that transpired. Warn them so that no others fall into this trap, Sergeant."

Yet as much as she knew he wouldn't leave his troops, she knew she wouldn't leave him, and her hand reached out to squeeze his shoulder. She waited until his gaze rose back to hers then shook her head solemnly. "You know I won't."

Their eyes met in a long moment before his gaze dipped down. "I was afraid you'd say that. And hoped it all the same. I can't save these men by myself, they – " His gaze slipped over to the men, and those piercing eyes widened in surprise. One of them was missing.

"Where'd Jenson go?" he asked, and Thia noticed his hand twitched towards his pistol in worry.

Thia hadn't seen him go off; last she saw the man he was

writhing in pain from a wound to the stomach that seemed quite severe. Yet in the dark she could see some trail of smeared blood upon the floor headed towards the stairs. And the struggle below had quieted.

"Oh no..." she fretted, her shoulders straightening as she looked back at her Lieutenant. "What are your orders, Sir?"

He had none; discipline was breaking down with him despite his facade of control. He rushed towards the stairs and down, and she followed.

Below they found the man cutting loose the cannibals. Those freakish men who had become so starkly pale, but so hale and hearty despite their long time spent tied and bound. Despite their state, all of them were fitter than ever from being below the surface of the earth for so long. It was as if they were growing stronger below rather than weaker. And the injured man was cutting them loose as they calmly smiled and waited.

"Stop man! Have you gone mad?!" the Lieutenant bellowed, yanking on Jenson's shoulder and pulling him away from the pale man. "These men have lost their minds! They'll tear you apart without a second thought!"

In his condition, it wasn't hard for the Lieutenant to dislodge him. Jenson fell to the floor and grabbed his side in pain. "I'll be dead 'fore long anyhow!" he wailed, rolling onto his side and quaking with hurt and fear.

"Explain yourself man! Suicide is no resort. Not when we've still got a chance!" the Lieutenant bellowed, pleading for the man's own life with him.

"Don't you understand, Lieutenant?" came the words of the sobbing Jenson. "We're dyin'. All of us! If it ain't from the wounds, or the madness, it'll be hunger in the end!" He said, glaring up at him and Thia both. "The only ones that ain't dyin' are them!" he said, jabbing a finger towards the pale cannibals. All of them so eerily silent with blood still dried on around their mouths.

The Lieutenant took hold of Jenson and shook him. "That isn't living, man! Their minds are lost! They've not uttered a civil word in days! They… they devoured your own brother while he still lived and screamed for mercy!"

Thia's face fell to the broken, injured man and felt such pity. She had a will to continue living, but she could understand suicide under these circumstances. But to endanger everyone else as well, to free those pale ones onto the underworld…

It made her shoulders tense and her gaze turn icy, even if he did have stranger delusions about what they would do.

Jenson's gaze went hard. "I'll take that over dyin' slow, bleedin' out my gut like a stuck pig. Waitin' for death to claim me as I cower in fear of the madness outside."

The Lieutenant didn't look as hard and hurt as she did. Instead the man looked sad. So very, very sad.

All of that ceased to matter though once the three Pale Ones spoke up in unison. Their voices eerie and inhuman, speaking in time and none sounding like the men had in life. Instead, their voices were much richer, deeper. Charming. At times a chant, a soothing hymnal, others discordant and strange.

"Disciples of the Great Mother, gather.

"New meat has come.

"A harvest to become a feast.

"We shall be bannermen of a new form of life. Rid yourselves of humanity, for it is but a tattered old rag upon you that makes you ugly and frail.

"Weak and afraid.

"Join us.

"Praise be to the Mother.

"She shall consume the world and give birth to it anew.

"Better."

The Lieutenant stared in silence but Thia grabbed his shoulder tight, shaking him from his stupor. "We have to go.

Now. Fast." Her voice was frantic, and she tried to tug him with her, begging him to move.

He stood firm, refusing to budge. "Who is the Great Mother?" he asked in an authoritative, demanding voice, refusing to give ground. "What does she want?!"

Before Thia could try again their voices rose up once more.

"The Great Mother is purity. Is grandeur too great to be fathomed by mortal minds. She is God. She is the creator of God. She is all things. And she sees this world and deems it unfit. It must be remade. It must be made perfect to be worthy of her so that she might walk it. Her disciples made immaculate, that they might comprehend her grace."

"Lieutenant! We have to go now," Thia pleaded, taking a step backwards. "Please, it doesn't matter who she is."

The Lieutenant stepped back, his brow furrowed, thoughtful, but fear was creeping into him. Even the once-suicidal Jenson looked afraid as their eyes and mouths moved in such perfect unison.

"Is that horrendous… she-devil we saw the Great Mother?" the Lieutenant asked, persistence and curiosity driving him despite his fear.

"From her own womb she was born into this world. But an avatar. One of many. This world is not yet ready for her as she truly is, and she seeks to create a vessel that will be suited to the task. Join us. Let us give praise and welcome her to her new home. Let us offer ourselves that we might aid in her coming."

A great peel of some blood curdling noise halfway between hysterical laughter and shrieking rang through the air, shook the walls of the tower, the whole city in fact! The Lieutenant grabbed at his ears to drown it out, and before she realized it, Thia was doing the same.

He turned to her and together they began to run, trying to get as far from that tower as they could.

$$\text{❅ } 44 \text{ ❅}$$

The impact at the bottom was rough, and she had lost time after striking the stone columns of calcified minerals at the bottom.

Though as she rubbed her head and tried to sort herself out, the surroundings became familiar.

The smooth, polished stone, the ovular shape.

She was back in the tunnels of the Whip-Legs.

Immediately she froze, growing more cautious. And not a moment too soon.

As she turned her gaze upwards, she noted her vision in the dark was returning, as she could see the tendrils of a Whip-Leg above her. Just a few inches from her own body.

Same as the one Tar'kul and her encountered before, she could see it suspended overhead. Motionless. Still.

It had not detected her. Even though she'd crashed down right beneath it. Could the things be deaf, too? They didn't seem to see too well either, at least in the dark. Though they'd made short work of the Dead-Lights. Was it light they were drawn to? Did they live in the shadows only to better see their prey?

She prayed she was right as she drew in a breath, trying to move beneath it and further into their den. It was dangerous, of course, and she had to be cautious, but she understood this. They were animals, and they needed sustenance to live. That made sense to her, and that brutish, unmalicious threat felt almost comforting in comparison to what she had encountered before.

The floors were smooth and rounded, though as she crawled along she noticed something.

During her slumber her legs had returned to her. The first sign was when she felt a pain in her ankle, likely from twisting it before. As she cleared the long, spindly limbs of the Whip-Legs, she could raise herself up onto her legs, albeit shakily. Though how much of that was the poisoning and how much was simply her hunger and weakness, she couldn't be sure.

And despite all the pain and anguish, she felt invigorated. She had a purpose, other than one of fruitless escape. She had to find Sharn, and she knew the girl had to be lurking in these areas nearby, away from the town and yet so near to it, protected from all beasts but the Whip-Legs, and though they were terrifying, they were easier to maneuver around. Still, Thia reminded herself not to get cocky and remain cautious as she moved through the winding tunnels.

❧ 45 ❧

ours of careful wandering through the maze started to take its toll upon Thia, however. Enthusiasm, especially in this dark, sunless world of the below, was hard to keep up. She'd come across several other Whip-Legs, roosting above in the tunnels, but she'd avoided them all.

Though throughout the entire process she'd found no sign of anything familiar. No sign of any way out even. Just more endless tunnels, up, down, to every direction, but none seeming to lead anywhere. How did these creatures navigate such a labyrinth?

She couldn't go on forever like this, not without food or water, so she knew she needed to find some sign of... something, and soon.

Her prayers were answered, but not how she would have expected it. The tell-tale signs of the Whip-Legs fast approach sounded through the tunnel before her, and she had to crouch down and hide as best she could to avoid the fast, oncoming creature.

As it sped past her she could hear another coming, then another.

It was like being caught along the edge of a locomotive engines path, but once they were gone she was left to wonder: What were they headed towards? Was it an intruder? Did Sharn by chance get detected?

Her choices were to go investigate or simply continue her aimless wandering with no sign of progress. Hoping to find something better before she died of thirst.

It wasn't a choice at all.

She quickly changed direction, following after them with a great urgency, trying to keep up with their fast speed. Adrenaline once again pumped through her veins, pushing her on beyond reason and hope.

No, that wasn't true.

She still hoped.

Thia couldn't keep up with them at their rate, but she saw where they went. And when she lost track of that guessed. Luckily another went by soon after, and after dodging that one too she continued her pursuit.

More twists and turns and she was making her way towards some unknown destination. Closer to whatever end she sought.

When she found it, it was not at all what she expected. She reached someplace familiar, near that entrance she had first stepped into the realm of the Whip-Legs out of fear of something worse.

Though what she saw out through that exit tunnel was both familiar and startling.

That great, undead-plant knight that had sought to stop her in the courtyard of Sir Reginald's castle was in the midst of battle with the Whip-Legs. Not only him, but other misshapen former humans, reforged in plant-matter, all warred with the Whip-Legs. And they were winning.

In fact, where the Dead-Lights had been swarmed over, Sir

Reginald's forces were armoured and organized. They were beating the communal creatures at their own game.

At the heart of their formation, their commander sat atop a necrotic horse, leading the assault with saber in hand. Their glowing lanterns making them a beacon in the dark, but unknowingly calling the Whip-Legs to them.

Thia's mouth dropped open and she pressed herself into the rock. This wasn't good. Was this why Jremy had been so agitated? Certainly he couldn't have known, but still, if they defeated the Whip-Legs, she wasn't certain what would happen. Would they storm the city? *Could* they?

The thought sent a shiver down her spine.

She felt like she might burst into tears, unable to find Sharn and Rufus and protect them from so many terrible things.

Though in her despair, one thing arose above the others: if she was back at the entrance, she could retrace her steps towards the crevice where she first found Sharn. Was the girl hiding out there perhaps?

Moving quickly, Thia did just that. Though as she went, she came upon the answer to why there were so few Whip-Legs at the battle.

In the halls she saw dead Whip-Legs. Not just some, but many. One living one, that looked injured, pulled away its comrade's corpse. Amid the slaughter, she saw one of Sir Reginald's disfigured and dismembered men. They had been inside already.

If they were now fighting outside, it only made sense that they'd pushed in, but were driven out, and now returned more organized, and prepared. It also explained why she saw so many fewer Whip-Legs in battle outside the walls than she had seen take on the Dead-Lamps. Their numbers were thinned in battle with the organized undead.

Making her way through the gore, she found the rough,

unhewn stretch of cavern and that familiar crevice where she'd rested with Tar'kul and saw Sharn for the first time.

There was no sign of the girl, but as she moved forward to step across the crevice she caught sight of something below.

Her first reaction was that it must be some of that dripping water she heard, though when she gazed down closely… there she was.

Though the darkness and shadows made odd work of her girlish face, her visage was that of an angel. There she was, the girl Thia had gone in search of. She must have found a little hideaway down in the crevice, because once Thia caught sight of her she ducked back inside of some cranny.

Thia didn't want to grab the attention of either the Whip-Legs or the undead, but excitement nearly made her call out the young girl's name. She bit down on her tongue, though, and smiled so broad. It was a genuine expression, one that wrinkled her eyes and hurt her cheeks with the force of it, and she started to move towards the child.

The walls of the rocky gap were wide enough to easily squeeze down between, but it would still be a treacherous climb through a dangerous space.

But she knew she could do it, even with her busted ankle. She'd persevere. She had to!

It was a treacherous climb, and Thia's hands often failed to find a grip, or found only an unreliable groove to hold onto. Though the heart pangs she experienced no longer chilled her as they used to. She was accustomed now to her life dangling by a thread.

When she made her way down to where the little girl hid, she found Sharn, huddled up on the floor in a little nest of bedding and some meager supplies. She gazed up at her with wide eyes, that were half frightened, half curious.

"Sharn," Thia whispered softly, lowering down to her knees and cringing a bit at the hard stone. "Are you okay?"

It was a miracle she had survived as long as she did without any help. She was no older than Rufus was.

As Thia used her name, however, the hardened young girl seemed to light up and then grow wary again. "Y-you know m'name?' she said, only her stammering keeping her from blurting out the words at that quick-fire rate her people did.

"I promised your mom I'd come take care of you. Keep you safe out here. And I know Rufus. I... I lived there for a while, Sharn."

The girl's hopeful expression at mention of her brother and mother was dimmed a bit at the last part. "I... I don't 'member ya none. An' you talk funny," she said. Though it was bluster, she was trying to act standoffish with her, Thia realized. She wanted to be tough. But she seemed a sweet girl at heart, with little stomach for anything truly mean or defensive.

"Do you remember seeing me here? Up above? I was with a friend... someone who might have looked scary to you." Thia didn't move closer to her, didn't want to scare her away or push her too hard or too fast.

The girl nodded her head slowly. "I 'member," she said softly, shifting onto her knees and looking closely at Thia. "Y're-ally talk ta m'mom? She okay?"

Thia smiled and moved closer, still being cautious and slow so as not to frighten her. "Yea, I did. She was real worried about you and excited when I said I'd seen you and you were okay. She was so proud."

The little girl's expression grew so bright and hopeful. "Is she comin' soon too?" she asked, and any warmth and pleasant-ness in the moment was being sucked into the abyss at that question.

Thia knew the truth of Sharn's mother. Knew she would never see beyond that cell ever again.

But she tried to stay hopeful and filled with joy, for the

young girl's sake. "She's not sure yet, Sharn. But she asked me to take care of you while she works out a plan."

It was a cruel lie. She knew that eventually, down the road, it would shatter Sharn's faith in her. But Thia wanted to shield her from the horrific truth as long as she could, and give the young girl something, anything to be happy about.

Sharn thought about it a second and then nodded, while smiling to her brightly. "That's good. Mum's real clever. She always comes up wit' th'best ideas," she boasted despite herself.

"I bet," Thia smiled. "Do you mind if I come over there and join you? We gotta be real quiet and hide here for a while, okay?"

Sharn nodded to her with a broad smile, scooting back onto her bed of old cloth like what Thia now wore. "We gotta wait for Rufus t'come anyhow," she said. "Shouldn't be long!" she declared with confidence.

Thia shifted to sit beside the young girl, making herself a bit comfortable and starting to tend to her twisted ankle. Though thankfully it was little more than a nuisance. "You know about Rufus coming?" How did she find that out?

The little girl's eyes were wide with curiosity as she looked up at Thia. "'Course I do. I'm waitin' here like I was told 'til he comes back ta join us," she said with a big bright smile. "S'prised ta see you here first, though."

"Join *us*?" Thia was confused, and becoming rapidly concerned. There was something she didn't know, something this little girl did. "Who told you we'd be coming, Sharn?"

"The scary fella," she said with a smile. "Yer friend."

Thia's eyes went wide and her heart swelled with... there weren't any words for it. Before she knew it tears were blurring her vision and she was swiping them away like a mad woman.

She'd held out hope, convinced herself it wasn't just delusion that kept her faith in him alive. And when she'd had that last dream, it was like she could feel herself getting closer to him and just never allowed that to register fully in her consciousness.

Tar'kul was alive?

"Is he here?"

The girl shook her head. "Nuh uh. He went inta Haven ta git Rufus an' you, he said. Didn't he get ya out?" she asked with her pale brow furrowed. "He said he was gunna rescue ya both, an' then we'd all go out togedder."

Oh no... Thia's face fell and she shook her head. "No, I got myself out another way. I thought that Tar'kul had died. But he'll get Rufus. He'll know I made it out, don't you worry. Now we need to be very quiet for a little while, okay, Sharn?"

She needed to concentrate. To reach out to Tar'kul through that strange link she barely understood. She hadn't felt him all the time she was in Haven but perhaps that was another side effect of the poison.

Sharn was surprisingly obedient, and kept perfectly still and quiet beside Thia as she focussed her mind.

Immediately she noticed a distinct difference in what she perceived, unlike anything in all her time in Haven.

Though the psychic abilities were hard to control and harder still to understand, she could feel the presence of Sharn's thoughts. Not understand them, nor read them clearly as she did Tar'kul's, but she could feel glimmers of her feelings, sparks in the aether darkness. The raw presence of the girl's emotions as if they lingered on the air.

She had never felt that in Haven. Not once.

As she stretched out her awareness she could feel more presences. The faint presence of the Whip-Legs she assumed, so basic and animalistic. Then other people. She assumed they must be people from Haven.

Though no Tar'kul.

Could she not reach that far? Or was what kept her from reaching him not the poison, but Haven itself? Was that strange shaft in the rock insulated from psychic abilities? Was that what had allowed them to hide from the Pale Ones all this time? Though if so, their faux-concern for their women was made all the more sick. They would've been in no danger of being summoned out of their hole while there.

Thia's head started to throb a little, though perhaps it was just hunger. Still, after what felt like a long time of trying, she was getting frustrated and afraid. What if he didn't realize she'd escaped? What if he'd gotten caught up in whatever had been happening at Haven when she'd left?

She sighed as she leaned back, looking over to Sharn and smiling a little, despite her frustration and despair. She'd been so quiet, so obedient. That would be an asset down here.

"Thanks, Sharn... I hope you don't mind my asking, but what has he been feeding you? Is there anything extra?"

The girl perked up at that question and immediately lifted herself up and unveiled a hidden stash beneath some of her bundle cloth. Immediately Thia recognized the curious material as Tar'kul's, the same stuff he had adorned his home with, that her old satchel was made from.

From within it Sharn produced the strange mushrooms and bugs, though her nose crinkled a little. "He says it's real important ta eat it, but I don't like it none," she remarked, holding it out to Thia.

Thia grinned a bit and practically salivated at the sight. "You don't know how much you miss it when it's gone." She started eating, having to force herself to ingest the crude meal slowly after having such bountiful meals provided for her over the past days. But those had been poison, and this? Somehow, she knew she had it to thank for much of her talents and luck down here.

The girl watched her with some surprised awe, and then tried to emulate her behaviour, taking little nibbles of the mushrooms. Though she never lost the distasteful expression. "It ain't sa good as th'stuff back in Haven. But it's better for us he said. Right?"

"Right," Thia agreed softly. "And you get used to it. Makes you healthy and strong."

At that the girl seemed to perk up and eat more of the underworld food, and Thia knew she was guided by a desire to survive and be strong. As young as she was, she had a powerful drive to succeed.

"Good girl," Thia said fondly as she finished off her ration and touched at her aching ankle. It wasn't so bad, she knew, but she still stood cautiously to test it. Just the fact that she could feel pain in her legs gave her a sense of joy and pleasure.

Thia went and drank some of the dripping water, quenching her thirst on the drippings from the world above.

"Listen, there's fighting going on up above, okay? I want you to stay here, but if anyone sees you, you have to run. Even if they seem nice. Unless it's Tar'kul or myself, you run and you hide. We'll find you. I'll find you. But first, I have to make sure he and Rufus are on their way. Do you understand?"

The girl rose up, alarmed by the idea of Thia leaving her. "B-but he said not ta leave!" she stammered out. "Said we was gonna make out gitaway from here! 'Long the river!" she said, pointing to the crevice.

Thia wrapped Sharn's hands in hers, looking down at her seriously with her blue eyes. "Did he know about the battle up top?"

Sharn nodded eagerly to her, eyes wide. "Said that made it the perfec' time ta go git ya both!" she remarked. "Said they'd be too busy ta notice 'im sneakin' in, so he could rescue ya an' come on back before they even noticed! Said 'e was real good at sneakin'!"

Thia smiled brightly and nodded. "He is. Okay, you stay here, then. But don't trust anyone but us, okay? *Especially* not the plant people. They talk like me, and they might try to act nice like me, but they are mean and will hurt you."

Sharn nodded to her eagerly. "Plant people," she repeated. "Don't trust 'em!"

"Good girl," she repeated and stroked her hair out of her face affectionately. Thia was only young herself, but she already felt some maternal instincts for the girl. Perhaps it was just because of the warmth that Rufus had shown her, for she certainly had no interest in children before that.

Thia took back to the crevice, though this time with her experience climbing down, and the vantage point of looking at it from beneath, she could make out the safe nooks and crannies to grab a hold of much better.

Climbing back up, she pulled herself into the tunnel above and could hear in the distance the faint echoes of fighting in the distance. Sir Reginald had re-entered the tunnels, it was apparent, and Thia's time would be running short.

She knew the way towards Haven, or at least thought she did. Jremy had said the tunnels change their shape, but he'd told her so many lies, how could she know that wasn't just another means of keeping her in place?

Tracing her way back towards Haven through the dark tunnels, she felt her dark sight return to its old intensity. She could see more clearly already. Was it just the snack that did it?

Whatever the reason, it was lucky it had returned, because before she heard them, she saw the rushing forms of some of the men from Haven. Their ratty clothes and crude weapons unmistakable. Though more remarkable still was that they ran with a Whip-Leg in their midst. Not as captive or trophy, but as if the creature were hunting *with* them.

She had time to duck out of sight in the cave, avoiding their sight and armed with the knowledge that she must've been on the right track after all.

Once the danger had cleared, Thia tread back out carefully, resuming her trek back.

The caves were easier to traverse than the tunnels; they seemed more distinguishable than the uniform tunnels the Whip-Legs seemed to call home. Though she was noticing a change… the tunnel she had taken with Jremy before, up high in the cave wall, it was no longer there. Only stone stood in its place.

So he had been telling the truth…

Though the longer she thought on it, about his atrocities and his betrayals, the more she doubted it. She found some grooves to grab hold of and lifted herself up to where the tunnel had been before. Once closer she saw the truth of the situation: more of that strange, spongy material had been used to block off the wall. It was coated with some matter that made it blend it almost perfectly with the stone.

So she was right; it wasn't that the tunnels changed, it was that Jremy's men were masking tunnels, creating their own labyrinth.

"Bastard," she cursed silently. He told her that he was protecting his people, but he was keeping them captive and lying to them. So that he could keep being king of his under-world hellhole.

But she didn't let her malice and rage overtake her. She wouldn't be seeking revenge. She simply wanted to see Tar'kul and Rufus again, and save the poor women if she could.

She hoped she could.

She wouldn't demoralize herself by thinking on how she might potentially save half a dozen or more crippled and enfee-bled women.

There was no time for that.

Though as Thia climbed up through the hole, she heard yet more footsteps coming from ahead. She had to tread lightly, carefully minding herself as she pushed into the labyrinth further.

Another strange spongy wall masked the other end of the tunnel, and as the footsteps receded she carefully pried it open enough to see through.

Outside was a big stretch of open cave that led towards Haven. Yet right before the gates to that hell hole, a miraculous sight graced her eyes.

It was Rufus, looking lost and confused.

Her heart leapt into her throat and she looked around cautiously before she practically started jogging towards the young boy. She was flushed with excitement, her smile broadening with each step. "Rufus," she called out in a hushed tone.

The boy looked to her with an astonished expression. "Ya got out?!" he said with disbelief, looking utterly shocked to see her there. His gaze falling to her legs, "An' yer legs! Ya kin walk!" he declared.

"Yes, now listen, Rufus. Did you see a scary looking man? With strange hair?"

Rufus' eyes widened but he nodded immediately. "He tol' me ta run to the crack in the tunnels ta find Sharn!" he said excitedly, then pointed back towards Haven. "He's back there, tryin' ta get inta Haven. I tol' him not ta! The guards are out keepin' watch!"

"Okay, here, follow me," she said urgently, leading him to the hidden tunnel entrance and pushing aside the spongy matter. "Be careful of the Whip-Legs, and avoid the plant people okay?" Thia continued on hurriedly telling him the path to Sharn as best she could, before patting him on the head. "We'll be there soon."

Rufus nodded to her. "I'll protec' her," he declared with more bravado than reason.

Thia closed the tunnel and headed off, back into Haven, hoping that Rufus could find his way safely.

❄ 46 ❄

Returning to that light-soaked tunnel was the last thing Thia should ever have wanted to do, but she couldn't leave Tar'kul behind.

The bright light stung her eyes unmercifully, even though it was nearly night time by their reckoning. Her eyes could no longer tolerate such bright lights, and after quickly readjusting to the darkness they refused to want to readjust back to the light.

Only with great effort and sufferance did she strain to look about, seeing the unconscious bodies of two Havenites. They must have been the guards that Rufus had referred to, and she could only imagine that it was Tar'kul that was responsible.

Looking up the winding path that was the village, she could see someone stumble from a cave-house with a scream, then run terrified into the upper reaches.

That had to be Tar'kul.

She tried to reach out, to touch his mind once more, even as she began to run towards the house as fast as she could while favouring one leg.

Her suspicions seemed to be confirmed, though; she couldn't

sense Tar'kul or even the man who just ran off. Haven seemed protected from psychic tricks.

Out of the hovel she heard the strained, guttural voice she'd only heard before on one occasion. Those vocal chords so unaccustomed or simply ill-suited to human language. "Thee ahh?!"

Thia burst into the home in time to see the dark visage of her long lost friend Tar'kul tearing through the meager possessions of the residents, trying to find some sign of her whereabouts. He must have been ravenous in his desire to find her, and the place was a complete wreck already, for he knew his time to search would be short.

"Come on!" she shouted at him, her eyes wide. She didn't have time to savour the joy that was flooding her body. "Before they catch us!"

She didn't waste any time on pleasantries, on welcoming him back into her life. There'd be time for that later!

Though when the tall, monster of a man turned towards her, his mouth hung open in startled surprise. His obsidian eyes hidden from her, as they were bandaged to filter out the blinding light.

"Thee-ahh!" he exclaimed again in his rasping voice, rushing towards her.

She took his hand and together went outside, where she immediately saw through the painful light that men were approaching from above. Several of them.

Together the reunited pair ran back towards the entrance, Tar'kul's hand squeezing hers as she led the way for the near blind man.

They were racing their pursuers, desperately trying to outpace them. Her ankle was holding her back, but Tar'kul helped prop her up, serving as a crutch to help her gain speed as they went.

Together they burst through the exit, back out into the cave system where her sight was restored. She led him towards the masked tunnel, enough of a distance between them, she hoped, to get inside without them seeing their route.

Once on the other side, Tar'kul ripped his bandage free, and his obsidian-gaze fell upon her.

She could feel a surge of his thoughts and emotions, and felt for a moment that he embraced her tightly. Though instead she realized it was just the longing he felt, and his memory of her rebuffs kept him from doing more than squeezing her hand.

And that was what she wanted, not then. Not because she was any longer repulsed by him, but because they weren't safe. Not yet.

She squeezed his hand back and took a moment to catch her breath. "I sent Rufus on ahead. The plant people are pushing in, though. We need to hurry."

Tar'kul nodded to her and together they carried on; their pursuers were still too close to tarry.

Coming out the other end of the tunnel, Tar'kul leapt down first, then caught her, making the trip down into the cavern beneath easier.

Though before they could turn, from out of the one of the side passages, Jremy and his sons appeared.

The towering giant's eyes went wide with shock at seeing her. "Don't go wit' 'im!" he called out to her, looking frightened for the first time Thia had ever seen. Frightened of losing his new possession.

Thia's blood turned to ice, and she faltered. Not because she didn't believe in what she was doing, in how terrible Jremy was.

No, it was because in that moment, she wanted to kill him. To hurt him like he'd hurt all those other women, like he'd hurt her. To punish him for turning his sons into monsters just like him.

"If you don't let those women go free," she snarled, "you will know true pain." And then her mind acted almost unconsciously.

She probed his thoughts with her own.

That fucking bitch! She's mine! I'll not let her get away! Not after all I spent winning her over! Not after all my trouble, it was an endless array of fast, self-centered thoughts that ran through his mind. The internal ramblings of a control freak gone mad. Though amid the noise she did hear something of actual value. *If she goes out that tunnel there's no stopping her. She can't do it! Gotta stall her.*

Her lashes fluttered excitedly and she relayed the information instantly, silently, to her traveling companion. She felt no pity, no affection for the man who had been her sweet and tender captor. Not now that she knew what he did. What he was.

Timed together, she and Tar'kul dashed through the side tunnel to Jremy's raging cries. The two of them racing down that rocky passage as the men pursued her.

Onwards they went, though it was different territory for her. She wasn't entirely sure where they went until the tunnel looped around and she saw that they were now back among the Whip-Leg tunnels.

Together they guessed at the right way, and ran down the smooth, ovular path.

Until the tendrilled limbs of a Whip-Leg came flailing before them.

They jumped back in startled surprise, avoiding the creature in time.

Though once they realized why, they were less relieved.

The Whip-Leg was dead, and out of an adjoining tunnel its killer loomed. The great knight of Sir Reginald's standing there, gazing upon her with his eerily glowing eyes beneath his visor. "Stop," echoed its booming, steady voice.

But that was the last thing on their minds.

They leapt over the corpse of the Whip-Legs and carried on, probing out the rocky crevice where the siblings waited.

Tar'kul scooped her up in his arms without warning, then crouched down, lowering her over the edge towards the little cave beneath. Though before she dipped that low, she could see their pursuers coming from both sides.

Jremy's sons and him had wound around another way and came from the other side.

Tar'kul spoke to her, his mental voice that familiar chittering. *"Go! Grab the ledge below! The girl will show you the way out!"* he insisted, and she could sense he had no intention of following her. He was going to try and stall the others and buy her time.

"I'm not leaving you again," she cursed at him, even as she reached for the ledge, helping herself down.

"You must! Or they will get you and the little ones! We can't all be saved," he pleaded with her, reminding her of that dream upon escaping Haven. Of speaking with the Lieutenant, telling him to give up on his delusions of saving all his men.

As Tar'kul dangled over that edge, helping her down, Thia put all her strength into pulling on his arm, yanking at him. Her stubborn refusal to let him sacrifice himself contradicting her own words as she pulled the tall, lanky man over the ledge.

It was brazen and caring of her, yet as the six-limbed Tar'kul plummeted over she had to scramble to find the strength to save him from falling into the hole beneath.

Thia tumbled back into the crevice, pulling Tar'kul with her as best she could, but he only partially made it. Two of his arms scrambled for a hold on the ledge while the rest of his body dangled over the edge as his limbs flailed, obsidian eyes wide with alarm.

"I'll pull you with me!" he protested, fearful for her.

"You will not," she swore aloud, her jaw clenched and her face reddened with the strain. "You've saved me enough!" Her words were mere grunts, panted out on hard breaths.

She'd been inactive for so long, but she poured all her willpower into supporting him, pulling him out of the maw of oblivion. The two kids clambered over to help, grabbing hold of the monstrous man's other arm, his two smaller ones clawing at the edge to try and help.

Meanwhile, up above, their pursuers arrived. The sight of Jremy and his sons looming over them, though as Thia cast an anxious glance upwards, she noticed they were frozen in place, and their attentions weren't locked upon the group of them below.

The distraction bought them time, and together Thia and the two kids pulled him up, giving Tar'kul enough leverage to grasp on and help get him the rest of the way.

He flopped onto the stone panting, his chest heaving as Thia ducked her head outside and peered up. There she saw the two sides clashing; Sir Reginald stood there, and his Knight leapt before him across the gap and into the throng of men as a close melee broke out.

"Now," Thia hissed at them, tugging Tar'kul up with both hands before shooing the children on. "We need to run. Fast." She sounded so certain, even though she was heaving for breath and her arms and legs were aching from exertion. She was grateful she'd taken the chance to eat when she still had it.

Tar'kul clambered up onto his four hands and knees, then rooted through the cloth, taking up the meager belongings that were accumulated there. *"There is a tunnel beneath,"* he chittered to her mentally. *"Won't be pleasant, but it leads out of here."* He got up and headed to the ledge again, carefully leading the way for the three of them.

It was a narrow ledge overhanging the crevice, and the fall would've sent one ricocheting between rocky cliffs all the way down.

They were going to get out of here. Thia could feel it. Escape was so close, and if she didn't snatch it now, it would leave her behind forever.

Still, she had the children go first, carefully and urgently helping them. "Don't worry, Tar'kul will get you if he needs to. Hold on tight." Yet she knew she'd have to be extra cautious. For her legs not to hold out just a little longer, for her body to be strong enough to help her along.

But as she glanced towards the dark pits of the underworld nightmare, she knew that, as usual, she didn't have a choice but to be strong.

The sounds of fighting rang out above them, but onwards they went without so much as a glance back.

Thia's ankle still ached, but she braced herself as she shuffled upon the stone ledge, carefully moving down the incline. The four of them all descended into darkness, blacker even than what they were used to.

Rufus slipped, teetering towards the edge, but Thia grabbed him, pulled him back against the wall and held him in place.

Tar'kul heard the motions behind him and called out to her inside her mind, *"Be wary! There is water below, but it is an unpleasant fall."*

"We'll make this, Tar'kul. I'm positive." There was so much more she wanted to say, but truly, she was surprised by how much his absence... the thought of his death... had affected her. The relief, the gratitude, even in her thoughts, was obvious.

In return she could feel his emotions, the strange warmth and relief he felt for her return. Even though in his heart he knew it would only be temporary, that her ultimate destination was a world he could never be a part of. Not again.

The two kids were remarkably quiet and resilient. Thia took a look at them and saw that while they held hands, all doubt seemed to have fled them utterly.

Down and down into the abyss, Tar'kul led the way. The tall, lanky man was able to reach both sides of the crevice for much of the journey, but as they neared the bottom, it grew wider and he too had to shuffle along slow and carefully.

When at last Thia could hear the faint movement of water, they were already nearly there.

The dark stream was barely moving, but it meandered off into the unknown gently.

Tar'kul turned back to the rest of them. *"We must go through the water. Here,"* he bent down, and near the bottom he produced a couple extra bundles of cloth. He passed one to the kids, then another to Thia. *"It's food. But it also floats. Use it to help travel down. It is a long journey, and you need all the strength you can save,"* he chittered.

Thia stilled as she accepted it, smiling a faint, affectionate smile at him. Her monster. Her friend.

Her fingertips brushed against his hand and she had to lower her eyes to the ground.

"I should have listened to you," she apologized silently.

That obsidian face of his, half man, half something else, looked at her with confusion at first. Then his lips formed into a smile. *"Could not tell you all then… speech was leaving me. Became harder to speak. Head hurt so bad…"* he explained, and it made sense. Unlike her, he relied upon his psychic abilities almost completely in his life below. The loss of them in that dead zone doubtlessly had other effects upon him.

Of course, Tar'kul had warned her before they ever set foot in Haven itself.

But there were humans living there. She couldn't have left, not after being deprived of human contact for so long. She never would have been able to live with herself.

And it wasn't all bad. She glanced at the two kids, and felt such relief that at least she was able to save them. To free them from that horrible place, and the abominable adulthood that awaited them both.

"They told me you had died."

Tar'kul's face contorted into one of blank confusion for a moment. *"I tried to save you. But they were too many,"* he explained, telling her of that moment during which was unconscious. *"They came at me in a big swarm. Though many fought over you, trying to take you back to their holes. They squabbled over you for a while. But in the end there were too many... and I had to go... and wait,"* he said, and she could feel the shame radiate from him. He'd used their fight over who got her to slip away. *"Knew they would not kill you. Before we ever got there, I could sense how much they wanted you... alive."*

With his gaze dipped low, clutching the satchel in his arms, he lowered his head. *"I am sorry for leaving you to them."*

Her gaze fell and she nodded solemnly. *"I don't blame you. But I wish I could have saved more... The other women..."* She knew she didn't have to describe it to him. The emotions, the things she felt, they were so strong and didn't have words.

They couldn't be explained.

But he had a connection with her that surpassed any, and she began to smile at that awareness.

The two kids shifted anxiously as the two of them looked at each other, smiling in the dark, sharing their private moment.

"Come," Tar'kul said, wading into the water. *"I will lead the way. Have travelled it once before,"* he explained before turning about, his coat floating on the water as he used the bundle of mushrooms like a float to help buoy him.

The siblings went next, gasping and squealing as the cool water bit through their clothing.

It was chilly, yet invigorating at the same time, dipping herself into the stream. There was so much more she wanted to say, to ask, but instead she chose to silently enjoyed the moment. The impending doom slipping away behind them, but new terrors loomed ahead.

❃ 47 ❃

Tar'kul had not been exaggerating. The journey was long; it seemed to have been hours since they set out and Thia's body was now as cold as the water. It wasn't freezing, at least. The temperature of the underworld was too tepid for that, relatively unaffected by the weather up above.

Still, carried along in the moving stream, her legs and arms had grown tired. The lack of warmth was making her body work harder, causing her to feel so famished.

Worse still, the crevice had become a narrow tunnel some hours back, and was growing tighter all the time. Thia barely had room to get her head above water anymore, often having to bob up and down to suck in air with a gasp.

Ahead of her, Tar'kul was having to fend for himself and reach back at the same time, trying to help keep the two much shorter kids afloat.

"Is it much farther?" Rufus asked, the chattering of his teeth audible through his words.

Thia of course had little idea, and Tar'kul's chittering mental voice was not heard in response. He probably wasn't eager to break it to them that the journey was much longer yet.

"Aw, c'mon Rufus," she gulped out between her bobbing in the water, but forced some cheer into her tone. "It's good for your body." Make him strong enough to handle the trials ahead, of which there were always so many. But she didn't want to tell him that, to crush his hope.

The two desperate kids were having a harder time than her, despite Tar'kul's aid. "I-it's s-s-so c-cold!" stated Sharn through noisy teeth.

Though before Thia could try to rally the kids once more, a sound carried down from the tunnel behind them. The water grew louder, no longer a mere soft babble. The trickle was fast growing, and as she looked behind she saw a cresting wave moving down towards them.

"Watch out, there's more water com – !" her voice was cut off as the wave pushed her forward, into the bodies of the two waifish kids, and the three of them were forced beneath the surface as pressure mounted.

The 'tide' rose so fast, whatever spring melt that fueled it having picked up a great amount of momentum abruptly back in the direction from which they'd come.

The tangle of bodies grew as they passed through the chilly stream, the three of them hitting Tar'kul's tall, lanky form.

With his six limbs, the obsidian-man clung onto the walls and stalactites for support as he grabbed at the three of them.

They couldn't have been beneath the water for long, but it came so suddenly it seemed to last an eternity, and the precious gasps of air they got as Tar'kul pulled them up to the now almost non-existent gap between stream and cave roof allowed them to prepare.

Tar'kul's mental voice chittered inside their minds, *"Can't hold on! Keep your breath! Swim with water, not against!"*

With their last gasps, the four of them went spiralling

through the water, the current whisking them through the narrow channel.

It was terrifying, but somehow, deep down, Thia found it a bit exhilarating at the same time. Perhaps she'd been beneath the earth too long.

That, or she was finally losing her mind. The sound of laughter seemed to echo at the back of her mind, but it was a mirage. It was gone as fast as it came and she dismissed it.

She clutched to all the chilly limbs she could, trying to maintain some semblance of control over her companions.

The world was awash in murky darkness, Thia's dark-vision giving her little sight into the water. Only vague shadows of the two children and Tar'kul could be seen, but she managed to grab the children—or at least one of them—and try to kick forward, to propel herself with the current.

They had to be close, right? Tar'kul wouldn't have sent them on this trip if they weren't.

His uneasy, chittering voice made her less confident. "Keep swimming! Do not slow! Keep moving!"

It was hard to swim; she'd not done it in so very long, and all her trekking through the underworld did not prepare her for that full-body activity. It put parts of her to use that had seen no exercise in years, it seemed, but she had no choice. Her body might give out, but not until she was dead.

Thia swam with all the energy and strength she could muster, pulling the children with her as best she could. While ahead of her, Tar'kul's strange, shadowy form swam in jerking motions, not like a man but like some bizarre creature of the deep. His six limbs kicking at once to propel him in bursts like an octopus.

Her lungs burned, her limbs ached, the old stale air escaped her mouth but she fought the urge to suck in the murky water. She had to hold on longer.

She couldn't do it, she realized. She couldn't take these children on her own. They were too much drag for her! So why was Tar'kul abandoning her to manage them alone? After all he'd done, all he'd been willing to sacrifice, why now was he leaving her behind to such a fate?

Panic set in, her heart pounding so hard, her lungs about to burst with its need for breath. She would cry, if she weren't so deeply immersed in the terrible, crushing water. Still, her face screwed up, and she had to force herself to press on. To hold on to them just a little bit longer, to grasp onto life for just another few moments.

Rational thought abandoned her; she didn't even reach out to Tar'kul to plead for help. Instead she just kicked with her oxygen-deprived legs and forced herself to carry on.

She'd lost sight of Tar'kul entirely.

She understood why shortly after as she tumbled out onto the waterfall, her resolve collapsing instantly as she sucked in sweet air and cascaded forward.

It was then she realized she only held Rufus in her arms, the poor boy held in such an awkward position it made him seem like two children.

Though as she careened over the edge of the fall, Tar'kul's long dark arms seemingly grabbed out of the air to grasp her, and she swung along an arch beneath him as he was suspended from a stalactite.

The tall man didn't hold Sharn, though. The little girl was out of sight!

"*Come to me!*" came Tar'kul's mental voice, calling to the young girl and not Thia for once.

Seconds passed like hours. The young girl flailed out in a mad tangle of slender limbs. Though she didn't have the velocity to propel her out, and Tar'kul had to lunge forward, weakening his hold upon the stone work to grasp her.

Thia watched it all as if in slow motion, the desperate Tar'kul reaching out with one of his longer arms, trying to grasp the girl's hand.

It seemed as if all was lost for a moment, but then he caught her, and fell down, one of his other arms losing its grip above.

The girl was saved, but he no longer had the strength or hold needed to keep his position, and as he swung back like a pendulum with Sharn dangling below, all four of them plummeted.

It was only then Thia realized why he had swum ahead in the first place. Why he had raced to get ahead and grab a position upon those stalactites.

Beneath the waterfall were many more of those stone spires, pointing upwards like needles. Marking their doom amid the cascading water.

The four bodies descended towards them, their trajectory set and inalterable now that their hold upon all solid matter was lost.

Yet they all went together as one interconnected mess.

They did not get impaled on rocks. It was only by great fortune that Sharn's weight and Tar'kul's swing back gave them enough of an arc to take them into the water beyond the stalagmites below. They crashed into the cold water there instead of the stone-spikes that would've claimed their lives at but a few inches more.

Together, the quartet flailed and swam to the surface, gasping and trying to get out of the spray of the waterfall so that their breaths were no longer tinged with murky water.

Thia coughed up more of the dirty water, her mind dizzy and her eyesight clouded.

Was she alive?

She could barely even tell if she was grateful for the fact anymore. It was all just getting to be too much. The stress of living in this hellhole, of fighting over and over again... Of struggling. The dizzying heights of exhilaration crashing down into exhaustion frustrating her.

She leaned back in the water and for a moment she just floated. Just existed.

Tar'kul gathered up the two kids, and then began to swim. "Come! Must get to island and rest," he implored her with the children in tow.

Though as Thia came out of her stupor she noticed their sacs were floating nearby her, their sustenance having followed them despite the disarray.

She gathered up the bundles, which was easy enough as they helped keep her afloat, and then turned to join Tar'kul and the children towards the island.

There she watched it in the distance, the smooth stone with its pointed stalagmites jutting upwards.

Though her eyes took in the whole of the cavern as well, the curious stonework. The dangling shapes that were so often macabre, like the two calcified protrusions that looked like a gored pig hanging from two hooks.

As her gaze settled back upon the island and her companions ahead, she noticed something else. The water level had risen noticeably along the walls. That island, though, had not been submerged a hair.

It wasn't an island of any usual sort. It was floating on the murky water. All her instincts developed in the world below had taught her to treat everything with suspicion.

She wanted this pain—this suffering—to stop. She'd hoped that the two children, that regaining the use of her legs, that having Tar'kul back... Shouldn't it have rejuvenated her will to live? Maybe she'd tricked herself into believing it had, for a brief moment.

So why did she feel so dispassionate? So tired of fighting?

Instead she could barely even muster up fear of that moving island, and simply looked at her monstrous companion.

"*It's floating.*" Even her thoughts sounded defeated, and Thia's brows furrowed a tad.

It should have come as a terrible surprise to her when a long neck emerged from the water, and a beaked, reptilian sort of maw swung slowly back around towards the three nearest. A squawk and a hiss cried out from the creature, and Tar'kul did his best to move back, but moving in water couldn't be so dextrous for any of them.

Only the warning Thia had given him saved him from falling victim to the snap of its maw, and gave him time to push the children back towards her.

Her hellish existence was to continue, it seemed, and she had to swim towards the kids, trying to get the floating mushroom bundles to them as quickly as she could. They couldn't swim well, and needed the support.

While ahead of them, Tar'kul faced off with the great, turtle-like beast that came for its meal.

Another dart of its beaked maw went for the tall man, but he avoided it again. Though only barely.

Perhaps that was his intention though, for this time when the beasts head reared back, Tar'kul clung to its long, sinuous neck. Water poured off him and the creature as they flailed about, trying to dislodge him from the monster's neck.

Thia grabbed up Sharn and Rufus, handing them the satchels, securing them to it. "Hold onto these, keep your distance," she warned them before swimming into the fray.

Tar'kul was holding his own against the creature, clambering along its neck towards its face. Whatever plan he had in mind was in jeopardy, however, because as Thia approached she saw two thin appendages rise up out of the water. They were so much like the Whip-Legs that she thought them related for a moment.

Was this some offshoot of the bizarre creatures? Adapted to the subterranean rivers and lakes? Did these creatures evolve down here just as they did above?

Such existential matters would have to wait for a safer time, and instead Thia waded in with little plan on her mind. Only the mystifying urge to face danger yet again.

She began to see what Tar'kul was going for as he climbed along the creature's neck. His smaller arms were trying to claw at what seemed to be the creature's eyes. Though it would be futile if those whip-like arms got at him first.

The arms snapped towards him, lashing his back and the stones that dangled above, evoking a cry of pain from Tar'kul and ruining his opportunity.

Thia flung herself into the battle, clinging to one of the whip arms and pinning it down with her weight. The appendages seemed to lack strength; they did damage through their whipping momentum, not through raw muscle.

With just the one limb snapping at him, Tar'kul was able to dig his clawed hands into those eyes, making the creature shriek in agony, its head and whip-limbs flailing wildly. A turtle's shriek is not a sound she ever wished to hear again.

Though as her companion created such a mess of gore, Thia noticed below that its neck protruded further… and betrayed a weaker point still.

It looked like greyish brain matter, soft and spongy at the base of its neck. Towing the whip-limb with her as it struggled against her motions, she got to it.

Though unlike Tar'kul, she had only her bare hands as weapons, and even the vulnerable mush of flesh didn't seem like it would be hurt a great deal by her battered and broken nails.

Glancing at the hide they'd mistaken for an island, she could see that the stalagmites at least were genuine. The creature must have sat motionless for countless centuries to form such a protective camouflage. Yet she saw in it the thing's undoing.

She climbed onto its shell, clambering atop it as Tar'kul bore the assault of both whip limbs once more, and she put her strength to trying to break off the calcified stonework.

Her biceps tensed, and she ground her teeth, trying to tear off a chunk of stone.

It came away, miraculously, and she nearly fell off the creature, sliding to her knees and plunging the jagged chunk of mineral into its tender flesh.

It was over in an instant. Her quaking, weary arms diving the makeshift dagger into its brain again and again, her body covered in greenish-grey blood and gore as she ended its life.

Then the great beast's neck and head crashed down into the water, and Tar'kul with it.

Another of hell's horrors. Defeated.

She didn't relax. She couldn't. Tears were streaming from her as she still pounded its body uselessly, no longer trying to fight it. She was just acting on instinct. Or was it emotion?

It was exhausting, and exhilarating, and she didn't have the time to sort out her incredibly conflicted feelings on life and mortality. Instead, there was just the need to do something. To save the people she was with, the people who she cared for.

So much anger and fear had welled up within her, and she knew she was losing it. Some rational part of her mind told her to relax, to pull back, but still she fought against the dead beast, her entire body trembling in her anxiety.

She lost track of time; it was only when the equally weary and worn Tar'kul climbed up and pulled her back into his arms that she realized what she had done. How she had lost all control. The creature's neck was floating away, clinging to its hide by only a sliver now it seemed.

Tar'kul's voice called out, croaking and gravelly, not inside her mind but formed with great strain. "It… okay," he assuaged her, and she realized he must have been trying with futility to communicate with her mentally through her outburst. "Caaalm… doowwnn," he said, four arms holding her tight against his chest.

But how could she?

Her mind was both frantic and blank, repetitive in its thoughts.

I'm going to die down here.

I'm going to die down here.

I'm going to die down here.

It was her worst fear, and yet now... it was almost like a lullaby. Like a promise. Something she'd been so frightened of, yet now... welcomed.

A stop to her struggle. To her constant pain.

Tar'kul held her through it all, for how long she had no idea. At some point she fell asleep, or passed out. Not much else crossed her mind.

❧ 49 ❧

Thia looked around her at the camp sight of the remaining soldiers. Though all that seemed to remain now were her. And him. The courageous Lieutenant.

He knelt before the grave of their last companion, freshly buried.

"If only we'd tried feeding on the mushrooms a little sooner… he needn't have died like this," the Lieutenant said, so much of the life drained from him. He'd been through a hell not unlike Thia's, after all. And even his military and officer training could prepare him for that. Not entirely.

He was still so tall and broad of shoulder, his hair grown longer and wilder, and so black. He managed to look more like the world above than she did at this point, she wagered. Some shred of his civility and dignity still remained, that made him both handsome and inspiring even in the depths of this dream-realm.

Though it was easier to appreciate such things here, when she knew she was safe from reality. It was but a dream, after all.

A vacation from her own pain and into the pain of someone else. Someone who deserved a better world, a better ending.

It still tugged at her heart, despite her trying to harden herself to such emotions. It wasn't easy to turn off the things that made her human, though. No matter how much she wished she could change that, her longing for a better life - for herself, for her friends, for her Lieutenant - it all remained, real or not.

"We couldn't have known," she offered, though she bit back so much of the sorrow in her voice. Instead she sounded hard and stony, like she wished she felt.

The Lieutenant rose up from his knees in an almost ghostly sort of manner, his shoulders a little slumped. He held one of those fungal blooms she now so clearly recognized; it was what Tar'kul had fed her, had saved her with.

"You're right," he said, gazing down at the oddly coloured mushroom, sizing up its sickly colour. "I never would have guessed they were. But desperation makes us do mad things," he said, before tossing it down onto the pile of the things that grew in their little hideaway.

"Lieutenant," she said softly, looking up at him. She had so much she wanted to ask, so much information she wanted from him, but instead her gaze fell and she breathed in the stink of their den deep into her lungs. "You have done very well here."

At her reassurances, his face lit up with a faint smile. It brought a certain vigor and handsome charm back to his under-world-stained face, and drew her gaze back to him as if beyond her control.

His jawline was showing the black, shiny makings of a beard, and it didn't look bad on him. She realized he had as much good looks in him as her lost beloved Edain. 'Striking', 'dashing', those were the words for such a man. He must have been a star of the officer pool as far as the ladies were concerned. A noble of great promise, who had lost all that when he set foot into the depths to save the lives of peasants above.

He placed a strong hand upon her shoulder, squeezing it reassuringly in return for her words. "Thank you," he said simply, and she could see the shimmer in his eyes as tears threatened to form.

"You were given an impossible task, and you never gave up. Even when I tried to tempt you to." Her voice lost some of its hardness, quivering a bit before she swallowed it back. "I've enjoyed getting to know you better."

The man's expression softened, but his grip tightened upon her shoulder. "And I you, Sergeant. No, John," he said, calling her by the name of whomever she replaced in this dreamscape version of events.

The Lieutenant cracked a smile as his gaze drifted off a little, "Y'know, I always thought the rest of you officers despised me. I heard the way some of your brothers would mutter, 'There goes Taran Coll. Ol' Tar-Back, the peasant-king.'" He shook his head and laughed. "An upstart with delusions of nobility. A peasant who earned his stripes against all tradition and decency."

"Taran." She couldn't help but mutter the name beneath her breath and felt her eyes burn. She had to swallow back her sobs, but it was proving nearly impossible.

She'd wondered, she'd suspected...

But to hear it spoken was something entirely different.

Her hand went to his cheek, and she knew it would be odd. Inappropriate, even, for John to be touching his commanding officer like this, but she didn't care. She needed to look at him, to feel him. To know that Tar'kul was a man such as this.

A man not unlike the one she had loved in times past. Both handsome and ambitious. Clever and courageous.

A man who once reflected on the outside all those things he had in such abundance on the inside. Summed up in one word: beauty. For even after time untold in the labyrinth of hell, he retained some measure of humanity, of decency.

He looked at her differently, though she surmised it was not because of the oddly familiar touch of her hand upon his cheek. Was Tar'kul—Taran Coll, an old British name if ever she had heard one—only now becoming aware that he was sharing his memories with her in a dream? Did the way her fingers stroked over his smooth skin and dark, glossy beard hairs feel too different to be mistaken for the camaraderie of his old, long deceased friend John?

How long ago had this all happened? So many decades must have passed with him alone. And what of John? When had he fallen prey to this wicked place?

"I wish I could save you," Thia murmured kindly.

Confusion twisted Taran's face at her words, "T'is my duty to save you," he replied quietly, his brow furrowed just slightly.

Her thumb ran across his cheek once more, her fingers stroking along his jaw, and her gaze met his, steadily.

For a long moment she studied him, his masculine beauty, his dignity, and that faint hint of something else behind his eyes.

Before she could over-think it, her lashes fluttered and she pushed herself in, her lips pressed hotly against his in such a passionate kiss that warmed her body despite the cool of the underworld.

The move took him quite by surprise, and he reeled a little, but his full, handsome lips were no more pleasing against hers for it. The way his strong arms grasped her shoulder and waist were comforting, and the gentle tickle of his sleek black beard was delightfully masculine.

It was Tar'kul as he had once been, a man she could easily have fallen in love with. Shared lust with. Admired and respected.

She was so lost in the moment, she didn't notice as her tongue explored his mouth so desperately that she was no longer kissing the dream-him of years-gone-by. That instead she was kissing the very flesh and blood Tar'kul of monstrous half-man proportions. The very surprised Tar'kul who awoke from his dream to find her upon him. Kissing him so passionately in the quiet of the underworld.

Though instead of alarm or recoiling from her, his arms—all four of them—wrapped about her in return as his inky black eyes gazed at her where dream and reality melded into one.

And even then, she didn't pull away. She wanted to comfort him, to give him some taste of what he'd deserved. He'd sacrificed so much in coming down here, more than she could ever possibly fathom. His transformation must have been horrifying for him, especially to experience it all by himself. And knowing he'd forever more be a monster to the world above...

So she consoled him, her arms wrapping around his neck, her tongue exploring his strange, inhuman mouth.

Yet those lips, those lips still so felt like the ones in his dream. Full and smooth, soft yet supple. Moist and warm.

She knew—simply knew—that the kids slept soundly, and it was but the two of them entangled in each other's arms. She could feel his emotions, the overpowering sense of joy at her kisses, her touches. The love. For as alien as he had become—and he was truly alien, his thoughts were even changed, become something different and a little stranger to read than those of humans like her and the kids—he did love her. The man within his warped flesh was filled with love for her. Strange, misshapen, but genuine love.

Two hands rubbed over her waist to her hips, while two more went up along her back to her shoulder blades. His strangely elongated tongue touching hers as they kissed and explored one another's mouths in full consciousness now.

Ever since she stumbled into this underground world, she'd never felt like she had full agency over herself, over her body, over her sexuality. But now, in the desperate and emotional moment of waking, she felt completely alert and aware.

Perhaps it was simply a statement of how fragile and lost she had felt, but right now, she needed this. Needed him, needed his strange body to hold her. To numb the fear and terror, even if only for a while.

To soothe both their frayed minds, to give them both something *human* to live for, if only another day.

She could barely recognize herself in how roughly she clasped her body to his, how eagerly she kissed his soft yet monstrous mouth. She was desperate for more, for him.

The large cavern-lake was moist, and her clothes had remained somewhat damp as she slept in Tar'kul's arms. The scratchy material of the miners clung to her form as she pressed to Taran's body, feeling his hard muscular form, with its corded sinew.

She had seen him for what he was, and perhaps that, coupled with her burgeoning psychic powers that let their minds embrace so readily, made it so easy to see him for what he was instead of what he had become. For even though his thinking patterns had changed somehow, she could still feel the real him at its core, and they reached out to one another from therein.

She could feel the desire in him for her stir as they made out so passionately atop the rocky shell-island. His hands cautious still after he had confused dream with reality once before and hurt her so badly because of it.

"I'm here," she whispered between kisses, her icy blue eyes meeting his inky black ones. "I'm here." Her hand went to his cheek, her thumb rubbing over his flesh and then back into his strange hair, feeling him out as who he was began to meld in her mind.

She knew she must have looked like a mess, her golden hair ragged and unwashed, her dress clinging to her soft form, her body feeling thick with grit of the underworld even after the swim. But his affection, his desire, was something pure. Something genuine.

It stirred something within her that she knew she'd never understand, and she pressed her mouth to his again, harder.

Her reassurances soothed him, eased his guilty conscience even, and he touched her more eagerly. The long years of isolation having done nothing to decrease his yearning for companionship.

Above, she was a woman of nobility, of wealth and scholarship and inheritance. A lady of promise. Yet below she was ragged and worn, destitute and hopeless, and this man loved her still.

She could feel the heart of such courage beat beneath his chest as he gently lifted her, cradling her in his arms as he laid her to rest upon her back. His many hands feeling her, pawing and caressing her thighs and breasts as their lips smacked in the quiet cavern. From out of the recesses of ancient memory he conjured the words up and spoke to her lowly, "I love you."

It made her quiver with the rush of emotions that flooded her, filled her mind, and she reached out to bring him nearer to her. To smother herself in his affection and love. It hadn't been easy for him to speak those whispered words, to push past the torture of the centuries on his mind.

She felt like she was losing it, and she'd only been down here a fraction of the time he had. Could she even qualify her stay here compared to his?

She forced the considerations away as she opened her arms to him, her body yielding to his many hands. It was strange, and wrong, and she didn't care. The trappings of high society, of morality, they'd all frayed and disappeared into the ruins of these demonic dwellings and haunts.

Taran's hands moved her dress upwards, exposing her pale, ivory thighs and hips as he lowered himself atop her. Comforting her with his towering form as she beckoned him inside her. His old trench coat, tattered and torn after their adventures, left little of his lean, muscled form covered.

She could feel the pulse of his manhood against her, the hung in his moist lips and tongue, the desire in his hands as he squeezed her breasts so completely in his long fingers. Letting those mounds—fuller from her rich diet with the miners—fill his palms.

She barely recognized her own body, but in a way, it was better. It was her new body, something more suited to the underworld hell, and to... this.

Affection. Lust. Desperation. Love.

Whatever it was.

She didn't speak, verbally or mentally. Instead she simply beckoned him with her eyes, coaxed him with her hands as her legs parted under her own power. It was a sweet rebellion, to control that motion, and she didn't hide her soft smile.

Thia could see him as he was, so handsome and charming. So committed and dashing. A trick of the mind, that made it so much easier, more pleasurable as he exposed himself to her in acceptance of her offering. He returned her smile, happy for her control, for her willing offering of physical love and comfort.

Her gaze dipped past rocky, sparsely haired abs towards the throbbing member that he pressed to her loins. She was damp and ready for him, not like the dry state she had been when she'd submitted to Jremy out of desperation.

Taran's lips parted and he gave a soft, quiet moan as he entered her, holding her close as he eased himself into her between those milky thighs.

She inhaled, in anticipation of the pain that never came. That sharp stabbing, that brutal sensation, was instead replaced with something pleasurable. Her slick body was receptive and her breath was stolen away by a soft moan.

She bit her lower lip, trying to hold the strange, excited sounds in.

Her head tilted back and her body arched as he pressed so

deep into her quim, and she didn't hide the blissful expression on her face.

Perhaps madness was taking her in truth, it was hard to care anymore. Hard to fight it when she looked up and saw such a handsome, dashing man. So much like her old beau Edain, but more seasoned, more rugged. It somehow only made it better as he rocked into her, holding her hip in place, feeling her tender breasts as he filled her. Kissed upon her lips and neck.

The soft grunts and moans of Taran a pleasant backdrop to her own pleasure as they made the most of their circumstances. The way he gazed at her so full of love and adoration, she did not feel like the ragged shell of the woman she thought she was.

Never had she made love. Her experiences with sex were often wrought with disdain or fear, and this was wholly knew to her. Something that she'd never even begun to understand, and her legs lifted, wrapping around him and hugging him to her.

"Taran," she whispered softly, her mouth finding his throat once again and kissing him gently.

Hearing his name—his true name—spoken aloud in the real world seemed to kindle more of his humanity from that deep place, where it only seemed to bloom in full inside his dreams. He moaned back into her ear, the soft slap of his loins to hers rising as he pumped his hips and held her tight.

"Thia," he returned to her, as if each affirming their humanity amid the sea of alien chaos and wickedness.

It was as if, for that moment, they found sanctuary from the monsters in their mind, those demons that filled their every waking minute and haunted their every dream. As though they were making some form of magic that protected them from the reality of their hellish existence, and Thia smiled as her body arched and rocked against his.

It ended much as it had all begun, slow and tenderly. Marked only by the light, erratic twitches of their coital bodies as they shared fluids and found satisfaction in one another.

Taran lay atop her and inside of her as he panted, showering her with soft kisses as reality fought to bleed back in. To show her the monstrous man that had sullied her flesh as this place sullied her mind.

Yet the gentle sounds of his affection, no matter if they were the soft male grunts of Taran, or the strange coos of Tar'kul, were genuine and comforting.

For a little while, she felt her damaged psyche begin to mend, and she fluttered her eyes shut to keep the monsters at bay for a little while longer.

$$\text{❈} \quad 50 \quad \text{❈}$$

After a peaceful night of being held by Edain in her dreams—who was really Taran—Thia awoke to the sounds of the two siblings chatting away excitedly over their morning meal of discoloured mushroom and bug guts.

She was still wrapped tightly in those strong, dark arms so comfortingly as she heard the two kids taking advantage of their first moment to reconnect. Since escaping Haven, there had not been a single moment of peace for any of them that wasn't spent in desperate slumber.

Thia had trouble understanding them, her sleepy mind barely able to keep up with their fast method of speaking.

"I jes' knew ya'd be okay, sis," said Rufus, holding his sister's hand. "You was always the cleverest back in Haven. Never lost a game a scratch."

The young girl smiled and squeezed his hand back. "An' I jes' knew you'd come'n meet me. Ma' said we couldn't risk goin' fer ya, but I knew… wouldn' be long. An' I was right."

Thia found herself relaxing, and then her shoulders tensed, her eyes opening wider as she felt that terror that always followed pleasure. The fact that she'd let her guard down, the fact that she was happy... It always led to disappointment down here.

But as quickly as panic had gripped her, she forced herself to cast it back down. To breathe out that gasp and just drink in that relaxing calm, if only for a moment.

Taran awoke then, perhaps sensing her momentary unease and holding her tighter. His voice spoke to her in Thia's mind and she swore it sounded somehow more human. *"Should eat and get ready. Not far now,"* he said, and there was a certain tone of finality to those words.

Not far? Towards the surface?

She was almost afraid to ask, but her blue gaze turned to his inky black one, and she whispered the words aloud, "To what?"

He stroked his many hands over her sides and shoulders, *"To the only way up I know."*

She had shared his past with him through visions, dreams. She'd seen how he had come down to the underworld, been forced to flee and hide. The way back had surely remained, hadn't it? But he'd never dared move back that way. Or else never succeeded in making his way through.

Her hand ran over his strange, obsidian flesh, and she didn't look joyful. It was a subdued understanding that she knew he'd long ago accepted. He couldn't come with her.

But she knew she'd find a way to save him from this place. To repay the kindness he'd afforded her, to let him live out the rest of his days with some comfort and dignity on the surface.

And then she broke the momentary spell, looking to the children and smiling in a plastic sort of way, "Have you two eaten your fill?"

The two kids nearly jumped at the sudden intrusion of Thia's words, so lost in their own reunion that they'd forgot the world around them had existed. Clutching each other's hands tightly, they looked at her wide-eyed before relaxing and breathing a sigh of relief.

Their nearly twin-like smiles were so refreshing. "Mornin'!" said Rufus, and together the two of them started eating, a task they'd obviously neglected in their mad scramble to talk with one another.

"Doin' it now, missus," said Sharn with a meek looking smile before biting into the mushroom at hand. She didn't even make a face at the meal.

The fear, the desperate anger and hopelessness that had accompanied her to sleep were no longer anywhere to be found. She didn't overthink it, but she knew that it had more to do with Tar'kul than she would care to admit.

"I'm glad to see you both together again," Thia smiled as she pulled down her dress and rearranged her clothing before moving from Tar'kul and joining them for breakfast.

The towering man slunk off to do his own preparations noisily as the three of them ate and chatted. Whatever it was he did for food, he made care to do it on his own time, it seemed.

The two kids, however, beamed at her excitedly. "You'll like 'er, Sharn," said Rufus, still holding the girl's hand. "She's a nice lady. Was sweet ta me back in Haven. Played games like you an' me used ta!" he said happily.

For her part, the young girl studied Thia with wide, curious eyes in silence. Her thoughts her own, lest Thia felt the urge to delve within her mind.

But Thia didn't feel comfortable prying, and instead stroked the back of Rufus' head. "You made the days there pass a lot better," she complimented him, popping more food into her mouth and chewing it thoughtfully.

Sharn did at last speak up again as the meal neared its end. Her voice sweet and soft, "Are ya takin' us somewhere close by? Are we gun' live wit' ya, missus?" she asked innocently, her long, curved lashes fluttering a little, betraying her attempt at serious inquisition with an adorable expression.

It was hard for Thia to even fathom why she'd panicked so badly the night before. Maybe this was it. Knowing how much she could care for these two kids, how much she didn't want to disappoint them or get them hurt or worse was what had set it off.

She wanted to save them, and the idea that she might be unable to terrified her. She thought back to that moment she'd realized she'd lost hold of Sharn, and even though she hadn't been able to even register it at the time, she knew the fear had crept deep within her battered psyche.

But then, how many more reasons did she need to lose her mind here? And could any one thing be held responsible for her breakdown?

"We're going to make our own home. Somewhere safe," Thia said and forced herself to swallow the lump in her throat. "I'm going to do everything I can to see to it."

The young girl stared at her as Rufus nodded, her question coming fast. "What's yer home like?" Straight to the point.

Her brother butted in immediately. "She lives up 'bove! Where they gots all sorta things, an' don't got no worries like we do," he said, starry eyed at the thoughts of a sunlit world on the surface.

Meanwhile, Sharn's eyes bulged at the mention of the 'up above'.

"I'm a long way from home down here," Thia put it gently. "I'm going to find my home, though, once I get above. And I'll take you with me, and you'll each have your own rooms if you like. And very nice food that will help you grow up big and strong." She paused and then grinned wickedly, "Just like these mushrooms! But even tastier!"

Rufus wrinkled his nose, "That won't be hard," he said giving the mushroom a weird look before forcing more of it into his mouth. He gave a bit of a grin after that, looking high spirited, still charged by the reunion with his sister.

Sharn looked thoughtful, however, and spoke up after a moment's hesitation. "Ma said she came from up above when th' men a Haven kidnapped 'er. Said it was hard livin' up there too." Judging by the expression on Rufus' face, that knowledge was completely new to the boy. "Hard. But no' s'bad."

Thia tried to hide her regretful wince at the reminder of the children's poor mother, and had to avert her eyes. "It is hard for some people." It was one of those things Thia had always known, and just as easily ignored. Guilt twisted her stomach but she pushed it aside, "But it wasn't for me."

Sharn's eyes dipped and peered around the surface of the water before flitting back to Thia. "So Rufus says… you'll be like… our new ma?" she asked cautiously, showing none of the enthusiasm that Rufus did as he nodded.

"She will! Right?" he said, looking between his sister and Thia. "Ya would be a great ma!" he declared.

Thia pet Rufus' head again, giving him another soft smile. "I'll take care of you, and do my best to keep you safe. I don't know what that makes me, but I don't want to replace your ma. Not like that."

Her carefully chosen words seemed to sit well with the pensive girl, and Rufus as usual was easily pleased with her.

It was about then that Tar'kul—Taran—returned to them. "We go now," he said, then gestured for Thia to follow him.

Around to the front of the floating monster carcass that they all lay upon like some great, immobile boat, he gestured for her to take a hold of one of the stalagmites. "Hold on tight. Then to me," he said, offering her two hands.

Carefully, he grasped onto her as he leaned forward, reaching out for another stone spire that stuck from the water. Grasping that he pulled the whole of the floating island towards it. It strained both their arms, but with the creature no longer living, it broke from its stationary place relatively easily and began to slowly drift upon the surface towards the tunnel ahead.

It was then that Thia noticed its head was missing, and she spotted it floating on the water not far away. That hacking sound she had heard from him earlier must have been him severing the neck and head entirely, removing that last little sliver of flesh that she had left intact.

As he gathered up the long, whip-like limb that had been the creature's appendages, she spoke to him, "What more will we have to face before we get there?" Thia wasn't certain even he knew, but her excitement was drowned out by her apprehension of what they'd have to face.

"*Not much,*" he spoke to her mentally. "*I checked the tunnel while you were captured. We are near the end now. Only one thing remains,*" he said with a certain tone of finality to his mental voice.

He used the monster arm like a lasso, and on a second or third attempt managed to snag it on another protruding stone from the water. Stepping back, he grabbed hold of a stalagmite on the turtle-like hide with two arms, and began to pull. Thia joined in by grabbing hold of him for extra support.

It wasn't long before they were casually drifting down the cavernous stream towards their destination.

That city which haunted both their dreams.

Even when it was safe to let go, she lingered nearer to him than usual. She'd found some strength in the night before, though she had a hard time looking at him. Seeing him as he really was.

"*What will we have to do? Sharn and Rufus...*" she trailed off, but she wanted to say that if grown, military men fell in that nightmarish place, what hope did she and two children have?

Tar'kul was quiet for a while, but when he spoke he didn't have much to offer her. He'd warned her the journey would be suicide from the beginning; she had insisted anyhow. "*Good food has made you safe from their mind tricks,"* he assured, though whatever solace she was supposed to take from that seemed hollow in the face of the raw brutality she knew the creatures could commit though sheer physical power, whether they were vulnerable to their mind tricks or not. *"Can only move through fast. Quiet. Waste no time. Look at nothing but path ahead."*

The cavern walls drifted on by slowly as he pulled them along, alternating between using the whip arm as lasso and whatever stone spikes within reach he could grasp with his bare hands.

"Do you think the children will..." she asked silently, dreading the answer. They were quick, though. Spry. Perhaps they had a better chance than any of them.

The answer wasn't forthcoming. Most likely because Tar'kul had nothing to offer. No wisdom. No insight. The infernal city was no less a mystery to him than her, despite his years of living below. Despite his personal experience with it.

The morbid ship upon which they sailed moved slowly down the tunnel. It was a lousy way to traverse the remainder of the water ways, but then even with the end nearly in sight, neither of them were eager to push on faster. Tar'kul's slow pace was a final moment of peace. Perhaps a time to reflect. To savour life while it lasted, no matter how miserable it had become.

The tunnel ceiling and walls seemed to pass Thia by like clouds, which they oft resembled. The bulging round spots, so random in appearance, more common than the pointed jabbing stalactites.

Their random patterns were often frightening, or jarring. Sometimes pleasant. As they drifted on down the stream together, she could pretend for a moment like she was laying back on the ground with Edain, watching the clouds pass them both by. Mineral formations upon rock looking like shapes of things both alive and alien.

There she saw a horse, charging out of the wall itself. Up

above and to the right Thia made out an image of a pumpkin, and what looked like a cow ready to eat it.

For a moment she found herself amazed that she could still think in such innocent terms. Such upper-worldly concepts. When all around her loomed such evil and alien presence, she was able to conjure from her imagination something as mundane as a sheep in the bulges of mineralized stone.

She felt that momentary calm, that newly restored feeling of attachment to human life, and it was due not to her time in Haven, but her connection with Taran. Of coming to know him as he was, a man of valour, honour and surprising warmth. For whatever he had become, he was among the finest of men once. Someone like the man Thia had given her heart in the innocent days of her life.

As her mind meandered, Tar'kul pointed to a rock formation. "*Soul Reaper,*" he chittered to her calmly, and she saw it there. The menacing creature represented in random stone patterns.

No matter how calm she felt, how at peace in that moment before, it was a reminder that his mind worked differently than hers now. Countless years of being beneath the surface of the earth left him with fractured psyche. And despite the momentary reprieve, she was fast following him.

❧ 51 ❧

The river came winding out of the rocky tunnel and out into the open air. The open air of the great cavern that was the underworld. Thia found herself struck by the perverse beauty of the place for a moment, and it nearly made her miss the sight of the drop off before her, where the slow moving water became a steep plunge.

Tar'kul didn't however, and he reigned in the makeshift vessel towards the side, waving her over. *"Come steadily,"* he cautioned her, taking her hand and helping her climb up onto the flat ground. The two children were next, holding their bundles of food as they leapt one by one onto the shore.

Once Rufus was across as well, Tar'kul vaulted over and left the craft to complete its journey alone. The carcass of the beast plunged over the edge, and for a brief moment it gave Thia a look at the tangle of strange, meaty flesh beneath its hard shell.

It made her glad she couldn't see that during the fight with it. It turned her stomach, all those strange bulges and vile, organ-like cysts protruding among tentacles, short and long.

The small landing stood atop a plateau, overlooking an eerie but breathtaking sight. Laid out beneath them was a great valley, what resembled grey fields of fungus straight before them, then to the right a narrow passageway that must have connected to the rest of the underground cavern structure. She could see why their options of entering the twisted city were so limited. It was a narrow path that could easily be blocked by anyone or anything.

The Pale Ones would undoubtedly be easily able to monitor it, if they cared to. Or if they had the presence of mind to do so.

Though what truly grabbed Thia's attention was the city itself.

She'd seen it in her dreams through John, but to actually behold it with her own eyes?

The odd angles of the structures that defied all reason, the curious glow of green in its stonework, or metalwork, or… whatever it was the unholy place was crafted from.

It resembled the underground town where she'd first met Tar'kul, but only in the vaguest sense. It was like seeing the world through the eyes of a deranged lunatic with a paintbrush. Nothing was right; it made her sick to her stomach to see it, yet it called to her even as it made her want to retch.

Comparing it to the mental image of it in her head, she saw that it had changed from the time Taran had first arrived. However many years ago that must have been—centuries? Was that was Tar'kul had hinted at?—it now looked bigger, greater, more like a citadel fortress than a city if she had to peg one descriptor to it. And why not? Human words would not do such a mad assemblage justice, no matter how many or few you could assemble. If she survived to write her memoirs, she reckoned she'd never accomplish the feat of sharing even a sliver of its insane majesty.

She felt as though her mind was dribbling out of her ear as she stared. Lifting a hand to her ear, she thankfully felt nothing leaking out, even though the feeling persisted eerily.

Tar'kul took her shoulder, then that of each of the kids, *"Do not stare,"* he cautioned them. His rough, chittering voice not holding the sense of urgency and alarm she was used to when he warned her of danger. Was he truly resigned to inevitable failure?

She'd dragged him back here. Seeing it through his dreams, filtered through time and perspective, it hadn't held so much power over her. But now she realized what she'd asked him to do.

She'd made him re-visit the place where he'd lost his men, his friends, and what else? Thia forced her gaze from the terrifying, stomach turning city and instead into the inky black pools of his eyes.

Those eyes of his would be unreadable to a normal woman. Should be. Perhaps it was their psychic link, but after so long with him she could read his feelings in his dark gaze. The sadness, the sorrow. The guilt. And the love.

"We go now, almost done," he said, the whip-like tendril now coiled about his arm and shoulder as he led her from the plateau down a narrow and treacherous path towards the valley below.

❧ 52 ☙

That final journey passed in near silence. Thia wished she could say it was determination or caution that made their party tread across that fungal field so quietly, but she knew better.

In the shadow of the great citadel city—no, she thought, remembering back to the scene of worshipful Pale Ones and their insane speeches, it was a Cathedral to a Mad God—they walked in forced awe. Averting their eyes as if on a holy pilgrimage.

The walls about the city were immense, uneven, asymmetrical. The wrongness of the place took her back to her first moments in this black underworld, even after all this time she'd spent getting used to it. The great gates loomed off further to their right as they approached it, but Tar'kul took them towards it at a low point and it was there his newly found 'lasso' came into use again.

He was able to hook it around a barbed point upon the wall, then using his many limbs clamber up its side towards the top.

Once there he hefted them up, one at a time before descending down the other side.

From their position Thia counted herself lucky that their view was blocked by a building and she could not make out more of the abominable city if she tried. And sadly, for a moment, she had.

Things had changed dramatically since the time that Taran had ventured through, and as they strode through the alleyways and out into the street with cautious steps, their every sound was amplified. Not as a trick of the ear or the quiet, but genuinely amplified. Some dark power made their every breath sound as if it rushed out from some unknown colossus looming over them, twenty times their size.

Though the children were so good and quiet, their whimpers of fear were like sirens when even their heart beats could be heard around them all.

How could they hope to tread through the city without being detected like that? She had to wonder. Though not for long.

The answer was that they simply couldn't.

Tar'kul's mental voice carried to them, *"We are not hidden from them,"* he stated plainly. Though the resignation had gone from his alien voice, no longer able to feel such apathy as he did his best to lead them through hell.

"Run with me," he beckoned, but before they could, Thia heard the sound of someone else run dashing from a building. Her gaze didn't move fast enough to make out who or what in the dull green glow.

The four of them held hands and began to run with the brave Lieutenant in the lead.

This time, she was determined to give Taran the ending he deserved. He had to save his troops. They had to survive, on top of everything else, to give him some measure of happiness and accomplishment in his life.

For so long she'd fought for survival, fought for herself.

When the two children had joined her party, she'd thought that she'd be fighting for them.

Instead, it was for him. The monster who had captured her, raped her, protected her, saved her... Loved her.

Dwelling on such things at so perilous a moment should've been dangerous; instead it kept her from turning her gaze to where it sought to look. She sharpened the distraction into a point of focus as they ran towards the heart of the city. For no longer was it blocked from her view, as once they tread upon its smooth, stone-like streets, all roads led directly to it.

It was a panopticon lorded over with some dark deity at its heart. She knew this not because she saw it with her waking eyes, but because the very aura of the place beat with a wicked heart that betrayed its nature.

The four of them were running, but as they tried to dash down one alleyway, they found themselves blocked on the other end by several Pale Ones.

Tar'kul was right, in that she no longer felt the perverse pull of those gorgeous men. Their power over her was eroded completely, though young Sharn was hesitant, and her brother had to tug at her to keep her moving.

Onwards they went, to the next, and before they were three strides down it, they faced a similar group of the pale, sculpture-like men.

"They are blocking us off!" said Tar'kul with alarm, and though his words were psychically conveyed, Thia heard them echo and reverberate off the buildings all the same.

Whatever dark magic had made the place, it kept them from even holding their thought-speech private.

There was but one way to go as they checked each alleyway, further and further towards the heart of that cyclopean city with its central eye, overseeing all.

She thought of turning back in the heat of the moment, but

there she saw them too. Coming out of the alleyways, forming a cordon to block their sole avenue of retreat.

Thia looked to one of the buildings they passed and the doorway, "In here!" she cried, her words echoed at a near deafening volume. Though as she dove towards the open doorway, she found herself smacking against a solid surface as it sealed up before her. The stone, or metal just spawned a solid film across the entryway that barred their passage.

She shouldn't have been surprised by the strange mysticism of such a hellish place, but it still managed to stun her for a second. Her blue eyes glazed over as anger and fear grasped for her heart, but she pushed it away before it could get a lasting grip.

At that moment they had no choice but to operate on pure instinct. Together the four of them ran on to the one direction afforded them: Straight to the heart of the city.

Immediately there in that great plaza, Tar'kul tried to lead them around the building and down another street. But that was closed off. The Pale Ones marched in ominous unison, herding the four of them. The creatures in such numbers their doom was inevitable.

At last, as their options waned, and nothing more remained to be done but run straight into the mouth of hell, Thia looked and beheld the heart of madness.

That splinter of another world. Just seeing it bestowed upon her some understanding. For that strange otherworldly shard, alien even to the deranged and perverse underworld. It was a sliver of another universe that had pierced her own, and it had corrupted it.

There was no other explanation.

She stumbled, but Tar'kul grabbed her, helping her up. "*Do not give up!*" he pleaded with her.

Though why he persisted began to baffle her then as dismay filtered into her maddened mind. What was left to resist?

Then, amid the echoes of Tar'kul's words she could hear—booming across the whole city—laughter. Her laughter. Was it her own mind? Her torn psyche finally ripped to pieces irreversibly?

When she realized she was physically laughing, her chest heaving, it seemed obvious.

The children wailed in terror and fell to the stones, then Tar'kul alone was the only one moving forward, pulling the three of them along with his many arms in such a foolishly futile display. Even at their slow, methodical pace the Pale Ones would catch them if he had to tow them all alone.

They rounded about that void-splinter, and he took them towards the steps of a great coliseum the likes of which Thia could never have envisioned.

Through the hysterical laughter and sobbing, they slowly ascended the smooth incline until…

Up out of that great dome rose a creature that dwarfed all others. Pale and sickly, she was like a termite queen writhing among her young, standing taller than the Tower of London.

Tar'kul stopped in his tracks too.

The creature smashed down upon the edge of the coliseum, destroying its own construct as shards of stone went flying in such a bizarre fashion. Some laid suspended in air, others crashed against the cavern ceiling and rested there, as if gravity itself meant little so close to the Void-Shard.

They stumbled backwards as all reality shook, and the enormous queen descended down. Its lumpy, writhing form ending at the top with something more horrific still. The form of a woman, cackling madly in perfect timing with Thia.

In perfect unison. Their voices commingled in harmony as if they were twins.

As if twins.

She stared. Her laughter ceased. Yet the queen continued. The All-Mother.

She squirmed atop that writhing mass, then twisted to the side. Thia saw then that almost half of the queen's body was deformed, dark and monstrous. Like Tar'kul's. But the other half… was like peering into a mirror. Pristine and perfect. The spitting image of her.

It made her cringe, more than the sight of the horrible woman digging her clawed hands into the pale flesh of her great mound, and clawing herself free of her own abdomen through a mess of blood and gore.

The four of them were stunned, with nowhere left to run, and their gazes fixated as the hideous woman fell from her own body in a mess, smacking against the stone as she continued to cackle.

They could do nothing but stare as she picked herself up, her lower body covered in slime and blood, but still so human. It was like she had moulted away that great mass.

The All-Mother. Thia knew it. Tar'kul knew it. They shared the term between them, its echo lost in the great ruckus of her maddened amusement.

The woman descended the great stairs slowly, and though she now stood no taller than Thia herself, her presence was immense. The contrast of her ivory human flesh with her dark, monstrous self was jarring. Her one eye blue and manic, the other inky black.

"You came to me, without one of my pretties needing to bring you," she said, stilling her manic laughter. "What a good girl you are," she said, her voice suddenly sounding hateful before the All-Mother's expression returned back to that twisted mockery of merriment.

There was no words for the depths of terror that ran through Thia's body. It was beyond anything she'd ever felt, and she'd tasted such horrors. She'd nearly died countless times, seen to the edge of human corruption and cruelty, felt the strange mysticism as it began to chip away at her psyche, and yet now that all felt like a sunny day on the surface.

Thia didn't know how long she stared, dumbfounded, but she reached out to Tar'kul. Not in words, not even solid thoughts, but she wanted him to explain.

Even though she knew he couldn't.

This was beyond mortal understanding.

Though the All-Mother looked so much like Thia, her limbs and neck twisted at such odd, inhuman angles. Her eyes shifting to study the group of them as her head angled impossibly.

"I've been anxious to meet you in the flesh since one of my boys brought me a taste of your essence," she shouted at them angrily, her pouty lips in a froth with seeming rage despite the innocuous words. The emotions, seemingly random, faded to one of warmth as she stroked a clawed, dark hand over her human half fondly. "I liked what taste of you I got," she remarked like a mother speaking softly to a child. "I was just dying for more."

Disgust roiled Thia's stomach, and yet it mingled with something unexpected. Relief? That this hadn't been all something predesigned, something with greater implications than simply... transmutation? She'd tasted Thia's blood through the Pale One that'd bit her and adopted her look, but there was no greater purpose to it. Or so it seemed.

Still, that quickly faded to the more immediate and impending doom, and Thia spoke to Tar'kul, silently even as it echoed over them. *"Take them."*

No sooner had the thought been expressed than the All-Mother shrieked at them. "Stay a while!" she screeched, and the children seemed to stumble from the power of her words, and Thia... she would be lying if she said she didn't feel it. As if the insane goddesses shout had physical power within it.

Tar'kul, however, was too busy staring at the strange woman

that had stolen much of Thia's appearance. And she could detect a strange mix of emotions in him.

Judging by the way she half-sauntered, half-hobbled towards him, the All-Mother did too. She reached out with her human hand, caressed his cheek as he gaped at her.

"You escaped my clutches long ago," she said in a soft voice, motherly. "Escaped when you should have lingered. Joined my flock." Instinctively, he seemed unable to resist momentarily nuzzling against that soft, pale hand so much like Thia's. "But I can forgive that," she hissed, the creatures emotions such a strange, confused mess, "since you brought me the final piece I was missing."

The final piece?

Thia hadn't realized her jaw had dropped, her eyes straining in horror and burning from not being able to blink or look away. She forced her eyelids to descend once, twice, clearing her gaze from the grit of the air.

She didn't want to admit this was the end. That it all fell apart so close to her freedom. Yet she'd never gotten her hopes up, never let herself believe in sincerity that she wouldn't die down here. Not since... how long ago? When did she lose all faith?

Was it with the plant people? With the Pale Ones?

Or did she ever really believe she'd escape, that she really stood a chance of returning to the peace and quiet of her scholarly young spinster's life?

Her hand went to Sharn's shoulder, squeezed it hard as if trying to convey an unspoken message, to give the girl some strength.

Perhaps thankfully the children seemed paralyzed by fear at the situation. The thrum of nothingness behind them, the chaos of the All-Mother before them. They faced a reality that dwarfed their awful little existence in Haven in ways unimaginable.

The All-Mother stroked Tar'kul's cheek and jaw so affectionately, cooing at him in a way that was loving and motherly before abruptly shoving him back down to the steps with rough, callous disinterest.

She swung her gaze back to Thia, ignoring the little ones. "Do you have any idea how hard it is to find suitable women here?" she hissed at Thia. "What ones that do wander here," she laughed abruptly, "my boys usually rough up too much to be useful to me. That, or they were never fit in the first place."

Suddenly she snatched at Sharn's head, ripped out some of her hair to the girl's screeches and sniffed it. "Useless!" the All-Mother sobbed, throwing it away distastefully. Her emotions shifted dramatically as she reached in and cupped Thia's chin and jaw. "But you… you're just what I needed," she said with another bout of manic laughter, this time up so close to her she could feel the monstrous woman's breath upon her face. Smell the fetid stench of the gore left over from her former body.

Seeing her do that, Tar'kul stood up abruptly, looking ready to race to her rescue, but something stopped him. Some invisible force. The whip dropped from his shoulder to the stairs. And Thia's hero just stood there, dumb. Helpless.

Thia knew how he felt. No matter how much she willed her legs to run, they were just as useless as they had been back in Haven. She'd had to crawl on her belly just to escape.

The memory brought something back, though. After all she'd been through since leaving her protected little room, she'd forgotten she had even taken it with her. That knife she'd used for the one non-stew meal she'd eaten with the family. The knife she'd managed to carefully strap to her thigh.

The knife she hoped still remained through her tumultuous getaway and swim down a subterranean river.

Thia could hear something like humming—or chanting—all around her, and when she looked aside, she could see the throngs of Pale Ones, nude and worshipping. Their Goddess had descended for some great purpose, and they watched with reverence.

Her first encounters with those gorgeous but deadly men had been so baffling. Their strange ability to coax from her such intense desire had seemed so arbitrary when she learned it did not affect the men. Now she knew it was because the All-Mother needed her kind. Needed a woman... for some nefarious purpose she couldn't yet grasp.

As she stared into a face that was almost identical to her own, Thia was struck by the eerie sensation of violation. As if this... thing from another realm was stealing her very identity.

As Thia pondered the mystery and possible answers—was she going to steal Thia's self in the world above?—the All-Mother grinned at her knowingly. It was then she could feel the un-woman worm through her thoughts like a maggot in meat. "You've taught me much," she admitted casually, her dark, monstrous hand stroking Thia's blonde hair, the human one lifting to cup her jawline, her thumb running over her cheek lovingly.

What caught her most off guard was when the creature leaned in and kissed her. Tightening her fingers in Thia's hair to hold her in place as she explored her mouth like a lover would. Dragging out the moment, making it slow and sensuous.

Until the All-Mother's thoughts pierced her mind, "*I'm ready. And I'll use your essence to finally walk the world above. Free of my tether. Able to birth the new world from my womb. Thanks to you.*"

No.

No!

Thia was trapped in this hell, and she was willing to die here, but she would not suffer to unleash this monster on the world above! Her hand delved for her skirt, hauling it up and groping for that weapon, but her face paled as she found nothing there but naked flesh.

It had to still be there! It couldn't... she couldn't do this to the bright, sunny world above! It couldn't be her likeness destroying all she wished to return to!

The cruel creature pulled away from her, lips still moist from their kiss as she laughed in Thia's face. "I would've stopped you anyhow," she said mockingly, a sneer upon the half of her lips that so resembled Thia's own.

Though the strength with which the All-Mother backhanded her was beyond anything Thia could have conjured. She crumpled to the stairs at the dark deity's feet, her world spinning from the blow, her neck twisted and aching. With such power the thing could've snapped her neck…

The children squealed and Rufus pulled away, while Sharn tried to hit the woman with her slender girl's arms.

Tar'kul twitched, trying with all his might to move, to resist, but he couldn't budge. Thia could *feel* his rage at the All-Mother, his frustration intermingled with impotence before the creature's power.

The half-formed woman swung about and turned its sinister gaze upon the helpless man. "Don't worry, my child," she cooed to him before curling her fingers in the air, making his body move towards her like a shabbily controlled marionette. The jerky motions and sounds of joints cracking made Thia wince as he lifted her head and watched through bleary eyes.

"Once I devour her, you'll be able to give yourself to me wholly and completely." She grasped Tar'kul's jaw, but no longer held it with any feigned kindness. Instead she twisted his head to the side so far that Thia knew it must've endangered snapping the poor man's neck. "You came back here for her after all. Once she's inside me – "

Sharn had grabbed up Tar'kul's whip and holding it in both hands she snapped it up around the All-Mother's neck and yanked back. She dared such a brazen act in her childish foolishness.

Thia could not help but admire the girl's tenacity, her spunk in the face of such hopelessness. Her slender arms able to yank the woman back off Tar'kul to her surprise, setting her off balance.

Breaking her focus.

Thia knew this when she saw Tar'kul move of his own accord once more, grasping his throat as he choked for breath. In her own desperation she felt along her legs, desperately searching for the—knife! She found it, tied to her calf by the ragged strip of cloth. Through her troubles it had fallen low, but still clung on.

Tar'kul lunged at the All-Mother, fists and claws pummeling at her as she reached her arms behind her in such an inhuman fashion to pluck up Sharn.

It was such a mess of bodies, but Thia slid her crude knife from place and forced herself up. She was moving so slowly, but time couldn't be wasted. Not when she witnessed the evil deity clutch her hands around Sharn's head and heard the girl scream.

Thia couldn't get there in time.

Tar'kul was kicked, and the sound of breaking bones was heard as he went arcing back through the air to strike at the Void-Splinter. No sound emitted as he hit it, but he fell to the ground limply. Lifelessly was the word her mind didn't dare use.

All around his still form, some sort of strange, greenish ether seemed to snake out from the splinter. Like a vapour of some sort it coiled around his limbs and seemed to try and pull him in… or pervert him further with its otherworldly taint.

Rufus grabbed onto the All-Mother's human leg and pounded at her, but it was in futility as she pulled the screaming Sharn out in front of her, dangling her by the head.

Thia had lifted her arms, and with all the strength in her she could muster she plunged the dining knife downwards, aiming straight for the thing's neck.

She missed.

But the spine was close enough, judging by the reality-shaking wail the creature sent out.

Everything went blurry. Thia fell to her knees. Clasped her ears, though it did no good. The sound was as much inside her mind as spoken aloud. The chaotic cries of pain and agony. The tension of the moment wavered awkwardly, leaving Thia confused and overwhelmed, unable to ascertain exactly what the effects of her actions were.

All around them, the Pale Ones replicated her misery, each of them trying to clutch at their backs in mimicry of their deity.

Were they all controlled by her? Linked to her consciousness? They were no longer organized, and were all to varying degrees closer to their group. Had the dark god split her attention by summoning them to her? Controlling each of them to come and claim control of the meager party?

If it was, that futile gesture seemed to be what saved her and Thia pushed herself back up only to be clawed at terribly by the woman.

Blood stained her view so badly she could hardly see, but she pressed back in, pounded her fist upon the demented creature as she scrambled for the knife.

They were a messy tangle, and Thia suffered grievous wounds in the melee. Yet she found the knife handle, wriggled it free from the woman only to plunge it in again. Again. Her mind filled with so many emotions that she felt as chaotic and sanity-stripped as the goddess who was stealing her identity.

Laughter filled the city as Thia continued to plunge that crude weapon again and again.

When at last Thia blinked the blood from her gaze enough to see, she witnessed the small, determined young Sharn, using the whip-appendage to choke the thing as tears rolled down her face.

She wasn't sure when she finished with the woman. The moment had become a haze of rage and violence. Yet when she wiped her face upon her sleeve and gazed around at the sea of collapsed, lifeless bodies, she felt the work was done.

Thia pulled Sharn to her, consoling the girl who collapsed into sobs. "It's okay, you did it," she said, trying to calm her down, her knuckles white from still tying the thing's neck shut.

As tears began to pour from her own face, she saw below… Tar'kul's body being dragged slowly towards that shard. That black slice of the abyss.

"No!" Thia screeched, and something in that tone was so unreal, so unlike what she thought she should sound like. It was filled with anguish, raw from her maniacal laughter and panted breaths. She let Sharn down as gently as she could before she rushed for her friend.

Thia nearly tumbled down the stairs in her mad dash, her head still spinning. But as she got to Tar'kul, the tendrils of green vapour began to reach for her too. She could feel their tug, even as she pulled at her friend.

Her weary, blood-stained arms pulled at Tar'kul's unconscious form, and she strained with all the energy she had left.

It wasn't proving enough though, as those long tendrils of strange essence grasped at them both, making her skin crawl with its ethereal touch.

Tar'kul spasmed and woke with a ragged cough. Immediately aware of the things that pulled at him, he began to claw at the floor to try and get away. "No!" he cried out in a raspy, broken voice, further damaged by the blows he'd taken.

"Taran! Help me, we can do it!" Thia pleaded, the two of them pulling away from the grasp of those ethereal tendrils.

Thia's muscles ached, but at last they managed to pull free and the cloudy green limbs disappeared as vapour in the air.

She didn't allow herself time for relief or gratitude, even as they threatened to slow her down, and instead she was immediately looking around for the next threat. The next way that death would try to grasp at her.

Thia couldn't hope to survive this, but she would go down swinging. She would do all she could.

Instead, all she saw were the still bodies of the Pale Ones... already beginning to decay. As if their bodies were but ancient dust, held together by the will of their All-Mother.

The city no longer resounded with every slight noise, every thought. And only the sound of the two kids, sobbing and clutching one another filled the empty space.

Tar'kul pushed himself up with shaky limbs, coughing and choking in air. *"Must go... must get you out before... before..."* he didn't know. No more than she. But so long of living in that hell made them sure something would come for them. It had to.

So despite her exhaustion, the fact that she was trembling like a leaf, she went to the kids. Kneeling down to their level, she put a firm and reassuring hand on either of their shoulders, forcing a smile to her lips.

"We have to go. You have to be strong just a little bit longer, okay?"

And the words were as much for herself as them.

Tar'kul was too badly wounded to help them much. He clutched himself as they walked hurriedly. The city seemed almost more eerie as they went through quiet streets. They no longer knew if anything still existed to follow them. To bring them harm. But having to assume... having to be careful all the same.

The journey was uneventful. The city was deserted. Even the short stretch across open underworld was surprisingly quiet. It gave Tar'kul and Thia time to find their way to that ancient passageway.

The whole experience with the underworld had been so jarring. Nothing operated according to the rules of the world above, and even that period of relative peace sat ill on the parties mind. To reach such a climax only to plummet immediately into a silent journey broke all flow to existence. But then, such was the reality of that place.

Thia felt like her body was about to give out, and the children were exhausted, but she was so close. And they could not risk lingering another moment longer in that hell.

The tunnel upwards was more confusing, as Taran hadn't the slightest of clue how he'd travelled down it in the confusion of the time. But upwards they went, until the light started to strain and hurt their eyes.

Tar'kul was the first to break. "*I can't go. Not any further,*" he said, shielding his eyes from the light with his arm. That dull glow was too painful for him to bear. And the most alarming part was just how much agony it caused Thia in turn.

It felt like her eyes were being seared out of her sockets, but she knew that wasn't the cause of the tears. She whispered quietly to the two children to let their eyes adjust before she went to him, shielding his eyes with her two small, calloused hands.

"Go back to your home. To the place you first took me. I will... I will come back for you, Taran. I promise. And without the Pale Ones..."

His eyes were shut and he cowered from the light, but he reached out to wrap his arms around her and embrace her. "*I will wait... for as long as I can hold on,*" he said. Though he never told her what he meant by that. Why wouldn't he be able to hold on? His injuries were bad, but they weren't that bad, were they?

She leaned in, her breath held as she lingered just inches from his mouth before it slowly dawned on her.

"Her... death..." Was that the death of him, too? Would he start to decay like the other pale ones? His former comrades?

There were so many unknowns, so little Thia understood about that bizarre underworld. So little she understood about what happened with Taran. How he had become like he did.

He stilled her mind by pressing his lips to hers, kissing her warmly. Lovingly. Savouring the moment before he uncoiled his arms and crouched back away into the darkness further. "*Go. Hurry to your home. Do not forget me,*" he pleaded before turning and vanishing down the tunnel.

And that was it. What more could she do but chase after him, abandoning the two children that were now her dependants, to go back into the hell she'd spent so long trying to escape?

Yet she couldn't deny that for a fleeting moment, she truly wanted to.

She swiped at the tears that ran down her cheeks and sucked

her lower lip into her mouth, tasting the remnants of his kiss. Lingering just a second longer to stare into the dark after him she forced herself away, back towards the glaring, painful light.

"We have to keep going. How are your eyes?"

The kids were doing fine compared to her, and her concern for that fact only grew as they ascended. Before they reached the end, she had to cover her eyes with her arm and let Sharn guide her along by the hand.

Thia never got to enjoy the sunlight as anything but warmth and pain. Even her freedom was bittersweet.

❧ 54 ❧

It was still a joy, no matter how unpleasant it was and how bitter the parting for Thia knew at last that she was free. Thought every attempt she made to adjust to the light failed, and brought only agony.

"What do you see outside?" she asked the kids, who in the time since emerging were doing better than her at adjusting.

"It's… it's so strange," Sharn said.

"Ain't nothin' but green an' brown everywhere," said Rufus, before amending, "an' white an' grey up above."

It wasn't anything she could navigate by, though with how little of the world she'd seen in her time growing up, it wasn't much of a change. Still, to know she'd done it, she'd made it to the surface after so much time below...

It felt like walking in a dream.

But in her dreams, the skies were always blue.

"We'll rest for now," she said wearily. For though she was anxious to get going, she knew they were all so very tired. And she needed time to not only recuperate, but hopefully regain her sight.

§ 55 §

The journey to her home had been a stumbling, unknowing mess through the countryside. Thia had relied upon two children who had never seen the raw light of day before in their lives to guide her as if she were blind. The tunnel had caved in as quickly as they left, as though it were fate, sealing in the horrors of the den beneath.

There was no turning back.

Yet Thia's homecoming did not come quick or easy.

The journey was long and arduous, even without the constant terror of the underworld at her neck. Still, though, she felt it. Lurking in her bones, in her muscles, in her joints. At every sound, she'd ask the children what they saw. At every stumble, adrenaline flooded her and primed her for battle.

Though the confrontation with the All-Mother had been so brief, and her escape from the underworld then relatively short and easy, the surface had proven anything but.

It took her weeks to get home in the state she was in, nearly two days spend wandering aimlessly in the wild before finding a village, then the rest spent travelling and convincing folk to help and finally months of legal wrangling to secure back her inheritance. Her home.

With two frightened and confused kids in tow, and her eyesight refusing to adjust back to the light of the world above, Thia's homecoming was subdued. Unwelcoming.

Worse still, she felt nothing of Tar'kul there.

She ventured down the tunnel she'd first taken, into the depths of hell, going to the edge where it had broken and left her stranded. She called out to him mentally, time and time again. But nothing.

And though the Pale Ones were gone, she still saw other creatures of the underworld roaming in the darkness when she stared quietly long enough. It was not safe there.

Yet still she found herself, sitting far enough away to be safe, staring with some strange longing. It was comforting, and isolated. It made her feel alone, but not nearly so alone as the land above. Here, in the dark caverns, perched above the horror, she felt some measure of peace.

Some part of her that she tried to push down, to hide beneath the veneer of happiness to be back on the surface, knew she belonged to this place. Her soul cried out for it, but every time she pushed herself away when it became too much.

❦ 56 ❧

Another day began for Theodora. The lone lady of the estate.

Rumours about her had spread like wildfire, vanishing out of her own home one night without warning. Returning over a year later with two children in tow. Her condition...

She'd had to tell the authorities she was abducted. There was no other way to explain her absence, her condition. She prepared Sharn and Rufus along the way, and they carried the tale admirably. After all, it was no lie. She had truly been abducted into Haven. Deceived. Abused.

The authorities went to investigate the cave and tunnel she'd crawled out of, but it was blocked. Their attempts to uncover it were brief and ended in failure with no sign of anyone.

With the revelations came sympathy, but only to a point. A lady, even one who saved two children from heinous abductors, did not return to accolades and understanding. Not when she bore the additional surprise of an illegitimate child growing within her. No matter how beyond her control it was.

If she believed in miracles, one would've had to occur to see that unholy spawn inside her to fruition. She'd gone through such misery, and in the end was starving and weary. She hadn't even noticed her state until she was back home at long last.

So the tales built up about her.

The initial sympathy quickly waned, as it was wont to do. Then when the search of the cave was called off with nothing found, it turned to vicious rumours. That she had run off with vagabonds and scoundrels, only to return when they died or were arrested elsewhere. Or that she had been abducted, but came to love them and bore their spawn willingly.

The idle thoughts of the nobility were prone to wild speculation. She ceased to care rather soon, regardless.

No, her 'day' began at night now. The only time she could stomach to see at all. With a gauzy bandage about her head to filter out the moon and candle light, she was able to walk her manor, tend to the children, write her thoughts down.

And pine for what she'd lost below.

It was almost a human's life. Part of her still felt she no longer was entirely human. Not quite.

Sharn and Rufus were as well-behaved of kids as she could dream of. And they adapted quickly to life above, all things considered. Though she spent much time trying to teach them proper etiquette.

The fact that the family only went out at night did not help the rumours, but when Sharn beamed up at her with those big round eyes, the small girl so much fuller now on a rich diet of fresh, healthy foods, how could she refuse? "Can we go out and play in the garden?" she asked, carefully pronouncing each word as Thia'd been teaching her.

Rufus stood by, looking like a proper young gentleman in his suit, "Yeah mama, can we?" He was slower to catch on, but he adored her. Truly embraced her as his mother.

Thia was still such a young woman, in her own rights, but all three of them were aged more than any of them ought to be. They'd seen things that no one else ever had, so how could they expect to be accepted under the best scenarios? How could they discuss wine and capers with the rich when they had survived such an ordeal?

So Thia had decided that it would be better to just embrace their oddness, to do what they must in their daily struggles.

Her daily struggles.

The children, they adapted so much better than Thia could have ever hoped, and she nodded at their enthusiasm.

"The garden it will be." And instantly she remembered back to the twisted and macabre plant people, idly wondering if they'd won their war with the Whip-Legs, what had started the fight in the first place, and what had happened to Haven. A twinge of guilt twisted in her gut at the thought of what would happen to the poor women, though she had no such pity for Jremy and his ilk.

Her heart had turned to stone where they were concerned.

The night passed pleasantly, or as pleasantly as it ever did. Sharn—or Sharon, as she was now known as—and Rufus playing in the garden, showing yet again that they adapted better to her world than she did.

Thia did not trust servants much anymore, did not want one viewing their odd behaviours and fueling the rumour mongers. So only a couple tended to the grounds in total, and kept their distance at most times.

After the jarring experience of giving birth before the midwife, she'd learned her lesson.

It all left her with more duties and tasks than any noble lady was ever saddled with, and by the time sunrise approached, she was exhausted. So very weary, as she was each and every day.

Her windows were double-barred and covered with thin

drapes to keep out the light, and still Thia could never get it as dark as she wished it. Only the weariness made sleep come any bit easy. She was thankful for that.

378

❄ 57 ❄

Months after their escape...

Often Thia walked the underworld in her dreams, usually to awaken sweating and panicked. Most often in tears.

That night it felt different.

Her shuffling gait across the underground landscape dragging on so slowly. The feelings of weariness and loss filling her, making the physical aches and pangs in her flesh seem a distraction.

The infernal city came loomed over her, but she didn't even lift her head. Not out of fear this time, but fatigue. Weariness.

As she moved through the city streets, the bodies of the Pale Ones were mostly dust. A few remained as skeletons. A couple even had some flesh to their bones. Perhaps, she pondered, their decay was relative to their age.

It was a macabre thought, the kind of musing that hardly even seemed to concern her in that realm. Who cared anymore? They were gone.

When she came to the center of the city, she paused, then for some reason beyond knowing she diverted to the body of the All-Mother.

That ambling gait of hers was slow and uneven until she fell to her knees before the body.

The woman had moved.

Thia reached out, turned her over, and looked into the mismatched eyes of the creature that had tried to steal her likeness.

She lived.

Her breathing was shallow, and the power of her height was drained away. Whatever dark, unholy powers she had were all but gone, and she stared up at her in a pitiable state.

The All-Mother's lips moved very slightly, but then the words went directly from one mind to the other. *"Save me... She's forgotten you already. Save me... and we'll be together. We'll have each other here... at least there's that left to us."*

The plea and its accompanying emotions sounded so sincere. So heartfelt. So desperate.

Thia's eyes watered, her vision bleary as she reached out and stroked that human half of her head. That portion of her so much like her own.

Even through the haze of the dream and the tumultuousness of the emotional turmoil, Thia knew she inhabited Tar'kul's being.

"I can truly love you," the All-Mother said to him. *"We're alike... I know how you suffer. Alone... different... I am older and more unique than even you, my handsome saviour,"* she said, reaching her human hand up weakly to stroke his cheek. But she failed in her pitiful state.

Tar'kul's shoulders and chest heaved with quiet sobs, and he wrapped his arms in under her. Thia could see nothing more through his vision. The tears were so thick, and his emotional state so confused the world was a mess.

He lifted the mangled and misshapen woman, clung to her.

Clung to her for all of her that was like Thia, that much she was certain.

"Good boy… we'll be together. Forever," she promised to him.

Thia's heart—her true heart—panged. Tar'kul had thought she'd given up on him, and fell prey to that abomination's words.

"I'll treat you better than she ever could," the All-Mother promised.

He shuffled down the stairs. Both his and Thia's heart broke in unison.

"What are you doing?" the mangled woman demanded, worry wracking her weak, mental voice. *"N-no – ! Not there!"*

Tar'kul cleared his gaze and Thia could see before them both, the sight of that Void-Sliver. That evil shard of another realm that lost little of its maddening effects, even through memory and dream.

"No! Don't do it! You'll be alone! All alone! Helpless and weak!" she pleaded with Tar'kul as he put what strength he had left into resisting the green tendrils of vaporous ether before heaving the load in his arms and tossing her to its mercies.

Her bloody, mauled body hit the stonework and rolled towards it. Her mental cries of anguish rose, even as her body was too weak to cry out or even flinch. The tentacles of another realm coiled about her… pulling her in… leaving her helpless against it.

"You're a fool! A weak and pitiful fool! I'm your only hope!" she wailed to him, making his mind recoil from the harshness of the mental chastisement.

The shard began to undulate as it pulled her into itself, rejoining the foul entity with its source, sealing her back into the matter of another universe from which she spawned. Her cries became a loud distortion until they were indistinguishable from the sound of rumbling. Of the earth around Tar'kul tearing itself apart.

He stumbled as he tried to move away. Then fell.

A stalactite came loose and shattered upon the roadway before him, and as he scampered to get onto his hand and legs, another great quake caused him to fall flat onto his back. The position gave him a view of the great coliseum, crushed beneath stone

❧ 58 ☙

Thia's eyes flew open with a cry upon her lips. "Taran!" Her baby awoke with a banshee's wail at the sound of his mother's scream.

He was alive. Tar'kul was alive. He had to be! Her entire time separated from him in the psychic-shelter of Haven, she'd not shared a single memory with him in her dreams. Thia couldn't pretend to have a perfect awareness of how it worked, but she knew that he lived.

She reached out for the crying child, shushing it even as she stood from the bed, beginning to rapidly pace the room, letting the details of the dream seep into her mind. It wasn't like a normal dream, something that was like grasping at smoke. These shared visions were seared into her mind as if they'd happened, and she began searching it for what to do.

He lived. He thought she'd given up on him, and even still he threw away his only chance for companionship. The All-Mother... She was so like him. A twisted mockery of humanity, warped by the underworld and by centuries of breeding her deranged army.

There was only one thing for her to do. She had to go down, back into the underworld.

❀ 59 ❀

Thia left the crying baby in the arms of Sharn and Rufus; the two kids were responsible and reliable, and she had no other choice.

When she went down those stairs this time, it was prepared.

She dressed in something practical, pants that would've scandalized her in public, and climbing rope she'd procured from the groundskeeper long before in preparation of Tar'kul's return.

Staring into the abyss she'd crawled out of was one thing. Climbing back into it was a whole other.

Thia trembled as she peered down into the darkness. The only place she didn't need to shield her eyes at all. The one place she felt at home anymore. Yet the place she still had greatest cause to fear.

She climbed down the rope after attaching it further up the stairs through an iron rod. Slowly she descended down towards the bed of mushrooms that had saved her life almost two years before.

As she reached the ground, she saw a discarded whip-like appendage, like the one Tar'kul had wielded all those months ago.

$\maltese$ 60 $\maltese$

Walking through the streets of that dead city was a different experience. The glowing spores that covered things now seemed like bright street lights, and she found more activity there than she remembered before. Small creatures skittering about.

The loss of the Pale Ones must have given way to opportunities for new life.

Thia made her way back to that familiar little hole in the wall, finding the familiar gray rope dangling down as her mental calls went unanswered.

Determination drew her up the wall, and she climbed through the hole to search the home.

It was so deathly quiet. She had no great hopes of finding him here. And then, when she did see him, his eerie stillness made her think the worse.

She ran to him, kneeling down and shaking his shoulder, pulling him over towards her. His body was so limp. "Tar'kul!" she cried out to him, stroking his cheek and trying to get a reaction out of him.

She pressed her ear to his face…

And heard the shallow sounds of breathing. So faint.

"Tar'kul, I'm here!" she said urgently, her hands fluttering around him as if looking for something to do, some way to save him from whatever invisible cause was making him look so close to death.

She reached out to him, mentally, as a barrage of memories assaulted her mind. She was back in this hideaway, the place he'd tried to use as a prison to keep her safe. Unharmed by the dozens of things that wished her doom.

And yet it was all tainted with her affection for the deformed man. Everything he'd done to her, for her, she looked at it all with a new light of respect, with understanding.

She didn't know if this was love, if that was what skewed her mind towards him so readily, but it was the reason she couldn't let him go.

"I have the rope. We can get out. You can... You can stay at the exit, and I'll give you everything you need."

She remembered the water she brought with her, and uncapped the canteen, pouring some into his mouth with care not to choke him.

He coughed.

His inky black eyes flicking open weakly as he looked up at her.

"*It's you…*" came his weak, chittering mental voice.

Thia forced a broad smile, but how tired he sounded made her heart break. "Of course it's me. I told you…"

Her words left her, both verbally and telepathically, and her lower lip trembled.

She hadn't noticed at first, but the piles of bloody bandages indicated he'd been seriously wounded for some time. When her eyes inspected him more closely, she saw the marks. The bruises and scars upon his obsidian flesh.

He had been too injured horribly, and judging by the signs of the whip he'd tried to get to her. Tried and failed.

This time he lifted his hand and lightly touched her cheek. Feeling the soft, smooth flesh of her pale skin. He wanted to say so much, she could tell. But he was weak, weary. And judging by his emaciated look he'd not eaten in quite a while.

"So glad… you made it back safely…" and he smiled at her.

There were so many pragmatic things she wanted to offer him. A comfortable place to rest, food and water.

Instead, she offered him a reason to hold on.

"Tar'kul." Her lips skirted over his monstrous brow while tickling him with her long, golden hair. She'd let it continue growing out and now it was almost to her bottom, and even pulled back the wispy strands still escaped to caress him. "I had a baby. Our baby."

The first emotion she felt swell in him was confusion.

She'd missed it in her absence, that psychic bond they had developed. So much stronger than anything she could have imagined. She could feel his emotions so clearly. His thoughts came clearer than words, as she felt their essence.

So as his confusion melted into something so much warmer, into such strange joy and elation… she got to feel it all. Feel the swelling of his love even bigger.

He was so weak, so badly injured, yet he began to push himself up with her aid. *"I want to see. To help,"* he said to her as she did her best to support his body, to prop him up with her own. He was so much gaunter now, his weight was no longer as intimidating as before. *"I want to leave… with you,"* he said.

Of course, he could never live a life above ground as a normal person. But then… neither could she.

She'd thought of the possibilities before. Of converting the large cellar and basement areas of her manor into something he could live in. Something a little more human than the underworld. After struggling with the light of day despite her best efforts, she even thought it'd be best for her.

A smile flirted over her lips and she gently touched along his forehead. "That was always the plan, wasn't it?" she said softly. "You need to eat first, though. Do you have anything left?"

Tar'kul responded to her with what amounted to a psychic shake of his head.

Thia had brought some food with her, for though she'd not intended to be gone long, she had no idea where her search for Tar'kul might take her. Or what might become of her.

Reaching into her pack she pulled out some of the dried meats for him, fed him, slowly.

She cradled him carefully, stroked his hair and kissed his forehead.

It'd be a tough climb back up for him.

❧ 61 ☙

One year later...

Thia sat primly in the chair of her study, the opulent room much as her great aunt had left it, for she rarely set foot inside the chamber. Her light-sensitivity still made the brightness of day unbearable. Though on rare occasions she emerged for important business, a dark veil always concealing her face.

It was quite peculiar, and it often put her guests off, but that was fine with her, for the young businessman from London was there to try and swindle her. She knew it.

"The townspeople this side of the river could use the employment, madam Suthers, and if you help fund the construction by donating the land, we can assemble the mill and bring some life to this corner of England. I'm certain as a lady of some known charity and benevolence that you would be willing to make a sacrifice on their behalf." He wore the most fashionable of suits, well-tailored with a stiff-collar and a snake-oil salesman's smile.

No, that was not fair. It was a perfectly charming smile, the finest of disingenuous smiles that nobody could see through. The way it crinkled the corner of his eyes like a genuine smile would.

It was genuine. Theodora just knew better than to think it had anything to do with helping the poor of the area. The mill was projected to be a fat windfall for his company, and all the more so if he could find a sucker willing to fork over the land needed for a pittance. Even more daring he actually sought to get her to donate the land. The rocky stretch of shoreline that was in her family for three generations.

Up until now, it was rather worthless.

It was a convincing ploy, for if she hadn't the power to probe the minds of people she would never have guessed it prime real estate for such a venture.

"It sounds to me, Sir, that I'd be making the sacrifice on your behalf, more than anyone else's," Thia replied with the most charming of smiles showing beneath the rim of the dark veil. "Wouldn't you agree?"

With a confident chuckle he shook his head and covered up the placard he'd brought showing the sketch of the future mill. "Madam, I'm afraid you grossly overestimate the value of the land and the profits to be had. This is purely a philanthropic venture on behalf of our partners. We estimate that in time the mill could be self-sustaining, but that is optimistic forecasting to be polite."

He managed to sound so calm and certain of himself, even though Thia knew he was lying through his teeth.

She uncrossed her heels and stood. Though she was a short woman, she had cultivated a presence about her that made her intimidating. Or at least, so Sharon and Rufus had told her, based on the talk of the townsfolk.

"Well, then, I see no reason not to share the risks and the rewards."

His brow furrowed and he looked at her as if she were

behaving quite amateurishly. All so convincing. "Perhaps it is best I speak with your solicitor, madam. I am afraid you do not understand the, ah… finer points of economics, and a gentleman's perspective might aid you. As I'm afraid without your donation or… a very reasonable purchase price, I shall have to return back to London to put the deal to a close."

The condescending prick was quite good at his act. Assuming Thia hadn't known the truth.

"Well that would be a shame for you, wouldn't it?" She spoke slowly, as though to a child, "If you're unaware of the value of that which I possess, then perhaps I could speak to someone who understands. Perhaps Dorian Filipott would be more amiable to my counter-offer."

She watched the young associate react with abrupt surprise. "That… Frenchman has spoken with you already?" he asked, sounding quite taken aback.

Thia could feel his thoughts reeling. Wondering how he could have been beaten to the punch on the investment plan.

"I suppose he's looking to move fast, though I wasn't happy with his offer either. However, knowing you're now interested in the same plot of land as he," she lied easily, "he will no doubt move quickly."

The young man looked flustered, at last his smug facade broken. "Madam," he began, hesitating as he struggled to invent excuses. "Whatever Monsieur Filipott said," that French word spoken with such disdain, "I assure you, he was having you on. He and his associates commit themselves to sabotaging our good faith deals to promote the English countryside."

It was a weak lie, but the best he could come up with on the fly.

"Well, regardless. Though I love, dearly, my country, keeping up with the help I need around the manor simply isn't cheap, nor is maintaining the lands. I require reasonably full coffers just

as anyone else. If that demands that I negotiate with a Frenchman, then so be it. Thank you for the offer, all the same."

Thia smiled a sickeningly sweet smile as she walked towards
one of the bookshelves, playing at being disinterested in further
conversation.

The ploy worked however, as before she could flip a page he
was stammering. "Well… I'm sure we could come to an arrange-
ment on a price for the plot of land. Something… generous, my
lady," he said, giving her some modicum of her proper due
finally. "I will have to confirm it with my partners of
course, but…"

She waited three seconds, letting them tick by slowly before
she finally turned to face him once more. "I am sure we can
work something out. A percentage of the mill, and I will retain
ownership over the plot to be leased to the company. **We** will be
partners in this."

He looked absolutely flustered, though Thia knew intimately
that she had him. Even as he struggled to look blown away by
her audacity she knew she could find acceptable terms.

It helped, knowing his every intention.

❧ 62 ❧

With business done, and the young man sent off feeling cowed and bitter, Thia strolled down into her basement. Her heels clicked upon the new stairs, freshly installed earlier that year.

The basement was nicely reinforced, with new doors and compartments. She had to unlock two doors on her way, the entryway kept secure so as to let nobody find out her secret.

As the heavy iron-reinforced door slid open, she immediately heard the sound of laughter. Sharon and Rufus were quite pleased, as they frolicked in the dim under-manor.

Such a tricky pest, came Tar'kul – Taran's – voice to her inside her mind. It resembled less of that chittering strangeness than it used to, though she could not see him about. Just the two kids playing.

He's unlucky to have come to me after my descent, Thia responded back, mentally. Even though they had all the privacy to speak in the world, it felt more intimate this way, not to mention clearer.

She strode across the darkness of the basement as she pulled off her veil and the dark blindfold beneath, her eyes quickly seeing in the darkness with a clarity she once saw the world above. Though she needed it not to find him.

He resided at the back chambers, in the baby's room. Or so they had come to know it as, though the child seemed far from deserving the title of "baby" anymore. For as Taran's held their curious child in his four arms, Theron was already nearly so big as Rufus was when she first encountered that boy.

Theron was a strange child to look at, but in his curiously dark features she could see so much of his father. And even a little of herself. His mental words calling out to his mother in a way that was so heartfelt, words could not do it justice.

We missed you, came Taran's words.

She went over to them both, to her family, and brought her lips to both of their foreheads, one after another. *I've missed you too.*

One of Taran's hands unfurled from about Theron and clasped Thia's, their son clinging to her exquisite dress.

Though as they shared their closeness, the gentle sound of the door shifting ever so slightly drew Thia's attention.

It wasn't the door up into the manor, but the **other** door.

That door at the back of the basement, so heavy and sturdy. Reinforced beyond the others, guarding against something more perilous than discovery.

It's nothing, came Taran's reassurance.

And surely it was. The air currents from below every so often made that heavy door shift. If only a little.

Yes, she said with a gentle smile to them both, the sound of the children's laughter rising again, *nothing at all.*

ALSO BY J.E. & M. KEEP

Series:

Possessed by the Vampire:

Claimed

Hunted

Caught

The Warlord:

The Warlord's Concubine

The Warlord's Queen

Her Master

Her Master's Madness

Her Master's Corruption

Novels:

War-Torn

Her Descent

When Dreamers Wake

Chanting the Ancient Lay

Corrupted Hearts

Magic Academy

Unleashed

Vile

Outcast 1 & 2

Novellas:

In Her Dreams

<u>Brutal Passions</u>

<u>The Enforcer: 1</u>

<u>The Enforcer: 2</u>

<u>The Fembot</u>

<u>Bound as the World Burns</u>

Shorts:

The Seductive Nymph

The Curious Nymph

Wherever in the White House: Saved from the Lizard Lady

The Angel and the Demon

Packing' It In

Packing' It In: Not All At Once

The Virility Elixir

The Elven Babe: Stuffed

The Elven Babe: Dragon

The Elven Babe: Demonic

Shifters in Heat

Dancing for the Vampire

The Queen's Secret Lover

The Fertile Elf

Beast and Beauty

Bundles:

Darknest: A Dark Fantasy Anthology

Erotic Dragons Boxset

The Elven Babe: Trilogy

Wicked Monsters Boxset

ABOUT THE AUTHORS

Joshua and Michelle Keep are best-selling authors of romance, fantasy and horror, located in Newfoundland Canada. Fifteen years of joint-authorship together has earned them an enthusiastic readership and a reputation for unique, well-written stories.

Exploring the heights of romantic love and the depths of darkness, they focus on characters developing, growing and falling for one another amidst an engaging plot. Working to make sure a Happily-Ever-After exceeds your expectations.

Full time authors now, in years gone by they were a historian and corporate-ladder-climbing supervisor, respectively.

෨෪෬

Connect with us:
admin@jmkeep.com
http://jmkeep.com
http://jmkeep.com/newsletter
http://pathforgers.com
http://twitter.com/jmkeep
http://twitter.com/jekeep